WELCOME TO FLORIDA

UNIVERSITY PRESS OF FLORIDA

Florida A&M University, Tallahassee
Florida Atlantic University, Boca Raton
Florida Gulf Coast University, Ft. Myers
Florida International University, Miami
Florida State University, Tallahassee
New College of Florida, Sarasota
University of Central Florida, Orlando
University of Florida, Gainesville
University of North Florida, Jacksonville
University of South Florida, Tampa
University of West Florida, Pensacola

WELCOME TO
FLORIDA

True Tales from
America's Most Interesting State

Craig Pittman

UNIVERSITY PRESS OF FLORIDA

Gainesville/Tallahassee/Tampa/Boca Raton
Pensacola/Orlando/Miami/Jacksonville/Ft. Myers/Sarasota

Front cover: Illustration by Andy Marlette.

30 29 28 27 26 25   6 5 4 3 2 1

A record of cataloging-in-publication information is available from the Library of Congress.
ISBN 978-0-8130-8094-9 (paperback)
ISBN 978-0-8130-7369-9 (ebook)

The University Press of Florida is the scholarly publishing agency for the State University System of Florida, comprising Florida A&M University, Florida Atlantic University, Florida Gulf Coast University, Florida International University, Florida State University, New College of Florida, University of Central Florida, University of Florida, University of North Florida, University of South Florida, and University of West Florida.

University Press of Florida
2046 NE Waldo Road
Suite 2100
Gainesville, FL 32609
http://upress.ufl.edu

For my two Eagle Scouts—
the Florida men who make me proud every day.

CONTENTS

PROLOGUE

I started crafting this prologue on a drizzly Saturday while driving on U.S. 19 through Florida. U.S. 19 is one of my favorite roads—not for the pavement itself but for what it rolls past. It encompasses so much that's symbolic of what I love about this place.

It passes by the government employees who perform as mermaids at Weeki Wachee Springs State Park and a ginormous manatee statue at Homosassa Springs State Park. It passes by a couple of fake dinosaurs, one of which is on the National Register of Historic Places (a historic fake—only in Florida!).

It intersects with "Follow That Dream Parkway," which commemorates where Elvis made one of his better movies and met a very young Tom Petty, inspiring him to try to be a rock'n'roll star. And it rolls over the Suwannee River, where as a kid I managed to be "accidentally" baptized.

All of this on just one road! Can you see why I contend that instead of calling ourselves the Sunshine State, we should call ourselves "The Most Interesting State"?

Like U.S. 19, the book you hold in your hand covers a lot of quirky territory. There are stories and columns about an elephant sanctuary turned jet-centric community, a comic book artist who went to jail for drawing dirty cartoons, a hippo that became an official Florida citizen, nudists coping with the pandemic, and a wealthy developer known for wearing alligator shoes with alligator eyes. You'll also find tributes to some of my fellow Florida writers, such as Tim Dorsey and Carolina Garcia-Aguilera.

You will see, over and over, bad puns, corny jokes, and obscure pop culture references. More importantly, you will see stories about ordinary Floridians fighting to save some part of the state that they hold dear.

Usually, they're up against forces that have more money and more clout. Sometimes they lose. Sometimes they win. Sometimes the best they can do is postpone defeat long enough for the circumstances to change.

My hope, as you read this book, is that you will come to appreciate Florida the way I do, and the way these warriors for our spectacular state do—as a special place that's worth doing all we can to preserve what makes it special.

Part One

TRUE FLORIDA STORIES

1

Destiny Takes a Hand

Florida Phoenix, December 10, 2021

Don't you just love a good Florida story? I sure do. Not just the short ones, like the one about the Gainesville driver in a road rage incident who accidentally ran over himself.

I love the longer ones, too, the ones that take a few twists and turns and wind up with a surprise at the end.

I heard a classic long Florida story this week from Audubon of Florida's Charles Lee. It sounded too good to be true but, when I checked it out, the details were even crazier than he'd told me.

This story has some dramatic twists and turns and, to everyone's surprise, resulted in a happy ending just last week. Well, it's a happy ending if you like the Florida grasshopper sparrow, a tiny bird with a call that sounds like a grasshopper, a critter so rare that it's considered the most endangered bird in North America.

If, on the other hand, you prefer a story in which developers win in the end, this story may not be for you.

It concerns a big chunk of land near the hamlet of Yeehaw Junction, where State Road 60 and U.S. 441 cross the Florida Turnpike. This is where the Desert Inn—a legendary tavern with a bordello on the second floor—stood for more than a century until a wayward semi driver demolished it a year ago.

At one time the "town," if you could call it that, was known as Jackass Junction. However, while building the turnpike, officials with the state Department of Transportation insisted it be renamed as something more dignified—hence the switch to "Yeehaw."

But I digress.

In 2004, a Delray Beach developer named Anthony V. Pugliese III plunked down millions of dollars to buy a vast swath of ranchland, citrus groves, wetlands, prairies, and forests near Yeehaw Junction from a rancher with the mellifluous name of Latt Maxcy. In 2006, Pugliese announced

A Florida grasshopper sparrow. Photo by Mary Peterson of the U.S. Fish and Wildlife Service.

plans to build a new city of 250,000 people within an area more than twice the size of Manhattan.

He called it "Destiny."

He also called it "America's First Eco-Sustainable City." It would, he promised, be full of biking and hiking paths, natural preserves, and lakes for boating. It would have "a smart-grid infrastructure" that would run the city and produce a "near-zero carbon footprint."

Sure, all this development would wipe out habitat for the endangered Florida grasshopper sparrow, but sacrificing that tiny bird was a small price to pay for a farsighted project such as Destiny, right? As the old saying goes, you can't make a humongous, highly profitable, allegedly nature-friendly omelet without breaking some endangered bird eggs.

"What we're really trying to do is create a model city," Pugliese told the Associated Press at the time. "Rather than just going out here, digging a bunch of holes in the ground, and putting a bunch of buildings on there for retirees, we basically want to create a city that is environmentally sensitive to its surroundings."

* * *

Pugliese is one of those classic Florida characters who, if they didn't exist in real life, would have to be invented by Carl Hiaasen. One *South Florida Sun-Sentinel* story called him "an eccentric developer who has been known to wear alligator shoes with alligator eyeballs." His oceanfront home was so grand it actually had a moat.

On his own website, Pugliese declared himself to be "a pioneer, an inventor, a writer, an actor, an artist, and a designer with the ability to create impressive and award-winning buildings." (I think his middle initial V stands for "Very Humble.")

I spent some time on the phone with Pugliese this week, and occasionally was successful in breaking the rapid flow of his words to slip in a question. Among other things, he confirmed the alligator shoes detail (two pairs, bought in Vegas "for kicks," which he would wear "whenever the environmental guys came around," he said).

Pugliese's hobby is collecting pop culture artifacts—for instance, the gun that Jack Ruby used to kill Lee Harvey Oswald, the Wicked Witch's hat from *The Wizard of Oz,* and Indiana Jones' bullwhip from *Raiders of the Lost Ark.* He also owned one of James Bond's Aston Martin sports cars or did until someone stole it from an airport warehouse. The *Sun-Sentinel* in 1999 noted that police suspected Pugliese of stealing the car himself to collect on the insurance but could find no proof.

This, then, is the guy touting an audacious development plan near Yee-haw Junction—not exactly the kind of gleaming metropolis that tends to attract swarms of well-heeled buyers. Could he actually pull off something like Destiny?

Skeptics were persuaded once they learned who Pugliese's partner was: Fred DeLuca, billionaire co-founder of the Subway sandwich shop chain. They had been partners since 2005. DeLuca invested some $111 million in the project.

These days Pugliese doesn't have much good to say about his erstwhile partner, whom he described as "almost like [the movie] 'Rain Man,' a genius but also a wacko." He's also angry that he couldn't get immediate approval from what was then the state's growth management agency, the Department of Community Affairs, which Rick Scott abolished after becoming governor.

"You can't stop development from coming in here, especially the way people keep moving here like crazy," the developer told me.

As Pugliese struggled with getting the permits for Destiny, DeLuca became suspicious of how Pugliese was spending the millions he'd contributed. He insisted he wouldn't spend another dime unless he could see a budget, a demand Pugliese thought was outrageous. The partners sued each other—Pugliese suing DeLuca for refusing to pay expenses and DeLuca suing Pugliese for the way he handled the money.

The dueling lawsuits revealed that the "model city" of Destiny was, like so many developments in Florida, built on a foundation of chicanery.

* * *

Under oath, Pugliese admitted that he and his business manager had created fake companies and phony invoices to bilk DeLuca out of more than $1 million. But he didn't do it for nefarious purposes, he said. No, they were doing this to build up a "reserve fund" to pay Destiny's expenses should DeLuca completely quit forking over the money.

"This may not have been the best way of doing this . . . but it was done for the best interest of Destiny," Pugliese testified. "And all of the money went into the Destiny project."

Except it apparently did not.

The Palm Beach County State Attorney's Office pulled the records and accused Pugliese of spending DeLuca's money on his own expenses. For one thing, they said, Pugliese had spent $12,000 for a chiller for his moat. He needed one because the water had been too warm for the fish and some died. The chiller was supposed to cool the poor fish down, like an underwater air conditioner. If only saving the Florida grasshopper sparrow were so easy!

I asked Pugliese about the phony invoices, and first he told me "They were real, but they weren't real," and then, "It's not fraud! There was no intent!" and then, "So we made up a phony invoice—big deal."

When I brought up the moat chiller, he called it "the most ridiculous thing." What really happened, he said, was that he had contributed four chandeliers worth $12,000 to Destiny's corporate office, and thus considered it an even swap to spend Destiny money on the chiller for his moat. Who among us hasn't done that?

In 2012, Pugliese and his business manager were charged with fraud, money laundering, and grand theft. Three years later, Pugliese pleaded no contest to conspiracy and grand theft and the prosecutors dropped the other charges. He spent six months behind bars. To this day he complains he was the victim of corrupt prosecutors secretly working for his nemesis, DeLuca, but he didn't appeal his case.

Five years later, Pugliese lost in civil court, too, as a jury found for De-

Luca and awarded him a judgment worth (double-checks math, counts on fingers, removes shoes to count toes) $23 million. Plus, DeLuca wound up owning the land.

DeLuca wasn't around for the final act of the lawsuit drama. He died of leukemia in 2015. His widow kept the suit going and thus reaped the reward.

Which brings us to the most recent twist.

In the course of all this criminality and legal wrangling, Elisabeth De-Luca "fell in love with the property and wanted to retain it in its natural state," said Jack Payne, who last year retired as the University of Florida's senior vice president for agriculture and natural resources.

That's why, after about a year of discussions with UF officials, Mrs. De-Luca last week donated 27,000 acres to the university, Payne told me. Her instructions were to use it as a "living classroom" and preserve it from development, and that's just what UF will do.

"This is a once-in-a-lifetime gift," Brent Sellers, a professor in UF's agronomy department, told me. On his first visit to what the university is calling the "DeLuca Preserve," he and other UF researchers spent four hours driving around, marveling at the ecological richness of the land. He still can't get over its size: "I still get lost when I go there."

The Florida grasshopper sparrows get to stay, undisturbed by bulldozers, as do the endangered red cockaded woodpeckers in the piney woods. There are probably other rare species out on that land, plants as well as animals. Nobody's done a full site assessment of what's there yet, but UF officials say that's next.

UF put out a triumphant press release about the donation, calling it "among the largest gifts of real estate ever to any university in the nation." The long and fascinating story of "America's First Eco-Sustainable City" was conspicuously missing from the release. The name "Subway" never came up, and neither did the words "alligator shoes" and "moat chiller."

If it were up to me, at the entrance to the preserve there would be a really large plaque, or maybe a couple of them side by side, to explain to visitors how this property nearly wound up covered in concrete like a lot of the rest of Florida until—glory be—it wasn't.

After hearing this story from Lee, I tried reaching Mrs. DeLuca through her attorney, but he was the opposite of helpful, as were the folks at Subway's corporate headquarters.

As for Pugliese, he scoffed at the hoopla over her donation. He contended it was done for a tax write-off and also to burnish the reputation of her late husband, a man he insisted was too cheap to ever give anything away.

Now that he's out of jail, Pugliese is producing a documentary asserting the failure and lawsuit loss and even his jail time were DeLuca's fault. I tried to suggest to him that maybe what happened was bound to happen, no matter what, but I don't think he wanted to hear that. He didn't like the idea that this was all a simple case of fate, or luck, or—oh, what's the word?

Oh yeah. Destiny.

2

The Cowboy Life

Flamingo, October 18, 2021

On a steamy August morning, as the temperature rose with the sun, Jim Strickland stood on a raised cypress board in a rugged cow pen at Blackbeard's Ranch near Myakka City, looking down on a series of brown, black, and reddish cows scooting through a cattle chute. They flickered by like images in a clattering movie projector.

Strickland, the ranch's managing partner, wore a sweat-stained cowboy hat, a once-white fishing shirt with the sleeves rolled up, rumpled jeans, and old gray sneakers spattered with mud. As the cows trotted past him, the 66-year-old rancher kept count. On every second or third one, he squirted a spray that would keep away flies for a week or so. When some of the cows hesitated, he'd slap them on the rump or the back lightly, urging them to keep going.

"Go on, baby," he said to one.

The fly spray and the gentle touch are just two of the ways he and his ranch hands try to relieve stress on their cattle to ensure they don't worry off some of their weight. Think of it as New Age cowboying.

Between squirts, Strickland reminisced about the good old days, back when he would load a Boeing 747 full of cattle and fly them to customers in Guyana, Pakistan, and Dubai. Nobody overseas ever knew what to make of him.

"I'd get on an elevator somewhere and someone would look at my cowboy hat and say, 'Are you from Texas?'" he recalled. "And I'd say, 'Texas? What's Texas? I'm from Florida, birthplace of the cattle industry in America!'"

Strickland was not exaggerating. In 1521, on Juan Ponce de León's second trip to the land he'd named La Florida, the Spanish explorer brought along some Andalusian cattle, something never before seen in America.

When the Spaniard landed in Charlotte Harbor, his ship carried four heifers and a bull, along with 200 settlers. But Florida's first conquistador

Cattle rancher Jim Strickland. Photo courtesy of Jim Strickland.

didn't stick around long enough to start a ranch. Calusa warriors attacked with a fusillade of arrows. One struck Ponce de León in the leg. It had apparently been dipped in the juice of the deadly manchineel tree. He died in Havana shortly afterward. The cattle, meanwhile, fled into the scrub.

From that inauspicious beginning grew an industry that did more than sustain the state's economy throughout most of the 19th and 20th centuries. This year marks the 500th anniversary of cattle ranching in the United States. Historians say that ranching shaped the Florida we know today both geographically and culturally, boosting one-time cow towns like Arcadia, LaBelle, and Kissimmee and cementing an attitude of independence and even a defiance of authority still around today.

Now ranchers like Strickland may be the ones who help save us from losing what's left of the things that make Florida so special.

* * *

In movies and TV shows galore, the cowboy is an American icon—laconic, direct, a man of action. Think Marshal Matt Dillon and "The Lone Ranger," Gary Cooper and "The Man with No Name." In reality, the first cowboys were vaqueros who spoke Spanish and tended cattle outside St. Augustine after its founding in 1565.

As the Spanish spread through North Florida, they brought their cattle, establishing ranches and training the local Native Americans to tend the herds too. Strickland can trace his ranching heritage back to just before the Civil War.

"I'm sixth- or seventh generation," he said. "Everybody in my family has loved the cattle business."

The first of his ancestors to go into ranching relocated here from Georgia around 1850, he said. Cattle ran wild in the woods back then, and anyone who could catch a few could become a rancher. Florida was mostly open range, without fences, until fence laws were created in 1949 because tourists started colliding with cattle on the roads. Plenty of white settlers had already moved here to take advantage of that open range.

"They knew all those cattle were here—it was one of the things that drew them to Florida," explained James M. Denham, a history professor at Florida Southern College and the author of *A Rogue's Paradise: Crime and Punishment in Antebellum Florida, 1821–1861*. "If you had cattle, you had status."

During the Civil War, some of the sharper Florida ranchers sold their beef to buyers on both sides. Afterward, they found customers in Cuba willing to pay for their steers with sacks of gold. There are stories that some ranchers raked in so much money from the Cuban trade that they used full sacks of gold as doorstops.

Strickland says his family never enjoyed such luxury. What they valued was the cowboy lifestyle—riding horses and roping cattle, working outdoors and communing with nature—so they stuck with it.

"We're barely making ends meet here," he said. "I've always been blessed to do what I love to do. I have literally traveled the world with my cattle."

* * *

In the old days, Florida ranchers trying to get their herds to market battled hurricanes, mosquitoes, bears, panthers, sinkholes, and rustlers while driving thousands of cattle across the rugged landscape.

They were bound for ships docked in places like Tampa, Jacksonville, and the long-gone community of Punta Rassa, near what's now the Sanibel Causeway. They'd load the cows on sailing ships bound for other parts of the country or for Cuba, then celebrate with a trip to the nearest saloon or bordello.

These days, the life of Florida's cowpokes is a tad easier. After Strickland and his helpers finished culling the herd, they loaded some of the cattle onto a double-level trailer to go to a buyer who's a repeat customer. The truck and trailer belonged to a man named William "Bushrod" Duncan from Arcadia.

Duncan wore a cowboy hat like Strickland, and, like Strickland, he's the son of a cowboy. In the 1980s his father, Jack Duncan, was still riding and roping at age 67, which earned him a write-up in the *Los Angeles Times*. The paper quoted Jack Duncan saying folksy things such as, "If you can't do it on a horse, it's probably not worth doing."

"He was a cowboy 'til the day he died," Duncan said, his mellow voice carrying a strong country twang. "He worked all day, came home and ate supper, laid down on the couch and passed away." His father was 72 at the time of his fatal heart attack.

Duncan, 66, started out chasing cattle through the woods with his father, but then injured himself during a rodeo.

"When I hurt my back, I just quit cowboying and took up driving a truck," he said. "It was easier on my back. . . . I'm still a cowboy to the core. I just can't ride [horses] like I used to."

Duncan has watched with sadness the decline of Florida's cattle industry as, one by one, the ranchers sell off their property. He understands why they do it.

"Them developers come in and offer you five times what it's worth," he said, "and people who've worked hard all their lives, that's hard to turn down."

Some ranchers do the developing themselves. Right now, the biggest landowner in the state is the Church of Jesus Christ of Latter-day Saints. Church officials are already planning for the future development of some of their Deseret Ranch, situated near the headwaters of the St. Johns River. The scale of development proposed there, without significant conservation, could seriously degrade the water quality of the St. Johns River. According to *Florida Trend,* they envision 220,000 homes, 100 million square feet of commercial and institutional space, and close to 25,000 hotel rooms where now there are cattle and wild palms.

Once ranchland is paved over, little remains to mark what was once there, although there are exceptions. When Al Boyd sold off thousands of acres of northern Pinellas County ranchland, the 17-foot concrete boot that marked the boundary of his Boot Ranch property remained. Now his land is covered in subdivisions and strip malls, and the big boot stands in the parking lot of The Shoppes of Boot Ranch.

Strickland's story is more tragic than Duncan's. His father was killed in an accidental shooting when Strickland was 17.

At the time, he said, "We owned a little land but leased a lot for cattle. I stayed a rancher because that's what I loved but had a lot of help along the way. Mentors were and are a blessing."

His father's ranch foreman "took me under his wing and taught me how to rope and so forth," he recalled. He and the other cowboys would ride horses to drive their herds from one part of the ranch to another part where they could feed. Then the cowboys would feed, too.

"The foreman would be driving a Jeep, and he'd meet us somewhere along the fence line and build a fire and cook us some lunch," he said. "Some of us would hold the cattle while the rest of us ate lunch, and then we'd swap."

Blackbeard's current foreman can't help with the cattle on this day because he's in quarantine, recovering from a mild COVID-19 infection. Strickland runs the ranch with just two regular employees—the rest of the cowboys are day laborers, temporary hires who bounce from ranch to ranch.

As Strickland sorted the cattle on this hot day, the crew helping him included a 71-year-old neighbor spattered with mud from head to toe and the 11-year-old son of one of the ranch hands who'd wanted to accompany his dad to work. Both of them wore cowboy hats, but only the boy wore cowboy boots. The 71-year-old waded through the muck in white rubber boots that he called "Lakeport loafers."

Both said they loved working with cattle, spending time outdoors and riding horses. Despite their age difference, they smiled a very similar smile.

Not present: Strickland's son, who lives in Paris with his family and works for the diplomatic corps. Years ago, after spending lots of time ranching, he told Strickland, "I see how hard you work for how little money. It's not for me."

"Did it hurt my feelings?" Strickland said, looking down. "Yeah, a little."

* * *

Like Strickland, Alex Johns grew up in the cattle business. Like Strickland's son, he understands how low-paying a profession it is.

"I've been involved in ranching from day one," said Johns, 47. "I was born into it."

He's now the natural resource director for the Seminole Tribe, which means he oversees a co-op that controls ranches from the Georgia state line down to the Everglades. Yes, he's heard the jokes about Indians playing cowboy, but points out that his tribal ancestors started tending the Spanish cattle five centuries ago, so they're not newcomers to the field.

Despite the romantic image of cowboys, "it's pretty hard work, long days and very hot and humid conditions," Johns said, "and they find out there's not a lot of money." As a result, he said, it's "harder and harder to find good help."

Back in the heyday of Florida ranching, from the 1870s to the 1930s, cowboys needed only a few tools to do their jobs: a reliable horse and a comfortable saddle, a rope for tying up the cattle, a leather whip for cracking over the herd's head, a cow dog to help keep the cows going the right way, and a good memory for brands. Plenty of them also carried guns and knives for fighting rustlers or rival cowhands from other ranches.

"People ambushed each other all the time," said historian Canter Brown Jr., author of *Florida's Peace River Frontier.* "It was a rough locale and a rough life."

The premiere cowhand of those days was the tall and lanky Morgan Bonaparte "Bone" Mizell, who couldn't write his own name but was renowned for his ability to recall every brand of every rancher in the region around Arcadia. (He was also renowned for his alcohol consumption. Once, after he passed out during a cattle drive, his compadres relocated his bedroll into a nearby cemetery. When he woke up and looked around, he said, "Judgment Day, and I'm the first one up.")

These days, ranchers rely heavily on technology unavailable back in Bone Mizell's day. The cattle have clips attached to their ears that can be scanned with a smartphone, providing a full history of each cow, Johns said. The Seminoles don't drive their cattle to market. Instead, they sell them via Internet auction, uploading a video of each cow. Spreadsheets track the history of the herd.

Strickland's approach is similar. As the cattle he was sending to market took their turns on a cow-sized scale, the ranch manager frequently reached for his iPhone. He used it for calculations on their total weight before loading them on Duncan's truck. He also sent texts and photos to his customers so they knew what they were getting.

After Duncan drove away, Strickland showed off the ranch to a visitor—not by straddling a horse but by firing up an electric golf cart. The cart bounced along through the pastures as the rancher pointed out wells equipped with pumps operated by solar and wind power and talked about analyzing soil samples to maximize the growth of grass for grazing.

Keeping the ranch gates open has required diversifying the products for sale, he said. In addition to selling prime cuts of its own beef to local restaurants, Blackbeard's now sells Miakka Prairie Honey, collected from beehives set up across the fence from Myakka River State Park. Another product:

eggs and meat from Blackbeard's Heritage Breed Chickens. The ranch is developing a line of Blackbeard's Miakka Goat Cheese, too.

The pandemic has made Strickland glad the ranch diversified. Last year, with so many restaurants shut down for months, he said, Blackbeard's discovered that the only steady customer for its steaks was the fast-food chain, Wendy's.

As often happens with an industry on the downslope, some nostalgic people try to re-create the glories of the past.

North Florida rancher and storyteller Doyle Conner Jr., for instance, said he got roped into leading the first Great Florida Cattle Drive in 1995. He asked ranchers throughout the state to lend to the drive a native Florida breed known as "cracker cattle," instead of the more common modern breeds of Brahman, Brangus, and Beefmaster.

The Seminoles and every county in the state sent representative cow hunters to drive a herd of 1,000 cattle from Yeehaw Junction to Kissimmee. In 2006, they repeated the event but reversed the route.

The organizers wanted to hold one this year for the 500th anniversary of Ponce de León's cattle arriving in Florida but postponed it due to COVID-19.

A few years ago, Strickland participated in what he said was "the world's fastest cattle drive" to promote the launch of the photography book *Florida Cowboys: Keepers of the Last Frontier* by Carlton Ward Jr. and an accompanying art exhibit at the Tampa Bay History Center. Dogs that he and other ranchers brought along to lend the drive some historical authenticity got into a fight in the street. The snarling dogs stampeded the cattle so that they bolted past their destination and had to be brought back to the history center.

Strickland would much rather look forward to the future than back at the past. That's why he likes Julie Morris so much.

* * *

Driving around the ranch, Strickland pointed out the different habitats—dry prairies, maidencane marshes, live oak hammocks, cabbage islands, and longleaf pine savannas. They all attract wildlife, some of it rare or endangered. That's why he wants to maintain them just the way they are. For ranchers like Strickland who don't want to see developers turn their land into a row of cookie-cutter homes, Morris has suggestions.

Morris, now with the National Wildlife Refuge Association, has been working to conserve ranchlands for decades to find ways to preserve native habitat on these properties and funnel some badly needed income their way.

Sometimes that means selling the development rights by giving the state or local government a so-called "conservation easement" on some or all of the property. Sometimes it means tapping some other state or federal program—or a combination of the two—to enable a rancher to continue the five-century tradition a few years more.

"When you look at these ranchlands from an ecological perspective, it's such an eye-opener," she said. That's why the recently passed law creating the Florida Wildlife Corridor is so important for the future preservation of this type of land.

Anyone who wants to hang onto habitat for everything from gopher tortoises to panthers knows "we've got to keep these ranchlands intact somehow. They're keeping Florida green."

At Blackbeard's Ranch, Strickland has made use of Morris' recommendations to reduce the pressure to sell out the way some neighbors have. Beyond saving habitat, he sees a bigger reason to try to maintain ranchland as ranchland: climate change.

That's why, he said, the future of Florida ranching and the future of Florida itself are intertwined. The future of ranches like Blackbeard's may depend more on the ability to preserve the natural landscape—particularly carbon-absorbing forests—than on how many cattle can be sold at market.

Development has its place, he said, but "condos and new houses are not going to help you with climate change and sea level rise, not the way green space can."

3

CIA Island

CrimeReads, December 1, 2021

On Florida's Gulf coast near Fort Myers lies a sparkling island named Sanibel with about 7,000 residents. The island is known for two things.

One is the dazzling array of seashells that wash ashore on its gleaming white beaches. For more than a century, shell collectors from around the world—including such big names as Thomas Edison, Edna St. Vincent Millay, and Raymond Burr—have visited Sanibel to search the sands for the finest coquinas, lightning whelks, and lion's paws. The locals joke about the popular tourist "dance" move, the Sanibel Stoop.

Sanibel's other claim to fame is as the home of novelist Randy Wayne White and his hero Marion "Doc" Ford, a marine biologist who used to be a spy. Through 26 novels (so far), Doc has been repeatedly called back into action to right wrongs, protect the weak, solve crimes, and so forth. The series has sold so well that Sanibel is also home to a seafood restaurant called Doc Ford's, where in addition to the grouper and crab cakes, you can buy Doc Ford shirts, hats, and hot sauce.

How, you may ask, did White—a former fishing guide turned author—come up with the idea of planting a globe-trotting ex-spy amid the landscape of laid-back, super-casual Sanibel?

Easy. He drew from real life.

Sanibel is the only place in America to be incorporated largely through the efforts of former Central Intelligence Agency employees. One even became the first mayor.

* * *

Florida has plenty of unusual communities. There's Nalcrest, built for retirees from the National Association of Letter Carriers (no dogs allowed!); Cassadaga, a haven for mediums that bills itself as the Psychic Capital of the World; and Gibsonton, home to so many ex-carnies and sideshow performers that it was featured in an episode of *The X-Files* called "Humbug."

But a town run by ex-spies? That's odd even for Florida.

White makes it clear he, personally, is not a former spy. He was never affiliated with any covert agency in any capacity. He's been a guide, a magazine columnist, and a novelist—that's all. What he knows about foreign countries he has gleaned from his work for *Outside* magazine.

But you can't live and work in a small town like Sanibel without picking up a few clues about the neighbors, he said.

"I moved here in 1975 to be a guide, and I heard all the stories about the CIA," White said.

One story that made the rounds: CIA agents who trained Cuban exiles for the Bay of Pigs invasion on nearby Useppa Island fell in love with the area and moved to Sanibel when they retired.

There is a factual basis to this one. Useppa was indeed the training ground for that particular foreign policy fiasco. The Useppa Island Historical Society's museum maintains a permanent exhibit about it.

But Porter Goss, an ex-spy who's been a friend of White's for four decades, says the Bay of Pigs is not the reason he wound up trading in his trench coat for cutoffs and flip-flops.

Instead, it was a more personal connection.

* * *

Goss, raised a Connecticut Yankee, graduated from prep school and Yale and spent two years working for Army Intelligence before he was recruited to join the CIA.

To prep this preppie for undercover work, the spymasters put Goss through a training course that covered "everything from lock-picking to very esoteric, mind-bending intellectual training," Goss told the *Miami Herald* in a 1987 story headlined, "A little intelligence goes a long way, politicos say."

He spent 10 years as a junior clandestine officer in places he can't mention doing things he can't talk about. A 2004 *Guardian* profile says Goss, who speaks fluent Spanish, was based in Miami during the Cuban Missile Crisis of 1962 and "had some interesting moments in the Florida Straits," and later he recruited and supervised agents targeting Communist infiltration of labor unions in Central America and Europe.

But around 1970, he fell seriously ill. Systemic blood poisoning caused a heart infection and kidney problems. After months in a London hospital, "my doctor said I needed a place with some peace and quiet," Goss said.

That's when one of his former bosses invited him to bring his family to Sanibel—which would soon be full of anything but peace and quiet.

* * *

Goss had vacationed on another nearby barrier island, Boca Grande, and found it to be "absolute heaven," he said, so persuading him to move his family to Florida's Gulf Coast didn't take much work.

The invitation came from Don Whitehead, a onetime political science professor who had a yen to write—and who also was an ex-CIA man who had been Goss' supervisor.

When Whitehead retired, he and his wife Grace had searched all up and down the state's Gulf Coast for a beachfront condo they could afford. What sold them on Sanibel was a comment from a real estate saleswoman that there were no condos on Sanibel and never would be.

With its natural beauty and slow pace, Sanibel seemed different from all the other places they'd lived. They had ended up building a modest one-story block home with a swimming pool.

"They found us a place to stay—a small house on a back lane—while I continued my recovery," Goss said.

Soon Goss and Whitehead were joined by a third ex-CIA man, another of Goss' onetime bosses, Fred Valtin.

As an agency employee in the 1960s, Valtin "helped the Germans establish a postwar government under the auspices of the CIA," his widow later told the *New York Times*. "He hung around with Willy Brandt and helped build the Social Democratic Party."

By the time he retired in 1973, Valtin was director of Planning, Programming and Budget of the CIA's Directorate of Operations.

Once they were all together on Sanibel, the three families spent so much time socializing, Goss' son Chauncey recalled, "I grew up thinking everybody worked for the CIA."

Just for fun, the three ex-agents started a boat rental company, keeping their meager profits in a shoebox. The fun ran out pretty quickly.

"It became very clear, when we were cleaning fish goo off the boats with no-see-ums eating us alive in the 90-degree heat, that this business was getting a little old," Goss said.

At Whitehead's suggestion, they started Sanibel's first homegrown newspaper. That's where the trouble started.

* * *

Because Sanibel was an unincorporated community, its future lay in the hands of the Lee County Commission. Lee County is named for General Robert E. Lee, even though he never set foot there. The commissioners meet beneath a portrait of the Confederate leader gazing down at them with a look of vague disappointment.

When Whitehead, Goss, and Valentin started the *Island Reporter* in 1973, Goss began attending the commission meeting. He would drive over to the county seat of Fort Myers to gather intel—or "take notes," as reporters call it. Then he would pass his observations along to Whitehead, who would write them up in newspaper story form.

It didn't take long to see that they had gotten involved in something even nastier than fish goo.

At that time, most Florida county governments were unabashedly pro-development. The Lee County commissioners went beyond that. They saw no reason to reject any development plans anywhere.

And they and their developer pals had set their sights on quiet, lovely Sanibel, even if it involved putting a string of tacky condominiums right on the beach.

"There was a growth-versus-no-growth division on the island at the time, but the black-hat developers were in the minority," Goss recalled. "But that's the group that held great sway with Lee County. Sanibel was the goose that laid the golden egg for Lee County."

The *Island Reporter* took an editorial stand: Sanibel should incorporate so it could chart its own course. Otherwise, say goodbye to the things that make the island so beautiful, they wrote.

The county commissioners and their developer friends struck back, painting a picture of the pro-incorporation forces as elitists who had their slice of paradise and didn't want to share it. They also argued that Sanibel was too small to be a city. To Goss it was pure propaganda, easily exposed as such by the feisty little newspaper.

"Don and Fred and I had seen this kind of action before," he explained. "If you're a CIA officer working in a foreign country, you're going to see how propaganda works, including some cases where you're involved in creating it. We knew how to expose some of these tactics."

Sanibel voters flocked to the polls and, in 1974, overwhelmingly supported incorporating as a city so they, not the Lee commissioners, could control the future of their island. When they picked their first council members, the council then selected Goss as the island's first mayor.

"I was everybody's second choice," he joked.

What that meant was that he was the one who was handed the legal papers every time a would-be developer sued the city for not approving a project that conflicted with Sanibel's new, restrictive comprehensive plan for future growth.

"The process server was a regular at our house," Goss said. "We'd usually offer him a beer and a sandwich."

* * *

Disgruntled developers blamed the federal agency that once employed their nemeses, complaining that the CIA was buying up property and would take over the island. But Goss makes it clear the trio operated independently from the agency, which is forbidden by law from carrying out operations in the United States.

"The CIA recruits leaders, and they train you to lead," he explained to the *Herald* for its 1987 story.

The paper noted that Goss had been succeeded as mayor by his fellow CIA retiree, Valentin. Meanwhile, the mayor of nearby Naples was a former member of the CIA's predecessor agency, the Office of Strategic Services, and in another nearby town, Cape Coral, there was another CIA retiree who had served as a council member and mayor.

By contrast, three of the county commissioners who had opposed the Sanibel incorporation were busted for, among other things, taking a boat ride with prostitutes, courtesy of the county's sewer contractor. The contractor was himself acquitted of bribery but later convicted of stealing $1.7 million from a public highway project.

In a nice irony, one of the people that Democratic governor Bob Graham appointed to fill out the term of one of the ousted commissioners was none other than Goss, a Republican. He would then go on to win election to a seat in Congress, where he spent eight years as chairman of the House Intelligence Committee, and then was appointed CIA director, where he served for two years before retiring all over again.

But did any of the ex-spies who retired to Florida ever hire Randy Wayne White as a fishing guide before he became a bestselling novelist writing about an ex-spy?

"If they were, they never shared that info with me," White said. "Who knows?"

Postscript: I first met Goss while covering his first congressional race. Because reporters are supposed to check the background of candidates, I called up the CIA and asked if Goss had actually worked there. Someone promised to get back to me. Eventually, I got a phone call from someone at the CIA who wouldn't identify himself. He told me, "I can confirm that Mr. Goss worked here—but that's all I'm allowed to say" And then he hung up.

4

The Buzz about Tupelo Honey

FORUM, Spring 2023

Start with the golden liquid itself.

Hold a jar of it up to the light and examine its beauty. Experts describe it as a light amber with a slight greenish cast.

Open the top and inhale. Some call its aroma "pear-like," and "hoppy."

Now take a taste of tupelo honey, the most magical—and most endangered—of Florida's homegrown culinary treats. Marvel at its floral, buttery flavor. Marvel that there's no aftertaste, no bitterness.

Marvel, too, that it exists at all these days.

"There are some things in this world that you can't mass produce, and tupelo honey is one of them," says Glynnis Lanier, whose family-owned business in Gulf County has been selling tupelo honey since 1898. Her husband Ben started off "in the bee yard" at age 6 and is now 65—and he's getting ready to hand it off to their son Heath, age 19.

As a concept in pop culture, tupelo honey is available all over. Turn on an oldies radio station and there's the Van Morrison hit titled "Tupelo Honey" from the 1971 album of the same name. In it the Irish singer-songwriter raves about how sweet his wife is.

The song itself is so sweet that on a 1994 episode of the TV show *Friends,* one of the characters proclaims it the most romantic song of all time. (His on-again, off-again girlfriend disagrees.)

Then there's the 1997 movie, *Ulee's Gold,* starring Peter Fonda as a Florida beekeeper whose specialty is tupelo honey. Fonda's performance won him a Golden Globe and an Oscar nomination. The Van Morrison song plays at the end.

There's even a chain of restaurants called Tupelo Honey Southern Kitchen, the name suggesting both regional authenticity and quality ingredients. The chain has locations in the South, Midwest, and West, but there's not a single Tupelo Honey Southern Kitchen in Florida. That's even though tupelo honey is the official honey of the state of Florida, so declared by the legislature in 2016.

Florida is the best place to find real tupelo honey, not some weak mixture with an inferior honey that falsely claims to be tupelo. You can taste it straight from the jar, drip it on some biscuits, or drizzle it over whatever you're cooking and make it taste better.

The only problem with real tupelo honey is that when you find it, you're liable to find it's all sold out.

* * *

Some people think tupelo honey comes from the same place Elvis did—Tupelo, Mississippi. These people are liable to also mistake noon for midnight and water for gasoline.

To get real tupelo honey, go to the small town of Wewahitchka in Gulf County, a 30-minute drive east from Panama City. How small is the town the locals call "Wewa"? The last census counted about 2,000 residents.

The humans are greatly outnumbered by the hundreds of thousands of honeybees in the hives.

Tupelo honey comes from only two tiny regions—the Apalachicola River basin on the Gulf Coast, and the area around the Okefenokee Wildlife Refuge on the Georgia-Florida line. Although other Florida towns, including Apalachicola, produce the honey, Wewa is the center of Florida's tupelo honey industry.

Wewa is not a rich town, not by a long shot. Jim Rish, who at 70 is the fourth generation of his family to be in the tupelo honey business, compares it to Dogpatch, the tumbledown hometown of comic strip hillbilly *Li'l Abner.*

Yet the honey sold there is far more expensive than any honey produced elsewhere. A 12-ounce jar on the Internet was recently priced at $29.

"It's always at least twice as much as other types of honey, if not more," said Rish, who on LinkedIn lists his position as "bossman" at Rish Tupelo Honey.

In a good year, the tupelo honey harvest can make a beekeeper a small fortune. Rish offered this example: A barrel of honey weighs 650 pounds. At a time when tupelo honey was selling for $15 a pound, he collected 22 barrels of it. That's a sweet $214,500 in all.

Tupelo honey "has a huge economic impact here," says Joel Whitmer, executive director of the Gulf County Chamber of Commerce. The only other industries in the county, he says, are timber, tourism, and fishing.

The golden liquid is so central to Wewa's existence that the town holds a Tupelo Honey Festival every May, a practice that started in 1941. There's even a Tupelo Honey Queen. Fans travel for hundreds of miles to buy as much honey as they can afford.

Vendors at the festival know that the best way to sell their product is with a free sample.

"Don't tell them what it costs—that'll freak them out," Rish says. "But once they taste it, they'll say, 'I've got to have that.'"

* * *

Bees make tupelo honey, of course, not the humans like Lanier and Rish who harvest and sell it.

They do this by collecting pollen from the green and white blossoms of the white tupelo gum tree. That greenish tint in the honey comes from leftover bits of the pollen, Rish says.

During the dozen or so days when the tupelos are in bloom, the keepers unleash their bees on the blossoms, trying to time it just right so that their swarms target only the tupelo, and not anything else. Wait too late and you could wind up with some gallberry pollen in the mix instead.

"If you harvest at the right time, you get a good grade of tupelo," Rish says.

Soon the hives and their wooden frames will be filled with honeycomb loaded with honey. When the bees have loaded up their hives, the beekeepers will tote the 90-pound boxes of honey-laden wood frames into their honey houses, which is the place for extracting and processing the honey. Rish's honey house dates back to 1902.

Each of the wooden boxes contains 10 frames. Beekeepers pull out each frame and, using an electric knife or a device called "a scratcher," slice off any wax caps the bees put on the sides of the comb. Then they slide the frames into an extractor, which works sort of like a top-load washing machine.

In a video that Rish paid $2,500 to make after a good year, he shows how the extractor uses a combination of steam and centrifugal force to sling the honey free of the comb. The honey rains down the side and flows into a filtering device to catch any wax, then pumps it out into barrels.

Because of its high fructose content, pure tupelo honey resists turning into crystals the way many other honeys do as they age. If you buy something labeled "tupelo honey" and it crystallizes, you've been suckered.

White tupelo trees grow in swampy spots around the South, the trees rooting themselves in places where they can drink their fill of the tannin-stained water.

"They need a lot of water, so they grow in the water," Lanier says.

Nowhere else do they grow as thick as they do along the banks of the Apalachicola and Chipola Rivers in the Florida Panhandle and in the Altamaha River basin of Georgia, say the Wewa honey experts.

Usually, the tupelo trees bloom for no more than two weeks from mid-April to mid-May. The length of the blooming period varies, though, making it just one of the dozens of variables that make tupelo honey such a challenge.

"I've seen it bloom for only one day," Lanier says. "Or for three days. You hope it blooms long enough to produce enough honey to get you through the year."

* * *

The first beekeeper to discover the magic of tupelo honey was a gray-bearded gentleman named S. S. Alderman who lived on an island in the Chipola River. A magazine for beekeepers called *Gleanings in Bee Culture* published an interview with him in which he talked about buying his first bees in 1872.

In those days, roads were few and often too rough for a horse-drawn cart to travel safely. Alderman transported his hives to the tupelos via a barge, with the honey the bees produced shipped out via waterway as well.

The first Rishes and Laniers came along a few years after Alderman, and in that order. Although the two families share a love for honey, the relations between them are more sour than sweet. Rish, for his part, refers to the Laniers as "Brand X."

The Laniers are so well established that Ben Lanier served as a technical advisor for *Ulee's Gold,* parts of which director Victor Nunez filmed on the family's property.

The Laniers' finances depend entirely on a successful honey harvest. Rish, on the other hand, has other sources of income: a disability check from his military service and a pension from when he was a Presbyterian minister in Texas.

"I don't have to work at all," he says. "I just do it because I want to. It's outdoor work. It's honest work. And it's a family tradition."

The older apiarists are now facing competition from younger folk like Pam Palmer, whom everyone calls "Miss Pam" because she used to be a middle school principal and guidance counselor.

When she retired from the school system, Palmer says, she was looking for something else to do—teaching yoga, perhaps. She noticed on Facebook that a parent she knew from her school years, a onetime carpenter named Gary Alderson, had left the construction business amid the 2008 economic meltdown and instead was trying beekeeping. She wound up joining him as a partner.

Soon love bloomed just like the tupelo trees. Now they're married.

"It's a sweet little love story," she jokes.

But as much as the couple loves running Blue-Eyed Girl Honey—named for their granddaughter—it doesn't pay the bills. They also run a home construction business and keep up with the bees in their spare time.

"We build houses to make a living," Miss Pam admits. "The honey business takes more money than it makes."

* * *

New or old, the tupelo honey makers face challenges far beyond what their forebears faced.

Since they became beekeepers, says Lanier, "a lot has changed."

Water flow has decreased in the Apalachicola River, partly as a result of suburban Atlantans further upriver watering their lawns and golf courses. That affects the tupelo trees.

So do the heavier, harder storms brought by a changing climate. In October 2018, Category 5 Hurricane Michael slammed into the Panhandle with a fury fueled by hotter-than-normal Gulf of Mexico water temperatures.

The previous spring had brought a bumper crop of honey, thanks to blossoms that just dripped with their loads of nectar, Lanier says. Everyone had high hopes for the following year. Then the storm clobbered them.

"Michael just tore this place up," Lanier says. "It took every piece of vegetation off of every tree."

A lot of beekeepers lost thousands of bees in the storm, Gulf County extension agent Ray Bodry says. But the extension agent surveyed damage to the tupelo trees and was amazed at how many somehow survived while other types of trees were obliterated.

But then something odd happened.

"The weird thing is that they were blooming in December," he says. "They continued to bloom through the early part of the winter. Then when they tried to bloom again in the spring, they couldn't."

That wiped out the 2019 tupelo honey harvest.

"The trees were under so much stress," Lanier says. "The tupelo trees have not bloomed good since then."

The changing climate has also hurt the population of wild bees, which are important to pollination of crops. To try to make up for that, some bee-keepers have begun renting their hives out as pollinators and trucking them around the country. Lanier says her family refuses to do that. They want to keep their bees close by, so they can keep an eye on them.

Climate change has also aided the spread of invasive pests on Florida farms, according to state climatologist David Zierden. The greatest threat to the bees these days comes from parasitic Varroa mites, first discovered among Florida hives in 1987. They were spotted in September, and by October they had shown up in 19 of the 67 counties. By 1989, they had spread to beehives in nearly 20 states.

The mites don't hurt the bees directly but transmit a harmful virus to them. They become crippled, unable to fly well. The mites are considered such a major threat that their full scientific name is *Varroa destructor*.

The mites can be killed off with a chemical treatment, but using it requires a delicate touch.

"A lot of stuff that will kill the mites will also kill the bees," warns Lanier. "Everybody puts so many chemicals in the environment, anyway, and the bees are so sensitive to everything. I figure that if it's not good for the bees, it's probably not good for you, either."

* * *

Then there's the controversy over colony collapse disorder.

In the winter of 2006, a Pennsylvania beekeeper who had shipped his bees to Florida became the first to report an odd phenomenon that soon began popping up all over the country. The worker bees in the hives disappeared, leaving behind the queen, some of the younger bees, and plenty of food. It's as if they went out for cigarettes and lottery tickets and never returned.

Hives can't exist without plenty of worker bees to maintain them, so the colony would simply collapse. Because the affected bees had disappeared, and the hives seemed normal, scientists were baffled. The mysterious disappearances have led to some wild theories.

"I had one lady tell me that the towers using 5G were making the antennas on (the bees') heads pick up these signals," Palmer says.

A consortium called the Bee Informed Partnership sent out survey forms to beekeepers across the country, seeking information on what was going on, says James Ellis, a honeybee husbandry expert and entomology professor at the University of Florida.

Only in the first year was colony collapse disorder listed in the top five reasons for bee losses, says Ellis, who created the university's Master Beekeeper Program. Afterward, poor nutrition, mites, and bad weather all ranked higher, he says.

Further research deepened the mystery. Turns out beekeepers from years past reported a similar phenomenon, calling it spring dwindle disease, fall dwindle disease, autumn collapse, May disease, and disappearing disease. They still haven't found the cause or causes.

To Lanier, this is just one of a multitude of threats to her family's longtime livelihood.

"It's a constant battle to keep your bees alive," she says. "It's a big risk every year whether you'll bring in a honey crop. Sometimes you make it. Sometimes you don't."

* * *

Lanier sees other threats, too. Georgia, for instance.

Georgia beekeepers have been making a lot of noise lately that they can produce tupelo honey that's just as good as Florida's, she says. A 2019 *New York Times* story on tupelo honey in both states suggested that Georgia's honey had overtaken the Florida standard that year.

However, her husband told the *New York Times,* "It's impossible to make good tupelo honey in Georgia."

Lanier says she's also concerned about the mixtures. Some major distributors are selling jars labeled "tupelo honey" that are around 50 percent tupelo and 50 percent some other, lesser type.

"Who wants 50 percent of something?" she asks, clearly offended.

Some threats are more personal. After Hurricane Michael battered their beekeeping operation, she says, Ben was walking in the swamp, checking the trees, "and he couldn't get his legs to work." Rushed to the doctor, he learned that "all three of his main arteries were almost 100 percent blocked," she says. That's why they needed their son to step in.

Between her husband's illness and dealing with the aftermath of the hurricane, she says, "it has been an ordeal the last couple of years."

Rish, though, is optimistic about the future. He says he worked with a team from Florida A&M University to design a trap for a pest known as hive beetles that seems to work well.

And he, too, is working with the next generation of his family. He made his son a sweet deal.

"Right now, we're partners," Rish says. "We're licensed hemp growers, too."

The hemp isn't a supplement to the honey collection, he explains. It's become a part of their honey operation.

"We found a way to infuse tupelo honey into hemp," Rish explains. Just as adding tupelo honey to your cooking improves flavor, adding it to the hemp "makes it taste better."

5

The Royal Story

Florida Phoenix, May 19, 2022

If you plan to visit the historic Central Florida community of Royal, I have two pieces of advice for you:

(1) Don't go there feeling hungry. There are no fast-food joints or other restaurants where you can order a Royal version of the Royale with Cheese.
(2) You better hurry. Powerful people are plotting its destruction as we speak. Their reasoning is that this is the price of progress, can't make an omelet without breaking some eggs, and all those other clichés.

I drove through Royal on Sunday afternoon, just to take a look at it before the shady politicians and greedy developers pushing the Northern Turnpike Extension obliterate it.

One of my passengers described the area as "rustic," which seemed like just the right word for this quiet slice of Sumter County. We saw cows. We saw farms. We saw a mix of mobile homes and single-story houses, none of them close to each other.

We stopped at the community center to read the town's historical marker. Royal's origin story is a standing rebuke to anyone who thinks Florida history started in 1971 when Walt Disney World opened.

Royal dates to the waning days of the Civil War. I got the whole story by spending about an hour talking to Beverly Steele, 66, who oversees the community center and is the keeper of Royal's history.

My hour talking with her seems about 59 minutes more than the Florida Department of Transportation spent researching what will be lost if they ram this unwanted road through Royal.

"This will destroy our community," she told me. "It's going to pave over two of our churches and my community center is in its path and it's going through most of our populated area."

It also takes aim at their cemetery, which Steele told me a DOT consultant said had no historical significance.

That's only true if you don't count the formerly enslaved people buried there.

* * *

Royal's original founders were recently freed slaves who had been living and working on a plantation bordering the nearby Withlacoochee River, Steele told me.

How could ex-enslaved people buy land? They didn't. They were handed ownership by order of General William Tecumseh Sherman, the man who gave Atlanta an extreme makeover.

Brace yourself, Buttercup. I am about to lay on you some of that "critical race theory" that Governor Ron "Welcome-to-the-Not-So-Free-State-of-Florida" DeSantis hates with such a passion.

In January 1865, Sherman issued an order giving all freed slaves under his jurisdiction—which covered some 400,000 acres across the South—the gift of 40 acres (and, later, a mule). That would get them started on the road to freedom.

America had stolen their liberty as well as their ability to choose where they lived and to get paid for their labors, their opportunities for education, and their right to be safe in their own bodies. The law said they belonged to their "masters," as if they were cows or chickens. Surely America owed them something to make up for that wholesale theft.

But after Abe Lincoln's assassination, his successor as president, Andrew Johnson, overruled Sherman (here's the CRT part). He ordered the return of the land to its white owners, even though they had rebelled against the United States.

By then, though, Royal had gotten its start and its residents had no intention of giving anything back.

"Royal quickly became known as a location where African-Americans could own property and engage in various business activities," Steele told me via email. "Faced with increasing restrictions elsewhere, Royal became very attractive in the years following Reconstruction."

As a Black community, Royal has faced some government decision-making that, if it was not racially motivated, sure gave that appearance. Its school remained segregated for about 20 years after the Brown v. Board decision. Meanwhile, the community was bisected by the construction of Interstate 75 in the '50s, although later an overpass reconnected the halves.

A child stands in a farmer's field in Royal in the 1960s. Photo courtesy of Beverly Steele.

(I contacted several Florida historians, and they said they'd never heard the Royal story before. One of them, by the way, wrote a book about antebellum Florida called *A Rogue's Paradise,* so it seems to me that not much has changed in the past 161 years.)

Most of the estimated 1,200 residents who live in Royal today are descendants of those freed slaves, Steele told me. They still live on their inherited portions of the 40-acre parcels their ancestors first settled.

"It's a beautiful thing for me to walk on the same land they walked on," she said. "They walked it in work boots, and because of them I walk it in three-inch stiletto heels with a tiger print."

Now here comes the DOT to stomp its way through the community like Godzilla.

This destruction is bad for Royal, of course. But the residents can take some comfort in the fact that the new highway will make some of Royal's neighbors rich.

One of them, by the way, has given gobs of cash to the governor and his political party.

* * *

State officials have been trying to build a northward extension of the Florida Turnpike since the spectacularly colorful Claude Kirk was governor in the

1960s. (Kirk once rode a horse to a news conference, brought a woman he called "Madame X" to his inauguration, and planted the state flag on the ocean floor, among other eccentricities.)

Charles Lee of Audubon Florida, whose career as an environmental activist started around the time Juan Ponce de Leon was sipping from our fountains, told me the DOT has tried to build this misbegotten project at least three times.

Each time, the turnpike extension plan has delighted developers who foresaw making big bucks and angered local residents who fought to keep their rural area rural. Each time, that vocal local opposition has defeated the developer-driven road, Lee told me.

Lee sent me some old newspaper clippings, which made for entertaining reading. I particularly liked the one in which a DOT official told the *Miami Herald* in 1999, "The traffic numbers are low enough that it doesn't meet any economic feasibility test."

This time, it wasn't the DOT that dug up this dead horse to beat it some more. It was the Florida Legislature.

In 2019, our fine lawmakers passed a bill calling for three massively expensive toll roads that would serve no purpose except as a payback for a large campaign contribution to the senate president from the Florida Transportation Builders Association.

Governor DeSantis was fine with this waste of time and money. He signed the bill and announced, with his usual keen political insight, "I think we need new roads in Florida to get around."

Then, when costs shot up because of the pandemic, the legislators passed a new bill last year repealing their edict for two of the roads but leaving in place the Northern Turnpike Extension. (The governor, with his usual keen political insight, signed this bill without comment.)

The folks in Royal first learned in December that their land was being considered for the turnpike extension route, Steele said. They started getting letters from lawyers specializing in eminent domain. Those are the cases in which the state seizes your land against your will and pays you whatever it can convince a court is fair.

This sort of rude awakening is not the best way for a government agency to charm property owners into feeling cooperative.

Shortly thereafter, DOT officials invited them to a public meeting to talk about it. They invited DOT officials to come to them instead. The message the residents delivered, according to Steele, was simple: "Stay out of Royal."

The DOT "is committed to refining the current alternative corridors to avoid and minimize impacts to communities and environmentally sensitive features to the extent possible as the project progresses," a turnpike spokeswoman named Angela Starke told me.

"As such, FDOT will refine the corridors to minimize the impacts to the community of Royal." (I would note that "refine" is not the same as "avoid.")

Meanwhile, though, folks like developer Carlos Beruff have already made plans to cash in.

Beruff, a Manatee County developer and onetime U.S. Senate candidate, has a long record as both a GOP campaign contributor and a guy whose concern for the environment ranks well below his concern for making a fortune.

Right now, for instance, he's under investigation for illegally trimming mangroves. Back in 2016, he told me he wanted to cut back those mangroves "for the obvious reason—the view!"

Beruff is a generous guy, though. For instance, Sumter county commissioner Roberta Ulrich—appointed to the commission earlier this year by DeSantis—"has raised the bulk of her campaign cash from a big-name GOP donor living outside the county," the *Villages-News* reported this month. That donor: Beruff.

I am sure his generosity had nothing to do with the speed with which one of his companies, SR 44 LLC, was able to win county approval for a change in its zoning. The change was necessary so Beruff could turn a 100-acre pasture near Royal into a site for a new freight distribution center for truckers.

Now a Citrus County couple, Jim and Lynda Fenton of Floral City, who run a citrus, strawberry, and cattle operation, are applying for a similar zoning change, with similar intent. But their property, at 600 acres, is much larger, and it's much closer to Royal.

Sumter County's own zoning report spells out what's going on: "The high demand for industrial land near the I-75/SR 44 interchange is in response to state plans to extend the Florida Turnpike through the area."

It's as if they're seeing all those trucks booming by on I-75 and picturing them full of money and pulling into their property instead.

I tried to contact Beruff and the Fentons about this, but they didn't return my calls. I suppose they felt awkward discussing how much profit they would make—and how they would lose out if the Northern Turnpike Extension were canceled again.

So now Royal residents are battling both the DOT's road plan and also the speculators who hope to start servicing 18-wheelers driving on the road that doesn't exist yet.

I haven't even mentioned the effects on the aquifer yet.

* * *

Sumter County's biggest and best-known community is the mostly white retirement mecca known as The Villages.

The Villages has gained national attention for its cases of voter fraud, its golf cart–related crimes, and its occasional instances of sex in public.

It's also one of Florida's major water guzzlers. Officials in The Villages suck so much water out of the aquifer to keep the golf courses green that sinkholes are constantly popping open.

Royal doesn't have that problem. But its residents do rely on well water, Steele told me. That flow from underground has been a major feature of the community ever since its founding.

In fact, when she was a young girl, everyone frequently congregated at a naturally formed water body they called "The Sinkhole."

"The men would go down and start fires and the women would start fishing, and by the time we kids got there, we could smell the fish frying," she said.

Now imagine the pollution running off a highway or a truck stop built on top of that, she said. The people who aren't forced off their land by the turnpike extension would likely see their wells contaminated by the pollution.

"People are not going to be able to live here in peace," she said.

It's an ugly scenario—one of many revolving around the Northern Turnpike Extension, which has once again ticked off a bunch of people in its pathway.

But the DOT's threat to dethrone Royal presents Governor DeSantis with a rare opportunity to use his keen political insight.

By signing both the 2019 bill and the 2021 repeal, DeSantis has officially endorsed this Northern Turnpike Extension not once but twice. It's his highway. In fact, I plan to start calling it the Ron DeSantis Road to Ruin— the "Ron Road" for short.

If the Ron Road does indeed steamroll through Royal, that will show that the "critical race theory" he despises so much is no theory at all. It's as real as his desire to be the Official Dreamy Hunk Poster Boy of *Fox & Friends*.

Lee pointed out to me that there is a clear alternative to the DOT's proposed pathway: widening I-75. That's what a local advisory committee wanted in the first place.

"No one would dispute the need to expand I-75, and it could be done with next-to-zero environmental impacts," Lee said.

By ordering the DOT to pursue I-75 widening instead of his "Ron Road," DeSantis could end the threat to this historic Black community and placate all those other turnpike opponents ready to break out their pitchforks and torches.

Then he could claim that Royal's continued survival is evidence that critical race theory is just liberal poppycock.

Of course, he'd have to explain the decision to all those disappointed developers. I'm sure they'll understand if he explains it right. He could tell them that line about making an omelet.

———————

Postscript: In August 2022, the DOT announced that, because of widespread community opposition along every potential route, it would "pause" its Northern Turnpike Extension plans and instead work on expanding I-75. So it's not dead, just in a holding pattern.

6

Stinky Town

Florida Phoenix, August 31, 2023

This weekend my wife and I helped our older son pack up and move to Jacksonville. He's starting a new job, occupying a new apartment, and driving a new (used) car.

It was a bittersweet trip. After we arrived, we heard about the Nazi who shot three Black people and then killed himself. In other words, it wasn't a propitious time to move to the town everyone calls Jax, but it was too late to turn back.

On the way there, my wife was reminiscing about a visit she'd made back in the 1980s. The smell, she said, was horrible. The whole place reeked. Thank heavens those days were over.

I had forgotten about that. From the 1930s to the 1990s, a pair of paper mills, along with a handful of chemical plants, constantly blanketed parts of the city with their foul emissions. Kids growing up there used to joke that the horrible smell proved Jacksonville really was "the armpit of the universe."

Although lots of people complained, nobody in charge wanted it to go away.

"Some of us say it smells like money," a mayor named Hans Tanzler once joked, pointing out how many people were employed by the source of the stink. This was a popular sentiment among the ruling class in Jax. They claimed the smell was just the consequence of all those jobs, and you couldn't have one without the other.

However, that money-making aroma also drove people away, according to Bill Delaney, a writer whose work frequently focuses on the history and culture of what's known as Florida's "First Coast."

Promising youngsters would flee as soon as they were old enough to hit the road. Meanwhile, executives of potential new corporate citizens would stop off in town, take one whiff, and head for someplace that smelled cleaner.

The city acquired a national reputation for its repellent odor. One local official said the city bore "the stigma of a stinky town."

Delaney, who grew up in Jacksonville as the son of a former mayor, said the stench always made him think of "fire and brimstone and the pits of hell."

It wasn't only that hellish smell that people disliked. The smoke billowing from those mills carried bad news for everyone's health, too.

Yet for 60 years, people had to put up with it because someone made money from the status quo. And then, when certain factors fell into place, everything changed.

It's not unlike what's been happening these days with our stinky, pollution-fueled, toxic algae blooms, hazards to both our health and our tourist economy. A lot of us would love to see some limits on the pollution that fuels the blooms, but so far the state has let us down.

History often offers us clues from the past to solving our current problems. That's why—in between preparing for Hurricane Idalia—I decided to find out how Jacksonville finally beat the stink.

* * *

Jacksonville was once known by the rather bland name "Cow Ford." It wound up adopting its current moniker to honor Andrew Jackson, Florida's first territorial governor (and so far, the only one to successfully run for president).

Jacksonville was mocked regularly on the recent TV comedy *The Good Place*. The show depicted it as a lawless swamp occupied by clueless dopes who crash their Jet Skis into manatees and spray-paint flamingos. On the show, the Jax airport is named for Randy "Macho Man" Savage, the patron saint of Slim Jims.

Actually, an impressive bunch of people have called Jax home. Harriet Beecher Stowe moved down after the Civil War. It's where James Weldon Johnson penned his most enduring poem. Labor leader A. Philip Randolph, who organized the 1963 March on Washington, went to school there.

There's quite a musical legacy, too. Pat Boone was born there. Ma Rainey honed her blues in the clubs in Jax. The Allman Brothers and Lynyrd Skynyrd invented Southern rock there.

One of the most important events in the city's history occurred in 1937. That's when a Russian immigrant named Samuel Kipnis told the local chamber of commerce he planned to open the city's first paper mill. He

A crane with logs at a Jacksonville paper company. Photo from the Florida State Archives.

promised it would produce a $1 million payroll for local residents and purchase 100,000 tons of wood a year from the region's tree farmers.

"When I become a citizen of Jacksonville, as I expect to in the near future, I will have the job of promoting goodwill for the National Container Corp. here," Kipnis said.

He made no mention of what the smell would be like.

In 1953, a company called St. Regis opened a second paper mill a few miles north of National Container, and within a few years had expanded its operation along the St. Johns River.

Other chemical plants opened nearby, and they contributed to the nose-scorching stew, as did the city's odiferous sewer plant, said Charles E. Closmann, who teaches environmental history at the University of North Florida.

The smell wasn't the only objectionable thing coming out of the smokestacks, either.

In 1978, for instance, what people described as a "sticky yellow film" fell from the sky and settled on hundreds of new cars at a car dealership near the paper mills. It caused an estimated $200,000 in damage. Then, in 1980, it happened again. As a result, BMW of North America stopped shipping 15,000 cars each year through the Port of Jacksonville.

As the city grew, so did the number of complaints—as did the number of national headlines. A 1983 Associated Press story reported "It Isn't

Roses You Smell When in Jacksonville." The story began, "In Jacksonville the problem is—well, the city stinks."

On particularly bad days the awful odor wafted up to 30 miles inland. But most of the time, it didn't affect the city's wealthier enclaves, Delaney said, making it easy for the powers-that-be to ignore what was affecting the rest of the city.

"It was a legacy of the Jim Crow era," he told me. "The poorer neighborhoods were always targeted for these kinds of things."

In the early 1980s, a retired Navy pilot named Walter Honour became the chief of Duval County's Bioenvironmental Services Department, and he tried to rein in the reek, Closmann said.

Political leaders didn't like that. They "forced him out of office," Closmann said. After his ouster, you could say the city was literally without Honour.

Jacksonville's elected officials were so tied in with the local power structure that they wouldn't rock the boat for some blue-collar concern, Closmann said. They clung to the foul aroma, despite the fact that it was so putrid even James Brown would have deemed it too funky.

They wouldn't even take action after a 1982 study published by the American Cancer Society reported that, between 1970 and 1975, Duval County had the nation's highest death rate from lung cancer.

But then, in 1985, came a pivotal moment for Jacksonville, Closmann said. One of the instigators was a fellow named Reagan.

No, not that one.

* * *

These days when television stations do what they call investigative reporting, it's often some minor consumer protection issue that needs to be straightened out. But back in the post-Watergate era, local TV did some serious investigations.

In the 1980s, Harry Reagan was editorial director of Jacksonville's WJXT-TV. He's still around, so I called him up to ask how the station's most famous investigative story got started.

"In the good old days of local journalism," he said, "we would periodically look around and say, 'I wonder why we continually have to put up with that?'"

That's how the subject of the Big Stink came up.

"The people in Jacksonville had given up trying to get rid of it," he recalled.

Reagan's news team started asking questions about the causes and effects. The end result of their legwork was a 30-minute, award-winning documentary called *The Smell of Money.*

The documentary—portions of which aired nationally—featured some of the people suffering health problems from the foul emissions. One older resident told the TV audience that every time he breathed in the tainted air, "You can feel it going down in your lungs, and it's just cutting, it seems, like, acid-like."

The documentary also showed the scientists' findings about the lung cancer rates and the cavalier attitude of city and corporate officials who ignored those impacts.

One interview featured a woman who had tried complaining about the smell to city officials. She said a strange man had approached her to warn that if she kept causing trouble, "something's going to happen to you."

From time to time, Closmann said, he has shown the old documentary in his UNF classes. The students start off making fun of the '80s fashions and hair—a target-rich environment for mockery, as anyone who's seen the band Flock of Seagulls could attest.

But soon his students get caught up in the story about a real-life battle between good and evil, he told me.

"It was incredibly dramatic," the professor said. "It was so well done."

The fed-up public, the scientific research showing the human health effects, and the hard-hitting media reports set the stage for finally vanquishing the Bad Air Monster. But one more factor had to be filled.

A champion.

* * *

In the world of fiction, whenever some evil is afoot, a champion arises to fight for what's right. The ever-popular Knight in Shining Armor trope dates to Medieval times (the actual era, not the Orlando restaurant) and continues today through *The Equalizer 3.*

The champion who arose to battle for clean air for Jax was one of the most unlikely to do so.

His name was Tommy Hazouri. He was an Arab-American glad-hander with an acerbic wit. He wore a toupee that couldn't have been more obvious if he'd adopted a raccoon and let it ride on his head. When a political opponent threatened to rip it off him, he quipped that she was "the queen of mean."

In 1987, Hazouri ran for mayor, promising to battle the people he called "the fat cats" and swap the city's notorious stink for the sweet smell of success.

"If there's one issue that transcends this city, rich and poor, black and white, it's the odor issue," he told the *Orlando Sentinel*. "Odor is the only issue keeping us from being a world-class city,"

His was no empty campaign promise, either.

In his first eight months as mayor, Hazouri demoted the city's ineffective pollution control chief, hired eight more employees to respond to odor complaints, pumped up his legal staff to take polluters to court, and formed a sort of "stink strike force" with the state attorney.

At his prodding, the city council passed a tough new anti-odor law. The law spelled out that if five people in five households complained of a smell and an inspector could track down the source, the city could fine the offender. The penalty: up to 60 days in jail and a $500 fine, with civil penalties up to $10,000.

Paper mill managers complained Hazouri was unfairly singling out their industry.

"You get a bunch of people together and the place will smell with or without a pulp mill," one told the *Sentinel*.

The polluters fought back in court. They said the city's ordinance was so vague it was unconstitutional. They lost and had to clean up their act or face hefty fines.

Of course, filling the role of the champion has its drawbacks, as Luke Skywalker could tell you. The Empire usually strikes back.

In Hazouri's case, the fat cats ensured he served only a single term as mayor. (He later won races for the school board and for city council.)

But the changes he made stuck for one simple reason, Delaney said.

"Nobody," he said, "wanted to be the mayor who brought the stink back."

* * *

Some of the factors that spelled success in Jax are harder to find these days. For instance, Reagan told me that the TV reporting he sees now doesn't really compare to what his crew was able to do in the low-tech '80s.

"There's just not as much good local journalism anymore," he said.

That's partly because the money for local newspapers and broadcast outlets has been cut waaaaay back, and there are far fewer reporters now than there used to be.

Science has taken a beating too, whether the subject is the safety of vaccines or the reality of climate change (at least we still pay attention to hurricane predictions). Scientists aren't the trusted figures they used to be, thanks to unscrupulous politicians who don't want the voters listening to anyone who might point out their failings.

Meanwhile the public in Florida has been distracted by ridiculous culture war issues so they won't notice the environmental damage done.

Nevertheless, three of the four factors are already present for dealing with our toxic algae blooms.

We've got scientific evidence of harm to humans as well as to marine life. There's been plenty of hard-hitting news coverage. And you better believe the public is growing fed up with the smell, the dead fish, and the repeated health warnings.

So far, what we lack is a champion.

Governor Ron "How-Soon-Can-I-Get-Back-to-Iowa?" DeSantis seemed to fill that role in 2019. He appointed a panel of scientists to tell him how to obliterate the blooms. But then he all but ignored their recommendations, perhaps because they would have inconvenienced his campaign donors.

Maybe, once he's finally done playing presidential candidate, he'll come back to Florida ready to tackle this substantive issue again. We'll know for sure if he shows up in Tallahassee wearing a raccoon on his head.

7

No Laughing Matter

Florida Phoenix, December 1, 2022

I have a confession to make. I'm oooooold. How old am I? I remember when Steve Martin was just a stand-up comic whose big schtick involved getting small.

These days Martin is the star of a popular Hulu TV show about a trio of snarky amateur detectives. In movies, he's played a well-meaning dope, a clumsy con man, a phony faith healer, a crafty movie director, and a desperate brain surgeon.

Just once he played a character who was truly evil, albeit in a comical way. In *Little Shop of Horrors* he's a dentist who loves inflicting pain on his patients, his nurse, and his girlfriend, usually while inhaling laughing gas.

In the end, the laughing gas kills him. "I'll asphyx—" he begins, then breaks into peals of laughter.

I thought about that performance last week while reading about a Florida chemical plant that's been around since the 1950s and is killing us all.

It was in a story in *Inside Climate News* that was headlined, "Who Were the Worst Climate Polluters in the U.S. in 2021?"

The opening paragraph is a real grabber: "U.S. greenhouse gas emissions climbed by 4.1 percent from major industrial sources in 2021, according to new data recently released by the U.S. Environmental Protection Agency. The increase is the largest year-on-year rise in emissions tallied across more than a decade of reporting."

The story went on to list the worst climate polluters. They included a coal-fired Alabama power plant that produces more carbon dioxide than any other U.S. facility, a Pennsylvania coal mine that produces more methane than anywhere else, and—because there is always a Florida angle to every big story—this plant in the Panhandle.

It's a Florida nylon manufacturing plant, and it tops the rest of the country in emitting nitrous oxide, aka laughing gas.

When it comes to the climate, laughing gas is no laughing matter.

"Nitrous oxide is 273 times worse for the climate than carbon dioxide on a pound for pound basis," the story noted. "Emissions from the facility in 2021 equaled the annual greenhouse gas emissions of 1.5 million automobiles, according to the EPA."

For some reason, this news did not strike me as funny.

* * *

I was amazed that I had not heard of this plant before. Its name was Ascend Performance Materials—Ascend, as in going up and awaaaaaaaaaaaaay.

Ascend is owned by a Houston-based private equity firm named SK Capital Partners that generates revenues of approximately $14 billion-with-a-B every year. In other words, they've got money to burn even as they burn the planet up.

But then I realized I did know this polluter. It's from my old stomping grounds up in Escambia County, which is no surprise.

Escambia is a fine place, with gorgeous beaches and lots of hard-working people. Some of them are working on this side of the law and some on the other side.

Unfortunately, Escambia has a major downside: Lots of polluters call it home. There are so many, you could easily put on a game show there called "Name That Polluter!"

According to a 2017 story in the *Pensacola News Journal*, Escambia County ranks 11th among all of the U.S. counties for disposing of the most toxic waste. No other Florida county made the national list.

Escambia is the site of one of the worst Superfund sites in the nation, nicknamed "Mount Dioxin." And there's a paper mill that's dumped so much of its waste into a local waterway that everyone calls it "Stink Creek."

But even among that tough competition, Ascend stands out. The 2017 story noted: "Of the total releases in the county, chemical manufacturer Ascend Performance Materials . . . contributed the vast majority."

Turns out Ascend is only the most recent name for the plant, which is the largest in the world for converting petroleum into nylon products for use in everything from carpet to cars.

Originally the Ascend facility, which sits on 2,000 acres by the Escambia River near where it flows into Escambia Bay, was known as Chemstrand. Then it became Monsanto, then Solutia.

Monsanto and Chemstrand—those are names I remember from childhood. I called up my parents, who still live in Pensacola. They told me that

An aerial view of the Pensacola nylon plant known then as Chemstrand and now as Ascend. Photo from Florida State Archives.

over the decades some of my own relatives had worked at Monsanto. It was a steady source of jobs for the community.

It was also a steady source of toxic waste, right from the start.

"The plant began operating in 1953, and almost immediately complaints about pollution were voiced," a scathing 1999 grand jury report noted. The 120-page report focused on polluters who ruined the area's natural bounty for their own gain and the regulators who routinely ignored and concealed violations.

Chemstrand's owners professed ignorance of any toxic waste. It was the corporate version of that running *Family Circus* gag where the kids claim that everything that's gone wrong is caused by "Not Me" and "Ida Know."

But studies confirmed that Chemstrand was one of the principal sources of the pollution fouling Escambia Bay in the 1960s, the grand jury wrote. Its discharges "led to the collapse of this estuarine system."

The company had to stop dumping its waste in the water. Instead, it began injecting it underground, which brings a different set of problems. Meanwhile, there were problems with what was coming out of its smokestacks.

Linda Young, a longtime environmental activist in the Panhandle, told me she worked at the plant one summer before going to college. Her job: gluing plastic daisies onto welcome mats.

"They gave us umbrellas for walking between where we worked and the cafeteria where we'd eat lunch," she said. The employees needed umbrellas because residue from the plant's smokestacks was "just falling through the air like snow, and it would burn your hair, your skin and your clothes."

* * *

In 2019, the *Pensacola News Journal* checked back on what had happened to all the problems identified by the 1999 grand jury report. Twenty years later, things weren't much better:

"EPA data shows the Pensacola area releases more toxins than almost anywhere else in America," the paper noted. It's as if the Chamber of Commerce were seriously trying to score the No. 1 spot, with a big assist from lax state and federal regulators.

As for the plant now known as Ascend, it had "been in noncompliance with the Clean Air Act for eight of the past 12 quarters and in noncompliance with the Clean Water Act for seven of the past 12 quarters, according to the EPA."

Young told me about how, a decade before that report, the county's utilities authority had sued the plant for tainting water supply wells with some nasty chemicals it had injected in the ground. However, a judge ruled that the water supply agency had failed to show that it had suffered harm (I guess the judge didn't drink water).

Young said she petitioned the EPA to crack down on the plant and also test more of the utility's wells, "but the EPA just looks away."

More recently, in 2021, there were not one but two fires at the Ascend site, the second within five days of the first. When I asked a company spokesperson named Alison Jahn how that happened, the answer she gave me was, "Inclement weather."

I should mention that Pensacola is one of the rainiest cities in the United States. I am not clear how that heavy rainfall could lead to a pair of industrial blazes, but I never got a better answer from Jahn. I guess only James "Fire and Rain" Taylor can explain that one.

Jahn spun me a pretty picture of the plant and its surroundings: "We employ nearly 1,500 people which amounts to over $100 million of salaries and taxes annually that are spent back in the community. . . . We're heavily involved in the community through our active employee base who volunteer with our Ascend Cares Foundation."

"Yes yes, very nice," I muttered to myself while reading her emailed response. "But let's get to the part about how you're killing the Earth."

* * *

Some people use laughing gas, aka nitrous oxide, as a casual party drug. In that context it has several nicknames: Hippie crack is my fave (because I'm old). You've probably heard of whippets.

Laughing gas was first synthesized by an English chemist named Joseph Priestly in 1772. I like to picture him as a budding comic who found a shortcut to audience appeal, although that's not in the history books.

Today, as Steve Martin showed us, it's primarily used as an anesthetic by dentists—I mean used on their patients, not on themselves.

We've known since 1991 that the laughing gas produced during the nylon manufacturing process is a danger to the planet. It pushes us further along toward a far warmer world, with more intense hurricanes, rising sea levels, bigger storm surges, and more toxic algae blooms and mosquito-borne diseases.

As of 2020, the EPA says, it accounted for about 7 percent of all U.S. greenhouse gas emissions from human activities. In addition to being nearly 300 times worse than regular carbon emissions, nitrous oxide molecules stay in the atmosphere for an average of 114 years. That's a loooong time, even for an oldster like me.

That's the bad news. Here's the good: Laughing gas emissions are easy to get rid of before they leave the plant's exhaust.

Most nylon plants around the globe, "alarmed by [its] potency as a greenhouse gas, joined forces almost 30 years ago and developed technologies to abate virtually all of their pollution," *Inside Climate News* reported in 2020. They've been "using low cost incinerators and chemical reactors to destroy 95 percent or more of their nitrous oxide since the 1990s."

But not Ascend! No, they do things the old-fashioned way. They're just letting those emissions rip like a rude noise from a whoopie cushion. Ha ha! Isn't that funny?

Apparently, that's how you make billions in revenue: You reject spending money on low-cost equipment to fix your pollution problem. Think of the savings! Too bad about the planet.

Jahn told me that Ascend finally began working on its emissions problem in 2018. That's more than a quarter-century after its competitors. I guess it took the company that long to figure out that maybe saving the Earth is a good investment, considering it's where their employees live.

By 2020, company officials promised that they would "implement a process this year for reducing its nitrous oxide emissions by 50 percent." They pledged that by February 2022, there would be "a well over 95 percent" emissions reduction.

It appears they were just joking about that.

Instead, *Inside Climate News* reported earlier this year, that emissions from Ascend's Pensacola plant "increased by 50 percent in 2020, EPA data show. Air permits filed with state regulators in Florida do not indicate that the company is moving forward with more ambitious reductions of the potent greenhouse gas."

Jahn told me this week that "we exited 2021 at an effective 50 percent reduction in site N2O emissions and expect further reductions in early 2023."

She didn't want to talk about how they're doing it or what the delay was about. I picture the company officials being like Steve Martin's dentist: unable to act because the laughing gas makes them too giddy. Meanwhile, climate change keeps getting worse.

The delay in fixing their emissions problem isn't hurting their owners' profits, though. In fact, I think you could say they're laughing all the way to the bank.

8

When the Butt Hutt Closed

Washington Post, June 7, 2022

LUTZ, Fla.—The bad news is, the Butt Hutt remains closed.

The popular lakeside bar at Florida's oldest nudist resort is still shuttered, even as the rest of the Lake Como Family Nudist Resort in Lutz slowly re-opens. The Bare Buns Café, for instance, now allows limited seating on the screened patio and under the pool deck canopy, albeit with everyone six feet apart—and please bring a towel to sit on.

Across the country, state and local governments are easing restrictions imposed to prevent the spread of the coronavirus. The virus continues to kill and new cases pile up, leaving businesses and communities struggling with when and how to resume operations. Florida's robust nudist industry is no different.

"We're in the first phase of our four-phase reopening plan, with phase four being everything goes back to normal—but whether we'll actually get to that, nobody knows," said Mike Kush, marketing director of Lake Como, founded in 1941 as the Florida Athletic and Health Association.

Florida's year-round balmy weather has made it a magnet for tourists with a taste for clothing-optional swimming, tennis, and volleyball. Florida has more nudist resorts than any other state—29 registered clubs, more than twice as many as California.

Like all other aspects of the tourism industry, Florida's nudist resorts have been hurt by the coronavirus and stay-at-home orders. Lake Como was open only to its 200 year-round residents; the 800 who visit regularly were locked out. The resort also canceled three of its biggest events, including its Dare to Go Bare 5K Run, which usually attracts 150 unclothed competitors.

Nobody knows yet how much money the resorts will lose this year because of stay-at-home orders and quarantines, said Erich Schuttauf, executive director of the American Association for Nude Recreation.

Roe Ostheim, 72, a 24-year resident of Cypress Cove Nudist Resort in Kissimmee, normally stays busy playing tennis, golf, and pickleball in the nude. For two months, she had to content herself with riding her bicycle around the resort—but she didn't mind.

"I feel safer in here than I do anywhere else," the Scottish retiree said, explaining that the resort's residents all know each other and look out for each other.

Ostheim said a few residents have complained about the resort keeping its gym closed, as well as a temporary requirement to wear a mask in common areas, but she is not one of them. She's glad that the golf course has reopened, albeit with some new rules: "Nobody touches anybody else's ball, and we all start on a different hole, alternating with the one, three, and five holes."

Her friend Carolyn Hawkins, 77, has lived at Cypress Cove for 40 years, and said she's never seen such a strange time. In the past, when other residents would stop by her house, she would gladly invite them in—but not now.

"I don't ever let anybody in my house," she said.

She helps supervise the resort's recently reopened pool, where swimmers are limited to 10 at a time and must stay six feet apart.

"That's a little challenging," Hawkins said, noting that the rules have sparked a little grumbling. "A lot of people are waiting to get in, but they also don't want to see it shut down again."

All in all, though, she was glad she was inside the resort when Governor Ron DeSantis issued his stay-at-home orders.

"I could hang out in my house with no clothes on, and there's no stress here," she said.

At Hidden Lake Resort, near the Panhandle town of Jay, visitors who had recently arrived from New York, Canada, and Illinois were allowed to stay on during the shutdown. It was safer than sending them home, said owner Jim Nowling. Meanwhile, nobody else was allowed in. Nowling said he had to cancel pages of reservations.

Hidden Lake is one of the smallest nudist resorts in Florida. It typically has about 35 people staying there over Memorial Day weekend, Nowling said. That marks the end of their busy season, which begins in October and goes all winter and into the spring.

With just a handful of guests over the past two months, the 800-acre resort was particularly quiet. Nowling said they lit a bonfire most nights and held potluck dinners.

Hidden Lake and the other resorts began reopening in mid-May. Doing so has meant some changes. For instance, people who normally wear nothing are now walking around wearing masks.

"We'll have tan lines, but in a different place," Schuttauf joked.

Some popular resort amenities—bars with live music, like the Butt Hutt, for instance—are still deemed too risky to reopen. Others are once again accessible, but with limits.

At Cypress Cove, management announced that only three people at a time will be allowed in the outdoor hot tub, and then for only 15 minutes at a time. Six can occupy the indoor hot tub, but still for only 15 minutes. Meanwhile, only 10 people at a time can occupy the pool, and for a maximum of 30 minutes per person.

The Caliente Club & Resorts in Land o' Lakes, which bills itself as "the hottest nudist resort in the country," posted a long list of new precautions ahead of its May 11 reopening: new hand sanitizer stations, increased cleaning, menu boards rather than handed-out menus, disposable cutlery in the restaurant, and thermal imaging cameras to check body temperature.

Lake Como and Caliente are both in Pasco County, which has so many nudist resorts it's become known as the "Nudist Capital of the U.S." Pasco officials have embraced the nudist resorts because they generate hundreds of thousands of dollars in tourist taxes.

Nudists may not have pockets, but they do have a lot of money to spend. A 2017 study by Saint Leo University, paid for by the nudist association, estimated that 2.2 million nudists visit resorts and beaches and take nude cruises, contributing more than $7 billion to Florida's economy.

Nudism first caught on in the United States 90 years ago, brought over by German immigrants who believed the best way to commune with nature was in one's birthday suit. The nation's first resort for nudists opened in New York's Hudson River Valley in 1931 and drew 200 members as well as police raids. A judge acquitted the members of lewd behavior, ruling they had done their best to avoid exposing the public to naked bodies.

In the 1940s, the nudism movement spread across the country, particularly once resorts began including pools and RV parking. Now they range from expensive lodging with glitzy nightclubs and four-star restaurants to facilities with few amenities beyond nature trails and a high fence.

Nudism, however, isn't necessarily any more or less dangerous than a clothed lifestyle when it comes to the coronavirus.

"I don't see wearing clothing as being much of a risk factor," said University of Florida epidemiologist Cindy Prins. As for whether swimming and sunbathing can block the virus' spread, she said, "it depends on whether you're doing social distancing."

"It's generally safer to be outside than inside," said Marissa J. Levine, director of the Center for Leadership in Public Health Practice at the University of South Florida. Other than that, she said, nudism offers no real advantages in warding off the virus.

Prins and Levine did agree that one special instruction that Caliente's management offered its residents might not be as effective as it hoped.

"Being wonderful and social we know our members and guests often greet each other with a hug and a kiss," the Caliente notice said. "In this time, we might suggest a variation. . . . We might suggest embracing the butt bump. It's more fun than the elbow bump and doubles as a great move on the dance floor."

Prins said: "I would recommend—not."

————

Postscript: I wrote a lot of pandemic-related stories in 2020 and 2021. This was by far my favorite. By the way, the Butt Hutt has now reopened.

9

That Dam Reservoir

Florida Phoenix, July 2, 2020

This happened 20 years ago, but I remember it like it was yesterday.

I was on a boat, floating along a muddy shoreline. A handful of ibises, egrets, and wood storks foraged near a stand of gaunt cypress trees growing along a slope. Each tree bore a dark band about three feet up from its roots. The dark mark showed how high the water usually stood.

Beyond them, in what was once a river channel, I could see miles of stumps. They belonged to cypress trees that had not been cut but rather squashed by a monstrous tank-like machine built solely for this purpose and called a "Crusher-Crawler." Some of the stumps were enormous.

This was a dried-out version of the 9,500-acre Rodman Reservoir—or as some fans of the reservoir insist on calling it these days, "Lake Ocklawaha."

No matter what you call it, it remains the subject of Florida's longest-running environmental wrangle. The fight's been going on so long it's become like the tangled lawsuit at the center of Charles Dickens' novel *Bleak House*—people have been born into the fight and died out.

To create the reservoir, the U.S. Army Corps of Engineers built what was originally known as the 7,200-foot-long Rodman Dam in 1968, halting the flow of the wild Ocklawaha River as part of the controversial Cross-Florida Barge Canal.

The canal was supposed to be a triumph of geometry over geography, giving ships a way to slice straight across Florida rather than go all the way around through the Keys. The fact that it would also cut into the Floridan Aquifer and make the state's primary source of drinking water an undrinkable briny mess was just a bonus.

Fledgling Florida environmental groups, led by a scientist-turned-activist named Marjorie Harris Carr, won a court order to halt canal construction.

In 1971 then-president Richard Nixon killed it for good when he cut off federal funding. But the dam remained, inundating 9,000 acres of the Ocala National Forest, smothering 20 natural springs, and blocking migrating manatees, striped bass, and other marine life.

Governor Lawton Chiles, a Democrat, vowed to tear down the dam. So did Governor Jeb Bush, a Republican. Neither succeeded.

Powerful North Florida legislators refused to approve money for dam removal because, they said, the stumps had turned the reservoir into a great fishing hole for largemouth bass.

(One of the Rodman's defenders, Senator George Kirkpatrick, was such a stalwart dam fan that it's now named for him. Meanwhile, in an only-in-Florida irony, the route of the aborted canal is now a recreational trail named after Marjorie Harris Carr—and thus the Carr Greenway abuts the Kirkpatrick Dam.)

Every three or four years, the state drains the reservoir to rid it of aquatic weeds. During each drawdown—including 20 years ago when I saw it, and this spring when it happened again—people who hate the dam take reporters and photographers out to show off what the river would look like if it were returned to its untamed state.

Meanwhile, fishing fans formed a group called Save Rodman Reservoir. Executive director Larry Harvey, a Putnam County commissioner, says they number about 450 people. Not all of them fish in "Lake Ocklawaha," though. Harvey told me he does not, because his house is on three other lakes that also offer good bass fishing.

When I asked Harvey what would happen to the supply of bass if the dam were removed and the Ocklawaha became a free-flowing river, he said, "We don't know what would happen."

But he was skeptical about the dam-less future. Given all the development that has taken over the Florida landscape since the dam was built, he told me, "I don't think we can go back to everything's natural state."

Another argument for keeping the dam, Harvey said, is that it holds back water that might someday be needed for regional drinking supplies. I asked him if anyone's drinking out of it now and he said no. I asked if the springs that are currently inundated wouldn't be a good source too. He said a reservoir is better.

* * *

Jim Gross, who now heads up the group that Carr founded, Florida Defenders of the Environment, contends the Save Rodman organization is just "a small group that holds the rest of the state hostage."

By contrast, 35 organizations, some with thousands of members, have now banded together to form a Free the Ocklawaha coalition, he said. They contend that emptying the reservoir would help with everything from manatee migration to keeping a rising sea level from turning the adjacent St. Johns River salty.

Gross and his allies are once again negotiating with state and federal officials about removing the dam, figuring out what steps to take and where the millions might come from. (They also have a federal lawsuit going, just in case.)

They have come close a few times in the past. In 2016, for instance, the head of the U.S. Forest Service said it was time to get all that water off federal forest land.

Meanwhile the St. Johns River Water Management District did a study that said any pollutants released from opening the reservoir would not cause irreparable damage downstream, as had been feared. But the November election that year meant someone different took over the Forest Service and the momentum for freeing the river faded, he said.

Gross said the bass fishing in the Rodman Reservoir isn't nearly as good as it used to be. A recent Bassmasters ranking of great bass fishing locations didn't include Rodman in its top 25 with Lake Okeechobee and Lake Seminole.

It wound up in a "best of the rest" category, sort of an honorable mention. However, the state wildlife commission does credit the Rodman for being the No. 1 water body in the state for trophy catches.

When I talked to Harvey and to Gross this week, I told each of them that what's going on with the Rodman reminded me of the Dead Lakes Dam on the Chipola River in the Panhandle. They both said they had never heard of it.

* * *

A sinkhole in the Chipola close to where it joins the Apalachicola River created the Dead Lakes, a 10-mile-long waterway near Wewahitchka. Cypress trees sank into the water-filled hole. Most of them died. The moss-draped stumps gave the lakes both their forbidding name and their eerie beauty.

After a three-year drought kept the Dead Lakes too low for fishing, the Florida Legislature approved building a dam on the Chipola. Built in 1960, the 18-foot-tall dam was supposed to boost fishing by maintaining high water levels, rather than letting the lake fluctuate on its own.

When the Dead Lakes Dam was new, fish corralled in the reservoir were much easier to catch than the ones in the free-flowing river. Anglers crowded onto a bridge overlooking the dam to catch a cooler full of fish, and then another and another.

But over time the lake filled with silt and weeds. Acres of fish spawning beds disappeared. Soon the remaining bass, bream, and shellcracker were so small they were hardly worth fishing for.

The solution: Tear down the dam. In 1987, the state hired a salvage contractor who cut slots in the dam and removed it a section at a time, allowing the impounded lake to draw down slowly. His bill: $32,000.

State fisheries biologists studied the Dead Lakes for several years after the dam was torn out. Without the dam, they found the lakes were healthier. There were more fish and bigger fish. And there were twice as many different kinds of fish as there used to be.

Of course, some people were unhappy about losing the dam. They tended to be the ones who'd had waterfront property while the river was dammed and lost easy water access when the dam was demolished.

If the Rodman is to be emptied out for good, the one person the anti-dam people need in their corner is Governor Ron DeSantis.

DeSantis has a mixed reputation on environmental issues—steering millions to the Everglades, for instance, while also approving an expensive toll road that will pave over the heart of Florida panther habitat. Perhaps if he sides with the folks in favor of killing the Kirkpatrick Dam, they could find something else to name near the Marjorie Harris Carr Greenway.

How about the Ron DeSantis Ocklawaha River Landing and Manatee Observation Area?

———————

Postscript: As of June 2024, the dam remains intact.

10

Orange You Sad about the Citrus Industry?

Gravy, September 2023

Not long after our first child was born, I drove to a nursery to buy a tree. My dad had planted a tree when I was born, so I was determined to do the same. He went with persimmon, but I picked one that seemed more fitting for a Florida family: a citrus tree.

What could be more Florida than that? Oranges adorn most Florida license plates. Orange blossoms are the official state flower. Orange juice is the official state beverage. There's even a county named "Orange" and another named "Citrus."

I brought home the spindly tree, dug a hole in the backyard, and set the root ball in it. The tree grew well. By the time our second child came along, it had begun producing fruit—juicy little tangerines with a sweet, sharp twang.

From time to time, I'd herd our two toddlers into the backyard to help me pick the little flavor grenades. They liked helping with the retrieval, but only my wife and I ever ate the tangerines. Our kids never enjoyed the tart taste the way we adults did.

As the boys grew older and busier with schoolwork, sports, and other activities, our trips to the backyard to gather fruit dropped to near zero. I'd still pick a batch during the growing season—September to April, with the peak around the end of October. My wife and I would eat some, but we'd give the rest away.

Then, sometime after 2016, the tree changed. It didn't produce as much fruit, and what it did put out didn't taste very good. Soon it stopped producing anything and eventually toppled over, dead.

It had fallen prey to a bacterial disease called "greening" that began ravaging the Florida citrus industry in earnest in 2005. It is spread by a bug no bigger than a piece of orzo, and since its arrival in Florida it has laid waste to thousands of acres of groves.

By 2023, it had infected more than 1 million trees, driving many long-time growers out of business. It is the most serious of several diseases that can infect a citrus tree. That means not just backyard hobby trees like mine are at risk; the entire Florida citrus industry is in peril. As the groves disappear, so does a major totem that's long been a part of the state's image.

During the glory years of the citrus industry—the 1990s—growers harvested 240 million boxes of fruit a year. Last year's harvest, 41 million boxes, was the lowest since World War II. The most recent crop forecast predicts this year will bring in a mere 16 million boxes.

Some growers talk confidently of overcoming the greening challenge the way they've overcome others over the years: the hurricanes that have knocked over thousands of trees, the freezes that killed crops planted too far north, the other diseases such as canker that wiped out harvests.

They're also battling an even more insidious foe: Changing American tastes. Younger consumers have stopped drinking orange juice at breakfast—or even eating a traditional breakfast in the morning. The disappearance of demand may be what ultimately thwarts any revival of the industry.

"What could possibly bring it back?" asked Florida historian Gary Mormino, who is skeptical about talk of a comeback. "Will people suddenly start to like orange juice again?"

* * *

About a 20-minute drive from my house, on the other side of the soaring Sunshine Skyway Bridge over Tampa Bay, there's an exit for U.S. 19 that rolls into a stretch of rural Manatee County.

On one side of the road is Rosie's Produce Market, with small signs staked out by the road advertising honey, fresh blueberries, and other delights. On the other side is a building that looks like it was zapped via time machine from an earlier century. Out front, tacked to a power pole, is a big orange disc with a face painted on it. Out back is a grove of gnarled trees.

The Citrus Place is a family-run fruit stand in Terra Ceia, open since 1972. Its founders, Ben and Vera Tillett, had been high school teachers. They set up shop originally as a U-pick grapefruit grove. Eventually, they expanded into retail, selling a wide variety of citrus along with souvenirs, sandwiches, and fresh-squeezed juice.

The Tilletts would unlock their front door on the last Monday in October and close down the last weekend in May. Plenty of tourists always stop by, but most of their business comes from locals who crave their farm-fresh, unpasteurized orange juice.

When the couple first opened The Citrus Place, it was just one of half a dozen similar businesses in Manatee County. Now it's on the verge of becoming the last of its kind, not just in Manatee County but in nearby Sarasota County as well. Their last rival, Mixon Farms, recently announced that it is closing after 85 years in business and selling the property.

"The citrus industry is in a lot of turmoil now," said Sid Tillett, 65, who started working at his parents' establishment when he was 14. He took charge when his father died four years ago at age 87. Greening has taken a toll on his production, too, and not just with the trees it killed.

"Even the trees that are still alive are not producing the quality or quantity of fruit that they did 20 years ago," he said. "The virus has weakened the tree. They're not putting out as much fruit, and the fruit is not as good."

That's the greening at work, sucking out what makes citrus so pleasant to eat. Blame that little bug that's done such a thorough job of spreading the disease.

The *Diaphorina citri,* or citrus psyllid, looks kind of like a cross between a moth and a termite. It feeds on stems and leaves of citrus trees, meanwhile passing on Huanglongbing, the bacteria that causes citrus greening. By attacking the tree's vascular system, the disease clogs the flow of sap and drastically reduces the transport of water and nutrients to the fruit, which turn out small and sour.

First identified in China in 1919, greening spread to Africa, Asia, and South America before reaching Florida. According to the USDA, the psyllid first turned up in South Florida in 1998, and the disease it carries was first detected in a pair of homeowners' trees in Miami in 2005. By 2014, greening had spread to every Florida county with a citrus grove, as well as to groves in Louisiana, Georgia, South Carolina, Texas, and California.

"This disease effectively reduces the quantity and quality of citrus fruits, eventually rendering infected trees useless," the USDA reported in 2006.

There is no cure for greening, but scientists have been experimenting with greening-resistant trees, as well as with putting bags or screens over the young trees to keep the bug out. Tillett has heard that some growers are building netted enclosures around their trees to protect them from the psyllid. The cost: $40,000 an acre. With six acres to cover, he's not sure he can handle such an expensive solution.

Does that mean the end is nigh? Tillett wouldn't speculate. But he did make one observation focused on his customers' changing tastes.

"When we first opened, the only thing we sold was grapefruit," he said. "Then our juices became the top seller. You know what's our top seller now? Our major seller is ice cream."

* * *

Despite its pervasive presence among the state's symbols, the orange is not a native of Florida. Like two-thirds of the state's residents, oranges came from someplace else—specifically, Spain.

Spanish explorers carried the fruit aboard their ships because their crews could eat them to ward off scurvy. They would plant the seeds in pots on the ship and transplant the saplings wherever they landed, according to Erin Thursby, author of *Florida Oranges: A Colorful History*.

Florida's earliest groves date to 1565, when Spanish explorer Pedro Menéndez de Avilés founded St. Augustine. The groves the Spanish planted around that region were intended strictly for local consumption.

But by the late 1700s, a slippery St. Augustine businessman named Jesse Fish—described by one historian as a "land dealer, slaver, smuggler, usurer, and cunning crook"—had found a way to send Florida oranges elsewhere. He became the first to export oranges out of state, shipping them to the Carolinas.

After the Civil War, the writer who helped start it, Harriet Beecher Stowe of *Uncle Tom's Cabin* fame, bought a house and grove near Jacksonville, in a town called Mandarin, overlooking the St. Johns River. She wrote numerous dispatches to Northern newspapers extolling the balmy breezes and lovely vegetation, calling Florida "The Mediterranean of the South."

Stowe, the most popular writer in the nation at the time, urged her readers to visit her new home state to aid its recovery from the economic disaster of the Civil War. She virtually invented Florida's tourism industry—and touted its citrus, too. Local boat captains sold tickets to ride the river past her house in hopes of spotting the famous author. The visitors sometimes invaded her grove and walked off with any fruit they found.

She wasn't the only author to tout Florida citrus. In 1928, Marjorie Kinnan Rawlings, who won a Pulitzer for *The Yearling*, bought a 72-acre grove near Cross Creek. In her book about her home, she talked of stepping from the impersonal highway to enter into the grove and feeling "out of one world and inside the mysterious heart of another." Present-day visitors to her home, now part of Florida's state park system, are encouraged to pluck

Orange Picking Time in Florida

A Florida postcard touting the citrus industry. Photo from the Florida State Archives.

oranges from her trees, but I have tried them, and they don't taste very good.

World War II changed everything, both for Florida and for citrus.

Before the war, California led Florida in orange production, but few people drank orange juice as part of their breakfast routine. Once again, though, the fruit's vitamin C content became important to fighting scurvy.

"Part of the war effort was finding ways to ship oranges to the troops overseas," said Mormino, author of *Land of Sunshine, State of Dreams: A Social History of Modern Florida.* "Before the war, they had canned orange juice but nobody liked it. Florida became the location of a Sunshine State version of the Manhattan Project."

The result of that concentrated science project: frozen concentrated orange juice, which became a hit with families thanks, in part, to the new-fangled freezers sold as part of kitchen refrigerators. In postwar America, no one had time to squeeze enough oranges to make juice for their family. Now, thanks to concentrate, they didn't have to.

"The most functional sentence in the English language is: 'Mix with three cans of water and stir,'" Mormino said.

How popular was the new product? "Citrus production in Florida increased from 43 million boxes in 1945 to 72 million in 1952," the Florida State Archives noted. "About half of all fruit became [frozen concentrate] in the 1950s."

Florida's citrus growers bought national ads pushing the idea of orange juice as the perfect breakfast drink, both tasty and full of health benefits. They hired celebrities such as Bing Crosby, whose endorsement boosted sales for Minute Maid for thirty years. Growers planted groves galore.

About 30 minutes from Orlando, in the town of Clermont, a couple of tourism promoters built a 226-foot spire known as the Citrus Tower. When it opened in 1956, the view it offered of the orange-filled countryside was breathtaking.

"From the top of that tower you could once see 12 to 16 billion citrus trees," said Mormino. "Today it's all gone, unless you spot one growing in someone's backyard."

* * *

The industry's shrinkage has been dramatic. As of 2000, Florida groves occupied 832,250 acres according to the USDA. Twenty years later, that number has dropped by roughly half to just 419,542 acres. Some growers, out of desperation, are trying other crops, such as olives, pomegranates, peaches, avocados, or even hops. Others are just giving up.

Freezes have knocked out some of the groves over the Florida citrus industry's lifetime. For instance, the "Great Freeze" in 1894 destroyed most of the crop. Drought and hurricanes have dealt hard blows too, particularly in recent years. Hurricane Ian's path in 2022 touched roughly 375,000 acres of citrus groves across the state, inflicting an estimated $675 million in damages.

"Mother Nature's been pretty hard on us the last year or so," said Matt Joyner, executive director of Florida Citrus Mutual, the state's largest association of citrus growers.

Joyner, a seventh-generation Floridian, grew up working in a family-owned grove. He has watched the rise of greening and the decline in groves and production. A decade ago, Florida Citrus Mutual had 8,000 members. Now it's down to 2,000. As the oranges disappeared, a new Florida crop took their place.

"There are a lot of places that historically were nothing but citrus groves, and now you see a lot of rooftops," Joyner said. "The days of raising a family on just 200 acres of citrus are gone."

Oranges like sandy soil, and the trees sprout best in elevated spots atop ancient sand dunes in the state's central and southern peninsula. Those areas are also an ideal place to build subdivisions, shopping centers, office parks, self-storage warehouses, and apartment complexes. Every time a freeze, storm, or disease knocks out a grove, developers are waiting to make a lucrative offer to the weary grower.

When the developers take over, they tend to make a wholesale change to the character of these rural areas. For instance, in a sparsely settled spot near Fort Myers, the 4,000-acre Old Corkscrew Plantation grove used to produce one out of every 100 oranges grown in Florida. But it went bankrupt, and a Canadian bank foreclosed on the property.

In 2016, a Texas agribusiness giant called King Ranch bought the grove for $29.5 million and within two years was working with a developer to create a new town there called "Kingston." The plan calls for 10,000 dwelling units, 240 hotel units, and 700,000 square feet of commercial space.

That's a big change for a quiet, rural area that was supposed to be kept at a low density because of its value in recharging the region's groundwater supply. Neighbors who treasure their peace and quiet have done their best to fight the plan, calling it "nuts," but, so far, the pro-development forces have won every round.

What remains of Florida's citrus industry these days tends to fall into one of two categories, according to Joyner. It's either part of a multinational conglomerate or a multigenerational, family-run farm of 800 to 1,000 acres that may also be involved in cattle ranching or growing other crops to make ends meet. Nevertheless, Joyner said he's optimistic that this dwindling pack of growers will somehow find a way to bounce back from the current crisis. He's far from alone in making that prediction.

"Our citrus industry is one of the most resilient agricultural commodities in the world," insisted former Florida Agriculture Commissioner Nikki Fried, who served from 2018 to 2022.

But as someone who's been drinking orange juice with his breakfast for five decades, it's hard for me to shake the sense that this is whistling past the graveyard. Instead, it feels like, after 500 years, we're witnessing the slow-motion demise of Florida citrus.

A lot of people now skip breakfast, according to The Food Institute, or they grab something on the go, preferring coffee to orange juice. The supposed health benefits are now regarded as mere marketing hype, with The Food Institute pointing out, "A single 12-ounce glass of O.J. contains an incredible 9 teaspoons of sugar, about the same as a 12-oz. can of Coke."

Recently the kid whose birth prompted me to plant that long-gone tangerine tree graduated from the University of Florida law school, so my family drove up to Gainesville to cheer him on. As we zoomed along Interstate 75, we passed the usual billboards advertising roadside attractions—strip joints, fireworks stands, and so forth.

There was one in Ocala featuring citrus. I've been driving past it for years. Oranges used to be the centerpiece of the billboard's design, but not anymore. Now, I noticed in passing, the big centerpiece was its live baby gators. The citrus had been shoved to the side—almost like an afterthought. The oranges cling to the edge of the sign, barely hanging on.

11

A No-Wake Zone in Stillwright Point

Florida Phoenix, July 8, 2020

Six months ago, back when we could still safely leave the house, I drove down to Key West to give a talk about books. On the way back, I stopped off in Key Largo to look at the 215-home Stillwright Point neighborhood.

Outwardly, there is nothing remarkable about Stillwright Point. It looks like most other "finger canal" neighborhoods around Florida, where a developer has dredged canals along a waterfront and piled the fill atop mangroves to create slivers of land that look like grasping fingers. Waterfront homes in Stillwright Point go for six-figure prices.

What makes Stillwright Point remarkable is that last fall its roads remained inundated with brackish water for 90 days straight. At times the flooding—caused by a combination of king tides and rising sea levels—reached a foot deep.

Picture it: Three months of living in a mini-Venice minus the singing gondoliers. Residents had to pull on a pair of waders just to walk down the street. Anyone who tried to drive through the flood wound up with salt-damaged mufflers, brakes, and rims. A few homeowners put up handmade "NO WAKE" signs out by the road.

When I was there, I could still see standing water in some streets, looking like big puddles from a hard rain, but it no longer covered the entire road. I chatted with Patrick Cummings, 34, whose three kids were playing in his front yard. This wasn't the first time their streets had been underwater for a while, he said, but it was by far the worst. Whenever the neighborhood floods, Cummings said, "it traps us all in here."

I thought about the folks in Stillwright Point last week when the *Miami Herald* reported that the U.S. Army Corps of Engineers had come up with a plan to help such low-lying areas of the Keys. For a mere $5.5 billion—billion with a B—the Corps would elevate 7,300 houses, "floodproof" another 3,800 buildings, and tear down about 300 homes, whose owners would need a new place to live.

Two thoughts occurred to me when I read that story: (1) That's an awful lot of taxpayer money to fix one county; and (2) the Keys are far from the only place in Florida facing this soggy problem.

On that same drive from Key West, I cruised down Fort Lauderdale's East Las Olas Boulevard, where you'll find the grandfather of all Florida finger-canal subdivisions with serious flooding problems. A developer named Charles Green "Charley" Rodes invented finger canal construction in Fort Lauderdale during the 1920s land boom.

He used dredges to create a series of canals and fill-dirt cul-de-sacs between East Las Olas Boulevard and the New River for a project that he originally named after Venice (although some accounts say he pronounced it "Venus"). The finger canals multiplied how many waterfront lots he could sell to suckers—er, customers.

I chatted with Las Olas Isles subdivision resident Stephen McGowan, 55, who has spent the past 21 years watching the king tides fill his street and creep up his sloping brick driveway every fall, even on sunny days. Every year, the water rises a couple of inches higher, he said.

"Is it climate change?" he asked. "I leave that for the scientists."

* * *

While Fort Lauderdale may be where finger canals started, they reached their apotheosis in another Florida city, Cape Coral, billed in the 1950s as Florida's "Waterfront Wonderland."

The construction by Gulf American was so poorly planned that while the company built lots of houses and a country club with a dancing fountain called Waltzing Waters, the developers forgot to include water lines, sewers, schools, and supermarkets. The one thing they had plenty of were canals—400 miles of them, the most of any city on Earth.

Recently, a nonprofit group called the First Street Foundation noted the downside of that achievement when it released a new database showing the flood risk from rainfall, river flooding, or hurricane storm surge for more than 142 million homes and properties across the United States.

To create the database, the foundation worked with more than 80 hydrologists, researchers, and data scientists. The No. 1 state for flooding risk is Florida, of course. And the No. 1 city in the nation facing a serious flood risk is Cape Coral—not quite all of it, but 111,237 parcels, which works out to 86 percent of the total properties.

Cape Coral won this dubious honor because it was "predominantly built on canals at very close to sea level," Jeremy Porter, director of research and development at First Street Foundation, explained in an email.

I tried to talk to someone in Cape Coral's government about this but got no response to my calls and email. Perhaps they were too busy bailing the water out of City Hall.

Tom Ruppert, a coastal planning specialist at an organization called Florida Sea Grant that works to conserve coastal resources, says climate change is exposing the flaws of Florida's century-long binge of rapid but sloppy growth.

Finger canal subdivisions were built to be about a foot above sea level, which assumed that sea level would remain constant, he said. Of course, it did not.

While that type of construction has fallen out of favor, he said, other types that are still in vogue in Florida continue courting disaster, such as slab-on-grade foundations surrounded by lots of impervious surfaces that don't absorb rainfall.

Despite the obvious peril from rising seas, nobody in charge in Florida seems fired up about combating climate change right now. Instead, they talk about "resilience" as if it were some magical incantation and not a euphemism for spending millions of taxpayer dollars to fix problems that developers caused.

"All we're doing is propping up anybody with a vested interest in maintaining the status quo," Ruppert told me.

Meanwhile, notes Jane West of the pro-planning group 1,000 Friends of Florida, local governments continue approving building new homes in flood-prone areas. For instance, in Vilano Beach, near St. Augustine, she said, builders are being allowed to put up new houses on lots where houses were recently washed away by a hurricane storm surge. The task of selling these homes is eased by taxpayer-subsidized flood insurance.

"It's certainly a mixed message," West told me. "Continuing to build in vulnerable areas does not make sense."

This week I checked a website called "realtor.com" and in spite of all the flooding problems, there are vacant lots for sale in Stillwright Point. For a mere $129,000, you too can buy property that you may sometimes be unable to access except by boat or paddleboard.

Maybe the best we can do is try to educate the folks who insist a water view is worth any risk even as the seas rise. To that end, I think the Florida Legislature should require real estate agents to hand every buyer of waterfront property a pamphlet on how to deal with repeated flooding, featuring tips on how to dry your sodden carpets, how to get mold out of your baseboards, and what's the best bait to catch the fish that will be swimming down your street.

And once they read the pamphlet and sign a form saying they understand the risk, they get a free pair of waders and a professionally lettered "NO WAKE" sign to put out by the mailbox.

12

Plane Crazy

Florida Phoenix, November 30, 2023

Look! Up in the sky! It's a bird! It's a plane! It's a bunch of planes! And a helicopter too! And the noise is making all the horses go bonkers!

This is what life is like for the people who own farms around the Marion County community of Jumbolair Aviation and Equestrian Estates.

Jumbolair, near Ocala, is a gated enclave for the wealthy owners of private planes. It boasts of having "the largest licensed, private runway in North America." Its most famous resident is onetime Sweathog and cross-dressing *Hairspray* musical star John Travolta, who parks his Boeing 707 right in his own driveway.

Now Jumbolair's owners want to expand it. They want to build 241 houses and 205 townhomes on about 380 acres. They want to add commercial businesses. They may even open the runway to non-residents.

"There is a desire to build hangars on common areas of the property and commercial areas of the property and rent those hangars out to residents and possibly people who do not live in the subdivision," one Marion County official wrote in a memo about the proposal.

To nearby residents, that means even more planes and helicopters thundering over the surrounding pastures, scaring the livestock, polluting the air, and occasionally dumping the fuel into their "springs protection area," tainting the aquifer and waterways.

You can see why local ranchers don't think this is so super, man. You could even call them "neigh sayers."

"There are people out here who have lived on their property for generations," said one neighbor, Jonathan Rivera-Rose Schenck, who's a comparative newcomer. Expanding Jumbolair so dramatically "doesn't really fit in the community at all."

"There are so many safety concerns, it isn't even funny," another of the neighbors, Amy Agricola, told me this week. What's worse, she said, "they tried to push it through under the radar and get it approved."

John Travolta's house in Jumbolair. Note the jet in the driveway. Photo from Florida State Archives.

It's another twist in the history of a parcel of land that already has a pretty wild backstory—one that involves everything from elephants to exercise machines to buried bags of cash.

* * *

Jumbolair's list of past occupants tells you a lot about how bizarre life can be in Florida.

Early on, the place was a horse farm owned by socialite Muriel Vanderbilt of the fabulously wealthy Vanderbilt family. She used the property to train her thoroughbred racehorses. Desert Vixen, born on the ranch, later was inducted into the U.S. Racing Hall of Fame.

Another owner, briefly, was Jose Antonio Fernandez of Miami, whose drug-smuggling operation was so large he had to buy his own bank to hide his profits. He pleaded guilty in 1985 to racketeering, conspiracy, drug trafficking, and fraud. Workers later discovered bundles of crumbling $100 bills buried on the property and (allegedly) turned them all over to the FBI.

Next up was Arthur Jones, who made his fortune creating and selling the Nautilus exercise machine. An avid aviation fan, he built the 7,550-foot runway for his fleet of planes.

In 1984, Jones used one of those planes to rescue 63 baby elephants from a scheduled cull of the herd in Zimbabwe. As a result, he turned the property into an elephant sanctuary. There were also rhinos, a silverback gorilla named Mickey and, after a while, quite a few crocodiles.

The elephants were the source of the name, since the land was now a lair for Jumbo.

Jones, in his 50s, had married a Revlon "Charlie Girl" model named Terri, then 18, who grew up in Seffner. She was his fifth wife (out of six, if you're keeping up with the Joneses) and regularly flew to Tampa to get her hair done.

The couple even appeared on *Lifestyles of the Rich and Famous,* where, by one account, the cantankerous Jones pulled a gun on host Robin Leach.

In 1989, the couple divorced. Jones' ex-wife retained custody of Jumbolair and remarried, this time to a jewelry store owner. Terri Jones Thayer, as she was now known, then created Jumbolair Aviation Estates: 38 residential lots with deeds that provide access to her ex-husband's runway and taxiways to every back door.

"It's like a cross between *Dynasty,* James Bond, and the Crocodile Hunter," she told a *St. Petersburg Times* reporter.

In 2013, a new owner took over: Frank Merschman, founder of Big Top Manufacturing, an airplane hangar and fabric structure maker in Perry and a resident of Jumbolair since 2007.

A year later, Merschman bought another parcel of Jumbolair from a holding company owned by a member of the Qatar royal family. The broker: Donald Trump's longtime attorney, Michael Cohen, who received a $100,000 brokerage fee. He failed to pay taxes on it, which was one of the reasons Cohen wound up behind bars.

By 2019, Merschman was ready to be rid of Jumbolair. He asked for $10.5 million and, two years later, agreed to sell for $1 million less.

The new owners: Robert and Debra Bull of Melbourne. Bull is founder of CMS Mechanical, a national commercial heating and air conditioning company. He's also an avid boat racer.

None of the neighbors knew what a drastic change the Bulls had in mind for Jumbolair until the signs went up.

* * *

Alyson Scotti was driving by Jumbolair one day near the end of last month when she noticed a row of yellow signs along the property boundary. But the lettering on the signs was too small to read from the road.

"I pulled over and went to read them," she told me. When she saw they were about a proposed rezoning, she looked up on the county's website what the Bulls wanted to do. Her reaction to what she read: "Holy cow, they're building a city!"

This was on a Friday afternoon, October 27. The signs said the rezoning was scheduled to be voted on at the next Planning and Zoning Commission meeting on Monday, October 30.

In other words, only a weekend stood between the Bulls and what seemed like a definite slam dunk.

Upset at what she saw as an attempt to slip something past Jumbolair's neighbors, Scotti started using her phone and computer to alert everyone about what was going on. She managed to round up quite a few people, many of whom emailed county officials about their objections and signed a petition against Bull's plans.

At that point, the county staff was recommending a yes vote on both the rezoning and change in land use.

"Mr. Bull and his wife wish to integrate the upscale aviation neighborhood with our beautiful equestrian community to create a premier aviation equestrian oasis, supported with some limited commercial uses," the county staff's report said, making it sound like the Bulls would create a haven for flying horses like Pegasus.

But by the time the meeting opened on Monday, the staff had changed its tune. They told commissioners they recommended denial. One major concern: increased traffic on the narrow local roads.

Bull's Ocala attorney, Rob Batsel, started off his presentation by thanking the county staff for a comprehensive report but then added, "I preferred the staff report that came out on Friday and recommended approval."

Batsel played down the changes the Bulls had proposed, telling the commissioners, "We're not asking for too much. We think the property owner is entitled to the highest and best use of the property."

Meanwhile, the opponents had packed the meeting room. When it was their turn to speak, they did not hold back. They, too, worried about the roads. But many more mentioned their concern about the increased aerial traffic thundering overhead and the environmental consequences.

One of them, James Nelson, called Bob Bull "a noise bully" who frequently flies his copter over his neighbors' property just above treetop level. He accused the Bulls of planning to ruin a quiet area "just so a millionaire can make more money."

In the end, the planning commissioners voted 3–1 to recommend the county commissioners deny the Bulls' proposal. Seeing the reversal of the Bulls' fortunes happen so quickly, Schenck told me, he almost felt sorry for Bob Bull—until later that evening.

"He flew his helicopter over my house for 20 minutes starting at 10 p.m." he said. "My wife told me, 'I feel like I'm in *M*A*S*H*.'"

He said Bull has repeated the noisy visit every day since then.

"It drives the horses nuts," he said.

* * *

The Marion County Commission is scheduled to discuss the Jumbolair rezoning and land use change next week, on December 5. The commissioners are not bound by what their Planning and Zoning Commission recommended. They could hand the Bulls everything they want on a silver platter.

But the Bulls are apparently nervous about what's going to happen. I say this because they had their attorney invite all the opponents to a convivial little get-together in one of Jumbolair's hangars on Tuesday night.

"We understand it can be unsettling to receive a letter about development 'in your backyard,' but assure you that our goal is to create a wonderful addition to the neighborhood," Batsel wrote in his invitation.

Schenck said he saw about 75 people in the hangar. Bob Bull was there too, he said, but never spoke, not even when Schenck tried to ask him questions. Instead, Bull's attorney and engineer ran the show.

Schenck said the main message the pair delivered was: This massively disruptive development, much like the Marvel movie villain Thanos, is inevitable. Therefore, you should stop fighting it. (If you watch Marvel movies, you know this approach did not work out well for Thanos.)

Batsel also insisted that Bull isn't pushing this project for the money. According to Schenck, that bizarre assertion prompted a lot of people to ask, "If he's not in it for the money and the neighborhood doesn't want him to do it, then why exactly is he doing it?"

They got no answer. I suppose you could say Batsel and Bull didn't want to address the elephant in the room.

Finally, Schenck said, he and a friend had enough of that Bull—um, I mean hearing about what Bull wanted. They left about 20 minutes before the scheduled end.

But then they stuck around outside the hangar door. They did that so they could buttonhole everyone else as they left, asking them to sign the petition to be submitted to the Marion County commissioners next week. They all did, he said, and now the number of signatures has hit 500.

That suggests that the hangar hangout was much less effective than the Bulls expected.

I've tried repeatedly this week to pry a comment out of Batsel or the Bulls, without any success. I kept thinking, "Surely they'll want to respond to the angry neighbors." But no, they didn't even tell me to not call them Shirley.

I wouldn't count Bull out at this point. He seems determined to win permission from Marion County to expand Jumbolair, no matter what.

But as he tries to bring this unwieldy craft in for a landing, he better expect a LOT of turbulence. And he should probably end his helicopter harassment. Otherwise, thanks to Florida's Stand Your Ground Law, he might face some serious anti-aircraft fire.

———————

Postscript: In February 2024, after Travolta announced that he also opposed Bull's plans, Bull pulled his rezoning request.

Part Two

FLORIDA MEN AND WOMEN, UNITE!

13

A Pain in the Butt

Florida Phoenix, November 25, 2020

Jackie Lane knows a lot of people think she's a pain in the butt. They wish she would just shut up and sit down. Stop causing so many problems for the paper mill near Pensacola. Stop putting people's jobs at risk.

"The community is not particularly fond of environmental activists," she told me this week. "There's a lot of opposition."

She doesn't care. She soldiers on, year after year, battling for her beloved Perdido Bay, an hourglass-shaped estuary that straddles the Florida-Alabama state line near Pensacola. She's not at all shy about saying what she thinks about anyone who threatens it. She is, as my daddy used to say, "rough as a cob."

Lane and her husband Jim, an engineering professor, moved to a home on the bay's northern end in 1975. They raised their kids there. They went swimming twice a day, every day. They fished for flounder, redfish, and mullet and enjoyed dining on what they caught.

"Not anymore," she said. Nowadays she sees nothing but the occasional catfish, and the last time she tried swimming in Perdido Bay she emerged feeling like her skin was on fire.

She first noticed something was wrong in the mid-1980s.

Before she got married and started having children, Jackie Lane had earned a doctorate in marine biology from the University of South Florida. When she first moved to Perdido Bay, she was amazed by the clams she found there and began studying them.

"There were so many clams you could put your foot down on the bay bottom and one foot would cover 10 clams," she said. "They were that thick."

Then, in 1986, "they all died," she said. She checked with officials from what was then known as the state Department of Environmental Regulation, who told her, "Well, it might be because of the paper mill."

Well, of course it was.

* * *

Built in 1941 in the then-rural enclave known as Cantonment (pronounced can-TOHN-ment), the paper mill has been owned by a succession of companies: the Florida Pulp and Paper Company, Champion International, St. Regis, and now International Paper, the world's largest paper company.

When I was growing up in Pensacola in the 1960s, everyone joked that the stench from the Cantonment paper mill was so bad that pilots from Pensacola's Navy base never worried about getting lost. If their instruments went out, they just popped open their airplane canopies and sniffed their way back home.

The air pollution wasn't the worst part. Year after year, the mill dumped millions of gallons of polluted waste into a stream called Eleven Mile Creek, which flows into the poorly flushed northern segment of Perdido Bay.

People joked that the tributary's real name was "Stink Creek." A friend of mine said he remembers the smell being similar to "dirty athletic shoes stored in a gym locker too long and then sprayed with industrial strength antiseptic cleaner."

According to a history written by Lane's group, Friends of Perdido Bay, after the mill began operating the water in the bay turned brown, seagrass died, and the fish began to disappear.

The bay's degradation chased away commercial shrimpers who earned a living there back when the water was clear. As for the clams, Lane said, they died because the paper mill had accidentally or on purpose dumped the contents of one of its settling ponds, sending a big dose of its waste cascading down the creek all at once.

A 1999 report by a local grand jury said no matter who owned the mill, not once in its history had that polluting paper factory "ever fully met state water quality standards. We found instead a pattern of violations, studies, and promises to improve, followed by more violations, more studies, and more promises and so forth—all of which was accommodated and/or constructively approved by [state regulators]."

International Paper acquired the mill 20 years ago. After checking a dictionary, I think the correct word for the new owners' relationship with the Department of Environmental Protection would be "cozy."

An example: Then-DEP secretary David Struhs cut a deal for his agency to lend $56 million at below-market interest rates to build a treatment plant and pipeline that would primarily be used to redirect International Paper's waste.

Jackie Lane by Perdido Bay. Photo courtesy of Jackie Lane.

Such loans, which use federal tax dollars supplied by the EPA, are supposed to go to public utilities, not to a private company. To get around that requirement, Struhs made some calls and persuaded the Escambia County Utilities Authority to apply for the loan with the promise that International Paper would repay 80 percent of it.

With the deal secured, Struhs resigned as DEP secretary. He'd gotten a new job as the vice president for environmental affairs at International Paper.

State law says the DEP should only allow pollution to be dumped into the state's waterways if it's in the public interest. During one 2007 court hearing, a DEP employee testified, "We considered International Paper's interest as public interest." It's the Florida version of "What's good for General Motors is good for the country."

The DEP has taken such a benign attitude toward the company that when its 2010 pollution permit expired five years ago, the state let it continue pumping 24 million gallons of pollution out every day.

In May, the agency at last meted out some punishment for the continued violations of water quality standards, requiring the company to pay $190,000 in penalties, implement a $1 million environmental mitigation project, and pay a $10,000 fine each time it falls short of the requirements. (International Paper's revenue for the 12 months ending September 30 was $20 billion, so they can probably scratch together these payments from the change in the CEO's couch cushions.)

"We wish to make it very clear that the department's expectation is that you will work as expeditiously as possible to address the ongoing compliance issues at your facility," said the DEP—while still allowing the mill to dump 24 million gallons of pollution a day.

* * *

The death of all those clams in 1986 drew Lane and her husband into fighting against the mill's dumping, a fight that had begun with other activists going to court in the 1970s. She was in her 40s at the time she enlisted in the battle. She's now 77 and still fighting.

Her husband died in 2012 but that didn't stop her. Other allies faded away over the years as well, even as she has carried on.

"A lot of people have gotten old and died," she said, but "we've also gotten some new folks and contributions that pay for quite a bit of testing."

I asked the corporate spokesman for International Paper to tell me their view of Lane's long-lasting crusade against their company. His response: "International Paper is committed to protecting the environment as healthy and sustainable watersheds are essential to our community and our business. Concerning the administrative challenge, we are unable to comment on ongoing litigation."

In other words, they can't talk about Lane suing to stop them because she's still suing to stop them. She just went through a Zoom court hearing earlier this month, facing off against attorneys for the DEP and the company all by herself. (The DEP did not respond to my request for a comment on its long history of not holding International Paper to account.)

"The people from the mill have always been pretty nice," Lane said. But she said she has gotten a lot of flak from the mill's union, and from Democratic politicians supported by the union, as well as from the industries that sell products to the mill, such as the chemical plants and the forestry folks.

She says she quit her job teaching at Pensacola Junior College because she grew tired of the trolling from students and other teachers.

The county's pro-business Republican commissioners are no fans of hers, either. One of them, to show that Perdido Bay is as clean as could be, stood waist-deep in the bay and drank a glass of its water.

"Yeah, he's an idiot," Lane said, proving she could never be a State Department diplomat.

When Hurricane Sally passed nearby in September, it splashed a big glop of the bay bottom onto her property. She had it tested. It was contaminated with cancer-causing dioxins, mercury, and other toxic pollutants. Perhaps the commissioner could consider all that stuff "flavoring."

Lane says she understands the community's desire to keep the paper mill open and running, supplying steady jobs: "Nobody wants to see that paper mill close—but nobody wants it in their bay, either."

I wanted to tell you Jackie Lane's story this week because, while she may be a pain in the butt, she and other activists like her seem to be doing more to protect Florida from pollution than certain agencies that have "protection" in their name.

So whether you're gathering with your whole family this Thanksgiving or eating alone to avoid coronavirus, be sure to say a prayer of thanks for all the pains in the butt like Jackie Lane. Without them, we here in Florida would be up Stink Creek without a paddle.

14

The Mayor of Margaritaville

Florida Phoenix, September 7, 2023

The first time I encountered the Mayor of Margaritaville, he was playing a concert at my college back around the Cretaceous Period. Despite the passage of so much time, I will never forget the experience.

What made it so memorable was not Jimmy Buffett's laid-back musical stylings, or the dazzling craftsmanship of his Coral Reefer Band. No, what I remember the most about that concert is hearing one of my classmates singing along VERY enthusiastically with what she thought was a song titled, "Why Don't We Get Drunk at School."

Buffett died last week at age 76. He was widely mourned as Florida's troubadour laureate by both the Parrot Head faithful and more casual fans who grew up hearing his music as the soundtrack of their lives.

The obituaries cited his hits, such as "Margaritaville" and "Cheeseburger in Paradise." They also talked about how a flat-broke folkie who'd once played for tips in Key West had parlayed his songwriting talent and savvy into a showbiz empire worth $1 billion, involving everything from books to beer to beach resorts.

What hardly any of them mentioned, though, is his impact on one particular Florida environmental issue.

This dates to his 1981 album *Coconut Telegraph*. There's a song on that album called "Growing Older but Not Up." The lyrics mention feeling like an old manatee heading south as the weather grows colder.

"He tries to steer clear of the humdrum so near," Buffett warbles. "It cuts prop scars deep in his shoulder."

A month after the album hit stores, Buffett played a concert in Tallahassee, and that song was on the playlist.

After the concert, he was chatting backstage about that song with a new fan. They both agreed that manatees needed help. The singer offered to spearhead a new organization to help protect them.

Jimmy Buffett shows off his personalized "Save the Manatee" license plate, which features an unintentional misspelling of his name. Photo from the Florida State Archives.

And that's how the Save the Manatee Club was born, with Buffett as its co-chair.

* * *

Some celebrities seem to adopt a new crusade every month—the rainforest for January, whales for February, and so on. They commit to causes the way they commit to matrimony.

Not Buffett.

He retained the post of Save the Manatee Club co-chair right up until the moment he expired, a span of 42 years. He took office the year *Raiders of the Lost Ark* hit theaters and didn't leave until *Indiana Jones and the Dial of Destiny* came out.

And it wasn't a ceremonial position either. Buffett actually did things to help manatees.

Buffett first encountered manatees when one swam near his boat and he thought, "Whoa! What was that?" Over time, he came to regard them as a symbol for the best of this state he'd adopted as both his home and muse.

"To me, the manatee represents what we all like about Florida—kind of cruising in warm, clear water and not bothering anybody," he said once.

He'd seen several that bore scars. Ever since Ole Evinrude invented the outboard motor in 1907, boats had been colliding with manatees and leaving deep gashes.

By 1949, so many had been hit that an Everglades National Park biologist named Joe Moore discovered he could use their scar patterns as a way to tell individual manatees apart. Scientists now use a computerized version of Moore's scar catalog to track manatees.

Buffett's concern about the damage being done to the manatees is evident in his song. And when he performed it at the February 1981 concert in Tallahassee, that line caught the attention of one particular concertgoer—the most powerful politician in Florida.

* * *

Bob Graham had been governor for two years. A Harvard Law grad, he's the son of a former state senator whose family developed the community of Miami Lakes.

Running for governor, he'd focused on the issues of education and the death penalty—not the environment. But he'd just gotten slapped upside the head by evidence of the importance of that issue.

The *Sports Illustrated* swimsuit issue was the magazine's most popular seller each year. The cover of the 1981 iteration featured a bikini-clad Christie Brinkley posing on Captiva Island. Inside, there was a different kind of bombshell: a lengthy piece about how Florida seemed to be doing its darndest to kill off the natural attributes that made it special.

"The sad fact is that Florida is going down the tube," the magazine warned. "Indeed, in no state is the environment being wrecked faster and on a larger scale."

That magazine story had just hit newsstands when Graham's daughter Suzanne asked her dad to take her to the Jimmy Buffett concert. Graham, never the hippest guy in the room, asked, "Who's Jimmy Buffett?"

Graham found himself enjoying the concert, and then took his daughter backstage to meet the star. (One of the perks of being the chief executive is that you get a backstage pass.) That's how he wound up chatting with Buffett.

When I interviewed Graham and his aides for my book *Manatee Insanity: Inside the War Over Florida's Most Endangered Species,* I asked if, when he met Buffett, Graham was thinking about how to counter that *Sports Illustrated* story. They all denied it. But I think it's fair to say that the decline of Florida's environment was on his radar when Buffett mentioned helping manatees.

"I volunteered my services to be involved at that point in an awareness campaign of the plight of the manatee in Florida," Buffett testified in a lawsuit some years afterward. "And I made the governor aware of my intentions and offering of my services."

Buffett spelled out that he wanted to do more than be a big-name cause endorser.

"I don't want to just be a token celebrity," he said. "I want to be involved."

Graham suggested forming some sort of manatee awareness committee. And he said later, "it took about three milliseconds to decide he should be the chairman of this new effort."

Buffett didn't think Graham was taking him seriously. But after the concert, one of Graham's aides, a man named Ron Book, arranged a meeting with Buffett. He was under orders from Graham: Hash out with Buffett how he'd like to organize this manatee campaign.

"A lot of people have forgotten how a lot of the progress we've made on manatee protection was due to him," Book, now a lobbyist and the father of Senator Lauren Book, told me this week. "I give Jimmy all the credit."

* * *

For their meeting, Book brought along a manatee expert, a biologist named Patrick Rose, to provide some scientific expertise.

Rose recalls they met in the lobby of Palm Beach's fanciest hotel, The Breakers. He said the singer brought along a woman named Sunshine Smith who struck him as being "free-spirited." She also had sharp business instincts. Smith became the original proprietor of Buffett's Margaritaville store in Key West and Buffett's manager.

Buffett agreed to cut a series of public service announcements asking boaters to watch out for manatees, play a benefit concert, maybe sell T-shirts with those lines about a manatee with scars.

Then Buffett suggested something more substantive. He proposed they post manatee warning signs at boat ramps, dive shops, and marinas (and later donated $35,000 to start the postings).

"He was never just a spokesman," Rose told me this week.

About a month after their backstage meetup, Graham publicly announced he was forming a Save the Manatee Committee and appointing Buffett as chair.

"You can't but help like a manatee," Buffett said during the March 1981 press conference. "And their only predators are people who aren't aware of the problem."

Graham expected "a total love-in" at his announcement. Then a reporter

threw him a curve. How could the governor square his law-and-order political stance with Buffett's songs about drug use?

Graham, caught unprepared, made up an answer. Rather than glorifying
drugs, he said, Buffett's songs "point out the problems, the distress, the human tragedy of the use of drugs." (Fortunately for Graham, no one brought
up the weed-tastic name of Buffett's band.)

Graham admitted later that that was "a totally dingbat response." But it
guaranteed he wouldn't be asked anything more on that topic.

The manatee effort proved to be the start of a long friendship between
the singer and the future U.S. senator who became known for his environmental advocacy. At a subsequent Capital Press Skits performance, Graham
showed up dressed as Buffett. He was then joined onstage by Buffett, wearing Graham's trademark suit with a tie decorated with silhouettes of Florida.

* * *

Buffett turned out to be a creative thinker about the Save the Manatee Club.
According to Rose, Buffett was the one who came up with the organization's
most effective fundraising program, dubbed "Adopt-A-Manatee."

When you adopt a manatee, you do not, of course, receive custody
of an actual manatee. Instead, for a modest amount—$15 at first, now
$25—adopters receive a personalized certificate and a biography of the
manatee chosen, as well as regular updates.

Within a week of Buffett announcing the adoption program in 1983,
more than 1,000 people had signed up. Because of Buffett's involvement,
Reader's Digest ran a story that sparked national interest in the manatee
adoption program.

This did more than merely raise money for what eventually became the
independent, nonprofit organization Buffett had hoped for.

Those adopters felt invested in the fate of their individual manatee.
School children in Arizona, your maiden aunt in Minnesota, some fan of
marine life stranded in landlocked Wyoming—they all were now rooting
for their manatee to make it.

When the Florida Legislature approved selling a "Save the Manatee" license plate to raise money for manatee research, Buffett was awarded his
own personalized plate. In a classic case of Florida at work, though, the
plate he was given misspelled his last name, implying the state was now
serving a manatee "buffet."

* * *

Not all of Buffett's duties to help manatees were pleasant ones.

By 1999, the Save the Manatee Club's directors had decided to sue both the state and federal government over their failure to protect manatees under the Endangered Species Act and the Marine Mammal Protection Act.

Fine, Buffett said when he was told. But first, he wanted to warn Florida's new governor, Jeb Bush, about what was going to happen.

Rose—by now executive director of the Save the Manatee Club—scheduled a meeting with Bush for himself and Buffett. An aide assured Rose that Bush would be fully briefed on their purpose before they arrived.

The first few minutes went well, Rose said, right up to the point where they mentioned the word "lawsuit."

"Lawsuit?!" Bush shouted, leaping to his feet.

"I could see everything just drain out of him," Rose said. "He had not been briefed."

The pair fumbled through the rest of the meeting with the clearly steamed Bush. Afterward, during a press conference outside the governor's office, Buffett said Bush displayed "a great sense of humor."

Rather than talk about the leaping governor, Buffett took a more diplomatic approach, mentioning that "there's a great opportunity for cooperation."

The "cooperation" didn't last. A coalition of environmental groups led by the Save the Manatee Club filed the two suits less than a year later. Both the state and federal government settled out of court, agreeing to new measures to protect manatees that sparked a widespread revival of the population.

Buffett's next bit of celebrity diplomacy involved another backstage meeting.

* * *

For more than six years, waterfront developers and boating interests had worked together to convince the Florida Fish and Wildlife Conservation Commission that manatees were doing great. Now, in 2007, they were about to get their wish.

Despite the fact that 2006 had proven to be the deadliest year ever for manatees, they said manatees no longer needed the protection provided by being classified as "endangered." It was time to take them off the endangered list and repeal some of the protections that hurt their business.

Buffett was slated to play a concert in Tampa right before the wildlife commission vote. He invited then-governor Charlie Crist to introduce him to the 20,000 rowdy concertgoers.

The contrast was dramatic: Buffett in T-shirt, shorts, and flip-flops, shaking hands with Crist in a white shirt, dark pants, and shoes as shiny as the chrome on a new car. But Crist praised Buffett for being just like him.

"He has Florida in his heart and he loves her like I do," Crist told the cheering crowd.

What the crowd didn't see was that for 10 minutes backstage, Buffett had talked to Crist about what was wrong with the wildlife commission move.

After talking to Buffett, Crist called up the wildlife commissioners and told them to back off because "it would put this creature in jeopardy." They didn't vote it down, just postponed a decision indefinitely, much to the chagrin of the developer and boater lobbyists.

With Buffett gone, who can possibly do that sort of thing now?

I asked Rose, who is now 72, if the Save the Manatee Club is trying to line up another Florida-based singer, actor, or sports star to fill Buffett's flip-flops. Dwayne "The Rock" Johnson? Ariana Grande? Serena Williams?

He didn't really have an answer for me.

"We're going to stay strong and carry on," was all he could say.

Listen, manatees need all the friends they can get these days. There's been a massive die-off thanks to pollution-fueled algae blooms wiping out seagrass beds. Meanwhile boat collisions continue to claim lives and leave scars. According to the *Miami Herald*, 72 manatee deaths so far in 2023 were linked to watercraft.

Finding another Buffett will be difficult. But maybe every time we hear one of his songs, we should think about what we could do for manatees, from slowing down our boats to cutting our use of lawn fertilizer to buying a manatee license plate.

That would be a more constructive way to honor his memory than drinking a margarita, eating a cheeseburger, or getting drunk at school.

15

Lift Every Voice

FORUM, Spring 2022

On a warm and wet September evening last year, the first football game of 2021 was about to start. The two teams lined up on the field at Raymond James Stadium, each in their respective end zones—the Tampa Bay Buccaneers on one side, the Dallas Cowboys on the other.

Before the National Anthem, they listened to a different song, one that some call the Black National Anthem. It was a live rendition by the Florida A&M University's Concert Choir of "Lift Every Voice and Sing."

This was far from the first NFL game to feature the song. The NFL played an Alicia Keys recording of it before the start of all of its Week 1 games during the 2020 season, as well as ahead of Super Bowl LV and the draft in April.

The place where the anthem means the most, though, is Jacksonville, the Florida town where it was written and first performed more than a century ago.

> *Lift every voice and sing*
> *Till earth and heaven ring*
> *Ring with the harmonies of Liberty . . .*

The author of those stirring words was a Florida man, and a remarkable one.

* * *

The list of professions that James Weldon Johnson held is lengthy. In addition to being a songwriter, he was an educator, a novelist, a poet, a lawyer, a baseball pitcher, a diplomat, and a civil rights activist. And he did all that as a Black man navigating a post–Civil War world set up to extend white supremacy.

"He was a Renaissance man," says Liz McDonald McCoy, executive director at the Friends of James Weldon Johnson Park. Creating a park in

James Weldon Johnson, who wrote the lyrics of "Lift Every Voice and Sing." Photo from the Florida State Archives.

his honor is one of the ways his native city has honored its most famous resident in recent years.

Johnson was born in 1871 in the Duval County town of La Villa, later annexed by Jacksonville. His father was the headwaiter at a hotel and pastor of a small church. His mother was the daughter of the first Black man elected to the Bahamian legislature, and she had become the vice principal of the segregated Stanton School. Johnson attended Stanton until he was 16. He had one brother, John Rosamond Johnson, whom he referred to by his middle name, and an adopted sister.

Johnson's father taught his children Spanish, which helped when he let a Cuban exchange student stay with the family. When the teenaged Johnson took the train to Atlanta University, the exchange student went along. A conductor was ready to evict them from the "whites-only" section of the train until he heard them speaking Spanish to each other. That was Johnson's first encounter with overt racism.

In Atlanta, Johnson became a star pitcher for the university baseball team, a prize-winning orator, and a skilled woodworker. When he graduated, he was offered a scholarship to Harvard, but he turned it down to return home to Jacksonville and become the principal of his alma mater. He pushed for the school to add high school classes, becoming the first high school in Florida to provide classes for Black students.

In 1895 he founded the *Daily American,* Florida's first Black newspaper. In 1897, without ever setting foot in a law school, he passed the Florida Bar, becoming the first Black Floridian to do so.

Then, in 1900, for a celebration of Abraham Lincoln's birthday, he penned the inspirational poem "Lift Every Voice and Sing." His musically inclined brother, Rosamond, composed the tune to turn those lyrics into an anthem.

* * *

Johnson was not a fan of anthems. He often heard them in church, and even ones written by his brother stirred his dislike. In his 1933 autobiography, *Along This Way,* he joked that "it would not be gross injustice to give the composers of most anthems written for church choirs a light jail sentence for each offense." But this one was born of necessity.

Johnson was scheduled to give a speech for Lincoln's birthday. He thought about writing a poem about Lincoln, too. But he couldn't compose both in the short time available before the ceremony, he confessed in his autobiography.

Then he had the idea of writing a song, to be sung by a Stanton children's choir. An anthem, in fact, with lyrics by him and music by his brother. The two had no great ambitions for the song, he wrote later. They regarded it as "an incidental effort, an effort made under stress and with no intention other than to meet the needs of a particular moment."

After that famous opening—which he judged "not a startling line"— Johnson continued on "grinding out the next five." Then he came to the end of that stanza, where it says, *Sing a song full of the faith that our dark past has taught us/Sing a song full of the hope that the present has brought us.*

At that point, he wrote later, "the spirit of the poem had taken hold of me."

He turned the first stanza over to his brother to compose the music while he kept going on the next two. As he paced back and forth, "I could not keep back the tears, and I made no effort to do so," Johnson wrote. "I was experiencing the transport of the poet's ecstasy."

Finishing the lyrics gave him a feeling of "contentment—that sense of serene joy—which makes artistic creation the most complete of all human experiences."

Rosamond jotted down the musical score and then contacted a publisher he knew in New York to get it copyrighted and printed. Then the copies went to the children's choir members to memorize.

"A choir of 500 schoolchildren at the segregated Stanton School, where James Weldon Johnson was principal, first performed the song in public," the NAACP says on its website.

This should have been a time of triumph for both brothers. Instead, they soon left their native city, driven out by a near-death experience.

* * *

It happened in the wake of Jacksonville's Great Fire of 1901, explains Dr. Wayne Wood, historian at large for the Jacksonville Historical Society.

A spark from a small wood-burning stove caught some Spanish moss on fire as it dried outside a mattress factory. Over the next eight hours the blaze spread through 146 city blocks, destroying more than 2,000 buildings, killing seven people, and leaving almost 10,000 people homeless.

Johnson tried to convince the white firefighters to save the Stanton High School, Wood said. After all, the school was big enough to house Black families that were burned out of their homes. But the firefighters, looking dazed by the scope of the blaze, ignored his pleas, and let the building burn, Wood says.

In the wake of the fire, Jacksonville had no civil authority. Instead, militias from all over the South converged on the city to impose martial law. Suddenly the city where Johnson was known and recognized, the city with a reputation for treating Blacks fairly, was a smoking ruin, and its streets were full of armed white strangers. They saw only his skin color.

A female journalist from the North came to visit the burned-out town. She had written a story about the fire and wanted Johnson's opinion about the piece. Johnson met with her in a riverfront park. She was Black but very light-skinned. Johnson's complexion was darker.

As they talked, Johnson wrote later, he became aware of men yelling and dogs snuffling around nearby. Uneasy, the pair got up and started back toward downtown—only to be stopped by armed men in uniform. A streetcar conductor had reported seeing Johnson, a Black man, consorting with what appeared to be a white woman.

"They seize me," Johnson wrote in his autobiography. "They tear my clothes and bruise my body, all the while calling to their comrades, 'We got 'im!'" Meanwhile, Johnson wrote, he could hear the crowd yelling things like, "Kill the black son of a bitch!"

"As the rushing crowd comes yelling and cursing, I feel that death is bearing in upon me," Johnson wrote later.

Before he could become one of the 4,400 Black Americans who were lynched between 1877 and 1945, though, an officer intervened. He placed Johnson under arrest and took him to the provost marshal of the town. The provost marshal happened to be a member of the Florida Bar and recognized Johnson as a fellow attorney. He believed Johnson when he said the journalist was not legally white. He was released.

At first, Johnson was ecstatic about escaping his predicament. When he got home, the only person he told about what happened was his brother, who was horrified. Only then did Johnson fully appreciate the horror himself. The memory didn't recede after one night.

"For weeks and months, the episode preyed on my mind and disturbed me in my sleep," he wrote. "Shortly after the happenings just related, Rosamond and I decided to get away from Jacksonville as quickly as possible."

* * *

They traveled to New York, where the pair composed hundreds of songs for Broadway shows. One of those songs, "Under the Banyan Tree," was performed 40 years later by Judy Garland and Margaret O'Brien in the movie *Meet Me in St. Louis.* They helped to ignite the Harlem Renaissance that later would bring to prominence Zora Neale Hurston and Langston Hughes.

Johnson became treasurer of the Colored Republican Club in New York and wrote songs that advocated for the election of his fellow New York Republican, Teddy Roosevelt. That, according to Jacksonville activist and former senator Tony Hill, led Roosevelt, as president, to appoint Johnson as the United States consul to Venezuela, in effect making him the ambassador. Three years later, Roosevelt's successor, William Howard Taft, named him to fill the same role in Nicaragua.

While he was a diplomat, Johnson married Grace Nail, the light-skinned daughter of a wealthy Black real estate magnate from New York.

"Her delicate patrician beauty stirred something in me that had never been touched before," he wrote of his first sight of her.

After they wed, she learned Spanish and joined him in civil rights advocacy, as well as serving as a hostess for cultural gatherings in their home. They had no children. They remained a devoted couple until his death.

Diplomacy left him time to write, and in 1912 he published anonymously a provocative novel titled *The Autobiography of an Ex-Colored Man.* For its narrator, Johnson created a light-skinned biracial man who, after witnessing a lynching, makes the choice to pass for white. He republished it in 1927 under his own name, and it caused a sensation.

That was the same year he also published a poetry collection called *God's Trombones,* in which he finds rhythmic beauty in the language of Black preachers delivering sermons. Both books remain in print to this day.

In 1916, Johnson left the world of diplomacy for the field of advocacy. He became a field secretary for the NAACP, which at the time was a white-led civil rights group based solely in Northern states. He expanded the organization into the South, adding thousands of new members, and advocated for a federal anti-lynching law.

He also organized more than 10,000 marchers in the NAACP's Silent Protest Parade of 1917. The march became "the first major street protest staged against lynching in the U.S.," according to historian Anthony Siracusa of the University of Mississippi.

In 1920, Johnson became the NAACP's first Black executive secretary, cementing Black control of the civil rights group. He used that position to fight against segregation and voter disenfranchisement.

After a decade leading the NAACP, he resigned to teach creative writing at Fisk University in Nashville. In 1934, Johnson became the first Black professor at New York University. It was his last first. He died in 1938 at the age of 67 while riding in a car driven by his wife when the car was hit by a train. He was killed and she was seriously injured.

But his anthem, the one he wrote four decades earlier with his brother, lives on.

* * *

First came the children—the 500 Jacksonville youngsters who memorized all the words.

Although both Johnsons left town the following year, "the schoolchildren of Jacksonville kept singing it," Johnson wrote in his autobiography. "Some of them went off to other schools and kept singing it; some of them became schoolteachers and taught it to their pupils."

The song spread like the wildfire that had scorched so much of Johnson's hometown.

"Within 20 years, the song was being sung in schools and churches and on special occasions throughout the South," Johnson recounted "In traveling round, I have commonly found printed or typewritten copies of the words pasted in the backs of hymnals and the songbooks used in Sunday schools, YMCAs and similar institutions."

In 1929, the NAACP officially adopted it as the "Negro National Hymn," giving it an official role in marches, graduations, and celebrations. It is routinely sung as part of Martin Luther King Day ceremonies.

If you search YouTube, there are versions by Ray Charles, Aretha Franklin, Melba Moore (featuring Dionne Warwick, Anita Baker, and Stevie Wonder, among others), an a cappella solo by John Legend, and a soulful duet by Al Green and Deniece Williams. As part of her popular "Homecoming" concert at Coachella, Beyoncé sang it. Perhaps the most moving version is one recorded in 2020 by gospel guru Kirk Franklin and his choir.

And now the NFL, under fire for its racial disparity in hiring and promotions, has made it a part of televised football games, spreading a song commonly known among the Black community to white audiences who are likely not as familiar with its soaring rhetoric. The release of former Buccaneers head coach Jon Gruden's racist, misogynist emails guarantees the song will be around for at least another year.

The song is so potent that in 2021, U.S. representative James Clyburn, D-S.C., filed a bill that would declare it to be the national hymn for every American. If passed, the bill would put Johnson's song on the same level as the "Star Spangled Banner" in the hope it would help unite the country after centuries of racial turmoil.

"Nothing that I have done," Johnson wrote, "has paid me back so fully in satisfaction as being the part creator of this song."

16

An Un-bear-able Problem

Florida Phoenix, May 26, 2022

June 1 marks the official start of hurricane season, or as I like to call it, "Mother Nature's annual reminder that Florida is trying to kill us." Hurricanes making landfall, shark bites, sinkholes, lightning strikes—we lead the nation in all of these deadly categories.

Yet people keep flocking here like lemmings, trying to fill up every last green spot on the map.

Can you blame Florida for this hostility toward humans, considering all the awful things we've done to the state? Our manatees are starving, our waterways are struggling with toxic algae, and human-caused pollution is at the root of both.

One of the worst examples of humans' inhumanity to nature popped up last week in an Ocala courtroom. Before I tell you about it, a warning: If you have a weak constitution, you may want to sit down. It will churn your stomach—and not just because of all the donuts involved.

But this is also a heartening story because of how this crime came to light. It shows how one very determined person—in this instance, a Florida woman who'd been badly injured—can make a difference for the environment.

First, though, I need to explain something to you newcomers: In addition to panthers, alligators, and manatees, Florida's list of native species includes black bears.

They're highly intelligent animals with a great sense of smell. Picture the cartoon Yogi, but without the green tie, porkpie hat, and penchant for pilfering food from park visitors.

Yogi would tell you that being a bear in Florida is no pic-a-nic.

Florida's bears are smaller than grizzlies, reaching a maximum of only 750 pounds (compared to more than 1,000 for their Western relatives). Their diet is mostly berries, acorns, and insects. They once roamed all over the state, but their population dwindled to just a few hundred by the 1970s. That's when the state listed them as threatened.

Florida Fish and Wildlife Conservation Commission biologists estimate that around 4,000 bears now roam our forests and swamps. That's fewer than the number of manatees, but more than the number of panthers.

Yet bears were taken off the state's imperiled species list in 2012.

That's when the trouble started.

* * *

Our bears don't generate as many headlines as our gators, which every spring show up looking for love in all the wrong places.

Most bear-related headlines concern how, like a reverse Goldilocks, they wind up somewhere unexpected—swinging in a hammock, for instance, or chilling in a hot tub.

The one time our bears made international news was 2015. In a series of incidents, bears attacked and mauled five people. The bears were hungry and had wandered into areas where they found people—and loose garbage can lids. (One Central Florida man, claiming he was "the Bear Whisperer," had been feeding them by hand—until one of his neighbors was attacked.)

The bears began rooting in garbage cans because the state was letting people harvest their preferred food, saw palmetto berries, from Florida's 37 state forests. The berry-pickers paid $10 for the right to collect an unlimited amount and sell them to companies marketing them as a questionable cure for prostate problems.

Although the state halted the unlimited berry-picking in state forests, the fish and wildlife commission decided the best solution was to shoot a lot of bears. They decided to hold the state's first bear hunt in 21 years.

Tens of thousands of people wrote in to urge the commissioners not to hold a hunt. When I asked chairman Richard Corbett, a Tampa mall developer, why the board was ignoring the public's wishes, he suffered what my cracker grandmother used to call "a conniption fit."

"Those people don't know what they're talking about," Corbett snapped. "Most of those people have never been in the woods. They think we're talking about teddy bears: 'Oh Lord, don't hurt my little teddy bear!' Well, these bears are dangerous." (Amid the subsequent uproar over his comments, he resigned.)

You could argue that the hunt was wildly successful—from the hunters' point of view.

Wildlife officials shut down the hunt after the second day because hunters had killed so many bears so fast. They were already close to racking up what was supposed to be the week-long quota. The final tally was 304 bears shot dead—including 36 mother bears, still lactating.

However, because the hunt proved so unpopular with the public, you could say the black bears gave the agency a black eye. The commission has yet to schedule a second hunt.

Among the folks galvanized into action by that misbegotten hunt, though, was a woman from the Central Florida town of Geneva named Katrina Shadix.

* * *

I think it's fair to say that Shadix, 53, is obsessed with bears.

She signs her emails "Beary Best Regards." Her Facebook page features pictures of her holding a bear cub named Merlin at a West Virginia bear rehabilitation facility. She runs an organization, which she named Bear Warriors United, that sends free bear-proof straps for garbage can lids to anyone who asks.

Shadix, a onetime medical assistant, told me her activism on behalf of bears got a big push when she was rear-ended in a car crash. The crash messed up her back.

She got a large settlement as a result—$300,000 which, after various expenses, left her with $120,000. She used that to launch her organization, despite her injuries.

"I'm in constant pain but no one knows," she said. When she speaks at wildlife commission meetings, "I put on a smile and act like nothing's wrong."

She had already been part of the throng arguing against the hunt. While the hunt proceeded, she told me, she was supposed to be home recuperating from surgery.

Instead, she said, she strapped on a back brace and with help from a friend tottered out to one of the hunt check stations. She'd missed the dead bears being brought in, she said, but "locked eyes" with a yearling cub that had been orphaned.

"That's when I made a promise I will do everything in my power to make sure there is never a bear hunt again," she told me.

Shadix was full of enthusiasm and determination, but she faced a steep learning curve. Sometimes there's a difference between what feels right for humans versus what's best for wildlife.

Some of the things she said and did got under the skin (so to speak) of some older environmental activists. She made missteps. She ran for a seat on the Seminole County Commission but lost to the pro-development incumbent.

But she kept plugging away, smiling to hide the pain.

"She's a terrific advocate," said Kate McFall, head of the Florida chapter of the Humane Society of the United States. "We need more like her."

When someone heard about poachers going after bears in the Ocala National Forest, that person passed the tip to Shadix. She said she passed it to the wildlife commission.

* * *

The poachers posted the evidence of their crimes on Facebook, Instagram, and Snapchat. Their videos, taken in the national forest, showed packs of dogs chasing bears, sometimes driving them up trees, sometimes attacking the bears directly.

"This bear thought he could fly," one poacher, from Union County, wrote on a video of a bear jumping down from a tree, only to be set upon by the pack. The poachers killed at least one bear and skinned it.

They were training the dogs to pursue bears because that made them valuable to hunters in states where such pursuits are legal.

But setting dogs loose on a bear—while featured in the classic Florida book and movie *The Yearling*—is not legal here now. Even during Florida's bear hunt, the wildlife commission said no to using dogs.

There's a famous story about Teddy Roosevelt refusing to shoot a bear that had been tied down, thus launching the "teddy bear" craze. I bet these poachers would have been fine with killing Teddy's bear. They weren't big fans of ethical hunting.

Wildlife officers spent 11 months investigating the poachers. They infiltrated the gang, Shadix said. They put a tracking device on one man's truck. They got GPS locations from the poachers' phones.

They even got video of three of them digging through a dumpster behind a Jacksonville Krispy Kreme. The dumpster divers were gathering discarded donuts and other pastries to use as bait to lure the bears to their doom. This is not the kind of recycling we need in Florida.

Shadix said wildlife officers passed along monthly updates, as long as she kept quiet. She told me they obtained some crucial evidence when one of the poachers got divorced. His ex-wife told investigators that he had bear meat stashed in his freezer, labeled with a date after the end of the official hunt.

In December 2018, state officials announced the arrest of nine people on charges that ranged from conspiracy to animal cruelty to bear-baiting. Shadix posted on her Facebook page that she was relieved she could talk about the case now, and in all capital letters wrote that the arrests were "THE BEST CHRISTMAS PRESENT EVER."

Four years later, the courts are still grinding through these cases. The ex-wife pleaded guilty in 2020 and agreed to testify against the others. So far, four other defendants have cut deals for probation.

What got my attention last week was No. 6 of the nine defendants, William Tyler "Bo" Wood, 32, of Lake Butler, pleading guilty. His penalty: 364 days behind bars, plus 10 years of probation. He has to pay a hefty fine and (this may hurt the worst) surrender all of those dogs he trained.

This comparatively light sentence came in spite of the fact that, last fall, Wood was convicted in a Utah court of illegally capturing a bear after his dogs chased it to the point of collapse. He didn't get any jail time in the Utah case, just 18 months of probation.

How's your stomach doing now? Churning like an off-kilter Maytag?

* * *

Shadix told me she's been tracking poaching cases around the state since starting her organization. She said she shows up in person to witness what happens in court.

If you don't like how light these penalties are, imagine how angry she's been.

The first trial she attended, four years ago, was for a Sopchoppy man who admitted to killing five bears. He told the authorities he'd been shooting them because they were eating his corn.

When she learned his penalty would be less than the penalty for littering, Shadix decided that needed to change. The solution, she thought, was to get the Florida Legislature to fix the law.

Yes, that same legislature that's been kowtowing to developers every chance it gets and pushing clearly unconstitutional culture-war bills while ignoring real crises. But Shadix was not discouraged.

"I'm a Democrat, but I went to my Republican representative," she said. "I looked for the most alpha male Republican I could find."

Her choice, Representative David Smith, had been a Marine Corps helicopter pilot. He agreed with her that the poachers were getting off too lightly.

If it were up to me, all these poachers would be dipped in that delicious Krispy Kreme honey glaze and locked in a cage with one of their victims. But they say politics is the art of the possible. Smith's bill merely increased the penalty from $500 to $750 and extended the time hunting licenses could be suspended from one year to three.

This mild boost for bear protection passed both houses of the legislature unanimously and Governor Ron DeSantis signed it into law. (For some reason, the Pope did not report this rare pro-environment outcome as a bona fide miracle.)

Yet poaching continues, Shadix said. She's watching a Collier County case this week involving a Golden Gate Estates man who gunned down a bear cub that people in the neighborhood had affectionately named "Bailey."

And she said she's heard reports of a gang killing bears in the Panhandle—not for quote-unquote sport, but for money. She said certain bear parts can be sold for thousands of dollars to companies that ship them to Asia for use in folk medicine.

Honestly, folks, it doesn't sound to me like the bears are the big problem here. It's us silly lemmings, moving into their habitat, building houses, and occasionally shooting at them.

If you choose to live where they live, don't shoot them. Don't be surprised if one tries swinging in your hammock from time to time. And no matter what, don't leave out any pic-a-nic baskets.

17

For the Shell of It

Tampa Bay Times, September 13, 2019

JACKSONVILLE—Harry Lee has a basement full of shells. He has several glass-topped tables around his riverfront home that also display shells. His bookshelves are packed with books about shells, and one wall holds blue ribbons from winning first place at shell collector shows. He often wears a shirt that's covered with pictures of shells.

He has searched for shells at beaches around the globe, as well as in mountains and beneath the ocean. He even goes out into his backyard to search for shells. Once he found one in his backyard that was previously unknown to science. It's one of the 36 species of shells Lee has officially named. There are 18 species that scientists have named after him—*Nassarius harryleei,* for instance.

Lee, 79, has spent more than seven decades collecting shells—more time than he spent in his day job as a doctor, which was only 32 years. At one time, he was credited with having the largest private collection of shells in the world, worth about $1 million.

But now he's giving it all away, a little at a time.

It started nine years ago. About once every couple of months, Lee loads a bunch of his shells into the trunk of his two-door Chevy and drives 90 minutes south to the Florida Museum of Natural History in Gainesville. The museum staff unloads the shells to add to their own growing collection, now the third-largest in the nation.

"I'm in a distributive mood, rather than an acquisitive mood," said Lee, the author of a book called *The Marine Shells of Northeast Florida.*

By taking his shells to the museum, he explained, "I hope it's good enough to be of use to future generations." After all, he said, "you don't live forever."

Florida is full of obsessive collectors and their artifacts. There's the man with the most vintage Walt Disney memorabilia, and the one with the largest collection of fossilized poop, and the guy who has the world's largest collection of hamburger-related merchandise.

Lee's collection means more than just a successful acquisition of unusual items, according to John Slapcinsky of the Florida Museum of Natural History.

"It shows that a lot of science can be done by amateurs," Slapcinsky said. "People think they can't contribute if they aren't professional scientists, but they can."

* * *

Lee began collecting shells when he was six, but not the way most kids do. He didn't go to the beach and bring home a pocket full of whelks, cockles, and cat's paws.

He lived in New Jersey, far from any beach. At that age, he didn't get along well with his siblings, so his parents would often bundle him off to his grandmother's house for a day or so to separate the combatants.

One day his grandmother, a widow, took him across the street to meet her neighbor, Max Hammerschlag, a retired scissors-maker and a longtime fishing buddy of Lee's late grandfather. He welcomed the boy into his home and proudly showed off his collection of shells.

When the show ended, "I think I immediately demanded a curtain call," Lee said. "They looked so orderly and beautiful."

Before the boy left, Hammerschlag gave him a shell to take with him. Lee thinks it might have been a shell from a Cuban land snail, which he called "implausibly colorful—like they were hand-painted."

He was hooked, seeing in the shells not only beauty, but a key to the natural order.

He returned often to Hammerschlag's home, learning not only the names of the shells but also the proper way to describe them and fill out scientific tags showing where they had originated. Shells became his great passion, even as medicine became his career.

He and Kitty met as students at Cornell—he studying to be a doctor, she to be a nurse. As they talked in a New York bar where Cornell students hung out, she recalled, he brought up shells.

Still, she said, "I guess I didn't realize how serious he was about them."

Before long they were married, with two toddlers and living in Ethiopia. Lee was studying snails and the parasites that they pass along to humans—and in the process collecting snail shells. Then, in 1973, he was offered a job at a Florida medical practice. All he could think about were all the shells he could find.

He persuaded his wife to move to Jacksonville, via the Pacific Ocean. They made more than a dozen stops along the way in such shell-rich locales as Australia, Fiji, Tahiti, and Hawaii. They carried one suitcase for the kids' diapers, he said, and two dedicated to shells.

"It was," says Mrs. Lee, "a little unbalanced."

* * *

Over the years, Lee built up his collection partly through trades and purchases, and partly through going out himself and picking up what he saw.

"He'll get down in the mud and dig for them," said Slapcinsky, who has gone on several shell-hunting trips with Lee.

The rarest shell in his collection is known as a "sacred chank." Unlike most shells, which coil to the right, his sacred chank's coils go to the left. Collectors call that a "reverse." According to Hindu scripture, Vishnu hid a sacred text in one of those one-in-600,000 shells with reverse coils. The one in his collection, he said, came from a sketchy fellow who claimed to be a descendant of Lord Calvert, founder of the Maryland colony.

Lee's waterfront home has provided him with lovely views for years. But its proximity to a tributary turned into a liability in 2012, when floodwaters rose high enough to pour into the basement.

Half of Lee's collection stayed above the water line. The other half suffered damage to the tags and display, which required five volunteers working with Lee for six months to set them right again.

"That which was inundated had to be rehabilitated," Lee said.

Lee has a website featuring photos of mollusks that biologists all over the state use as a guide. He's not done with his research yet, either. Often when he brings shells to the museum, Lee wanders over to another part of the campus where he can borrow an electron microscope to continue assisting a scientist with examining tiny fossil shells. He peers through the eyepiece at specimens that were dug up from a sand mine in Sarasota County. Many are from species now extinct, he said, but he can see the similarities to their modern-day descendants.

Although Lee's collection delights other shell fans, his own family has not quite embraced his obsession.

None of his three children collect shells. One is an attorney, another is a biologist in a different field, and the third shares his wife's passion, horses. They run an equestrian center called Hadden Loch and according to Lee, his wife is happy to be doing anything related to horses, even shoveling manure.

"It's difficult for me to understand her passion," he said, looking perplexed. Then he smiled and added, "Of course, the feeling is mutual."

18

The Parks Man

Florida Phoenix, December 30, 2021

Do you have a Florida bucket list? I do, and every new year is a chance to check my progress. I crossed another item off it the other day when I stopped in at Ellie Schiller Homosassa Springs Wildlife State Park. I was there to see Lucifer.

The 210-acre state park in Citrus County features a "wildlife walk" that allows visitors to see panthers, manatees, roseate spoonbills, and its star resident, Lucifer, aka Lu the Hippo.

Lu is a holdover from the days when the park was a roadside attraction. For Lu to continue living at Homosassa Springs after the state took over, then-governor Lawton Chiles officially declared the popular hippo to be an honorary citizen of Florida.

Pro tip: Do NOT stand in Lu's "splatter zone." Trust me on this.

When people ask me what's so great about Florida, I always make sure to mention our state park system. From the soaring dunes of Topsail Hill in the Panhandle to the depths of John Pennekamp in the Keys, Florida's state parks provide a natural alternative to the artificial glitz of our theme parks.

They have a major economic impact, too, serving more than 28 million visitors and generating $2.4 billion in direct economic benefits to local communities. And some of them show off our quirky side, such as Falling Waters State Park, named for a 73-foot waterfall that disappears into the ground, and Weeki Wachee Springs State Park, which employs its own school of mermaids.

Until recently, the guy in charge of this vast domain—175 parks, trails, and historic sites spanning nearly 800,000 acres—was Eric Draper, a tall, soft-spoken Florida native who had lobbied for Audubon's Florida chapter until his appointment in 2017.

Draper just retired, so we spent some time on the phone recently discussing his four years overseeing some of Florida's greatest assets, important both to our ecosystems and to our tourism industry.

Eric Draper, former Florida State Parks Service director. Photo courtesy of Eric Draper.

Draper assured me he didn't decide to hang up his khaki uniform because of some raging conflict with his bosses at the Florida Department of Environmental Protection. He just felt it was time, he said.

"I'm 68," he told me. "I've got a couple of years left to take an active role in things, and I missed advocacy." He said he hopes to spend the next few years helping local governments find financing for projects to fix the state's water quality woes. (Good luck to him on that.)

Draper said he enjoyed his tenure overseeing the state park system, learning its great challenges (many driven by climate change—more on that in a bit). He also got to see its strengths, including the 1,035 full-time rangers and 500 or so part-timers staffing the parks. All of them deserve to be paid more than they are, he said.

"I hated hearing the expression, 'They do it for the love of the job,'" he said.

You can't recruit new rangers based on an expectation they will do the job just because they love it, he said. That's why he pushed for starting salaries to be raised from $26,000 a year to $27,000, he said, even though it meant overcoming what he called "inertia" in the DEP.

Draper told me he was surprised by how many cultural and historical treasures are in the park system. The oldest parks date only to the 1930s, when the Civilian Conservation Corps built them as make-work projects during the Depression. But some of the properties they protect are far, far older than that, such as the Mound Key Archaeological State Park and Bulow Plantation Ruins Historic State Park.

Over time, Draper grew to appreciate some of the lesser-known state parks, naming Fakahatchee Strand Preserve State Park as his favorite.

"I had the most amazing experiences at Fakahatchee Strand," he said, "standing in knee-deep water and seeing all the orchids and the birds."

He was amused by some of the things that happened, too, such as the time when this former coat-and-tie lobbyist took a powerful legislator on a tour of the Homosassa Springs park.

"He kept looking over at me, in my uniform shirt, like he couldn't get over it," Draper said, chuckling.

As for Lu's splatter zone, he said, "we steered clear of that."

* * *

Draper, one of five children of an Air Force sergeant, was born at Mac-Dill Air Force Base in Tampa. He told me he "developed a deep passion for the environment while camping and canoeing around Florida during high school and college."

He moved to Washington to work with an organization called Clean Water Action. In 1990, he joined the Nature Conservancy, which sent him back to Florida to help pass the Preservation 2000 land-buying initiative.

After a second tour of duty in D.C., this time as a senior vice president for the National Audubon Society, he returned to Florida in 1999 to work for the state Audubon chapter. This time, he stuck around. He became executive director in 2009, a position he held until he was appointed to the $115,000-a-year parks director job.

Draper took over at a time when the park system had gone through what airline pilots refer to as "a little turbulence." That's the term they use when the passengers have been thrown all over the cabin and are actively tossing their cookies.

The park system had been run previously by Donald Forgione, who became a park ranger in 1983 and worked his way up to director in 2010, the first person ever to do that. Then, in January 2011, Rick Scott became governor and suddenly the park service began being squeezed and manipulated like a fresh pack of Silly Putty.

Legislators who said they were working at Scott's behest proposed Jack Nicklaus be allowed to build golf courses in five state parks. One newspaper columnist declared this to be "The Worst Idea in the History of the World." Waves of bipartisan ridicule led them to withdraw the legislation.

Next, Scott's DEP secretary proposed letting private companies build new campgrounds and run them, starting with allowing recreational vehicles in the most popular park in the system, Honeymoon Island, near Dunedin.

Nearly 1,000 people showed up at a Dunedin public hearing, and I'd estimate 999 of them were opposed to the idea. I don't mean they merely disliked it. They talked of forming a human chain to keep the RVs out of what they regarded as "their" state park.

(Draper agreed with me that this was a sign of how people view their local state park as something precious belonging to the community: "People love them!" he said. "That's a great thing.")

Dropping that idea, Scott's DEP then proposed raising money for buying more park land by declaring some state lands surplus and selling them. Again, local officials objected—many had worked hard to preserve that land. Nine months later, the agency ended the program without having sold a single acre. The two DEP officials in charge both resigned.

Next, Scott's DEP secretary proposed allowing hunting, cattle grazing, and timber harvesting in some parks to boost their money-making potential. The parks were already raking in enough money to pay 85 percent of their expenses, but the DEP boss wanted 100 percent.

One of the many opponents of these proposed changes was Forgione. After six years as parks director, he was abruptly demoted, with no public explanation. The reason, Draper told me, was that he'd dared to buck his bosses. Draper said he would have done the same, despite the consequences.

To replace Forgione, Scott's DEP tapped a controversial Public Service Commission member named Lisa Edgar. She held the post just long enough for her name to be painted on the office door, then resigned and was charged with DUI and hit-and-run.

The position remained vacant for nine months, adding to the turmoil. Then, in a surprise move, the inexperienced Draper got the nod.

In his years at Audubon, Draper had made his share of enemies, usually because of his willingness to cut deals to achieve his organization's goals. Environmental activists usually divide into two groups: the Die-Hards, who refuse to bend or back down, and Deal-Cutters like Draper.

I wondered at the time if the Scott administration picked Draper primarily because one of the Die-Hards had labeled him "the worst environmentalist in Florida." But he told me, "I was recruited for my environmental credentials, not in spite of them."

After he and I talked, I rooted around for critics of Draper's leadership at the Florida Park Service. Mostly I got shrugs. Some of his former enemies had forgotten that's where he'd gone.

The worst criticism I turned up was someone who accused him of being "a placeholder" that Scott's people brought in to settle things down. Draper was downright offended when I told him about the placeholder comment, to the point that he sent me copies of his five-year plans.

"It is ironic, since most people thought I pushed too hard," he told me. "When I became state parks director there was no plan, and the only direction from above was to refocus on the FPS mission."

* * *

It's hard to argue with his results.

In 1999, 2005, and 2013, Florida's state parks won the gold medal—the top prize—from the National Parks and Recreation Association. In 2019, Draper's second year in charge, Florida's parks won their fourth gold medal—the only park system in the nation with that many wins.

"I have nothing but wonderful things to say about Eric Draper," said Tammy Gustafson, president of the Florida State Parks Foundation, which raises money to support the parks.

As for Draper's former employer, last month Audubon Florida gave him its 2021 Teddy Roosevelt Award "for a career of leadership on behalf of Florida's environment."

For his part, Draper feels he spent too much time "responding to the urgent rather than focusing on the important." The former includes figuring out how to fix a roof or obtain more vehicles as opposed to coming up with a broad strategy for dealing with climate change, leaving those decisions to each park.

Climate change is "a huge issue" for Florida's parks, he said. For instance, Tomoka State Park in Ormond Beach is one of the coastal parks where rising seas are rapidly eroding public property. Honeymoon Island is another.

As climate change warms the world's oceans, the hotter water makes hurricanes stronger. One example: Hurricane Michael, which in 2018 wreaked havoc at a variety of Panhandle parks, even inland ones such as Torreya State Park and Florida Caverns State Park.

Draper acknowledged that the changing climate heightens the risk to the parks of severe drought and rampaging wildfires, too.

Yet, so far, Governor Ron DeSantis and our legislature are inclined to do nothing about the causes of climate change. They'd rather spend millions of tax dollars on structures to adapt to it—at least until the water goes even higher. They don't want to indulge in what DeSantis referred to as "left-wing stuff" that would lessen our reliance on fossil fuels in transportation and building.

As 2022 dawns, put this on your Florida bucket list: Go see our coastal parks before they're washed away, then badger your legislators and other elected representatives to change their ways. They need to get busy saving our publicly owned beaches, forests, and preserves by cutting our state's greenhouse gas emissions.

I am in favor of doing anything that will focus their attention on this issue. That includes luring them into Lu the Hippo's splatter zone and not letting them leave until they say, "Yes." Sometimes, to get things done, you have to speak a language politicians understand.

19

The Seersucker Evasion

Florida Phoenix, January 28, 2021

The first time I met Rick Scott was a few months after he became governor of Florida. Back then, it sometimes seemed his vocabulary consisted entirely of one word: Jobs! He said "jobs" in answer to everything. How's the weather today? "Jobs!" Do you think the Buccaneers will win Sunday? "Jobs!" What's 2+2? "Jobs!"

I buttonholed him at a conference and tried to ask him about a proposal by his administration to open our state parks to more profitable yet destructive uses than camping and canoeing and hiking. I thought he'd squawk, "Jobs!" Instead, he changed the subject to ask why I was wearing a seersucker jacket.

I was wearing seersucker because it was summer and hot outside. As for the parks question, I eventually got Scott to answer. He strongly defended what he was doing to ruin the parks. Shortly afterward, a massive crowd showed up at a public hearing and screamed about it, at which point he flip-flopped and announced he was now against the idea.

I bring this up because last week, Scott, now Florida's junior U.S. senator, weighed in on a subject he spent eight years avoiding: climate change.

Florida, as you may know, is the state most vulnerable to climate change. It's hot and getting hotter, even at night. We're getting more rain and more powerful hurricanes. And sea level rise is putting water in some streets and homes for more days every year.

On the day Joe Biden was sworn in as president, one of his first official acts was to sign an executive order saying the United States would rejoin the Paris Agreement on combating climate change.

On Twitter, Scott had just congratulated Biden on being inaugurated—but now he snarled his displeasure about Biden's order.

"POTUS is throwing the U.S. back into the Paris Agreement just to appease his liberal friends," Scott tweeted. "This deal does nothing to hold real

The author trying to question then-governor Rick Scott, who prefers asking questions about the reporter's seersucker jacket. Photo courtesy of Craig Pittman.

polluters like Communist China accountable and unfairly puts U.S. taxpayers on the hook."

At least he was finally talking about climate change. That's more than he did in eight years as Florida's governor.

* * *

You remember what happened, don't you? For four years, Florida's governor had been Charlie Crist, then a Republican, but one who recognized the threat that climate change posed for his native state.

Crist convened a climate change summit in Miami. He issued executive orders that called for cutting power plant emissions, using alternate fuels, and rewriting building codes to require more energy efficiency. He even blocked a coal-fired power plant from being built near the Everglades.

But then, in 2010, Crist made the ill-considered decision to run as an independent for a U.S. Senate seat, losing to Marco Rubio.

He was replaced in the Governor's Mansion by Scott, a Texas native whose prior claim to fame was for taking the Fifth Amendment 75 times. This was during a deposition in a civil suit involving his work with a company that became known for the largest health care fraud in American history. (The suit was not directly related to the fraud, but that investigation was pending during the deposition.)

And just as he didn't want to talk to lawyers back then, he didn't want to discuss climate change either, except to say there wasn't any.

"I've not been convinced that there's any man-made climate change," Scott told reporters.

He junked Crist's initiatives, all in the name of pursuing jobs jobs jobs. Worse, he cut the budget of the state's environmental regulators who were in charge of clamping down on pollution and repeatedly vetoed funding for the agencies crafting a response to climate change, the regional planning councils.

When he ran for reelection in 2014, his response to climate change questions was to dodge them with a tactic just barely a step up from discussing seersucker.

"I'm not a scientist," he'd say. Then he'd change the subject to how much money the state was spending on Everglades restoration and scoot for the nearest exit.

Some former state workers said he'd gone so far as to ban the use of the term "climate change," which Scott denied. In his defense, I have to point out that he never fired the state climatologist or eliminated university programs that studied the subject. Maybe it was easier to ignore it than to punish them for flouting an order.

The truth came out at the end of a 2014 cabinet meeting, although few noticed. Susan Glickman, the Florida director of the Southern Alliance for Clean Energy, shouted out to Scott to ask what his plan was for dealing with climate change. As Scott scooted toward the exit, he blurted out, "No plan."

Glickman rounded up a group of climate scientists who signed a letter to Scott offering to lay out the evidence for him. After some political maneuvering, Scott agreed to listen to them for 30 minutes. But he had a plan—a variation on the Seersucker Jacket Stratagem.

"He spent the first 15 minutes on introductions," Glickman told me this week.

Seated in a circle, the five scientists, accompanied by Glickman, made their case and called for Scott to display leadership on the issue. In response, the *Miami Herald* reported, Scott "would not comment, question, or commit to whether or not he believes the warnings by the experts deserve his attention."

Instead, Glickman said, "he jumped up at 27 minutes" and scooted for the exit. He'd run out the clock without being cornered on coming up with a plan.

Later, a Palm Beach television station pressed him for an answer and apparently the reporter was not wearing seersucker, because they got a response. Scott said the state's emergency management division would handle any flooding problems—period. Nothing on curtailing greenhouse gases or steering new power plants to places away from the coast or raising highways and bridges so they're not inundated when storms hit.

Scott squeaked back into office for a second term. Thus, for eight years, as storm surges around Florida crept higher and the temperatures rose and more people suffered from heat-related ailments, Scott did absolutely nothing. Zero. Zip. Nada.

Between him and his successor, Ron DeSantis, "we've lost a decade for taking dramatic action on climate," Glickman said.

Some smart aleck (OK, it was me) pointed out in a *Tampa Bay Times* story the irony in this lack of action: Scott owns a $9.2 million waterfront mansion in Naples. It sits a foot above sea level and about 200 feet from the water, on a stretch of the coast where the water has been rising at the rate of about eight to nine inches over the past century.

He's got a personal stake in fighting sea level rise but apparently would rather let his house fall into the Gulf than do something about it.

Now that he's a senator, Scott has begun to at last acknowledge that climate change exists. For instance, if you search his official website for the term "climate," you will find this statement: "Climate change is real and requires real solutions."

To my surprise, his use of those words didn't set off an earthquake or a tsunami. Perhaps it's because he said that sentence in a speech in which he was condemning the Green New Deal as a threat to American jobs (there's that word again!).

Somehow, in his speech, Scott never got around to discussing what he views as "real solutions." It was a curious omission when addressing our emissions.

He clearly doesn't like the Paris Agreement, even though it is exactly what its name says: a voluntary agreement among 196 nations to try to bring down their carbon emissions by 2030. Every nation sets its own emissions goals. There's no penalty for not meeting them. It's like the Pirate Code in the movie *Pirates of the Caribbean*—more of a guideline.

In other words, when the senator tweeted that the Paris Agreement "does nothing to hold real polluters like Communist China accountable," what he didn't mention was that it doesn't hold the United States accountable for missing the targets, either.

In a subsequent tweet, Scott scoffed at a proposal from newly minted treasury secretary Janet Yellen for a carbon tax that charges polluters for their carbon emissions and redistributes the proceeds to Americans. That, too, was a ruinous idea, he said. But once again, while announcing what he was against, he failed to say what he was for—if anything.

"Rick Scott may have changed his tune on climate change, but his actions show he hasn't had a change of heart," Glickman said.

Surely that can't be true, I thought. I asked the senator's staff to spell out what "real solutions" for climate change he does endorse. Here's the emailed response I got, in its entirety:

"Senator Scott believes that taking care of the environment and working to create a better economy are objectives that can and must be pursued at the same time. You can't afford to take care of the environment if you don't have a strong economy. Getting our economy on track so everyone in this country has the shot at the American dream is Senator Scott's focus. President Biden's proposal [sic] liberal agenda would bankrupt this nation and take away the ability to invest in things Americans care about—like the environment."

Got that? Doing anything to fix our worsening climate is bad for the economy, so we should essentially do exactly what Scott did as governor—nothing.

I don't know about you, but I have this feeling about Senator Scott. It's a strange feeling. It feels like Scott's repeated avoidance of endorsing any plan to fix climate change means he's not doing something important. But what is it? Oh yeah, now I remember.

His job.

20

Two Toms and Three Ks

Flamingo, July 19, 2021

When I was a teenager in Pensacola in the 1970s, I pursued the rank of Eagle in the Boy Scouts. One of my merit badge counselors was a tall, pale, white-haired man in his late 70s named Theodore Thomas "T. T." Wentworth Jr.

He's the only person I've ever met who ran his own museum.

On Saturday afternoons, my mom dropped me off at old Mr. Wentworth's roadside attraction, the T. T. Wentworth Jr. Museum, so we could check off merit badge requirements. At the time, "museum" struck me as a grandiose name for what looked like a dusty repository of oddball knickknacks.

He and I would start off going over the requirements I needed for, say, the Citizenship in the Community merit badge. But after 20 or 30 minutes, my counselor would bolt to his feet and announce, "Let me show you something!"

And off he'd go, dragging me along to look at some item from his collection, which began in 1906 when he stumbled upon a gold coin at the beach that turned out to date back to 1851.

He had a petrified cat! And bricks dating back centuries! And a wooden propeller from an old biplane! Do you like swords? He had a wall full of them! There were old newspapers in frames and license plates that hadn't been valid for decades, and did I mention the petrified cat?

He must have shown me that darn cat 10 times, each time acting as if it were brand new. I got to where I hated that cat, but he never remembered that I'd already seen it.

I never made Eagle, but that was my fault for being lazy, not that of the easily distracted Mr. Wentworth. Back then he seemed like a nice guy, if a tad eccentric. After I outgrew Boy Scouts, I hardly thought about him again until 1989, when my mom mailed me a clipping from the *Pensacola News Journal.*

"Historian and collector T. T. Wentworth, 90, dies," proclaimed the banner headline atop the front page. The story, which included tributes from

T. T. Wentworth Jr. in his roadside museum, holding one of his artifacts. Photo from the Florida State Archives.

the governor and other notables, reported that among longtime Pensacolians, Wentworth was known as "Mr. Tom" and "Mr. History."

In the 1920s, the story said, Wentworth had been elected a county commissioner—the youngest in the state—and then served as tax collector for 12 years. In the 1930s he helped to launch both the local library and the Pensacola Historical Society. He had led a public drive to save some of the area's historic buildings, including Civil War–era Fort Pickens.

The obituary told me that in 1983, he had donated 250,000 items from his collection, valued at $5 million, to a historic preservation group that had opened a museum in the old Pensacola city hall—the largest historical collection ever donated by a private individual in the state, perhaps the nation, according to the paper. To salute his generosity, the museum took his name, calling itself the T. T. Wentworth Jr. Florida State Museum.

"I just hope it will always be like it is today, a big thing for Pensacola," Wentworth said upon the occasion of his donation.

But that's the thing about history. You think it's all settled, but it's not. Our perspective on it changes over time. New discoveries show old things in a new light. The status quo winds up being upended.

And so last year the old Mr. History was exposed as someone who was heinous and hateful, creating an uproar over whether the museum should change its name. The man who revealed his secret is Pensacola's new Mr. History, who also happens to be named Tom.

* * *

Tom Garner is a genial, soft-spoken white guy in his late 50s, the son of a postal carrier. Like me, he grew up in Pensacola, amid an amalgam of influences and attitudes—a Southern Bible Belt city that's also a port full of immigrants, a popular LGBTQ resort, and a Navy base where swaggering pilots train for dangerous missions.

Garner graduated in 1980 from Escambia High School, where a 1976 riot over white students flying the Rebel flag led to National Guard troops taking over as hall monitors. Garner says he missed all that.

Health problems prompted Garner to drop out of college eventually, he told me. He never went back. These days he and his wife run a successful gardening business. But he's better known around Pensacola for his other exploits in digging up dirt.

"I am not a professional historian," Garner told me. "I am what I refer to as a 'local historian.' Every community has them. They are individuals who fall in love with local history and become very well-informed about it."

His ability to burrow into historical records has benefited local environmental activists and journalists, according to Carl Wernicke, a former editor for the *Pensacola News Journal.* Wernicke, also a Pensacola native, befriended Garner while working with him to expose shady development schemes.

"He's very brave," Wernicke said. "He would have made a good reporter."

Garner's interest in history started in the same way as Wentworth's: with an accidental discovery in childhood. He was tossing around a football with friends as a middle-schooler when he spotted a bottle labeled "Hygeia."

He took his find to Old Christ Church in downtown Pensacola. At the church, a man named Norman Simons ran a historical museum—small but with artifacts that were well-organized and professionally displayed, unlike the Wentworth collection.

Simons, who in his crew cut and tie always looked like he stepped out of a photo from 1958, explained to Garner that Hygeia was the name of a Pensacola bottling company. Just from looking at it, Simons could tell the bottling plant produced this bottle sometime between 1900 and 1910.

Garner was astonished. The bottle filled him with a thirst to learn more about the area's history. Simons took him under his wing and taught him what he knew. Every time the Pensacola Historical Museum opened its doors, Garner would show up, pestering Simons with questions. Soon Simons was giving Garner small research assignments, teaching him to use microfilm to dig through old documents.

He introduced Garner to a professional archaeologist with the University of West Florida who trained him in archaeological fieldwork. Garner would go on to help start the Pensacola Archaeological Society.

I asked Garner if he'd ever met the other Tom or visited his original museum. He said yes, once, when he was in his teens.

"I went out there once on a Sunday afternoon," he said. "I remember there was a little old man out there, and he shuffled around behind me as I walked around the place."

Garner remembers seeing Wentworth's bricks, but not much else, not even the petrified cat. Unlike the collection Simons curated, it "was just a real jumble of stuff, good things in with junk."

After Wentworth donated his collection, Simons became the first curator of the T. T. Wentworth Jr. Florida State Museum.

Simons had one great passion: finding Pensacola's original Spanish colony. Garner recalls "many conversations" about that mystery. When Simons died in 1989, the mystery remained unsolved—until Garner, the amateur, figured it out.

* * *

Pensacola is the great also-ran of U.S. history. It was the first multi-year settlement in America to be established by European explorers. A Spanish explorer, Don Tristán de Luna y Arellano, landed there in 1559, six years before any Spaniards waded ashore in St. Augustine.

But five weeks after the Luna expedition landed, a terrible storm hit and smashed all the ships, which still carried the colonists' food supply. The survivors struggled to avoid starvation and finally abandoned the colony. That's why St. Augustine gets to brag that it's the oldest continuously occupied city in America.

UWF archaeologists had found the shipwrecks but no sign of the Luna colony itself. Then, one October day in 2015, Garner went to Subway for lunch and on the drive back he passed through an older neighborhood near where the ships were found. Simons had told him this area matched the few written descriptions of the colony's location, but no one had ever spotted any evidence.

On this particular day, Garner noticed one of the older houses had been torn down to be replaced by something newer. He stopped at what was now an empty lot and got out of his car, immediately spotting an olive jar neck and other artifacts on the ground—including some that to his practiced eye appeared to be from the right time period for the Luna colony.

He notified UWF's archaeologists, but they couldn't jump on the find right away. Two weeks later, he collected a few pieces from the site and brought them in. One of UWF's archaeologists sorted through everything slowly, then blurted out, "Holy moly!"

For discovering the long-lost Luna site, Garner was hailed as a hero. His discovery was written up in *The New Yorker* and other national publications. He landed a position with the UWF excavation crew, too, working as a liaison with the area homeowners to ensure access to the site. UWF included him in all its official press releases and documentation.

Six years later, though, he was out.

* * *

In 1861, Confederate soldiers plotted an attack on Pensacola's Fort Pickens, but called it off because of bad weather. That's how Fort Sumter became the place where the Civil War began. Otherwise, Pensacola saw little action during the Civil War.

Yet 30 years later, in 1891, a women's group erected a 50-foot granite monument to the Confederacy in the middle of downtown—an obelisk so large it was as if the Battle of Gettysburg had been fought there.

The Pensacola monument was among the first of its kind to salute specific Confederate leaders. One side of the monument honored the nameless soldiers who died to save slavery. The other three sides commemorated their leaders: Jefferson Davis, president of the Confederacy; Stephen Mallory, secretary of the Confederate Navy who lived in Pensacola after the war; and Edward Aylesworth Perry, an obscure Confederate general from Pensacola.

The monument was Perry's idea. As governor in the post-Reconstruction era, he pushed the poll tax and other tactics to squelch Black voting. Pensacola and other Florida cities had elected Black and Hispanic council members during Reconstruction. Perry revoked the charters of those cities so he could appoint all-white councils.

Perry died before the monument could be built, but his widow, a leader of the Ladies Memorial Association, carried out his wishes.

There it stood for more than a century, an ever-present reminder of the city's racist past and one politician's ego. Then, in 2020, as other cities across the South took down their treasonous statuary, the Pensacola City Council announced it too would consider removing its Confederate monument.

Garner wanted to contribute to the discussion. He'd been doing a lot of research on the history of racial violence in Pensacola. Some of the findings he delved into were horrifying, involving not just lynchings but rumors of mass murder. He'd also come across some interesting documents in the Wentworth collection.

People who objected to tearing down the monument claimed doing so would be erasing history, as if monuments were the only resource for learning about the past. Garner wanted to point out that the history Pensacolians embraced had already erased important facts because of who was telling the story.

Garner wrote a long letter to the city council. He planted the bombshell in the 12th paragraph.

He began by saying the time was right to pull down the Pensacola monument. Then he went on to explain how the racism of leaders like Perry had, in that monument and other historical plaques and memorials, skewed or distorted the facts of Pensacola's story.

After calling the roll of other inaccurate historical markers, he brought up the Wentworth Museum. He noted that Wentworth was remembered as a businessman, a county official, and a devotee of local history. Then he hit the detonator.

"T. T. Wentworth, Jr. was also Exalted Cyclops, Escambia Klan number 57, Invisible Empire, Knights of the Ku Klux Klan," Garner wrote. "Documents record the founding of Escambia's Klan in 1920, with Wentworth as its first Kligrapp, or secretary. In 1925, Wentworth was elected Exalted Cyclops, or president."

"These documents, held in the museum archives, are from Wentworth's personal files," he continued. "Among the many Klan-related items in the files are Wentworth's Klan membership cards, correspondence between Wentworth and the Grand Dragon, Realm of Florida, and an invoice for Wentworth's specially ordered satin Exalted Cyclops robe."

This, he pointed out, was the man who had controlled telling the Pensacola community's history—a KKK leader. That's why there was no room in the narrative for anyone who wasn't white.

Garner's letter didn't just go to the council. His friend Wernicke arranged for it to be published in the *Pensacola News Journal,* along with the footnotes, ensuring it would have maximum impact on public opinion.

The letter sparked a front-page news story on July 13, 2020, headlined, "T. T. Wentworth was KKK leader in 1920s. Now UWF Historic Trust looks to change museum name."

One person who cheered Garner's discovery: Local Black historian and storyteller Robin Reshard, a friend of Garner's.

"I think what Tom did was put a face on the institution of the Klan—a well-known . . . face," she said. "He was the best person to tell it, and at the best time."

Sure enough, the council voted to remove the Confederate monument. But Garner's letter set a lot of other changes in motion.

* * *

Rob Overton, the executive director for the UWF Historic Trust, which runs the Wentworth Museum, was visiting family in Houston when the Klan news hit.

As soon as he heard about Wentworth being a Klan leader, "I headed home and started working on a press statement." His initial reaction, he said, was, "The sky is falling."

His other reaction: "I wish Tom had come and told me about it."

Neither Overton nor anyone else in the museum's management knew the extent of the Klan documents that Garner had found in their archive.

They were not part of the original collection Wentworth had donated to the state. Wentworth had kept those in his house, where members of his family lived for years after he died. Once those relatives were gone, the bank serving as the estate's executor invited the museum staff to look through the house for additional exhibits.

"It was two floors and an attic, and there was stuff everywhere," Overton told me. The power was mostly off, so no air conditioning or lights. "We'd go out there with flashlights and boxes one day a week, starting in 2016. We got the last of the boxes in 2019."

They put all the boxes into freezers to kill any bug infestation and await the deed of gift from the family, he said. Only then could the museum staff and volunteers begin cataloguing the contents.

Garner just happened to be in the museum doing research when UWF's longtime archivist, Jacqui Wilson, noticed a box of documents that seemed to have something to do with the Klan. She didn't have time to go through it then, but she knew someone who did.

"It was just the two of us there in an empty office, and she sets it on the table and says, 'Knock yourself out,'" Garner recalled. "I opened up the box and my jaw fell on the floor."

The documents unveiled more than just Wentworth's scandalous past. They offered "an unprecedented window onto the workings of a Florida Klavern during the 1920s," according to a report released in July by a group of historians and others connected to the museum.

Wentworth's files showed how the secretive group operated and how deeply it reached into government. Members included state legislators, the superintendent of education, a judge, even the city harbormaster. People wrote to Wentworth asking for the Klan to intervene in their personal troubles, such as punishing a spouse for cheating. Because he was the local Klan leader, the police chief gave Wentworth a card granting him police powers within city limits.

In 1927, Wentworth sent a letter to a Klan leader in Atlanta in which he gave a summary of his Klavern's activities. It became the first history written by Mr. History.

He complained about how some people in Pensacola—Catholics and foreign-born residents—persecuted the local Klansmen via business boycotts. Bank officials refused to give a Klan-connected businessman a loan. Wentworth included dramatic stories of an attempt by the Knights of Columbus at stabbing a Klansman "with a keen-edged pocket knife" and a mob attack on an unnamed Klan leader in the city's court, with their target driving them back "with a thirty-eight nickel-plated revolver."

Wentworth didn't hide his membership. When the Klan ran ads in the local paper, the bills went to him. Between 1923 and 1925, Wentworth published pro-Klan articles in his *Tom Wentworth's Magazine,* touting "true Americanism and Protestantism."

"This is really his voice," said Jamin Wells, the University of West Florida professor who has spent the past year digging through all the Wentworth documents. The Klansman he described facing a business boycott and threats of violence was clearly Wentworth himself, Wells said.

When Wentworth joined the Klan in the 1920s, the organization had distanced itself from the bloody violence of its early years—or so it seemed.

"It was seen as respectable, from the white side," said Michael Butler, a Flagler College history professor and the author of *Beyond Integration,* a history of the Panhandle's civil rights struggles. Members were "professors and civic leaders, ministers and bankers. Belonging was a mark of patriotism. It was the 1920s equivalent of joining the Lion's Club, if the Lion's Club was an expressly racist organization."

But what most Klansmen did not know when they joined is that "it was essentially a Ponzi scheme," Wells explained.

Once someone like Wentworth joined, the organization started hitting him up for money. He had to pay his dues. He had to pay for his robe. He had to round up other people who would join and pay those fees as well, Wells said.

The documents and contemporary news accounts show the Klan had never really stopped being a violent organization. Wentworth's Klavern ordered a Greek restaurateur to leave town or else. There are hints in Wentworth's correspondence that he and his colleagues burned down a Black-owned hospital.

Around 1930, Wentworth had apparently lost interest in the Klan. He got a letter from the state chair reminding him his dues were unpaid. The files contain nothing to show Wentworth replied.

But he didn't come clean about it, either. Fifty years after he let his Klan membership lapse, "when offered the opportunity to discuss this history . . . Wentworth claimed no direct knowledge of the Pensacola Klan and provided inaccurate information to a reporter," the historians' report said.

The report notes: "With a few notable exceptions, Wentworth did not collect material related to African American history nor did he meaningfully include the African American experience in his histories of Pensacola."

* * *

When Garner saw what was in the box the UWF archivist had handed him, he pulled out his cell phone and took pictures of the documents, then put them back. He didn't tell her about the pictures, either.

He says he didn't tell the archivist about what he was doing "because I wanted her to have deniability" should there be a backlash for exposing the secret life of Mr. History.

If I had found what Garner discovered, I would have shouted it from the rooftops. But Garner sat on the information for nearly six months.

He didn't mention it to university officials, his fellow historians, or anyone else. He said he planned to offer to help the archivist catalogue everything, but two months after he found the Klan documents, the pandemic forced the closure of the archives.

"I had no plans to share the photos with anyone, particularly not the media," he told me. Only the Confederate monument debate prompted him to reveal Wentworth's real history.

After Garner's letter ran in the newspaper, along with his photos of the documents, the archivist who showed the papers to Garner abruptly retired.

I asked Overton if she'd been pushed out for showing Garner the Wentworth documents before anyone else had seen them.

"That's a personnel matter and I can't get into that," Overton told me, then added, "We have policies in place, and we have to abide by those policies."

A representative of the Florida Archivists Association said she'd apparently been pushed out for doing her job. I contacted the archivist to ask her about her retirement. She said she'd have to think about commenting, then hung up. I didn't hear from her again.

Then, when I asked the university for pictures of Garner, a public relations person said he was no longer an employee there. That was news to Garner.

The loss of the position didn't hurt him financially. His gardening business took off during the pandemic. But the loss of a job connected to the archaeology site he found left him feeling sad and hurt.

"Working at the Luna site, being part of the Luna project, was never about the job," he told me in a long text. "It was something I loved and that I believed in. I still do."

* * *

Sharon Yancey has the unenviable job of speaking on behalf of Wentworth's descendants. Her connection to the man is not direct—her aunt married Wentworth's oldest son but died three years ago.

She has some personal memories of him, though. She remembers how he'd show up for a family dinner and be "holding court, waxing eloquent and ready to eat." She recalls how "he'd walk into a room and people would see him and say, 'Oh, it's T. T., let's gather over there and listen to him. . . . He always had a story to tell.'"

She grew up hearing about how generous he was, how many people he helped over the years. Garner's revelation of his racist past rocked the whole family, her included. However, the one thing that did not surprise her was that the revelation came from things he'd saved—things someone else might have destroyed or thrown out.

"That man never threw anything away," she told me. "Was he a hoarder? Probably."

As the founder of a Christian ministry for children, though, she cannot defend what he did. It's "antithetical to everything I stand for," she explained.

She served on the board that advised Wells about his report for UWF, as did Garner, who found her quite impressive. She is now working to create some sort of healing event for the community, she told me.

The family is "very sad" about Wentworth's past, she said, but they would not oppose an effort to take Wentworth's name off the museum. Their namesake gave away all rights to his collection, she said, so the family feels like it's none of their business.

But there are white people in Pensacola who think otherwise.

When Overton's organization brought up the idea of taking Wentworth's name off the museum, some decried it as the worst kind of cancel culture. Others contended that misdeeds from such a far-distant past should have no effect on the present and that the Christian thing to do would be to forgive him for a youthful indiscretion. A year later, the controversy continues to rage on social media.

"I knew T. T. Wentworth. . . . This man that I knew for over 60 years was not a racist," a former public official convicted of bribery wrote recently on a Facebook page for people from Pensacola. "Mr. Wentworth was a good man, and the University of West Florida and the Press distorted a good man."

Nevertheless, UWF Historic Trust's board voted unanimously to take Wentworth's name off the building, although not off the collection he donated. The Florida Historical Commission followed suit in February. But the university's own trustees were not as ready to cut ties with a blatant racist.

One trustee, economic consultant Robert Jones, who is white, argued that Wentworth's other good works might outweigh his Klan support.

"My dad, who was a historian his whole life . . . once said to me, 'Robert, it takes an awful lot of "attaboys" to overcome an "oh shoot,"'" Jones told the other trustees. "The life of T. T. Wentworth seemed to have a great big old 'oh shoot' and that's his membership and leadership in the Pensacola Ku Klux Klan. I ask you, are there enough 'attaboys' to make up for that one big old 'oh shoot'?"

After a long debate, trustees voted 5 to 4 to approve the name change. Media reports at the time said the next and final step would be the approval of Governor Ron DeSantis and the cabinet, but in April officials with the Division of State Lands decided that wasn't necessary.

At the end of June, the Wentworth sign came down, to be replaced by one proclaiming the building to be "the Pensacola Museum of History at the University of West Florida."

In July, UWF posted digital images of all of Wentworth's Klan files so the public can see what they say. Anyone who reads them will see there's no ambiguity about the connection between "Mr. History" and the racist organization.

It's just as real and ugly—and far more disturbing—than that petrified cat.

Part Three

I HAD THE CRIME
OF MY LIFE

21

No. 1 in Raiford

Crime Reads, January 8, 2021

In 1986, a dark-haired mother of three applied for a job at a Miami private detective agency. When the boss asked why she wanted to work there, she lied.

"I told them my husband had left me and I had to pay the bills," said Carolina Garcia-Aguilera.

The ruse worked. He hired her.

The truth, as often happens in Florida, was stranger than fiction.

Garcia-Aguilera was an aspiring mystery novelist, one who started reading Sherlock Holmes stories in Spanish as a seven-year-old in Cuba. She wanted to write books about a female private eye in Miami, but she had run into problems with knowing how the business worked. For research purposes, she decided to get a job as a female private eye in Miami.

"I became a PI so I could write the books," she said.

A decade later, in 1996, G. P. Putnam published *Bloody Waters,* her first novel about private detective Guadalupe "Lupe" Solano, a self-described "Cuban-American princess" who stands just a shade over five feet tall and carries a Beretta in her Chanel purse. She's tough and tenacious, but she also has a weakness for fine food, expensive clothes, and going to bed with any man she finds attractive. *Kirkus Reviews* hailed Garcia-Aguilera as "a talent worth watching."

Six more Lupe Solano novels followed and sold well enough to be translated into a dozen languages. In her *New York Times* column, Marilyn Stasio praised Lupe for her "snappy style and a healthy self-confidence in her professional skills." She was even profiled by the *Times.*

The fifth Lupe book, *Havana Heat,* won the Shamus Award for best private eye novel in hardback from the Private Eye Writers of America, an award previously won by such luminaries as Sue Grafton, Bill Pronzini, Robert Crais, Lawrence Block, and Don Winslow. Garcia-Aguilera was the first (and, so far, only) Latina author to win that particular prize. Unfortunately, the awards dinner fell just after 9/11, so it was canceled.

"You know how I found out I won? I got a fax," Garcia-Aguilera said. "It wasn't very dramatic."

Her books brought her other kinds of acclaim. At the Florida State Prison in Raiford, she said, the Lupe novels were "the most popular books to check out."

Not everyone was a fan, of course: "I was excoriated for her sex—all the men." But Garcia-Aguilera didn't care. "I don't give a damn. It's my book. . . . I wanted her to be able to do whatever she wanted."

That's why, instead of going with the stereotypical down-at-the-heels gumshoe, she made Lupe the daughter of a well-to-do building contractor. Lupe's no antisocial loner, either. She and her two adult sisters—all of them named for Catholic saints—live in her widowed Papi's mansion in an upscale waterfront section of Miami called Cocoplum. They are waited on by two elderly servants who accompanied the family when they fled Cuba.

Lupe drives a Mercedes and keeps bottles of champagne in her office fridge. Her clients tend to be members of the Cuban-American elite who are willing to pay top dollar for her discreet help.

Each book features Lupe tackling an investigation that takes some wild twists and turns, but it's grounded in the kinds of things real detectives do: digging through a target's trash, running license plates, doing surveillance work.

The Lupe Solano mysteries quickly found an audience among those excited to see someone who shared their Cuban heritage writing in a genre dominated by white male authors.

"When I discovered the Lupe novels, it felt like coming home," said Alex Segura, who counts Garcia-Aguilera as a major influence on his series of books about South Florida private eye Pete Fernandez, which concluded in 2019 with *Miami Midnight*. Her novels were the push "I needed to find to nudge me along my way."

"I recall just melting into the page," said Raquel Reyes, who co-chairs Florida's annual SleuthFest convention and serves as a board member of the Florida chapter of Mystery Writers of America.

The seventh Lupe Solano novel was published a decade ago, and Garcia-Aguilera moved on to other genres, tackling romance and erotica. She kept her PI license current, just to maintain what she called "street cred," but that was her only connection to the world of crime.

Mystery authors Carolina Garcia-Aguilar and Raquel V. Reyes. Photo courtesy of Raquel V. Reyes.

But in a December interview, the 71-year-old author said she wasn't done with Lupe just yet, or vice versa. She said she has written an eighth book in the series and her agent is shopping it around to publishers.

For fans such as Les Standiford, founding director of the Florida International University creative writing program and editor of *Miami Noir* and *Miami Noir: The Classics* (both of which feature stories by Garcia-Aguilera), this is thrilling news.

"Anyone who hasn't discovered Lupe Solano yet," he said, "now's the time to do it."

* * *

Standiford, who in the 1990s wrote a nine-book series about a Miami building contractor who turns amateur sleuth, remembers first meeting Garcia-Aguilera at a party several years before her first novel was published.

She talked to him about his books and then mentioned working as a private investigator to do research for her own writing, which astounded him. He had heard of detectives who became writers—Dashiell Hammett is the best known—but never a wannabe writer deciding to become a PI first. On top of that, she struck him as the opposite of a hard-nosed private eye.

"She's bubbly. She's vivacious. She's funny," said Standiford.

Reyes, after hearing Garcia-Aguilera talk about her PI career at a conference, drew a different conclusion: "Some of the stories she told us, I would not want to mess with her."

Her background prepared her for this. The Havana where she grew up was a violent place. "During the revolution there were gunshots outside my house all the time," she told the *Orlando Sentinel* in 2002. "I spent a lot of time reading under the kitchen table."

A year after Fidel Castro seized power, when she was 10, her family fled Cuba with just the clothes on their backs. They lived in Palm Beach for two years, then moved to New York.

She came back to Florida, though, to study history and political science at Rollins College (also the alma mater of PBS kids' show star Fred Rogers). She put herself through college in part by writing papers for other students, in particular the soccer team.

"It taught me how to do research on stuff I wasn't familiar with," she said, laughing.

After graduating from Rollins, she studied languages at Georgetown University in Washington, D.C., until she got married. Her husband's job took them to Hong Kong, Tokyo, and Beijing. When they returned to Florida, she earned an MBA at the University of South Florida in Tampa. By then she had divorced her husband and decided to move to Miami to be closer to her siblings.

She took a social worker job at a large public hospital for two years, remarried, had her third child, and worked toward a Ph.D. in international studies. Meanwhile, she also served as a guardian ad litem, someone appointed by the court to represent the best interests of an abused, neglected, or abandoned child in legal proceedings.

Her work with judges and attorneys helped when she needed references for her private eye business, and in creating supporting characters for her mystery novels. But getting into the business herself proved to be the most important move.

The detective firm that first hired her "was not the highest caliber of PI firms," Garcia-Aguilera said. "The fact that they hired me should tell you a lot about them."

Nevertheless, she learned a lot there, lessons that would help her both in her PI work and in creating Lupe Solano's world.

She learned, for instance, that people who are trying to dodge arrest might stop to change their clothes, but they hardly ever change their shoes. She learned to shoot straight and keep her gun clean and oiled. She learned how to interview people. She learned that clients often lie because they don't want to be viewed in a bad light. And she learned all about surveillance tactics.

"There's nothing like sitting in a car in the pitch blackness doing surveillance with your bladder screaming because it's about to burst," she said, laughing. "My motto is, if you see a bathroom, use it, whether you need to or not."

Unlike Lupe, she didn't drive a Mercedes. Instead, she was usually in a Volvo station wagon "with a dog in the back and all the kiddie seats." Sometimes she had to ask her fellow detectives to babysit her kids while she was on a stakeout. She would keep a phone close by in case her daughters needed their mom's help with their homework.

Garcia-Aguilera decided to quit and start her own agency, partnering with a former Alcohol, Tobacco, and Firearms agent. The office they opened was in such a sleazy part of Miami, she said, that "we were always happy when our cars were still in the parking lot at the end of the day." (Lupe, by contrast, works out of a neat little cottage in upscale Coral Gables.)

This was during the height of the "cocaine cowboys" era in Miami, when drug dealers had shootouts on the interstate and even massacred rivals at the Dadeland Mall in broad daylight. She tried to focus on financial crimes, figuring those would be easy work. She was wrong.

"Every case we took on, even if it was finding out whether someone's dog pooped on your lawn or not, turned out to involve drugs," Garcia-Aguilera said.

By the '90s, though, financial crimes were on the rise, requiring her expertise in tracing assets, detecting fraud, and uncovering money laundering. Still, she wound up pursuing some cases "where there was a body on the ground."

Their agency did handle domestic cases, which she said could be very lucrative yet also very unnecessary. Florida is a no-fault divorce state, so there was no need for their clients to prove infidelity, she said.

"They just wanted to screw with their spouses," she said. "One time a man hired me because he thought his wife was having an affair. I found out she was having an affair with his brother. I provided him with the proof on video. So he threw a big family barbecue, and then he announced, 'Hey, let's watch a video!' and he showed that video to everyone, with the grandparents and the kids there and everything."

Garcia-Aguilera sighed, then said, "That's the day I stopped doing domestics. There are consequences to these things, and I didn't like it."

Some cases were grislier than others. She had a jailhouse interview once with a man accused of killing, dismembering, and then barbecuing his neighbor. After listening to the killer describe marinating the body to tenderize the meat before cooking it, she wrote in her notebook, "Get the recipe." (She used this in a short story published in *Miami Noir* called "The Recipe.")

She got so caught up in her private eye work, she nearly lost sight of the reason she'd signed up for it. Then she got a reminder.

"One morning my husband said to me—as I was leaving the house at 3 a.m. for a stakeout—'When are you going to finally start writing that book?'" she said. "So I finally started writing *Bloody Waters*."

* * *

The opening pages of *Bloody Waters* offer the perfect introduction to Lupe.

She's at a firing range, working to improve her accuracy and musing to herself on gender roles: "It doesn't take a genius to figure out guns were invented by men—no woman would ever abuse her hands that way. If a woman had designed the first gun, she would have found a way to ensure that her nail polish wouldn't chip during reloading."

But then she scoffs at the girlie-pink guns being marketed to women: "Really, what's the point of a cute gun? . . . Guns are for killing—whatever their color, shape or size."

Lupe's narration is a major attraction for readers. She manages to be sardonic but not cynical, self-aware but not self-important. She's also extremely knowledgeable about Miami's high and low culture, navigating easily between the high-society doings of the richest of the rich, the glittering nightlife of super-hip South Beach, and the no-tell motels and back-alley crack dens where her cases sometimes take her.

"She sees the city for what it is, a flawed, blended, and corrupt place with lots of divisions," Segura said.

Reyes said she delighted in seeing Lupe Solano drive down streets she recognized and eat at restaurants she'd visited. More importantly, she said, Garcia-Aguilera captures the Miami Cuban attitude and the pervasiveness of the Catholic Church in Miami's private and public life. (Lupe's favorite sister Lourdes—named for Garcia-Aguilera's mother—is a hip nun who insists Lupe keep three Catholic medals pinned to her bra for protection against evil.)

"She nails it—she nails the details," Reyes said.

Yet the realism of the Miami setting and atmosphere is accompanied by the kind of outlandish situations you won't find in other mystery novels.

In one book, Lupe's client is a high-priced call girl who's also supposedly a virgin. In another, Lupe is hired by the mother superior of one convent to investigate whether another convent is trying to pull off a phony miracle. In *Havana Heat,* the one that won the Shamus, Lupe's client is a rich old woman who demands she locate a long-missing tapestry and smuggle it out of Cuba in time to show it to the client's even older mother on her deathbed.

Of course, Standiford pointed out, "that's part . . . of the happy accident of living in Florida," where the outlandish tends to be the norm. Sometimes, the best story ideas come from just reading the morning papers.

The odd situations push Lupe to try unusual tactics. For instance, to investigate the convent, she dispatches one of her female operatives to set up a hot dog cart across the street, while dressed in a thong bikini (bikini-clad hot dog vendors were a common sight by the roads of South Florida in the 1990s). Inside the cart is a camera to snap pictures of the cars entering and leaving. All goes well until a county code inspector shows up to check her license.

Although the author and her heroine share a profession, there are differences. Garcia-Aguilera is taller (five foot five) and carried a Colt .45, not a Beretta. And unlike the fun-loving but single Lupe, she's a proud mom who dedicated each of her books to her children.

Garcia-Aguilera can't directly tap her PI experiences for her novels because her clients are promised confidentiality. Thus, she flips the gender or finds some other way to obscure the source material, she said. She joked that her favorite research is checking the menus of the restaurants she mentions.

"You'd think they'd offer me free meals" in exchange for the shout-outs, she said.

Garcia-Aguilera has surrounded Lupe with a fascinating supporting cast. There's Leonardo, her cousin and office manager, who's intent on converting much of the office into a gym and who shows up for work in skimpy exercise clothes. Barbara, a tough female sailor who stalks the waterfront with a machete strapped to her leg, makes memorable appearances in two books. Then there's Sweet Suzanne, a statuesque blond who runs a high-priced call girl ring and enjoys meeting up with Lupe to swap gossip over a high-calorie lunch.

Garcia-Aguilera never plots out her books in advance, preferring to let the characters speak to her and guide her writing. Sometimes that leads to trouble. She got stuck trying to come up with a good ending to *Havana Heat,* much to her agent's consternation. Her deadline loomed. Then, while taking a shower one night, the answer came to her.

"I barely dried myself off before I ran down the stairs to write it," she said.

One constant in each one of her books is her guarantee that there will be a minimum of three murders "or your money back." That's the reason the word "bloody" appears in several of her titles.

Still, she said, "I might have gone a little overboard in the new one." She's reluctant to say much about it yet, but the title sounds perfect: *Miami Madness.*

––––––––––

Postscript: I am sad to report that, as of January 2025, Miami Madness *remains unpublished.*

22

The Bard of Apalachicola

Flamingo, June 6, 2022

With one phone call in early 2015, John Solomon and his sleepy Panhandle town became celebrities.

He was working at the Apalachicola Bay Chamber of Commerce and Visitor Center when he answered a call from a woman in Tennessee. The caller identified herself as Dawn Lee McKenna, an aspiring mystery writer who wanted to pen a novel set in Apalachicola. She was looking for someone who could tell her about the town and its surroundings. She was also looking for someone who could fill her in about the local sheriff's office there in Franklin County.

"Well," said Solomon, "I'm pretty sure I'm your dude."

He explained that he'd been the local chamber's executive director for about six months and knew a lot about Apalachicola and the region it's in. Then he told the author that he had started that job after retiring from the Franklin County Sheriff's Department after 20 years.

McKenna, delighted, had a lot of questions for him. I mean a lot.

In June 2015, McKenna published *Low Tide,* the first book in what would become her Forgotten Coast series, which she labeled as "semi-noir, darkly funny and atmospheric suspense."

She described Apalachicola in that first book as "one of the few places left that actually felt like Florida, with its century-old brick and clapboard shops and houses, the marina filled with shrimp and oyster boats, and people who couldn't care less about Disney World."

In her second installment, *Riptide,* she painted a fuller picture: "Apalachicola was a throwback to an earlier time. . . . It was primarily a fishing town, famous for its Apalachicola oysters and Gulf shrimp. . . . Tourists came for the oysters, the fishing, the beaches of St. George Island and the nine hundred historic buildings turned into gift shops, nautical art galleries and restaurants. The town had one traffic light, a passing acquaintance with severe weather, and fewer than 3,000 residents."

McKenna's series focuses on a fictional detective, Lieutenant Maggie Redmond. She's white, in her 30s, five foot three, with dark hair and a ton of self-doubt. Maggie is a single mom who grew up in Apalachicola and lives in a cypress stilt house her grandfather built in the 1950s. She used to be married to a shrimper, and, as the series begins, she remains friendly with her ex while raising their two kids, a teenage girl and a younger boy.

Maggie is one tough cookie. By the third book, she's shot two criminals dead—one of them a drug dealer who's trying to strangle her, the other someone who's already wounded a colleague and is waiting to gun her down too.

As the series begins, she is investigating what appears to be a suicide on the beach and meanwhile contemplating beginning an affair with her boss and best friend, Sheriff Wyatt Hamilton. Maggie is hiding a big secret about her connection to the dead man. That leads to her being drawn into a strange relationship with the local crime lord, a wealthy and always polite Louisiana-born seafood dealer named Bennett Boudreaux.

In the acknowledgments to *Low Tide,* McKenna gives Solomon a special shoutout for helping with her research. He also appears as a character in several of the books, doing exactly what he does in real life.

Solomon says he made a deal with the author that she could put him in the books, but only on two conditions: "I got to be myself, and I don't die."

Solomon is one of several real Apalachicola residents who pop up in minor roles throughout the fictional series running a coffee shop or overseeing hotel check-ins. Despite the boilerplate disclaimer about "all persons, living or dead" being fictional, even Apalachicola's real mayor at the time, Van Johnson Sr., shows up in the series. Real Apalachicola businesses get special shoutouts, such as a waterfront seafood restaurant Boss Oyster.

While McKenna's books paint a portrait of Apalachicola as a picturesque fishing village/beach town, they also show it as the home to killers, drug dealers, kidnappers, abused women, human traffickers, and corrupt cops and politicians. There are enough grisly discoveries to fuel a couple of seasons of *Forensic Files.*

McKenna's characters display a dark sense of humor about those discoveries. In *Riptide,* a shrimper pulls up his net and discovers he's caught a severed foot. When someone asks the elderly medical examiner what he makes of the foot, he replies, "Well, it's not a candidate for reattachment."

Solomon joked that McKenna did a fine job of depicting the town, "except she boosted our crime rate by about 500 percent. We had one murder in 10 years, and she had five in a few months."

Yet the books are also fairly wholesome. "There's no cursing, no gratu-itous violence, and no sex," McKenna's mother, Linda Maxwell said.

Despite her crime-soaked descriptions of the town she calls "Apalach," around the time book number three came out, Solomon noticed a strange phenomenon:

Fans of McKenna's series started showing up at the visitor center.

They wanted to see the Forgotten Coast they'd encountered in her books. They wanted to see the places she wrote about and meet the real people she'd mentioned. It was as if Jessica Fletcher fans began showing up in Cabot Cove to see the settings of the murders she'd solved.

"They tell me, 'We've read all the books, and we had to come see every-thing,'" Solomon said. "I actually signed some autographs one time."

Six years later, the flow of McKenna's books has ceased, but the flow of McKenna-reading tourists hasn't. Solomon figures two or three groups a month stop in at his office on their sightseeing visits, some of them armed with maps and notes.

They want the full Dawn Lee McKenna Experience.

* * *

Last December, I was having brunch with a friend in Tallahassee, and we were discussing Florida crime writers. We rounded up the usual suspects—John D. MacDonald, Carl Hiaasen, Tim Dorsey, Randy Wayne White. We mentioned a few who aren't as well known, such as Carolina Garcia-Aguilera and Tom Corcoran.

Then my friend said, "I really love Dawn Lee McKenna's books."

"Who?" I said.

She proceeded to tell me all about her, including the part about the read-ers showing up in Apalachicola. I was astounded.

I figured other people more attuned to the latest thrillers must have heard of this. I contacted Oline Cogdill, a longtime Fort Lauderdale mystery book critic who's won a Raven award from the Mystery Writers of America. She was as clueless as I was.

"You've stumped me," she said, admitting that she, too, had never heard of McKenna.

But some of McKenna's fellow writers told me they definitely knew her work, although they had never met the author.

Claire Matturo, a Sarasota native and the author of such Florida-set mys-teries as *The Smuggler's Daughter,* praised McKenna's writing and knack for capturing what makes Florida so special.

"I grew up further south on the Florida coast, but I can spot a fake Floridian a mile away in fiction, and she's the real deal," Matturo said.

McKenna never made the *New York Times* Bestsellers list or even got a mention in any metro newspaper's book section. Yet she became a bestselling author. It was McKenna's choice of publishing format—the e-book—that made her such a hit with readers while keeping her name a secret.

"There are people you've never heard of who are killing it on Kindle Unlimited," explained Tamara "Tara" Lush, a St. Petersburg–based author who has published both romance and mystery novels in a variety of formats, most recently *Grounds for Murder* and *Cold Brew Corpse*. "Some of them are making $10,000 a month, because there are mystery and romance readers who read a book a day and they're looking for new content."

Readers pay Kindle Unlimited $9.99 a month for access to Amazon e-books. Some of the e-books are published by Amazon, which provides them to Kindle Unlimited subscribers free of charge. The authors then get payments from Amazon based on the number of downloads for their books.

Some, like McKenna, also publish paperback editions. But the big money is in the digital downloads. In February 2021, McKenna posted on her Facebook fan page: "Do you guys realize that you've bought over 250,000 copies of my books? . . . Add in the millions of pages read in Kindle Unlimited, and it's more like 640,000. You're the best readers any author could dream of having."

One of the most successful Kindle Unlimited authors is Melbourne native Wayne Stinnett, Lush said. His adventure novels feature an ex-military charter boat captain, and they're largely set in the Keys.

Stinnett, a Marine Corps veteran, worked as a deckhand, commercial fisherman, divemaster, taxi driver, construction manager, and truck driver before penning his first novel. Stinnett said he'd never met McKenna in person, but they became friends while chatting in an online forum for authors. He enjoyed a Southern romance novel she'd written, *See You*.

"I convinced her to try writing a mystery," he said. "Within five or six months she had two books ready to publish."

To show her gratitude for his encouragement, McKenna not only thanked Stinnett in *Low Tide*'s acknowledgments but also gave Stinnett's name to one of her characters.

"I was a crusty old oysterman," he said, chuckling. "So I made her a Key West fortune-teller in one of my books."

Stinnett emails out a regular author newsletter for his fans. He used that to endorse McKenna's first novel about Apalachicola, which helped to spark her sales.

"I had a pretty good following," he said. "She did phenomenally well."

Stinnett's version of what happened makes McKenna sound like an overnight smash. But according to her family, that skips over years of preparation—some of it involving a cookbook.

* * *

McKenna had such an innate feeling for life in a Florida beach town because she grew up in one, said her daughter, Kat Scheideler.

She was born in Pompano Beach, just north of Fort Lauderdale, an only child whose father disappeared when she was just a baby, according to Maxwell, her mother.

"She loved the ocean," her mother said. "She was pretty fearless about jumping in from anywhere."

For a time, Maxwell held a treasure-hunting lease in the Keys and she and the future author lived aboard a boat. Once, to visit relatives, they drove thousands of miles from Key West to the Panama Canal. On these trips, McKenna would have a book to read, or she'd be making up her own stories, her mother said.

"She started writing, seriously writing, when she was 14 and wrote a book," her mother said. The initial version was good, Maxwell said, but she kept tinkering with it and somehow she never got around to deciding it was ready to send to a publisher.

She really wanted to be a scriptwriter. Once, as a teenager, she ran into Martin Sheen at the Burt Reynolds Dinner Theater in Jupiter and handed him one of her screenplays, her mother said. He must have read it that night because the next day she saw him, and he praised her work. (Sheen and his electric blue eyes became the model for Boudreaux.)

When McKenna gave birth to her first child, her mother said, she dropped out of college and moved to Tennessee, believing it to be a better place to raise a child. She found work, albeit unfulfilling, in the food industry, eventually becoming a restaurant manager to support herself and her children after splitting with her husband.

"She had a hard time working for other people, and she didn't like supervising other people too," Maxwell said.

The turning point came when she discovered ghostwriting could pay her bills, her mother said. These writing jobs didn't pay well—$1,200 to crank out a book in a week or so—and her name never appeared on the cover. But McKenna learned she could write fast, she could focus on the job despite distractions, and she could produce work that was good enough to publish.

"She ghostwrote 30 books," Scheideler, her daughter, said. "Sometimes we wrote them together—cookbooks and exercise books, mostly."

One of those ghostwritten books was a *Hunger Games* cookbook, she said. "We went all out. We made all the recipes up ourselves."

All along, though, she had in mind writing a book of her own. She wanted it to be set in the kind of Florida beach town she knew as a child, her daughter said. She spent years plugging various descriptions into Google, trying to find just the right town.

When I asked why not just make something up, as most authors do, her daughter explained, "Because she wanted it to be real."

When she found Apalachicola and connected with Solomon, everything clicked. She used Google Earth to walk the streets of the town until she knew the place as well as anyone could, her mother said.

"Her ambition was to make enough money to not have to write for other people," Maxwell said. That goal turned out to be surprisingly easy to meet.

"The first book sold ridiculously well," Scheideler said. McKenna was stunned by her success, sometimes holding up her first royalty check from Amazon as if it were a trophy.

The second one came out later that same month. "Released today and already a bestseller," McKenna tweeted.

McKenna helped mentor another writer, one about as different from her as possible. Dan Mason, who writes under the name "Cap Daniels," stands six foot five and weighs 275 pounds. He looked like a giant next to the petite McKenna. Unlike Stinnett and Blackwell, Mason met her face-to-face, and they even ate dinner together.

"Every word I wrote after meeting her I wrote knowing that she would read it," Mason said. "It made me a more attentive writer."

Despite the praise from other writers and her fans, McKenna never took herself too seriously. In her eighth Forgotten Coast novel, *Lake Morality,* she has a character refer to "that author lady" who keeps visiting the town, then adds, "I don't think all her tires are properly inflated, if you know what I mean."

* * *

At the end of each of her books, McKenna asked fans to subscribe to her newsletter. Some 100,000 people signed up, her daughter told me. Those personal connections helped to foster a sense of family among the writer and her readers.

On her Facebook page, McKenna admitted that she was often trying to find something entertaining to say because she felt her books were "a lot more interesting" than she was in her private life. Sometimes she just posted video clips of music from her church in Kingsport, Tennessee, to which she was quite devoted.

While McKenna did well with e-books, her self-published paperback editions, produced under the imprint Sweet Tea Press, had a harder time finding readers.

Her cousin, Chrystal Hartigan, who had worked in music promotion, took some of them to beach town bookstores up and down the East Coast, trying to interest them in selling the books that did so well on Amazon. Only a couple of stores outside of Florida were at all interested, she told me.

One place her printed books do sell well: Apalachicola's one and only bookstore, which doubles as a knitting supply store: Downtown Books & Purl.

"These things fly out of there," said owner Dale Julian. "Everybody who's local has read them, and in many cases there are walk-on parts for real people."

Sometimes tourists visit the bookstore who aren't already McKenna fans, she said. They just want something short to read on the flight home to Chicago. Julian always recommends the first of McKenna's series.

"Then they call me two days later from Chicago," she said. "They tell me, 'Put the other nine in a box and send them to me. Here's my credit card number.'"

Others are already fans, visiting the scenes of the crimes they've read about. "They come in and say, 'I want to see where the body was found,'" Julian said.

The bookstore has been around for 20 years, but Julian said she'd never seen anything like the crowds that showed up for McKenna's appearance at the store.

"It was hot, hot, hot," she said. "Everything started at 1 p.m. with a lunch with the local book club. Then at 2 p.m. we started the signing. The overflow crowd stretched halfway down the street. What was supposed to be a two-hour book signing turned into four hours. Then she went down to the coffee shop that's featured in the books and invited any of the readers who wanted coffee to go with her. She got in a golf cart and rode around with her readers. Meanwhile I was ready to go lie down in the stockroom."

The signing was crazy, but the cruise was even crazier.

A travel agent pitched the idea to McKenna: A trip on a cruise ship, the *Empress of the Seas,* with her fans. Those who paid to go would enjoy exclusive access to McKenna to quiz her about anything.

She was uneasy about it, but said yes, Stinnett said.

"She didn't like being in the limelight," Stinnett told me. "Going on the cruise was very, very stressful for her. She was self-conscious about her looks."

About 150 fans signed up for the trip, Scheideler said. They were all given T-shirts that proclaimed, "I'm With Stoopid," and featured a drawing of Maggie's rooster. Despite her personal unease, McKenna spent as much time with her fans as possible.

The author's popularity fueled her determination to do a lot more with her gift. She started another series of books, these set in the Panhandle too, but in the 1970s. She planned for Sweet Tea Press to publish books by other authors, not just her.

And after Hurricane Michael hit Apalachicola, she created a charity called The Unforgotten Coast Fund to help the town's businesses recover. She planned to write seven more books in the Forgotten Coast series, for a total of 17, using special events to raise money for the fund.

But the series stopped at 10 because the unthinkable happened: McKenna stopped writing for a whole year in 2020.

* * *

McKenna had survived several bouts with melanoma when she was in her 20s, her mother said.

"She thought she had punched her cancer ticket," she told me.

But then, in 2016, she was diagnosed with breast cancer. She underwent surgery and chemotherapy, in the meantime still cranking out her fiction.

She could cook and clean house and do laundry and even deal with raw sewage seeping out from under her rented home, her mother said. Somehow, she still made time to write, her fingers flying across the keyboard.

She thought she'd beaten cancer a second time. But then, in November 2018, she told her fans: "Okay, you readers who have become my friends and family. . . . The verdict is cancer, metastatic to the bones from the breast cancer. Treatable, but not as yet curable."

Now she had a lot to say on Facebook. She recounted her biopsies, chemotherapy treatments, and loss of hair, in between mentions of her favorite comforts: Kraft macaroni and cheese, John Cusack movies (her favorite was *Grosse Point Blank*), and snuggling with her cat.

Now she struggled to keep up with the demand she'd created. Her health problems made it impossible. She called it "the Year of Not Writing," confessing in her newsletter, "For the first time in my life, I couldn't write a word. At least, I couldn't write anything worth reading. This led to me watching my career flash before my eyes, certain that y'all would forget about my books."

Even her charity work suffered. She wrote on the Unforgotten Coast Facebook page: "I haven't been able to do the cool fundraisers or produce the book-related merchandise readers have been asking for."

In April 2020, McKenna pasted on her Facebook fan page a picture of a book cover for something called *Beam Sea,* with this caption: "Making no release date promises because things are just wonky, but guess which book decided to start writing itself again?"

Months passed before she mentioned *Beam Sea* again, noting in January 2021 that "tomorrow I will be back to work on #11 in the FC series." In a February response to a query on Goodreads, she wrote, "I'm currently working on *Beam Sea,* the 11th book in the Forgotten Coast series. Hopefully we'll release in March, if health and time cooperate."

July rolled into August with no sign of *Beam Sea.* Then, in October 2021, her mother broke the worst possible news to the readers of McKenna's newsletter.

Beneath a large photo of McKenna's cat, Maxwell wrote: "Miss Lady, her irascible cat, is still waiting on the center of her bed, but my daughter, Dawn Lee McKenna, slipped away quietly last Saturday morning, September 25. She was surrounded by her four children and spent her last precious moments giving and receiving love."

She asked that subscribers stick with the newsletter, which she promised would continue, adding, "Not all of Dawn's tales have been told." But there have been no more newsletters, and no new books.

* * *

When fans show up in Apalachicola these days, Solomon said, one question they always ask is, "Do you think we'll ever get that 11th book?"

They want to know what happens next with Maggie, Wyatt, and Bennett Boudreaux, not to mention Stoopid. McKenna's death left them with the ultimate cliffhanger. The characters still live in the readers' imaginations, even as their creator has ceased to exist.

Her family is well aware there's still a strong appetite for McKenna's books. Her daughter said that Blackwell would continue the series he co-wrote with her mother, but Blackwell told me he can't, not without McKenna. He also squashed any rumors he'd be the one to finish *Beam Sea*: "I'm not able to write in her voice."

McKenna herself was apparently having trouble doing that, toward the end.

"I know she wrote 3,000 to 4,000 words," Scheideler told me. "But she said she hated them. She was kind of a secretive, sneaky person. . . . The problem is, she was so special to us, there's no way to do her justice with that series."

Maxwell and Scheideler told me they've talked of creating audiobooks, tapping a new market, but their plans haven't progressed very far. As for finishing *Beam Sea*, "we are definitely entertaining the idea," Scheideler said. They just haven't figured out how.

When McKenna died at age 58, no one was ready for it. The family posted no obituary, an odd omission for someone who made her living with words. No funeral home handled the body.

Instead, Maxwell said, they simply cremated the body and held a hastily organized memorial service for her at Hope Community Church's camp, an outdoor setting McKenna adored. Stinnett and Mason were there, but no one from Apalachicola was able to attend on such short notice.

As for her ashes, her daughter said, some of them will be turned into jewelry for family members and some will remain in an urn she plans to keep.

But some of them she plans to take on a sailing trip into Apalachicola Bay. She wants to scatter them in the place that made Mckenna's dream of being a successful author come true.

23

A Paltry Penalty

Florida Phoenix, September 18, 2021

Say what you will about Florida (and many of you have), but we've sure got some unusual crimes here. A surprising number of them involve reptiles.

You have probably heard about the guy who, in 2016, tossed an alligator through a Wendy's drive-thru window in Royal Palm Beach. Last year, Sanford police recovered a five-foot pet iguana named "Smog" that had been kidnapped (lizard-napped?) from a smoke shop.

Earlier this year, someone stole 13 Argentine tegus from a reptile breeding facility in Punta Gorda, and, so far, the owner has tracked down six of them, a feat of amateur detective work that I think rivals anything Jessica Fletcher pulled off in *Murder, She Wrote.*

But the reptile crime I heard about this past week was not one I have ever seen prosecuted before.

The charge: 22 counts of destroying gopher tortoise burrows in Marion County.

The scene of the crime: Del Webb's Stone Creek, a gated, 55+ "active adult" community in Ocala with an 18-hole championship golf course and a "resort-style pool, fitness center, spa, multiple game courts, a full-time lifestyle director, and more."

As for the name of the defendant, it's not a person. It's a company called Pulte Homes.

Pulte Homes is no fly-by-night outfit staffed by Cletus the Slack-Jawed Yokel and his 1972 John Deere backhoe. This is a nationally recognized corporate entity based in Michigan with branches that stretch from Massachusetts to California.

The company boasts on its website, "Over 70 years of experience go into the building of every Pulte home, and our construction standards are set high to meet expectations."

Yet those "high" construction standards were low enough that the company wound up facing 22 criminal charges. Twenty-two is a lot. A prosecutor told me that that's enough to eliminate the possibility of it being an accident.

The victims were particularly vulnerable, too. Gopher tortoises are classified as a threatened species in Florida. Their burrows provide a home for more than just those homely helmets-with-feet. They offer a refuge for 300 additional species, some of which are endangered.

By destroying those burrows, Pulte's work crew killed any tortoises inside, as well as all the other species using those burrows as a place to hole up.

I asked Jeff Goessling, an Eckerd College biology professor who co-chairs the Gopher Tortoise Council, how many gophers might have been using those 22 burrows. Between 10 and 30, he said.

Killing off so many tortoises at once seemed like a throwback to the days when builders would prepare a construction site with a tactic a veteran biologist told me about called "rub the scrub." Heavy equipment would obliterate any evidence of tortoises, burrowing owls, or any other ecologically important critter that had ever lived on a piece of property slated for development, so they wouldn't have to slow down for any permits.

I have tried repeatedly to get someone from Pulte to answer my questions about this case, but to no avail. I guess they don't want to talk about it—it's too embarrassing for them, poor dears.

Court records show Pulte initially pleaded innocent to all 22 misdemeanors, but then on August 25 pleaded guilty to every single one of them.

The penalty: a fine of about $13,700, which Pulte paid on September 3.

"Oh, gee, I guess they're going out of business now," St. Petersburg gopher tortoise biologist George Heinrich said sarcastically when I told him about the case. "That's a joke. Those guys have that much money in their petty cash drawer."

Still, I was surprised Pulte Homes would commit such a crime—not because of their high standards, but because they got caught doing something similar a year ago.

* * *

It happened last October.

Pulte Homes had a contract to buy 44 acres of undeveloped, wooded land in northern Pinellas County, the state's most densely populated county. Finding a chunk of undeveloped land that size in Pinellas is as rare as finding a product in Publix in October that's not flavored with pumpkin spice.

Pulte's contractor "drove a bulldozer near threatened gopher tortoise burrows," the *Tampa Bay Times* reported. The Florida Fish and Wildlife Conservation Commission issued Pulte Homes and its contractor "warnings for the violation . . . and ordered work on the land to stop for 28 days."

A Pulte vice president named Scott Himelhoch told the wildlife commission's investigator that the contractor had been hired to "clear a path into the property to allow access for a truck to conduct soil testing," not to kill tortoises.

Himelhoch said he had no idea—none!—that there were any gopher tortoises on that sandy, well-drained forest property. But an environmental consultant the company had hired to survey the property had unfortunately marked some of the burrows with orange tape, making them pretty hard to miss.

After the bad publicity and 28-day stop-work order, Pulte Homes' deal to buy the property somehow fell through. Oh darn!

Pinellas County, Dunedin, and a combination of private donors and nonprofit groups scrambled around and raised the money to buy it for preservation. No other developer will ever get a crack at those tortoise burrows.

What Pulte did next makes me suspect that this was not the first time the company flouted the rules intended to protect gophers, but just the first time it got caught.

The second time Pulte got caught happened in April. Once again, a bulldozer working for Pulte got too close to a tortoise burrow—and then apparently drove right over it and 21 more in the Stone Creek subdivision.

Shortly thereafter, Pulte's own environmental consultant, a company called Kimley-Horn, phoned a wildlife commission gopher tortoise biologist to report the burrow destruction. All the burrow openings had been filled with dirt, all the trees ripped out by the roots, and at least two tortoise carcasses were left behind. One of them had been brutally chopped in two.

A wildlife commission investigator named Aubrey Ransom checked out the tip, documented the destruction, and interviewed the supervisor at the site, Michael Piendel. Ransom subpoenaed all of Kimley-Horn's records, which included an email trail between Kimley-Horn and Pulte officials about the site.

What to do next required a decision by the state attorney's office in Ocala.

I spent 30 minutes on the phone this week discussing this case with Chief Assistant State Attorney Walter Forgie, who oversaw Pulte's prosecution. He said the last time his office had charged a builder with this particular crime was more than a dozen years ago.

Although prosecutors could have charged Piendel with destroying those 22 burrows, he told me, "we ultimately chose to prosecute the corporation because we wanted them to be held accountable. They're the ones profiting off this."

The Pinellas County incident helped persuade them to go after the company rather than its employee, he said. And that earlier case ensured the prosecutors would seek the maximum penalty allowed by law (such as it is).

Pulte did have an old, but still valid, wildlife commission permit to smother gophers (more on that in a minute), but that permit didn't cover this particular section of the property. Pulte officials said the crew had just gotten mixed up about what was what. The emails between Pulte and Kimley-Horn showed that excuse was as flimsy as the fabric in some celebrities' see-through dresses at the Met Gala.

Pulte officials couldn't claim ignorance about the presence of the tortoise burrows for the same reason that excuse didn't fly in Pinellas. Among the evidence found at the scene: two flags labeled "GT," indicating the location of gopher tortoise burrows marked by Kimley-Horn.

I asked Forgie if he thought the $13,700 fine would be enough to deter Pulte from pulling the same stunt a third time.

"I hope so, but only time will tell," he said after some hesitation. "I certainly hope it sends a message that they're going to be held accountable."

I asked Goessling the same question. He predicted homebuilders like Pulte won't be deterred from doing it over and over.

"The fine of a few thousand dollars won't outweigh the sale of a couple of million-dollar homes," he said.

*　*　*

When the charges were filed, Pulte made an unusual choice for its defense attorney.

Instead of picking someone with experience handling criminal cases, it hired Ken Wright, a Winter Haven land-use attorney who also happens to be a former chairman of the state wildlife commission. Maybe the next time I get a speeding ticket, I'll hire the former head of the Florida Highway Patrol to challenge it.

Wright's environmental track record is—oh, let's be kind and call it "diverse." On the one hand, while chairing the wildlife commission, he helped protect manatees from the boating industry and waterfront developers who wanted to take them off the state endangered list.

On the other hand, he served as general counsel for the Orlando-Sanford

Airport Authority, which outraged environmental groups by destroying three bald eagle nests. He served in a similar capacity for the Orlando Expressway Authority, which faced a public uproar over its plans to bury more than 400 gopher tortoises during highway construction. Ultimately, that agency backed down and relocated the tortoises. (Wright declined repeated requests for comment.)

The expressway authority held a valid permit from the wildlife commission to bury those gophers, just as Pulte had a valid permit to suffocate gophers on another part of its Stone Creek property.

For 16 years, the wildlife commission handed out permits for burrow destruction to developers willing to write a check into a fund for buying tortoise habitat. By the time the "pay-to-pave" program ended in 2007, after biologists reported that the tortoise population had gone into a nose-dive, the state had handed out 94,000 such permits with no expiration date.

Now, as I wrote in a column last year, "the state's rules say any developer who wants to build on land occupied by gopher tortoises is required to hire someone to track down every burrow and move the tortoises somewhere else before they can clear the land. According to Melissa Tucker, deputy director of the wildlife commission's habitat and species protection division, the state has so far issued 1,600 permits to relocate about 60,000 tortoises in the past decade."

But earlier this year, the *Orlando Sentinel* reported that this more humane gopher tortoise mitigation system had also become an unmitigated disaster.

The move-'em-out rule "has spawned an industry of for-profit refuges, consultants, and agents who capture and transport the animals, all fueled by tens of millions of dollars in developer payments," the *Sentinel* reported. "From inspections of refuges late last year and last month, wildlife commission officials are alleging that they learned of mass deaths of tortoises and extensive evidence of improper care."

The state's investigation of the removal permit system has thrown everything into an uproar just as the state's development industry is pushing to build more homes and strip shopping centers and storage warehouses on tortoise habitat, Goessling said.

Some people regard this as a catastrophe. I contend it's a prime opportunity for reform.

When the Florida Legislature next convenes, I propose they pass a bill that would offer tortoise-killing builders like Pulte Homes a choice when they get caught.

We can call it the "Let's Make a Deal" bill. I picture a judge gazing down at quivering Pulte executives and telling them, in Wayne Brady's voice, "Thanks for pleading guilty—now it's time to PICK! YOUR! PENALTY!"

Option A: The company pays a fine of $1 million for each tortoise burrow destroyed. That per-burrow amount doubles if the number of burrows destroyed totals more than 10. Thus, in the Pulte Homes case in Ocala, instead of $13,700, Pulte would have faced a penalty of $44 million. Now THAT is how you send a message.

Option B: The guilty party pays the current maximum of $500 per tortoise burrow—but anything that the company builds on that piece of property has to prominently display a permanent, easily readable plaque that says, "This building was constructed by slaughtering an imperiled species that was valuable to the ecosystem."

To let the tortoise-protection law remain as lax as it is now would be, I think, a real crime—and not one of those funny ones that we like to laugh about.

24

Dirty Pictures

Legal Examiner, October 20, 2022

Michael Diana seems like an unlikely movie star. He's got a sallow face and long, stringy hair. He's so soft-spoken he can be hard to understand. He's got an odd criminal record in Florida.

But that criminal record is the reason for his stardom. In 1994, when he was 25, Diana became the first artist in American history to serve jail time for obscenity. When he walked into his cell at the Pinellas County (Florida) Jail, another inmate asked what he was in for.

"For drawing cartoons," Diana said.

"Damn," the inmate replied. "They'll throw you in here for anything!"

Now there's a documentary about his strange case. *Boiled Angels: The Trial of Mike Diana* is available on Amazon Prime, where anyone with an Internet connection can see both Diana's controversial drawings as well as the surreal path that justice took with his prosecution and punishment.

And in a twist, the documentary is responsible for finally putting his court case to rest.

* * *

It all started with a serial killer.

In the late 1980s, Diana, the son of a science teacher and a homemaker, was working as a convenience store clerk and living in Largo, Florida. He spent his off-hours drawing disturbing cartoons about rape, murder, and child molestation—all based on things he'd seen on the nightly news. He would use a copier to mass-produce the drawings and put them together into comic books he'd sell via mail order to perhaps 300 subscribers. He titled his comic books *Boiled Angel.*

Then, in 1990, detectives stumbled across a copy of *Boiled Angel No. 6* while investigating the grisly slayings of five college students at the University of Florida. The graphic drawings of murder and mutilation made the detectives suspect the cartoonist of committing the killings. They even sent officers to take a blood sample from Diana, who was quickly eliminated as a suspect. (The murders were actually the work of a drifter named Danny Rolling, who became known as "the Gainesville Ripper." The Rolling case was later cited as the inspiration for the *Scream* movie franchise.)

Still, detectives looking over his bizarre depictions of cannibalism and other horrors believed they showed crimes Diana might commit in the future.

A Pinellas County deputy, using an assumed name, purchased a copy *of Boiled Angel No. 7* through the mail. After some delay caused by prosecutors trying to figure out what to do about Diana, they charged him with three counts of obscenity.

Although Diana self-published his work, his arrest so outraged the comics community that the Comic Book Legal Defense Fund ended up spending more than $50,000 supporting his legal fight. That included hiring one of the Tampa Bay region's best-known free speech attorneys to defend him.

The shaggy-haired Luke Lirot had not built up his reputation by defending artists and writers, however. His clientele consisted primarily of strippers, and his arguments generally concerned whether their dance routines were protected by the First Amendment. Still, he was convinced Diana was being railroaded on ridiculous charges, and he lined up witnesses to say so—including Diana himself.

* * *

The March 1994 trial turned the normally quiet entrance to Pinellas County's misdemeanor courts into a media circus.

Anti-obscenity protesters showed up to wave signs for the television cameras and express shock about the drawings they would never have seen had Diana not been prosecuted. Meanwhile the defendant would arrive arm in arm with his new girlfriend, a club DJ who called herself Suzy Solar and who delighted in doing outrageous things to get the attention of the camera crews.

During his trial, Diana testified that he did not intend to sexually arouse his readers, which is one of the legal tests for material judged to be obscene. Instead, he said, he wanted to horrify the readers.

"I make it as ugly as possible," he said. "I want to make it really terrifying, because these things really terrify me."

Because another test for obscenity is that it has no artistic merit, Lirot brought in experts from San Francisco and New York to attest to the artistic

Michael Diana became the first cartoonist in America to be jailed for publishing obscene drawings. Photo courtesy of Michael Diana.

aspects of Diana's drawings. The lead prosecutor, Stuart Baggish, professed himself unimpressed. In his closing argument, he told the jury that Pinellas County "doesn't have to accept what is acceptable in the bathhouses in San Francisco, and it doesn't have to accept what is acceptable in the crack alleys of New York." What counts are local standards, he said.

The prosecution's witnesses included a Florida novelist named Sterling Watson, whose book *The Calling* featured a scene of a professor leading a gang rape, and who testified that he found no artistic merit in Diana's work, as well as a local psychologist named Sidney Merin, who testified that Diana's drawings showed a mind that could easily progress from imagining horrible crimes to committing them.

Merin, whom the criminal defense bar had long ago dubbed "Sid the Squid" because of his ability to squirt ink into the jury's face and confuse them, had not interviewed Diana prior to delivering that opinion.

The jury's deliberations took a mere 90 minutes. They found Diana guilty on all three counts.

The verdict came in on a Friday afternoon, but Pinellas County judge Walter Fullerton—who bore a striking resemblance to George Carlin—said he wasn't ready to pronounce sentence. He could have sent Diana home and told him to come back after the weekend.

Instead, Fullerton sent Diana to cool his heels in the county jail for three days before bringing him back into court.

After his weekend behind bars, Diana learned the sentence he'd drawn: three years of probation, a $3,000 fine, and 1,000 hours of community service.

Fullerton also ordered him to undergo drug testing (even though no one had accused him of being under the influence), take a journalism ethics course, get a psychological exam, stay away from minors, and draw nothing obscene.

That last condition meant that every time he put pen to paper, Diana had to think about what a probation officer would say about his choice of images.

Lirot appealed, citing a number of irregularities, including the fact that the judge called a recess right in the middle of Lirot's closing argument—something even Baggish found odd.

Ultimately a higher court tossed out one of the three counts, because it concerned a comic book called *Boiled Angel Ate* that Diana hadn't even drawn at the time he was charged. He had just promised it to his subscribers.

The appeals court also tossed the requirement that he take a drug test. But the appellate judge upheld the other two counts, and Lirot could not get any higher courts interested in undoing the conviction of an artist found guilty of drawing dirty pictures.

* * *

Although the Florida court system had punished Diana, in a way it had also done him a favor, plucking him from obscurity and making him nationally known.

Before long, the ex-inmate was appearing on TV talk shows, displaying paintings at the Museum of Modern Art, and delivering speeches in Amsterdam and Berlin. A rock groupie even cast his private parts in plaster—she'd done the same thing to Jimi Hendrix, she said.

By the time his appeals had run their course, Diana had quit his convenience store job and moved to New York, where he shared a rent-controlled Lower East Side apartment with a member of a band called "The Voluptuous Horror of Karen Black."

Why New York? Because, he said, he'd been invited by *Screw* publisher Al Goldstein to appear on his show, *Midnight Blue,* which taped there.

It didn't hurt that while he lived in New York, he could draw whatever he wanted without worrying about a probation officer raiding his home in search of obscene material.

A few years ago, Diana befriended a comics geek who called himself Mike Hunchback and a film director and historian named Frank Henenlotter. The trio began getting together once a week for a movie night, Hunchback said. Hunchback was well aware of Diana's claim to fame, he said, but Henenlotter was not.

"Then, after about a year of us watching movies together, [Henenlotter] looked it up and he was pretty knocked out," Hunchback said. The director immediately decreed that he had to make a documentary about Diana's case. Hunchback signed on as co-producer and Diana said he was willing.

Despite Diana's quick agreement, "it was not an easy undertaking," Hunchback said.

The production required shooting footage in multiple locations—not just Florida, but also Texas and Canada, Hunchback said. They were able to locate and interview Baggish, no longer a prosecutor, as well as Suzy Solar and one of the leaders of the groups that protested against Diana. They talked to Diana's parents, brother, and sister.

They lined up punk legend Jello Biafra of the Dead Kennedys to narrate. Acclaimed fantasy author and comics creator Neil Gaiman agreed to let them film an interview with him in his home. They even got to talk to legendary horror director George A. Romero before he died.

The filmmakers wove Diana's story into the whole history of comics, starting with the controversial EC Comics imprint of the 1940s and 1950s and the underground comix movement of the 1960s and '70s. They put it into the context of changing national mores in the 1980s and the rise of 'zine culture, too.

The biggest hurdle to getting the movie made was their star.

"Mike is an artist, not a public speaker," Hunchback said, who described his friend as "the sweetest guy in the world" and also "a loveable oddball." Getting him to speak up, and to tell his own story in something other than his usual matter-of-fact tone, "was the most difficult thing."

The other complication is one they discovered when they wanted to film some scenes of Diana back in Florida. It turned out he was a wanted man.

Between his moving to New York and the twists and turns of his appeals, he had lost track of where he stood on completing his probation. A quarter century after his trial, now bald and approaching 50, he was still not done with the case.

"I was still wanted in Florida on a violation of probation warrant and felt like I was sneaking around," Diana said.

No Florida deputies flew to New York to apprehend the ink-stained scofflaw. But whenever Diana would fly overseas for an exhibit or a lecture, his return home would lead to delays. Invariably, the Division of Homeland Security would hold him when he got off the plane, alerted to the presence of his outstanding warrant. Usually, Diana said, they would turn him loose once they found out Florida authorities wouldn't pay to extradite him over a mere misdemeanor.

The filmmakers enlisted Lirot's help to get Diana's legal obligations cleared up. They covered the costs for him getting records showing he'd taken a journalism ethics class at New York University and had undergone a psychological exam years before. Dealing with so much red tape was not Diana's forte, Hunchback said.

"I had to babysit the guy," he said, laughing. "I had to call him up and say, 'Hey Mike, you need to get up and go do this today.'"

Finally, in February, Diana convinced a court that he'd completed all the conditions of his probation and the warrant was withdrawn. He was a free man—the perfect ending for the documentary.

These days Diana continues painting and drawing the same things that once landed him in so much trouble, although he has yet to produce the real-life massacre that police feared. He's even partnered with a company called Threadlist to put his drawings on coronavirus masks to sell to fans. The horrors that once landed him in jail now seem to fit right in with everything else going on in 2020.

Diana has never married or had children. He frequently watches *Adult Swim* shows on the Cartoon Network or images in video games. To him they don't look all that different from his sketches in *Boiled Angel.* And nobody is screaming for anyone to go to jail over those.

"Everything seems more open now," he said.

25

So Long, Serge

CrimeReads, December 13, 2023

I am sad to report that we lost author Tim Dorsey at the end of November. He died at his home in Islamorada in the Florida Keys at age 62—far too young, if you ask me.

Tim, a bear-sized guy who frequently wore colorful tropical shirts, was the rare writer who was as funny in person as on the page. We served on quite a few book panels together, including one at the 2018 Bouchercon called "Doing Crime the Florida Man Way." He always made me (and the crowd) howl with his quick-witted cracks.

Tim had a spectacularly twisted sense of humor, as anyone who ever read one of his 26 novels could tell you. Starting with *Florida Roadkill* in 1999 and continuing through this year's *The Maltese Iguana,* Tim's books detailed the life, loves, crimes, and travels of Florida-obsessed homicidal maniac Serge Storms and his perpetually stoned Sancho Panza, Coleman.

Twenty-six books in 24 years is an impressive output, notes Carl Hiaasen, who has written 13 wacky Florida crime novels for adults in 37 years.

"What a body of work he had," Hiaasen told me. "He was very prolific—uh, not that I'm jealous or anything."

Each of Tim's books ties together a wide array of unlikely plot strands. For instance, in *Clownfish Blues,* he managed to include scenes involving the practice called "worm grunting," a stop by the Florida town known as the Psychic Capital of the World, jiggly-cam reality-show antics that aren't real at all, attempts to manipulate the state lottery, the proliferation of professional sign spinners, the sex lives of furries, and the way the old *Route 66* TV show somehow contrived to visit Florida even though Florida is nowhere near that famous highway.

The plot is usually set in motion by some trivial pursuit dreamed up by Serge that eventually puts him and Coleman in a position to pull off a ridiculously violent rescue of some innocent party. In *Naked Came the Florida Man,* for instance, the duo set out to visit the homes or final resting places of

Tim Dorsey and Craig Pittman at the 100th anniversary celebration for John D. MacDonald in Sarasota in 2016. Photo provided by Ellen India of the Sarasota County Public Library system.

such notable Florida authors as Zora Neale Hurston, Stetson Kennedy, and Marjorie Kinnan Rawlings. Serge says he wants to highlight those cultural heroes to counteract the spate of "Florida Man" stories, which he notes correctly often involve someone who's naked.

Of course, Serge and Coleman are the living embodiment of Florida Man—overconfident, often felonious, frequently buzzed, and typically oblivious to consequences.

Usually, Tim would slip in some scenes that directly reference real "Florida Man" headlines. There was the one about the guy who tossed an alligator through a Wendy's drive-through window. And the one about the fellow dressed as an Easter bunny who wound up in a street brawl. And the one about the astronaut in a diaper. And the one about guys on probation lining up to use a convenience store microwave to warm up their phony urine samples before submitting them to be tested. It was fun to read the Florida papers and guess which stories would wind up in Tim's next novel.

"I get criticized for being outlandish," Tim told me two years ago during an interview for my *Welcome to Florida* podcast. "But it's always the true stuff that people think goes too far."

He'd also occasionally turn Serge loose with a wild monologue about his views on society, religion, and so forth. One of his best occurs in *Triggerfish Twist* when, through a case of mistaken identity, Serge winds up delivering the commencement address at the University of South Florida's graduation ceremony in Tampa. He talks for three pages.

What most chuckling readers may not realize is how much research Tim put into each book. He drove all over Florida, following the route that he'd laid out for his characters. He'd visit oddball landmarks like the tree in Gainesville that was supposedly planted by Tom Petty, and even stay in sketchy motels that he'd then work into the storyline.

"I've got to go to the places in the book," he explained on the podcast. "I'll see things that keep it fresh."

Hiaasen, in discussing Dorsey's mad methods, shakes his head about that.

"He was much more intrepid about his research than me," Hiaasen said. "Some of the places he went, I wouldn't even go."

Real things that happened to Tim on these trips would wind up in the novels, and real people he'd met would be in there, too. For instance, baseball great Bill "Spaceman" Lee appears in *Tropic of Stupid*.

This started with *Florida Roadkill*. While he was making the road trip outlined in that first novel, Tim and a friend bought a pair of tickets from a scalper to see the Miami Marlins play the Cleveland Indians in the seventh game of the 1997 World Series (which the underdog Marlins won in extra innings). At the game, Tim ran into Pulitzer-winning *Miami Herald* humor columnist Dave Barry (soon to become an author of wacky crime novels too). Tim's over-the-top enthusiasm rattled Barry, so that he backed up a step. In *Florida Roadkill* it's Serge who encounters Barry at the big game and scares him. Serge, oblivious to his effect on others, concludes Barry must suffer from some sort of nervous condition.

The hyperactive, coffee-swilling Serge loves Florida so much that if he finds someone trying to ruin this paradise or exploit its most vulnerable citizens, he'll stop at nothing to stop them. That includes killing those very bad people in very creative ways, often involving some Rube Goldberg device he's created for the purpose. It's as if Groucho Marx took over the *Saw* franchise.

At one point, someone refers to him as a serial killer, and Serge objects to the term. He prefers to be called a "sequential" killer.

Tim's fans all have their own favorite of Serge's justifiable homicides. Some like the death-by-shrinking-jeans, or the electrocution via amusement park bumper car. Mine is the fate he designed for the maker of porn videos featuring women crushing small animals. He arranged for the guy to be crushed by Lu the Hippo, a real-life resident of Homosassa Springs

Preserve State Park once declared by a governor to be an official citizen of Florida.

That's classic Dorsey—quirky vigilante justice combined with sneaky lessons in Florida's often bizarre history and culture. On the podcast, I asked Tim what it was like walking around with a serial—excuse me, sequential killer in his head all the time, and he said, "I think that's a condition of living in Florida."

Believe it or not, Tim wasn't a Florida native. He was born in Indiana. But his mother quickly corrected that mistake and brought him to the right state when he was still a baby, so they could live near his grandparents. He grew up in a town in Palm Beach County called Riviera Beach.

"I had a great childhood!" he said. "I had a bike and I rode all over creation."

He'd go fishing, play pickup ball, or explore. He left the state to study at Auburn University in Alabama, but eventually returned to work as a reporter and editor at the *Tampa Tribune.* Journalism taught him how to write fast, and to write every day, no matter what.

He said he decided to write a novel "because newspapers paid just above the poverty line." In an early draft of *Florida Roadkill,* he killed everyone off, including Serge. But when he rewrote it, he reconsidered. Serge was such a fun character, and a way to say some things Tim wanted to say. Why not keep him around for another book or two? (He did kill off Coleman—and then brought him back a couple of books later with the silliest explanation possible.)

He had no expectation of selling that first book, but to his surprise a publisher picked it up.

"Before that first book had come out, I had written the second one," he said.

Tim's travels for research enabled him to make a lot of personal appearances at bookstores and festivals. He was always prepared. I once happened to see into the trunk of the big Cadillac road hog he drove. Unlike Serge, who usually has a trussed-up bad guy stuffed next to the spare tire, Tim's trunk was crammed with boxes of his books, plus samples of the Serge T-shirts, hats, and hot sauce he'd sell to his many diehard fans.

"He has a rabid following, with people getting tattoos of images from the books' cover art," one book event organizer told the *Palm Beach Post* in 2021.

One regular stop was the Miami Book Fair International, where Barry frequently recruits visiting authors such as Scott Turow to play with his comically inept band, the Rock Bottom Remainders. Hiaasen would play guitar but often became frustrated because Barry refused to share the song list in advance, so he had no way to practice.

But Tim never lost his cool, Hiaasen told me. That's because he'd picked the perfect instrument to play at these makeshift concerts: the triangle. No matter what the tune Barry called out, he'd simply ting-a-ling away, a broad smile on his face.

That's the way I'll remember Tim, playing his own distinctive instrument, coping with challenges in his own clever way, always smiling.

* * *

If you've never read any of Dorsey's novels, here are five to get you started. I chose them after consulting former *Miami Herald* book critic Connie Ogle, *South Florida Sun-Sentinel* mystery critic Oline Cogdill, and *Tampa Bay Times* book editor Colette Bancroft:

1. *Coconut Cowboy:* Besides the joy in watching Serge clean up a crooked town modeled on a notorious Florida speed trap, there's a delightful subplot involving a college student writing a thesis on how Florida is a harbinger of the future of America. His discussion of this thesis is both hilarious and completely accurate.

2. *The Pope of Palm Beach:* This may be Tim's sweetest book. Serge winds up doing several author events for a book he didn't write, and it's just as hilarious as it sounds (except for the part where a dead body winds up in the library after-hours book return slot). Tim said the oddball events on the book tour were taken from actual events on his own book tours.

3. *Shark Skin Suite:* Serge decides to help an ex who's now a lawyer, which at one point leads to him and Coleman putting on jackets that say BAIL BONDSMAN—FUGITIVE HUNTER and then rolling up on sleazy motels and seeing who tries to flee.

4. *Orange Crush:* Tim told me once that this was his poorest seller because Serge does not appear in the book until about the halfway point. That said, it's the funniest satire of Florida's sleazy politics ever written, reflecting Tim's experiences as the *Tampa Tribune*'s political editor.

5. *Florida Roadkill.* Why not start where it all began and see what hooked everyone? The book reads like a spoof of the movie *It's a Mad, Mad, Mad, Mad World* as a variety of violent parties pursue a briefcase containing $5 million. The one downside? Once you finish this one, you only have 25 more to go before you run out.

Part Four

WILD THING,
I THINK I LOVE YOU

26

A Whale of a Tale

Florida Phoenix, February 11, 2021

Nearly two years ago, I stood on the edge of an enormous hole in the sand at Fort DeSoto in St. Pete Beach, trying to remember to breathe through my mouth, not my nose.

This was not a contest to build the world's biggest sandcastle. It was more interesting than that. It was a scientific endeavor of a type I'd never seen before.

In the hole, about 100 yards from the beach, a team of biologists braved a horrible stench while excavating a rather large dead body—a whale that had been found off Everglades National Park about three months earlier.

At 38 feet, the carcass was roughly as long as a Greyhound bus, but somewhat smellier. (If you've ever ridden a Greyhound in Florida during the summer, as I have, you'll know what I mean.) It was also a key to understanding what's been called one of the rarest whales in the world.

When the dead whale first turned up floating in the water in January 2019, a dozen biologists converged on the 23,000-pound carcass. They hauled it ashore and spent a couple of days examining it, measuring it, and taking samples. Then they put it on a flatbed to be trucked across the state to Fort DeSoto for a temporary burial.

Now, under a broiling May sun, they were digging it back up. The time it spent underground made it easier to peel off the flesh and collect the skeleton. I saw people with master's degrees and doctorates wielding shovels. They were particularly careful in retrieving the eight-foot by four-foot skull.

Memories of that hot and sweaty day came flooding back recently when the National Oceanic and Atmospheric Administration—NOAA for short—announced that an examination of the skull, along with other evidence, had convinced experts that this is an entirely new species of whale that's been swimming around in the Gulf of Mexico for years.

"There's so much about the world's oceans and marine habitats that we don't know," Patricia Rosel of NOAA, the lead author on the scientific paper identifying the new species, told me this week. "There are new species of fish and corals being described every year."

Knowing this is a new species is a major step forward. The bad news: This new species is already considered endangered.

In fact, the one that turned up dead in 2019—the one that led to verification that it's a new species—was killed by human idiocy.

* * *

Did you even know that we have whales in the Gulf? I've lived on or near the Gulf most of my life but, until about five years ago, I didn't know about the whales. Even though I have been out in the Gulf dozens of times, I've never seen any.

But Rosel said that as far back as 2008, she and her colleagues not only knew about the existence of these whales but suspected they were something special.

The biologists would take boats out near where the whales had been spotted and shoot a dart into their skin using a crossbow or a rifle, she said. (Yes, that's right, scientists shoot darts at whales with crossbows—how cool is that?)

When they retrieved the dart, it would pull loose a small piece of skin that would provide them with the animal's DNA.

But, to verify it, they needed an actual specimen that they could compare to other whales, she said. That's why the one that turned up dead was such a boon to science.

While they were happy to have a whole whale to study, the reason it died remains the most disturbing part of the story. As the biologists cut it open and examined its insides, they discovered something that wasn't supposed to be there.

Inside one stomach was a square piece of plastic. Its shape resembled a cafeteria tray, but smaller and with a jagged edge.

You don't have to be Sherlock Holmes to know what happened. Chalk up another case of death-by-plastic. The square had sliced its way through two stomachs and wound up in the third one, damaging the whale's digestive system. Otherwise, the animal was healthy.

How did this hunk of hard plastic get into the Gulf and, thus, inside a whale? We can't say for sure, but to me it seems likely that some numbskull human tossed it in the water. I could even picture some yahoo skipping it across the waves to see how far it would go, completely oblivious to what would happen once it sank out of sight.

We humans tend to be clueless like that—self-involved and self-regarding but blind to the ramifications of our actions, particularly when it comes to plastic. We look at a vast body of water such as the Gulf and, instead of regarding it as a marvel full of mysteries, we treat it as a combination garbage pit/sewer. I have actually heard people claim that dilution is the solution to pollution, when clearly it is not.

Last fall, the environmental group Oceana surveyed dozens of government agencies, organizations, and institutions that collect data on the impact of plastic on marine animals The survey found that, since 2009, nearly 1,800 animals from 40 different species had been injured by swallowing or becoming entangled in plastic.

Nearly 90 percent were species listed as endangered or threatened.

"Incidences of plastic killing or injuring these animals were higher off the coasts of Florida and neighboring states than any other region in the U.S.," Oceana's Melissa Valliant told me.

NOAA scientists still don't know a lot about these whales, which they have dubbed "Rice's whale" after Dale Rice, the first person to suggest there was an unidentified whale species (in Latin, it's *Balaenoptera ricei*) in the Gulf.

"We're trying to understand what they eat, what their favorite food is, where they feed," Rosel said. "We think they feed near the ocean bottom."

Whaling ship records show that these whales used to occupy a much broader section of the Gulf than they do now. These days, they appear to swim in a very narrow corridor that stretches from Pensacola in the northern Gulf down to just south of the Tampa Bay area.

One reason for that narrowing of their habitat: The offshore oil industry has installed thousands of oil and gas platforms in the western Gulf, which creates lots of ship traffic to and from the coast.

The Rice's whales have abandoned that busy area for the quieter eastern Gulf where, thank heavens, oil drilling has so far been banned. The ban is set to expire next year, but Florida's two senators, Marco Rubio and Rick Scott, have introduced a bill to extend the ban another 10 years.

One question that biologists are still working to resolve is how many Rice's whales there are. They think a good estimate is fewer than 50. They also think there are far fewer than there used to be in 2010—again, because of human idiocy.

You may recall that 2010 was the year of the BP disaster. The Deepwater Horizon rig exploded, killing 11 crew members, and then sank beneath the waves. A busted pipe continued spewing oil from the bottom of the Gulf for another four months, putting gooey gunk on Florida beaches.

BP's 500-page response plan for a disaster was ridiculously bad. And by "ridiculous," I mean that, instead of actually investigating what was living in the Gulf, the company did a cut-and-paste job from their plans for other drilling sites.

Thus, for an oil spill in the Gulf, BP's list of affected animals included walruses, sea otters, sea lions, and seals, which are all far more common in Alaska. The only thing dopier than that is that federal regulators didn't catch this sloppiness until after the disaster occurred.

While it did mention whales, what the plan said was that they weren't permanent residents in the Gulf. Instead, they were listed for "seasonal use areas; migration routes."

Scientists are still learning what damage that oil spill did to the Gulf's marine life—killing dolphins, disrupting the reproduction of crabs, and causing ugly lesions on redfish—but they believe the Rice's whales suffered more than most.

Although the oil rig was outside their usual range, the oil that spewed out overlapped with where they live. The Rice's whales have no teeth for feeding. They have a substance called "baleen" that filters their food. Oil can get stuck in the baleen, making it tough for them to eat anything without swallowing oil.

Whales exposed to oil can suffer from lung and respiratory ailments, increased vulnerability to infections, and irritation of the skin or sensitive tissue in the whale's eyes and mouths.

As a result, biologists estimate that the BP oil from the Deepwater Horizon disaster killed 17 percent of the Rice's whale population. They also estimate that 22 percent of the females that survived suffered "reproductive failure"—in other words, they were unable to produce healthy, live calves.

When NOAA proposed adding these new whales to the endangered species list, you can probably guess the one group that objected: the offshore oil industry. They fear that protecting the Rice's whale will make drilling in the Gulf more difficult to carry out, and to them that's what's important— particularly if the drilling ban does end in 2022.

When I heard that, it occurred to me that maybe we buried the wrong thing on that sandy beach.

———————

Postscript: The ban on drilling in the eastern Gulf of Mexico has been extended to 2032.

27

To Kill a Panther

Florida Phoenix, February 17, 2022

They say that cats have nine lives. I am not sure that's the case with Florida panthers. Sometimes it feels like everything in the world is trying to snuff them out—everything human, that is.

In the 1950s, hunters killed so many panthers that state officials banned shooting them. In the 1970s, their primary habitat, the Big Cypress Swamp, was nearly turned into the world's largest airport (they were spared by, of all people, Richard Nixon). By 1995, there were so few left that inbreeding was producing major genetic defects.

Yet they have hung on like that kitten in the 1970s inspirational poster, and now there are about 200 slinking around what's left of Florida's wilderness.

That's still not a lot. And now a federal agency has decided it's OK to kill one.

Yes, you read that right. The U.S. Fish and Wildlife Service, the U.S. government agency in charge of protecting panthers and the one doing such a bang-up job protecting manatees, has imposed the death penalty on one of these rare cats.

I learned the story behind this bizarre decision by perusing about 400 government emails (What do you call a group of emails? A flurry?). I obtained them under Florida's wonderful Government in the Sunshine Law, which our legislature keeps trying to flush down the toilet like a batch of embarrassing White House documents.

Reading them kept me up past midnight, just like a good murder mystery, except in this case the murder hasn't happened—yet.

Who's the victim? Well, biologists studying panthers assign them all numbers, not names. It's a way to make sure they don't start treating these apex predators like pets. But a few panthers have made a name for themselves anyway.

Florida Panther 3, for instance, died accidentally while being captured, an incident that occurred during the early days of the state wildlife agency strapping radio collars on the big cats for research. That's the panther death that led to the discovery of the genetic defects. Its taxidermied remains are on display at the Florida State Archives in Tallahassee.

FP 62 was the first radio-collared panther to ford the Caloosahatchee River and prove panthers could live in other parts of the state besides southwest Florida. It roamed as far north as Disney's Animal Kingdom before its collar's battery conked out and we lost track of it forever.

Then there was FP 79, nicknamed "Don Juan" for his prolific breeding success. Er, um, we won't discuss that (blushes).

The panther I want to tell you about right now is FP 260. This cat experienced a brush with death, recovered, was celebrated for its successful release back into the wild, starred in a nature film and then—hoo boy! You can't see it, but I am shaking my head right now because of what happened next.

Beginning last fall, 260 became the center of a bizarre spectacle involving paintball guns, a pack of hunting dogs, and a politically connected rancher. As of February, we still haven't seen the end of it.

As a result of this high-profile conflict, the feds decided 260 has to die. The agency would prefer to capture this cat and stick it in a zoo forever, thus taking one of the 200 panthers back out of the wild and thwarting its potential to breed just as it reaches maturity.

But if no zoo is available, then the agency stands ready to dispatch 260 across the Rainbow Bridge. Or as the federal panther coordinator wrote in an email, "We will make plans for capture and euthanasia."

Florida's panther scientists disagree with that move. I would say "strongly oppose," but that seems like an understatement, based on the fiery emails they've sent.

One warned the consequences would include "public outrage" that would lead to "serious negative repercussions" for both the state and federal wildlife agencies. Another state employee wrote that she's been losing sleep over what the callous feds were about to do: "FP260 is not a criminal. He is a wild panther."

The federal Fish and Wildlife Service is ready to take such a drastic (and probably illegal) step for one simple reason. In the words of one state biologist, "FP 260 is the renegade panther with a taste for veal, unfortunately."

* * *

Florida Fish and Wildlife Commission biologists crouch over injured Florida Panther 260 after it was hit by a car. Photo by the Florida Fish and Wildlife Commission.

Years ago, the main cause of death for male panthers was other male panthers. They're territorial animals. When one male moves into another male's territory, a fight inevitably ensues, sort of like when my mullet-haired cousins from the Panhandle go to their local roadhouse.

But over the last 20 years, as new roads were built through panther habitat and lots of cars and trucks zoomed down those roads, the leading cause of death became vehicle collisions. In 2020, 19 of the 22 panthers found dead had been flattened by cars.

FP 260 nearly became No. 20 on the roadkill roll call.

Fortunately, after a car clobbered the cat in December 2020, someone who witnessed the collision stopped to check on the victim, thinking it was dead.

"Surprisingly, he found the cat still alive and made sure no other cars struck it," Immokalee rancher Liesa Priddy wrote on a Facebook post for her JB Ranch. "After a few minutes the cat made his way across the road and under a fence onto my ranch property."

Priddy called the Florida Fish and Wildlife Conservation Commission. Soon a team of biologists showed up, tranquilized the injured panther, and took it to the Naples Zoo for treatment and rehabilitation.

Priddy, in her Facebook post, wrote that it would be "released back in southwest Florida, ideally on someone else's property."

Fortunately, 260 didn't break any bones. Veterinarians cleared the cat for release after just two weeks. Biologists strapped a radio-collar on the panther's neck, named it FP 260, and turned it loose in the Florida Panther National Wildlife Refuge.

Having been hit once, FP 260 apparently learned an important lesson about avoiding a second such near-death experience. As excited biologists tracked its radio-collar positions, they saw it began navigating the area using underpasses.

"By using up to 12 different wildlife crossings, FP 260 has been able to safely access Florida Panther National Wildlife Refuge, Fakahatchee Strand State Preserve, and Big Cypress National Preserve without ever setting a paw on a paved road," a wildlife commission press release stated. The panther's adaptation was so remarkable that it was noted by a local TV report.

A short film called *Wildlife in Our Backyard* featured FP 260 too. In the movie, sponsored by the Florida Wildlife Federation and shown at several festivals, the narrator says that 260 "can show us what success looks like" for humans sharing the Florida landscape with wildlife. "He is successfully living and navigating the fragmented landscape. . . . FP 260's future is bright, demonstrating hope for all of our native wildlife."

By the time the movie hit the fall festival circuit, though, FP 260 had returned to the JB Ranch and started preying on Liesa Priddy's calves. Normally, panthers prefer to eat deer or feral hogs. But starting in October and running through December, FP 260 took down nearly a dozen of her heifers.

Priddy is a former state wildlife commissioner whose tenure was—oh, what's a good word for it? Controversial? Yes. Headline-making? Sure. The subject of ethics complaints? That too, but she was cleared.

She has been complaining about panthers attacking her cattle for more than a decade. She has never been shy about calling, texting, or emailing state and federal officials to demand they do something about her losses, and for a very good reason.

"It's nice for agency folks to empathize with ranchers who are losing calves; but it doesn't seem to register what we are really losing is dollars," she wrote in one email about FP 260 to a top wildlife commission official written in blood-red letters. "Our ranch loses at least $25,000 per year from this problem. Anyone you know want a $25,000 pay cut?"

In 2016, Priddy became the first rancher ever compensated by the federal government for losing cows to Florida's official state animal. But the reimbursement process is slow and full of red tape, she told me when she and I talked this week.

Now, in a matter of months, a single panther had chomped on at least 10 of her calves, and she demanded action, pronto.

"She understands that we do not typically capture, relocate, [or] haze panthers in most scenarios unless there is a human safety concern," state panther biologist Dave Onorato said in an October email regarding FP 260.

But as Priddy's calf losses mounted, her calls for help went to higher-ups including the chairman of the state wildlife commission and the head of the federal wildlife agency in Florida. As a result, the state and federal agencies broke from the "typical."

First, they tried "hazing." They used a pack of hounds normally employed to track the panthers for collaring the cats and chased FP 260 away from one of its kills, treeing it not once but twice.

Then they fired what are known as "shell crackers" using a paintball gun, a method usually used to scare off bears. When the federal panther coordinator, David Shindle, heard about the panther's appearance in the *Wildlife in Our Backyards* movie, he joked, "FP 260's future is bright . . . illuminated by the dazzling pyrotechnic displays of shell crackers."

That didn't deter the persistent panther. It would not depart Priddy's ranch.

For their next step, in November, state biologists tried relocation—capturing the cat and moving it.

"After anaesthetizing him, they transported him from the JB Ranch to the Fakahatchee Strand Preserve State Park," Onorato wrote in an email.

They turned it loose at a spot 18 miles south of the ranch. A little more than a week later, FP 260 returned to the free smorgasbord provided by Priddy's herd, in almost the exact same spot where it had been captured.

Shindle's job involves all 200 or so of the panthers, but he was giving this one his full attention. He made repeated visits to the JB Ranch, checking the places where FP 260's radio-collar had been pinpointed.

Once, he nearly stumbled into the object of the uproar. He joked that "I was so close that I looked into his eyes and could see his soul."

In a November report on that encounter and their options for dealing with FP 260, Shindle wrote that all the panther's attacks "have so far not included a potential human safety concern." Under their official Panther

Response Plan, the state and federal agencies still classified this as a low-risk situation—annoying and expensive, but not a threat to humans.

But then, in December, that changed.

* * *

Newspaper accounts of the 1800s and early 1900s are rife with wild stories of panthers attacking humans. However, the number of documented Florida panther attacks on people is exactly (carry the one, add the remainder) zero.

Even though our cars and trucks kill them with a sickening regularity, the panthers would prefer to slink off than tangle with us hairless apes.

Yet in December, Priddy told federal officials that she feared FP 260 would attack a human. That gave them the legal pretext they needed to declare it a threat deserving death.

Shindle, in a late December email, wrote that his agency had "determined that Florida panther FP 260 should be permanently removed from the wild on the basis of the following federal authority"—and here he cited a specific federal regulation on endangered species—which "provides for removing animals that constitute a demonstrable but non-immediate threat to human safety."

Then he wrote that if they couldn't find a zoo to take it, "the USFWS will exercise the above authority to kill this panther." Like Steven Seagal, FP 260 was now marked for death. (Cue suspense music.)

Shindle wrote that the leadership of the state wildlife commission—chairman Rodney Barreto and executive director Eric Sutton—"concurred with the above determination." They did so even though it is counter to what their own biologists want and constitutes a step that longtime environmental advocates say is unprecedented.

I asked Priddy about her fear of 260, telling her that, in my experience, she's never been afraid of anything—including reporters asking snarky questions. What made her fear this panther?

She told me it happened when she accompanied biologists investigating one of her dead calves: "The panther was still nearby, and I saw it looking at us."

How did 260 react to seeing humans so close? "It crouched, watched, and silently moved away," she said.

I told her that didn't sound like threatening behavior. She said she'd seen videos of cougars out West attacking their prey and knew that these big predators are "nothing to mess with." Then she said, "Who knows what goes on in their heads?"

One thing Priddy had not included in any of her emails, but that she told me when I asked, is that she has been reimbursed for the loss of eight of her 11 lost calves.

The Naples Zoo—the institution that cared for FP 260—paid her $752 per calf, which she said was last year's market price. That's a tad over $6,000. They would have given her money for the other three, she said, but that's all their budget allowed.

So, to sum up: Because one influential person who's seen some YouTube videos got n-n-nervous being close to a panther, and because she is out roughly $2,200 for the uncompensated loss of three calves, the might and power of the federal government stands ready to turn 260 into dead meat.

This cat, once hailed as a success story for its dogged survival, would become, to borrow the words of *Monty Python's Flying Circus,* "A stiff! Bereft of life, he rests in peace! He's shuffled off his mortal coil, rung down the curtain and joined the bleedin' choir invisible!! THIS IS AN EX-PANTHER!"

Fortunately, 260 so far is (to quote a different Python sketch) not dead yet.

The reason is simple: Calving season ended at the JB Ranch. Around the time some ill-informed muckety-muck in Atlanta or Washington turned thumbs-down on its future, the young panther with the ravenous appetite left, heading back to wilderness far from cars and humans. Thus, "killing the panther is not being considered," an agency spokesman said this week.

Its well-timed departure at least gives everyone time to reconsider this boneheaded decision. I can't understand what the wildlife service bureaucrats were thinking but, as Priddy said of panthers, who knows what goes on in their heads?

I asked Priddy if killing this panther or locking it away in a zoo forever, all on her say-so, would be a tragedy.

"No," she said. "There's plenty more to take its place."

28

Oh, Deer

Florida Phoenix, March 10, 2022

Have you ever seen a Key deer? They're like a regular white-tail deer but scaled down to the size of a big dog. It's as if someone crossed Bambi with Marmaduke.

I saw one for the first time in 2017 while driving through the Keys. This was a few months after Hurricane Irma plowed through the place. The roadsides were piled high with debris and every breeze carried a strong whiff of backed-up sewage.

First, I stopped at the National Key Deer Refuge visitor's center, which at the time happened to be in a strip mall on Big Pine Key, next door to a pack-and-ship place and a martial arts academy. I wanted to make sure the refuge was open and that the deer had survived the storm. The staffers said yes (which I now know was not quite true).

I drove into the refuge and, once I got far enough off the beaten path, I stopped and got out of my car. As I strolled amid the smashed trees and torn-up underbrush, I saw a couple of the deer foraging for food. I wouldn't call them "small" exactly—maybe a better word is "fun-sized."

The diminutive deer have been on the endangered list since the first one was drawn up in 1967, along with such better known (and bigger) Florida critters as the panther and the manatee. But just two years after I spotted that pair amid the post-hurricane wreckage, the Trump administration proposed taking them off the list.

What a silly idea, I thought then. There are no more than 1,000 Key deer. They get run over a lot. And they live on hurricane-prone islands vulnerable to a rising sea level. Surely, they are the very definition of "endangered."

But then last week I read a story in a British newspaper, the *Guardian*, that outlined just how the U.S. Fish and Wildlife Service under then-president Trump tried really, really hard to get Key deer taken off of that list. When that didn't work, the goal shifted to knocking the deer down a peg to merely "threatened."

"Wait," you say, "that sounds kinda familiar. Didn't the feds do that to another iconic Florida species?"

How perceptive you are, dear reader! I bet you remember everything you're supposed to buy when you go to the grocery store, too. (I'm lucky if I get out of Publix with fewer than two phone calls home for guidance.)

Yes, the Fish and Wildlife Service has already taken that same step with the manatee, ignoring the advice of scientists (1,000 dead manatees last year shows you how well that's worked out). And now that same agency is considering something similar with the panther.

That's why it's instructive to see, with the Key deer, how the feds twisted both the English language and scientific data to try to meet a political goal of dumping them.

It's all because of a WIG—and not the fabulous blonde kind that turns bald RuPaul into a Glamazon.

* * *

Key deer and panthers have something else in common: Both wound up on that first endangered list 55 years ago because humans kept shooting them. By the 1950s, these mighty Nimrods had shot so many of the deer that scientists said there were only a tiny number remaining—a mere 25.

The feds opened the deer refuge in 1958, guaranteeing the animals would have at least some safe habitat left, even as humans were building homes, stores, and roads all around them. But the refuge didn't guarantee their future, any more than buying a house guarantees you'll always have plenty to eat and drink.

Development outside the refuge eliminated a lot of the plants they regularly consumed and the freshwater ponds where they found something to drink. Meanwhile, the fearless deer kept wandering into people's backyards and walking right up to them, not unlike Fido begging for treats.

People gave them junk food, sometimes while sticking their hands out of their car windows to do it. Key deer began hanging around the roads, which meant they were more likely to be flattened.

They faced other challenges, too. An infestation of flesh-eating screwworms in 2016 wiped out 15 percent of the population.

And it turns out they didn't do so well during Irma, either.

"A lot of them were killed," a retired biologist named Novy Silva, who began studying Key deer back in 1971, told me this week. "A lot of them drowned."

Irma sent a massive storm surge sweeping across the Keys, he explained.

The surge not only destroyed the buttonwood and mangroves they eat, but left saltwater in a lot of the places the deer used for slaking their thirst.

The deer became badly dehydrated, according to Jan Svejkovsky, who helps run the organization Save Our Key Deer.

The need for fresh water became so dire, he told me, that they convinced refuge employees to set out brightly colored kiddie pools filled with water for the deer to drink. It was a desperate measure, like the biologists tossing out lettuce for the Indian River Lagoon's starving manatees this spring.

Remember that kiddie pool scene like it's an item on your grocery list. It will prove to be important later.

Despite Irma, despite the screwworms, despite all the cars that run them down, and the weirdo who tied up three of them and stuffed them in his car so he could take pictures with them—despite all that, some of the feds believed the Key deer could be booted off the endangered list.

The wildlife service's regional office in Atlanta had decreed that, while Trump was in office, they were going to meet what a 2017 memo from assistant regional director Leo Miranda called "Wildly Important Goals," or WIG for short.

As we all know, a wig is commonly used to cover up something you want to hide. This WIG met that definition.

To fully appreciate the absurdity of what comes next in the WIG saga, I recommend you cue up the B-52s single by that name and play it while you read.

"Our WIG for FY17 was to conserve 30 species by delisting, downlisting, or precluding the need to list them," Miranda wrote.

How do you "conserve" species by booting them off the endangered list, kicking them down the protection ladder to "threatened," or never letting them on the list in the first place? No explanation for that tortured use of the term was ever offered. It carries the flavor of the Vietnam-era claim of "we had to destroy the village to save it."

Among the 30 species that Miranda proudly cited as successfully meeting the WIG for the 2017 fiscal year was the Florida manatee. Manatees had never achieved the long-established criteria for being changed from endangered to threatened, but the agency cited computer models that said they'd be OK. Miranda's memo makes it clear the wildlife agency did that just to meet the phony-baloney WIG.

Miranda then targeted the Key deer for the same WIG treatment, but more extreme. He drafted a memo to the agency's top official, proposing "to delist the Florida Key deer."

Said the memo: "This determination is based on the best available scientific and commercial information, which indicates that the threats to this species have been eliminated or reduced to the point that the species no longer meets the definition of an endangered or threatened species."

The biggest lie in that sentence is the part about using "the best available scientific . . . information."

Miranda wrote that there were "uncertainties regarding what effects changes in sea-level will have on Florida Key deer." To make that assertion, he ignored a draft study circulated by the agency's own scientists just a year earlier that said, flat-out, "The Florida Keys are going underwater due to sea level rise (SLR). All SLR scenarios agree and depict this to happen."

More subtle, and thus sneakier, was a claim that Key deer would not lack for drinking water because they could handle a high level of saltiness. Here's the part where you should remember the kiddie pools and think of a different abbreviation besides WIG (Hint: It's spelled "B.S.")

The basis for that ridiculous statement was a passing comment in a 1974 paper from a researcher that he'd seen deer drinking from one pond with a high salinity level, Svejkovsky told me. Someone working with that researcher had seen deer tracks near a pond with an even higher salinity. Neither report was peer-reviewed. That was it. There have been no subsequent studies.

"They were looking for any way they could to include the Key deer as one of those 30 species in the WIG," Diana Umpierre of the Sierra Club told me.

The wildlife agency announced it would hold a public hearing on delisting the Key deer in August 2019—but it would not release the report spelling out why it wanted to delist the deer until after the meeting. That secrecy made it difficult to urge the service to flip its WIG and spare the deer. But environmental groups condemned it anyway.

"Stripping the Key deer of protections to meet an arbitrary quota is like kicking a critically ill patient out of the emergency room to free up bed space," Jaclyn Lopez, Florida director of the Center for Biological Diversity, told the *Miami Herald*.

The Sierra Club and Center for Biological Diversity sued to get access to all the federal records. In the meantime, the U.S. Geological Survey stepped in with a report that Miranda's recommendation had failed to consider the "best" information about what rising seas would do to the deer's island home.

In May 2020, the agency changed its WIG (I picture this happening in a smoky backstage dressing room filled with feather boas). Now it tried to knock the deer down to threatened. By February 2021, though, the environmental groups had won legal access to most of the records and were (sorry for this one, folks) wigging out.

By this point, Trump had left office, and the urgency to achieve those WIGs had disappeared like so many classified documents that later turned up at Mar-a-Lago. The wildlife agency employs a watchdog in charge of "scientific integrity," and last August he gave the Key deer down-listing report the equivalent of an F- in high school biology.

* * *

I tried to get Miranda—now the regional supervisor—to answer questions about all this. I was told he was unavailable. Maybe he was out wig-shopping. I bet he looks smashing in a bouffant.

Instead, I got a statement from the agency's spokesman, Chuck Underwood, saying they were not contemplating any change to the Key deer's endangered status now. Instead, they're doing a five-year assessment—nothing more.

When I asked the folks from Save Our Key Deer who would gain from dropping Key deer from the endangered list, the organization's president, Valerie Preziosi, said the answer was obvious: "People who want to overdevelop the Keys. They'll be able to develop huge tracts of land" that are now off-limits to protect the deer.

But their profit would be short-lived. Climate change is not going away, and that Keys land will be inundated soon, regardless of whether it belongs to deer or the developers.

Our fine legislature, which is OK with spending millions of tax dollars on walls, pumps, and pipes to cope with sea level rise, just shut down an attempt at dealing with the cause. Governor Ron "Barks-at-Teenagers" DeSantis refuses to take action, too, sneering that that's just "left wing stuff."

The way things are going, we're eventually going to need to relocate those poor deer to some dry land, Svejkovsky told me.

Here's my suggestion: Move the entire herd to Atlanta. Put them in the Fish and Wildlife Service regional office there. That's pretty far from any rising seas.

In order to make room for them, we'll need to relocate the wildlife service's regional office and its employees to the Key Deer Refuge—after making sure they can all swim.

Gee, I wonder if you can use a WIG as a PFD.

29

Welcome to Gatorland

FORUM, Fall 2023

About 1:20 a.m. on October 11, 2015, 24-year-old Joshua James pulled up to the drive-through line at a Wendy's in Royal Palm Beach and ordered a drink. When he drove forward and the restaurant employee handed him his drink, James did something that made him nationally famous, albeit under the name "Florida Man."

He tossed an alligator through the window, then drove away.

The armored reptile, which James had spotted by a roadside and taken into his car, was only about three and a half feet long. He thought it would be a funny prank to throw it into the fast-food restaurant.

The woman running the drive-through didn't think it was funny. When the gator went flying by her head, she jumped out of the drive-through window to escape. After a call to 911, a state wildlife officer showed up, caught the alligator, and carried it to a nearby canal, where he turned it loose.

Then, using surveillance video and records of a purchase made at a nearby convenience store, police tracked down James, who was arrested and charged with assault with a deadly weapon—to wit, the alligator.

Many Florida Man stories that make national news are alligator tales. The reptiles known to science as *Alligator mississippiensis* inspire endless fascination—and fear—in people.

These formidable creatures, which can grow to 14 feet long and weigh more than 1,000 pounds, are so well adapted for survival that they have remained virtually unchanged for at least eight million years—a rarity among vertebrate species.

And in Florida, they are ubiquitous, numbering more than 1.3 million. That is one alligator for every 13 or so residents.

They live in freshwater lakes, slow-moving rivers and, of course, soggy wetlands. But you will also find them in man-made bodies of water such as canals and golf course water hazards. A rule of thumb: If water covers an area larger than a mud puddle, you should assume that it contains at least one alligator.

That means they are sometimes literally living in our backyards, a strange and occasionally lethal juxtaposition of a savage prehistoric holdover alongside pampered 21st-century human beings.

But not everyone is as wary as they ought to be. One popular 2016 Florida story concerned a Lakeland woman fighting state wildlife officials to keep her pet alligator, Rambo. She would dress Rambo in costumes and perch him on an all-terrain vehicle for photos.

"Everybody tells me he is vicious, but I kiss him on the mouth," Mary Thorn, a former pro wrestler, told the *Lakeland Ledger*. State officials worked out a deal where she could keep Rambo but had to stop renting him out for parties.

A 2023 story about another Floridian and an alligator had a more tragic outcome. An 85-year-old woman in Fort Pierce was walking her dog near a pond when an alligator made a grab for her pet. She stumbled and the alligator dragged her into the water and killed her.

Stories about fatal alligator attacks make news. In 2016, after two-year-old Lane Graves was snatched by an alligator from the shore of a lake at Disney World as his father frantically attempted to save him, the heartbreaking search for the toddler's remains dominated the media for days.

But such attacks are rare. In Florida, a total of 26 people were killed by alligators from 1948 to 2021.

Our obsession with alligator stories reveals plenty about our state and how it has changed through the years. Alligators were once classified as endangered. Now they have made such a comeback that the state maintains a Statewide Nuisance Alligator Program—SNAP for short.

"We would consider the population to be stable now," says Allan "Woody" Woodward, a former alligator researcher with the Florida Fish and Wildlife Conservation Commission.

* * *

Scattered around Florida are multiple alligator-themed tourist attractions, including the granddaddy of the bunch, Gatorland. Owen Godwin Sr. founded it in 1949 in Orlando as the Florida Wildlife Institute.

Godwin stocked 16 acres of what had been a road construction borrow pit with alligators and snakes. He hired Seminole Indians to live on the property in a fake village and wrestle the alligators for the amusement of tourists.

The entrance to Gatorland. Photo from the Florida State Archives.

Renamed in 1954, Gatorland now covers 110 acres and draws between 500,000 and 600,000 customers a year. They pass through a cartoonish entrance that looks like a gaping gator's mouth to gawk at its collection of 2,500 alligators and crocodiles, plus emus, zebras, and other animals.

"People visit Central Florida for two things: that big old mouse and alligators," says Brandon Fisher, media relations director of Gatorland.

Park rangers at Shark Valley in Everglades National Park, where alligators often bask in the sun along the trail, tell stories about visitors who don't understand that the motionless animals are dangerous. One tourist wanted to perch her child on an alligator's back for a photograph.

Many of Gatorland's customers are equally clueless about alligators. For instance, Fisher says, "People ask us why we let all the little alligators run around loose; what they mean are the little lizards you see all over."

Tourists who can't tell an anole from an alligator aren't the only ones short on knowledge. Most people don't know that alligators can climb fences and trees. They can also run as fast as 11 mph and swim as fast as 20 mph.

Another little-known fact: Alligators are often classified as a "keystone" species, vital to maintaining the state's ecological systems. For example, alligators consume large numbers of predatory gar fish, which otherwise would prey on gamefish populations; the deep holes they dig become reservoirs for fresh water during dry periods and nurture many other species; and as they swim, they help clear invasive vegetation and keep waterways open. They are also our first line of defense against the invasive Burmese pythons taking over the Everglades, sometimes battling the snakes to death.

And then there's eye-shine. Florida photographer John Moran knew all about that and used it to capture an iconic image.

An alligator's eyes contain a layer of cells called the tapetum lucidum—a Latin phrase meaning "bright carpet"—beneath the photoreceptor cells in the retina. This reflects light and improves vision in low-light conditions, which is important since alligators often hunt at night. It also makes their eyes appear to shine.

One spring evening in 1990, Moran climbed a bluff overlooking Paynes Prairie Preserve State Park in Gainesville and scanned the watery scene before him with a flashlight. He had expected to see several dozen eyes shining back.

"I was stunned to realize I was looking at hundreds of pairs of eyes glowing back at me in the approaching dark," he recalls. With a camera held steady by a tripod, he picked his shot: "Focusing on the big gator in the foreground as a reference point, the nature of those 43 pairs of light-points becomes instantly apparent in the picture."

Moran's photo has been reproduced many times, including as a two-page spread in *Life* magazine. When he displays the photograph and is asked by admirers if he was afraid, he says no. He adds, however, that the purchase of a print automatically grants the owner permission to claim that he or she assisted on the shoot by knocking the alligators away with a canoe paddle.

"Animals that can eat you alive speak to our deepest dread," Moran says. "And the thought of being eaten in the dark only makes the drama more compelling."

* * *

Alligators held a special place in the culture of the Indigenous tribes that first populated what became the Florida territory.

"In much the way the tribes of the Western plain revered and made use of the bison, tribes of the Southeast ate alligator meat, used their bones, claws, teeth and hides and regarded them as so much more than beast," Rebecca Renner wrote in *Gator Country: Deception, Danger, and Alligators in the Everglades.*

Their name comes from what the Spanish explorers called them: *el lagarto,* or "the lizard." To the Spaniards, gators seemed like dragons—but they soon learned that the animals could be "both dragon and dinner," to quote Renner.

The first scientist to study the Florida alligator was pioneering naturalist William Bartram. who visited the St. Johns River in the 1770s and documented two alligators battling each other, noting of one that "clouds of smoke issue from his dilated nostrils. The earth trembles with his thunder."

One day when Bartram was paddling across a lagoon, several alligators attacked him, he wrote, "roaring terribly and belching floods of water over me." He also recorded that when a group of alligators bellowed, "the dreadful roar is re-echoed for hundreds of miles all around."

According to Kathryn Braund, an Auburn University history professor who has studied Bartram's writings, the explorer's tales were significant in the scientific classification of the alligator. "He made some mistakes but got a lot of the behavioral observations correct," she wrote.

Bartram's descriptions of Florida's fearsome swamp creatures mesmerized Northerners. The alligators soon became a cultural symbol, synonymous with the state of Florida but also linked to racial stereotypes, according to Virginia Tech history professor Mark Barrow, who received a National Endowment for the Humanities fellowship to complete his forthcoming book, *Gator Tales: The Making of a Florida Icon.*

Barrow, who grew up in Gainesville, has explored images and descriptions of the alligator in sources including newspaper archives, tourist brochures, souvenirs, and postcards. He says that after the Civil War, captive alligators in circuses, traveling shows, and amusement parks became marketing tools to draw in crowds. They were also the leading attraction at Florida parks known as "alligator farms" for visitors who began to discover the state in the late 1800s.

It became popular for tourists to take home baby alligators as pets—although "once they grew and became unruly," Barrow notes, most were soon discarded. (Among Barrow's rich trove of alligator trivia: the first episode filmed of *Leave it to Beaver* featured Wally and Beaver ordering a baby Florida alligator from the back of a comic book and hiding it from their parents in a toilet; the censors, afraid American audiences would be shocked by seeing a bathroom on the debut of a TV series, ended up delaying the episode until later in the season.)

Soon after Bartram's journals were published, assertions by whites that alligators preferred Black flesh began to spread, says Barrow. Over the next century, caricatures of cowering Black people being attacked by alligators proliferated on everything from stereo view cards, photographs, and sheet music to advertising.

"In the aftermath of the Civil War, as part of a campaign white Americans undertook to suppress and keep Black Americans out of power, 'alligator bait' became a pervasive racial slur," says Barrow. He points to a photograph showing a group of naked African-American babies with the caption "Alligator Bait," which was widely reproduced. "People put it up in their parlors and places of business in both North and South," he says. "Not until the modern Civil Rights movement did such racist images fall out of favor."

Barrow's book will also examine perhaps the most famous modern symbolic use of the alligator—as a mascot for his alma mater, the University of Florida.

*　*　*

At one point, explorer Bartram claimed, an alligator got too close so "I soon dispatched him by lodging the contents of my gun in his head." As more people began to arrive in Florida in the 1800s and 1900s, that was the most common response to seeing an alligator: blow its brains out.

"It was just a wholesale slaughter from the 1870s to the 1960s," says Kent Vliet, a retired University of Florida biology professor who began studying alligators in 1980. "We had about a century of animals being killed by the hundreds of thousands."

Beyond fear and a twisted sense of sport, Vliet says, much of the killing was for profit—to harvest the hides, many of which were sold to fashion houses in France and Italy.

An 1893 federal fisheries report found that alligator hides had become a lucrative industry, with Florida at the center of the trade. The report figured some 2.5 million hides had been shipped out of the state since 1880. Two Jacksonville firms handled more than 60,000 skins in a single year.

The alligator was being "systematically and relentlessly hunted in nearly every part of Florida," the report noted, suggesting that it was "only a question of time when this valuable fishery resource will become exhausted."

By the 1960s, Americans were becoming concerned about the potential extinction of several species. In 1967, the U.S. Fish and Wildlife Service proposed an endangered list that included animals from Florida: panthers, manatees, Key deer, and alligators. (A Florida man, Nathaniel Reed, was instrumental in getting the Endangered Species Act passed in 1973.)

Meanwhile, the widespread explosion of post–World War II development paved over or filled in much of the alligators' swampy habitat. As a result, activists persuaded state and federal officials to preserve key parcels, including Everglades National Park and Big Cypress National Preserve.

Once they were a protected species with some protected habitat, alligators bounced back. By 1988, Florida wildlife officials were so confident that the population had recovered that they launched an annual alligator hunt, with licensed hunters allowed to take up to two per person. (About half of the 2,000 hunters who participated in 2022 managed to bag their two. About 30 percent failed to get any.)

The state also licensed dozens of independent trappers to capture and remove alligators that had been declared a nuisance after showing up too close to a school or invading a homeowner's garage.

The trappers have, from time to time, complained about poor compensation for providing this state-funded service. When a crowd of upset trappers showed up at a 2012 wildlife commission meeting, one commissioner said the state should shut down SNAP. He explained that when he's faced with intrusions of "vicious cockroaches and ants," he calls, and pays for, the services of a private exterminator.

Another commissioner objected to that comparison: "Unlike roaches, gators do eat people," he said. "You can't just step on them."

* * *

Like humans, alligators can suffer from polluted habitats. Between 1980 and 1987, the gator population in Lake Apopka in central Florida declined dramatically. An investigation found remnants of DDT chemicals, many of which turned up in the reptiles' eggs.

"There were contaminants in Lake Apopka that affected the expression of gender and sexual characteristics in alligators," former state researcher Woodward explains. "The source was a bunch of vegetable farms on the north end of the lake."

To solve the problem, the local water management agency bought the farms and turned them into reservoirs, he says.

Natural habitat remains the biggest problem facing alligators, as more than 350,000 newcomers a year crowd into Florida, now the nation's fastest growing state, which already has more than 22 million residents.

Driven from the vanished swamps, alligators take up residence on developed property that encompasses bodies of water. "The more people move into these areas, there's going to be conflict," Woodward adds.

Some conflicts come from people treating the animals like pets. In 2012, an Everglades airboat tour captain who spiced up his tours by luring alligators close to his boat with marshmallows discovered that the big reptiles tend to bite the hand that feeds them. He lost his.

A 2019 study of alligator bites dating back to 1971 found that alligators mostly bite adult men who live in Florida year-round. Thirty of the bite reports came from people who encountered alligators on golf courses, including one man who frequently dove into water hazards to retrieve lost golf balls. He was bitten four times over 15 years.

Alligators are far from picky eaters and will grab food wherever they can. They have been known to scarf down anything from snails to possums to 20-pound dogs.

"If alligators had a PR firm, we'd try to put a stop to that," says retired professor Vliet, who added that the key to living near alligators is "to offer them the respect of staying away from them." He recommends maintaining a 40- to 50-foot distance.

* * *

As scary as alligators look, they may wind up saving your life.

Scientists have learned their blood contains elements that are highly resistant to bacteria, Vliet explains. That includes strains of bacteria known to be resistant to antibiotics. In one Louisiana study, alligator blood destroyed a significant amount of HIV, the virus causing AIDS.

Vliet says he is now working with scientists at George Mason University to identify those antiviral peptides and extract and isolate them. So far, they have found hundreds, perhaps thousands of them, each targeted to block a different strain of bacteria.

"[Alligators] are carrying an arsenal of peptides that can attack any bacteria that invades their bodies," he adds. Some of the blood samples being studied came from creatures at the St. Augustine Alligator Farm Zoological Park.

Although the Defense Department has been funding the research with an eye toward the treatment of wounded soldiers, it could also help injured or infected people who have never set foot on a battlefield.

Anticipating the day when alligators will be helping to heal humans, don't bother them by invading their space. Just tell them: "See you later."

30

A Ghost of a Chance

Florida Phoenix, February 3, 2022

Did you know Florida is full of ghost stories?

You wouldn't think a place this sunny would have so many shades, but it does. You can find ghosts all over, from the haunted Pensacola Lighthouse up in the Panhandle to the infamous "Robert the Doll" in Key West. Why, on a good day in Tallahassee, you might even find the ghost of good sense (but don't count on it).

I know we're closer to Valentine's Day than Halloween, but I mention our ghastly, ghostly presences because I need to tell you about our most famous ghost, one that's been the star of a book and a movie.

I'm talking about the ghost orchid.

You've heard of the ghost orchid, right? It was featured in Susan Orlean's 1998 bestseller *The Orchid Thief,* as well as the 2002 Nicolas Cage–Meryl Streep movie based on it, *Adaptation.* How often does Hollywood make a movie about a plant? The only other one I can think of is the voracious people-eater Audrey II in *Little Shop of Horrors.*

Most of the year a ghost orchid resembles nothing more than a leafless green lump stuck to the side of a tree. But in the summer, when it blooms, it looks like an albino frog caught in mid-leap, a delicate apparition dangling above the dull foliage. One orchid expert I know calls it "sexy."

Juan Ponce de Leon dubbed Florida "The Land of Flowers." It's home to more than 100 native orchids. But only the ghost orchid shows up as a tourism promo on the side of U-Haul trucks.

In 1957, when Sarasota surgeon Carlyle Luer saw one (the flower, not the U-Haul ad), he was thunderstruck. He became an avid orchid grower, tracked down a ghost orchid in the wild to snap pictures of it, wrote the first guidebook to Florida's native orchids, gave up his medical practice, and co-founded Marie Selby Botanical Gardens, a scientific institution specializing in the study of orchids.

Luer wrote this of his blooming epiphany: "Should one be lucky enough to see a flower, all else will seem eclipsed."

For years, I wanted to see a ghost orchid, but I hesitated over the fact that the best place to see one was "the Fak," aka Fakahatchee Strand Preserve State Park. That's where both Orlean's book and the movie portrayed them growing in what she described as "a green hell."

To see a ghost, you'd need to sign up for a guided tour and wade through the swamp, meanwhile slapping mosquitoes and dodging gators. Even then, you might see nothing but the roots.

But then I found out that there's a place where you can see one without even getting your feet wet. You hike a mile down the boardwalk at Audubon's Corkscrew Swamp Sanctuary, turn left, point your binoculars about 50 feet up the trunk of a 500-year-old cypress tree, and BOOM! There it is, the biggest ghost in the state. In the summer it shows off multiple blooms.

So imagine my surprise last week to learn that the elusive ghost orchid is not classified as endangered. It's not anywhere on the federal list of species granted legal protection. It has the same protected status as a rutabaga—in other words, none.

I found this out because a trio of environmental groups filed a petition with the U.S. Fish and Wildlife Service to add the ghost orchid to the endangered list—finally.

Only 1,500 or so remain in the wild in South Florida, a decrease of up to 50 percent, according to the petition from the National Parks Conservation Association, Institute for Regional Conservation, and Center for Biological Diversity. (There are some in Cuba, but they're doing poorly too.)

I read that and did a double-take.

"Wait a minute," I said to myself (and maybe the leaping ghost of Dr. Luer). "They're in state and national preserves. Unlike most Florida endangered species, their habitat is protected from development. How can their population be in decline? And why aren't they already on the endangered list?"

When it comes to plants, I have what gardeners call "a brown thumb." However, I do know some plant experts, so I called them. I talked to the signers of the petition. I even sent an email to Orlean.

She replied that she liked the idea of adding ghosts to the endangered list but feared there might be unintended consequences—by attracting still more flower-stealers.

"I think it's clearly warranted and seems like a good way to create some awareness," she told me. "I just always worry that there are a few people who see endangered status as a motivation for getting their hands on something. Let's hope the value of giving the ghost this protection outweighs the possibility that it makes them seem more alluring than ever."

That's right, the author of *The Orchid Thief* is concerned about causing more orchid thievery.

But it turns out that's not the biggest problem the flowers face.

* * *

If you're a scientist, you know the ghost orchid as *Dendrophylax lindenii*. That name dates to 1846, when it was first described by a half-blind British botanist named John Lindley.

There are more than 200 plant species named for Lindley, many of which he named himself. He once told a fellow scientist, "I am a dandy in my herbarium." But he didn't name the ghost orchid after himself. He named it for the rugged adventurer who found it.

In the 1800s, Europe was caught in the grip of orchid-mania, an obsession even stronger than modern fads like playing Wordle. People simply could not get enough of the gorgeous flowers. Eager botanists dispatched swashbuckling explorers to seek new specimens for show and sell.

The king of these Victorian-era orchid-grabbers was a hook-handed man named Benedikt Roezel. He was notorious for single-handedly (ahem) stripping entire jungles of all their flowers.

One of Roezel's rivals (try saying that three times real fast) was a Belgian botanist named Jean-Jules Linden. Like Roezel, he was an intrepid traveler unafraid to wade into swamps or climb trees to get what he was after. He became the first to discover the ghost orchid while exploring the wilds of Cuba.

What set Linden apart from those other "collectors" (note the use of ironic quote-marks) was that he took careful notes on the growing conditions for each new flower he found. That was right before he ripped it loose and packed it up to ship to the paying customers in Europe.

A lot of orchids tend to have some sort of wild story attached to them. Even the word "orchid" has a colorful background. It derives from the Greek word for "testicle," because some of the orchid's tubers resembled a man's naughty bits. People used to believe them to be an aphrodisiac. (They were not.)

In the case of the ghost orchid, you can sum up the wild backstory in a single word: Poaching.

"Due to its beauty and rarity," the petition states, "the ghost orchid has long been prized by collectors in Florida."

The most famous poaching incident is the one that Orlean turned into a story for *The New Yorker* and then a book: On December 21, 1993, a Seminole Tribe employee named John Laroche (played in the movie by Chris Cooper, who won an Oscar) waded into the Fak with three members of the tribe.

When they emerged, they were carrying pillowcases and bags containing 136 plants, including ghost orchids.

Laroche was a savvy nurseryman with such an eye for playing the angles that he should have been a pool hustler. He believed that if the Seminoles— who are their own sovereign nation—removed plants from a state preserve, the authorities couldn't arrest them.

He led the expedition and told his trio of accomplices what to pull down. Where the orchids were attached to trees, he told them to saw off the limb.

That was the flaw in his plan. (Oops, forgot to shout, "SPOILER ALERT!")

They were caught and wound up being charged with removing plant life from the preserve—not the orchids, but the sawed-off branches. All four pleaded no contest.

The penalty for their poaching wasn't even a slap on the wrist. It was more like a love-tap. If they'd been caught tampering with an endangered species, the sentence could have been far more severe.

The poaching did not begin with Laroche, nor did it end with him. Stig Dalstrom, who stars in a series of nature films called the Wild Orchid Man, visited the Fak in 2008 and 2009 to show his viewers a real, live ghost.

The ranger who showed the showy flower to him was Mike Owen, who in 2013 got married standing in 18-inch-deep water next to the first ghost he'd shown his bride. He told Dalstrom the preserve had lost so many ghosts to poachers that "we're probably going to have to stop the public ghost orchid walks." People would take the tour, then sneak back and swipe the flowers, he said.

When I talked to Dalstrom this week, he said the poaching occurs because the ghost "is a legendary orchid."

"The idea of possessing the biggest, boldest, best-known orchid appeals to some people," he explained. But to him it makes no sense because their growing conditions are so specific to the swamp they're in that they usually wilt when removed.

"People still try to get them," he told me, "but they can't keep them alive."

The poaching isn't confined to the Fak. In the summer of 2020, a staff member at nearby Big Cypress National Preserve discovered 15 to 20 ghost orchids had been stolen, according to Superintendent Tom Forsyth and botanist Courtney Angelo.

The staffer "could see the scars on the trees where someone chopped into the trunk of the tree just above and just below the orchids with a machete (or something similar) and removed the orchids while they remained attached to the tree bark," Forsyth told me via email.

They suspect these modern Benedikt Roezels located the orchids by checking the metadata on nature photographers' pictures, a disquieting possibility.

But according to the petition, poaching isn't the biggest threat to the future of the ghost orchid. Instead, it's what's missing from the Big Cypress, the Fak, and Corkscrew Swamp right now, something that's much more basic and troubling:

Water.

* * *

In April 2020, a wildfire swept through hundreds of acres of the Big Cypress. It burned to within six feet of one known ghost orchid and within 20 feet of a bunch more.

Normally, wildfires are good for the Florida landscape, but not this one. The National Park Service report on it noted, "The Preserve is currently way too dry to let fires burn. Wildfires at this time will burn too hot, too fast, and for too long."

Nobody had ever thought to petition for the ghost orchid to be classified as endangered before because they assumed it was already protected by virtue of growing on preserves, said George Gann, president of the Institute for Regional Conservation. He and the other petitioners were spurred to take action by the first population survey in years, which showed the dramatic decline.

Turns out the preserves have been under assault for years.

Decades ago, logging crews wiped out most of the cypress trees that give Big Cypress its name. Even worse damage has been done by workers who dug drainage canals outside the preserves to dry out the soil so farmers could plant vegetables or developers could build homes and stores. Then along came the recent off-road vehicle trails in Big Cypress that dug deep channels through the muck.

Now all that harm is being exacerbated by another human intrusion: climate change. By altering global temperatures, we've upset the normal rainfall cycle, ruining the high-humidity habitat for the ghost orchids.

For the past 15 years, the region around the Big Cypress has experienced one of its driest periods in nearly a century, said Melissa Abdo of the National Parks and Conservation Association. That drought makes conditions ripe for those out-of-control wildfires, too.

Our human nature is to focus on the dramatic Dora-versus-Swiper story of rangers battling poachers. But the bigger threat is more subtle, more gradual, and more permanent.

Poached flowers may grow back. Altering where they grow ends that possibility forever. Such a loss implicates all of us when we drive our cars, use fossil-fueled electric power, or vote for politicians who refuse to do any "left-wing stuff" to combat climate change.

Think of us as Audrey II, mindlessly gobbling up everything in sight. If we don't change our ways, these lovely orchids just don't stand a ghost of a chance.

Postscript: In September 2023, a coalition of environmental groups filed suit against the U.S. Fish and Wildlife Service to force the agency to put the ghost orchid on the endangered list at last.

31

The Mangrove Massacre

Florida Phoenix, June 8, 2023

Florida likes to call itself the Fishing Capital of the World—and not because we've got so many fishy business folks operating here.

According to the tourism promoters at Visit Florida, we rank at No. 1 in angling excellence in part because we've got "more than 7,700 lakes, 10,550 miles of rivers, and 2,276 miles of tidal shoreline" where you can cast a line.

But what if clueless people do something so colossally stupid that they chase all the fish away? What's that going to do to Florida's peerless piscine standing?

I heard a story last week about just such a stupid move in Port St. Lucie, and then I went in search of the fisherman who witnessed it. His name is Jim Dirks, and he's been fishing the same stretch of water by what's now known as the Sandpiper Bay Resort, near his home, for 44 years, reeling in snook, tarpon, redfish, and so on.

And now, he told me, he can't.

The resort's river frontage was full of magnificent mangroves, some of them sprouting more than 24 feet high. The mangroves provided habitat for the fish that Dirks liked to catch.

Then, one Sunday last month, Dirks and a fishing buddy went to their usual spot and were startled to see the riverfront denuded.

Someone had chopped down all the mangroves and hauled them away. It was a mangrove massacre with hundreds of victims.

"They cut them all the way down to the roots," Dirks told me. "Which pretty much killed them."

Without the mangroves, the fish that Dirks loves to catch have all vanished. His Sunday nights are now free, unfortunately.

Dirks told me he asked an employee of the resort's marina who had committed such senseless destruction. The response: "I can't say."

Furious, Dirks snapped pictures and then, the next day, he sent them to the state Department of Environmental Protection. After all, he said, "if you live in Florida, you know that mangroves are a protected species."

That's when things got interesting.

* * *

Two days after Dirks sent his complaint to the DEP, a pair of inspectors showed up at the resort to see the damage for themselves. Mangroves, as Dirks pointed out, are considered so vital to Florida's ecosystems that they are protected from this kind of rampant butchery by a 1996 state law. You're allowed to trim them with a permit, but not kill them.

The inspectors met with Mike Giarogalo, the property manager, who showed them around. What they saw was appalling.

"While on-site, it was noted that mangroves were significantly altered, and the trimmings/branches of mangroves were piled in, or adjacent to, roll-off dumpsters for later disposal," the inspectors wrote in their report.

A week later, two more DEP inspectors showed up for a fuller inspection. This time, according to the DEP report, they were shown around by two people: Giarogalo and Michael Mota. The second man was listed by the DEP inspectors as "a representative of the owner of the property."

Mota has been the subject of quite a few stories in the *Boston Globe*. The most recent one called him a "Rhode Island entrepreneur and Hollywood mobster enthusiast."

Those last three words mean that he's a fan of fictional gangsters, particularly the ones from the acclaimed HBO TV show *The Sopranos*. He's even put on fan gatherings celebrating that genre.

Think of it as being like Comic-Con but, instead of Marvel, the focus is the Mafia. Instead of dressing up as Captain America, you'd cosplay as Don Corleone.

He's so into mobsters that he's even launched a mob-themed cryptocurrency and distributed tokens bearing his face and the motto "In Mota We Trust."

Meanwhile, though, the *Globe* reported that "Mota is being sued by creditors and vendors in 10 lawsuits totaling more than $500,000 and has left furious investors and vendors in multiple states." Guess those folks don't trust him anymore.

He's supposed to be the president of Florida-based Bayport International Holdings, which promised to carry out a $90 million to $100 million veterans home project in Pawtucket. According to the *Globe*, though, Bayport is actually a defunct company.

The list of his dissatisfied customers includes fellow *Sopranos* fans who "say he overcharged them and promised them perks they could not access, and he has been accused of not compensating vendors and actors from *The Sopranos* who were involved in his conventions."

The newspaper quoted one former business associate saying of Mota, "All you need to know about him is that he runs a website with the word 'con.' Because that's what he is."

Someone with that kind of a reputation fits right in here in Florida!

After all, when Charles Ponzi was first busted for pulling the original Ponzi scheme up in Boston, where did he go when he got out on bail? Florida, of course, where he immediately got involved in a real estate scam. A lot of Ponzi's land turned out to be underwater—not in terms of financing, but literally.

Anyway, Mota helped show the DEP employees all over the place, and he or Giarogalo or both of them came up with an explanation for what happened to all the mangroves.

No, it wasn't a mob hit. The mangroves didn't get mowed down like Sonny Corleone on the Jones Beach Causeway. Instead, the weather got the blame.

* * *

There's a non-gangster movie that I think deserves a mention here: *All About Eve.*

In it, the title character pretends to be something she's not. At the film's climax, another character who has uncovered the truth tells her all the ways that she's a phony. At one point, as he's running through her long list of embellishments, he comments on one, "That was a stupid lie. Easy to expose."

I thought about that line when I read the next part of the DEP report, which said that "the reasoning behind the mangrove removal/cutting was because of a tornado that had impacted the mangroves."

The DEP report didn't say who came up with that excuse, but Mota told the *Globe:* "I DID NOT CUT ANYTHING DOWN. I know there was a tornado and storm that happened at the property."

Oh, well then, that exp—no, wait, that doesn't explain anything.

One of the reasons why mangroves are protected under state law is that big storms like tornadoes and hurricanes don't knock them down. They're flexible in high winds and their interlocking root systems absorb the energy from big waves. So a tornado would be unlikely to hurt even one, much less a whole forest of them.

A biologist with the Florida Department of Environmental Protection measures the swath of destruction at the mangrove massacre in Port St. Lucie. Photo from the Florida Department of Environmental Protection.

Add to that the fact that the felled trees found in the dumpsters were still as green as your beer at an Irish tavern on St. Patrick's Day. Clearly they had all been healthy when someone cut them down.

Then there's the most obvious problem with the tornado excuse: There is no record of any such weather disaster. Neither the National Weather Service nor neighbors such as Dirks have seen any signs of a twister tossing cows around.

"There was no tornado hit that property," Dirks told me, sounding disgusted.

Instead, Dirks said, the obvious answer is that someone speaking for the property owner ordered all those mangroves to be chopped down. That way, the trees would no longer obstruct the guests' view of the water.

He speculated that some out-of-towner who's not familiar with Florida figured there'd be no penalty for carrying out so much environmental devastation. That person, he said, probably thought, "Oh, these people in Florida are idiots and we can get away with it."

Despite his love for lawless thugs like Paulie Walnuts (my favorite *Sopranos* character), Mota told me it wasn't him who ordered the hit. In fact, he said he's not even connected to the property owner, a real estate investment firm.

The way he tells it, he just happened to be in the wrong place at the wrong time, not unlike Tony Curtis and Jack Lemmon's *Some Like It Hot* characters witnessing the St. Valentine's Day massacre. He shouldn't have been mentioned in the DEP report, he contends.

"My name was there in error," Mota told me via email. "I was on site that day consulting on another matter and gave them a tour."

When I asked more questions, he referred me to the property owner's attorney, Keith Lee, who sent me a prepared statement: "As this is an ongoing investigation by the DEP, we will refrain from making specific comments to tell our side of the story. At this point, I can only say that we care very much about the environment and the local community and feel terrible about what happened."

* * *

As I may have mentioned a time or 12, Florida's DEP in recent years has developed a reputation for lackadaisical or even non-existent enforcement of environmental laws. As a result, I generally have low expectations for the agency that some people have dubbed "Don't Expect Protection."

But Dirks said he's been generally pleased with the way the DEP jumped on his complaint about the mass mangrove mayhem.

I checked with the DEP office that dispatched the inspectors. Spokesman Jon W. Moore told me the investigation is still in progress, but on May 30 the district chief sent a warning letter to the property owner, Store Capital Acquisitions LLC of Arizona.

"This warning letter is the first step of the department's formal enforcement process and we have a number of enforcement tools we are able to use to address these violations," Moore said.

The letter itself says the case "may result in liability for damages and restoration, and the judicial imposition of civil penalties."

The "restoration" part of that sentence caught my attention, so I checked with two mangrove experts. One was Samantha Chapman of Villanova University, who has been studying Florida's mangroves for years. The other was Loraé Simpson of the Florida Oceanographic Society.

"They're not going to be able to replace all that," Chapman told me. "Restoring it is going to be tricky."

She pointed out that mangroves actually create land by the accumulation of fallen leaves and other detritus. Now that the mangroves are gone, "that land's going to sink. . . . It's going to be a mess."

She told me that in other countries that don't protect their mangroves—Belize, for instance—"they clear all the mangroves and the land sinks into the sea."

When I asked Simpson about restoring the mangrove growth, she predicted the owners couldn't regrow a stand so lush "within the next 25 to 50 years, if ever."

It's unfortunate, she said, that "mangroves grow in places where people want to live and they think, 'Oh, it's just a tree, it'll grow back.' It's all about having that view."

She also predicted that, without the mangroves filtering runoff and sucking up nutrients, the water quality in the river will decline just as the fishing has.

Dirks said that a few years ago, one of his neighbors hired some landscapers who mistakenly chopped down mangroves along 80 feet of the shore. The neighbor had to spend $14,000 to replant them and provide regular updates about the regrowth over the next 10 years, he said.

So when Dirks compares his neighbor's experience with the vast destruction at the Sandpiper, he has high hopes for even harsher penalties being imposed.

"Someone said, 'Cut down those mangroves,'" he told me. "I want that person to go to jail."

I don't know that I'd go that far. Maybe hit them with an enormous fine and a requirement that they at least try to put back what was cut down.

Maybe, to make an example out of them, we can take a lesson from the Corleone family. Take all that chopped-up vegetation out of the dumpsters and put it in that person's bed, just like the horse's head in *The Godfather.* They won't be sleeping with the fishes—just with the mangroves where the fishes slept.

———————

Postscript: In December 2023, the DEP announced it would order the resort to pay a $110,395 fine, replant 2,780 trees, and be monitored for five years, which I do not think will satisfy Mr. Dirks.

32

Adios, Oysters

Florida Phoenix, July 16, 2020

One thing that makes Florida such a special place is our food. The divine Key lime pie served in the Keys, the savory croquetas made in Miami, the *delicioso* Cuban sandwich that Tampa claims as its own invention, the tupelo honey produced in Wewahitchka—all these offer a taste unique to our state.

But one of our greatest Florida foods is about to be put off-limits for five years.

I am talking about Apalachicola oysters, those sweet and salty mollusks that are best served raw on the half-shell with a little lemon juice. There was a time when nine out of every 10 oysters eaten in Florida came from Apalachicola Bay, and one out of every 10 across the United States—but not anymore.

The Florida Fish and Wildlife Conservation Commission is scheduled to vote next week on banning the harvest of wild oysters from Apalachicola Bay starting August 1 and continuing through 2025.

When I heard about this, I was stunned.

The first raw oysters I ever ate, in Pensacola's Marina Oyster Barn, were Apalachicola oysters. The last ones I ate, at a now-closed Apalachicola seafood joint called Boss Oyster, were fresh from Apalachicola Bay. The thought of going without them for five years is hard to swallow.

Yet what's left of Apalachicola's oyster harvesting industry supports this move. Some contend it should have happened sooner.

"This is something that's been asked for before by the oystermen," said Georgia Ackerman, head of the Apalachicola Riverkeeper organization, an environmental group that also supports the shutdown. Healthy oyster beds are a sign of a healthy bay, because they filter out impurities in the water.

People in Apalachicola have been harvesting the bounty of their bay since the 1800s. Some families count four or five generations of oystermen among their ancestors.

An Apalachicola oysterman shows off his tonging technique. Photo from the Florida State Archives.

Between oystermen, local restaurant shuckers, and cannery workers, the industry supported more than 2,500 jobs. The humble oyster has become fused with the town's identity, to the point where the sides of Franklin County Sheriff's Department cruisers carry the slogan "Oyster Capital of the World."

Back when that slogan was true, oysters covered more than 10,000 acres of the bay bottom. Hundreds of oystermen would venture out in their wooden skiffs, long tongs at the ready to reach down into the brackish water and grab the shells. They had plenty of customers waiting to enjoy the delectable meat inside.

"Food critics and restaurant owners from Miami and New Orleans say Apalachicola Bay oysters are among the finest in the world, if not the finest," the *New York Times* reported in 2002. "Chefs of fancy restaurants in Charleston, S.C., where mediocre seafood will be sent back, prize them above oysters from their native coast."

As recently as 2009, Apalachicola's oystermen harvested nearly three million pounds of oysters. On a typical day, a single boat could pull 50 to 70 bags of oysters from the bay, with each bag weighing about 60 pounds. Multiply that by the 480 or so oystermen then working the bay on a regular basis and you can see why the city would brag about its slimy source of pride.

What made the oyster so plentiful and succulent was the delicate balance of salty Gulf of Mexico water and fresh water flowing out of the Apalachicola River and, to a lesser extent, Tate's Hell Swamp. But then the river flow began drying up.

A drought that began in 2010 and lasted through 2012, combined with increased usage of water far upstream to serve the growing population of Atlanta, limited the fresh water getting to the bay. That altered the balance and limited the growth of new oysters to replace the ones harvested. A decade later, some reefs "have become so degraded that there is little-to-no shell material left," a wildlife commission report says.

The saltier water also brought in predators called oyster drills, a marine snail that attacked the bay's oysters so that young ones didn't live long enough to mature.

Overfishing played a role too, according to the state wildlife commission. In 2010, when oil from BP's sunken Deepwater Horizon rig floated toward the Panhandle coastline, the commission announced it would close off oyster harvesting temporarily. As a result, some oystermen rushed out and grabbed as many shells as they could before it was too late.

Some of the blame also lies with the wildlife commission itself, according to one local government official. The agency was lax about cracking down on poaching and the illegal harvest of too-young oysters, according to Franklin County Commissioner Noah Lockley Jr., a former oysterman himself.

"They let 'em go wide open," he told me this week. "There'd be a limit of 15 bags and people were coming in with 20 or 25 bags and nobody said anything."

Last year, oystermen harvested less than 21,000 pounds of oysters from Apalachicola Bay. The oysters weren't the only thing that declined. The number of oystermen has dropped too, as fewer people could make a living from the water. Some even moved away because they could no longer make a living the way their ancestors did.

Lockley told me he's concerned a shutdown of the bay will put the remaining oystermen into the poorhouse unless the state comes up with money to tide them over.

But Shannon Hartsfield, an oysterman who heads up the Franklin County Seafood Workers Association, told me that there are so few oysters left that there are perhaps four oystermen still working the bay regularly. As of Wednesday, he said, "there aren't any."

His own son retrained to become a welder, he said, and moved to Georgia to get work. Other oystermen are cleaning houses or doing landscaping, he said.

"So many oystermen don't have a high school diploma," Hartsfield said. "They think, 'Oh, I'm just gonna do what my daddy did,' and go on the water." But because of the bay's decline, he said, the current bag limit for catching oysters is two, which means a weekly income of $400 "and you can't make a living on $400 a week."

The federal government declared Apalachicola Bay a disaster area in 2013, and the state launched several projects designed to slow the decline, but they haven't helped.

To make matters worse, two years ago Hurricane Michael slammed into the Panhandle with a nine-foot storm surge and 155 mph winds, wrecking some oyster houses and tossing boats across the highway onto dry land.

Another hurricane nearly killed Apalachicola's oyster industry 35 years ago. In 1985, Hurricane Elena nearly wiped out all the oysters in the bay. State officials shut down oyster harvesting to give the oysters a chance to recover, while they rebuilt and reseeded the reefs. Some experts predicted it would take up to 10 years, but in just 18 months the state found enough oysters had returned to reopen the bay.

Because it worked once, the wildlife commission is pursuing the same solution this time around, not only shutting down the bay until 2025 but also banning the possession of oyster-harvesting equipment while on the bay. A $20 million grant (from a pot of money that, ironically, came from the BP oil spill settlement) will pay for a major restoration effort.

Just like last time, some oystermen fear that once the bay is closed it will stay that way. But Hartsfield's organization supports the closure and is hopeful that, like last time, the reefs will rebound faster than expected.

The bay may never be back to what it once was, he said, "but I believe in a couple of years we're going to have more than 100 oystermen out there making a living again."

To me, this underlines a lesson we in Florida have to learn and learn again. In this state, the environment is the economy. If you mess up the environment, you will mess up the economy—and in this case, even tear families apart and uproot a cherished waterfront culture.

Edible oysters have disappeared from estuaries all over Florida, killed off by dredging and pollution. In places where we could once harvest a gracious plenty of tasty mollusks—Cape Haze, Matlacha, Chokoloskee, even Tampa Bay—that's no longer an option.

Here's hoping that the Apalachicola oyster won't join them, and instead will make a comeback from the endangered list.

———————

Postscript: The ban, if it works, will be lifted in 2026. Meanwhile, according to a 2023 story in Garden and Gun *magazine, "Though wild oyster harvesting has been put on hold, it is still possible to enjoy oysters grown in Apalachicola Bay through aquaculture farming. Currently, more than one hundred lease-holders have staked their claims and futures on the one- to ten-acre leased water plots in and around Apalachicola Bay."*

33

The End of Infinity

Florida Phoenix, June 16, 2022

There's nothing like a good shipwreck story.

The battle against nature, the human drama, the deadly consequences—those elements make for some compelling telling. Doesn't matter whether the story involves the doomed sailors of the USS *Indianapolis,* the desperate passengers of the SS *Poseidon,* or the fearless crew of the SS *Minnow.*

Florida has had so many shipwrecks (some of them accidental, some on purpose) that it's part of our lore. Early settlers used to cruise the beaches collecting anything useful that washed up from the wreckage—lumber, clothing, even cookware. Once a ship showed up loaded with hundreds of coconuts. Folks planted them, thus giving Palm Beach its name.

I heard about a pretty strange shipwreck the other day, a contemporary crash that may lead to a pretty big change for boaters in the St. Augustine area—or ought to. It involved a boat named *About Time.*

The crash happened near dusk on February 12, 2021. A captain and seven passengers were aboard the 54-footer. They were returning from a day of competing at the Northeast Florida Wahoo Shootout.

The boat was doing about 21 knots—24 mph if you're a landlubber—as it headed for the Conch House Marina in St. Augustine.

Nearing their destination, in the St. Augustine Inlet, the boat smacked into something—hard. The boat stopped dead in the water. So did whatever it had hit.

Suddenly the *About Time* didn't have much time. Both its twin engines shut down and the damaged boat began sinking fast. Water poured through a hole a foot wide as automatic alarms screamed.

The captain, Shane Ryan of Ponce Inlet, put out a mayday call and managed to get one of the engines started again after several tries. Thinking fast, he intentionally ran the boat aground in the mud flats off Anastasia Island

State Park. That way, it wouldn't go under. None of the people on board were injured.

When a pair of Florida wildlife officers showed up, the owner of the boat, Dayne Williams of New Smyrna Beach, blurted out, "I think we hit a whale. I saw fins and blood."

He was right. It wasn't just any whale, either. It was one of the rarest whales in the world.

And the boaters wouldn't suffer any penalty at all for killing it—and killing a second whale, too.

* * *

The next day, a dead whale washed ashore on Anastasia Island with "injuries consistent with a vessel strike, including fresh propeller cuts on its back and head, broken ribs, and bruising," according to Florida Fish and Wildlife Conservation Commission records.

Biologists immediately identified it as an endangered North American right whale. Around 350 right whales are all that are left of the species. That's down by nearly 100 from the 2018 estimate.

There used to be a lot more—thousands of them. Whaling ships of the 1800s nearly wiped them out, harvesting their oil for use in lamps.

Those 19th-century whalers gave the species known to scientists as *Eubalaena glacialis* its common name. They were the "right" whale to hunt because they move slowly, migrate near shore, and stay afloat after death.

Even though those whaling days are over, the remaining right whale population faces other perils. It has continued shrinking faster than a stack of plywood sheets at Home Depot the day before a hurricane hits. I'll get into why in just a minute.

Florida has lots of endangered and threatened species that live here full-time: panthers, manatees, and Key deer, to name a few. The right whales are part-time residents, but it's a pretty crucial time when they're here.

They spend their whole lives in the Atlantic Ocean. Part of the year, they're found off Canada and New England. Then—not unlike the snowbirds who invade Florida around Thanksgiving and drive around with their cars' left-turn signal blinking for miles before turning right—some head south for the winter.

From November to April, some right whales swim about 1,000 miles down to warmer waters off Georgia and Florida. That's where the females give birth to their calves. Once their calves are strong enough, they all swim back north.

Infinity's calf, lying dead on the beach after being hit by a boat, is measured by two biologists with the Florida Fish and Wildlife Commission. Photo by Florida Fish and Wildlife Commission.

The whale that the *About Time* clobbered was one of those calves. It was about a month old and 22 feet long.

A coalition of federal, state, and non-government scientific agencies collaborate to keep an eye on the right whales while they're calving. The calves are really important to ensuring this species has a future. If a calving season passes with no calves born, everyone freaks out.

The group had spotted this particular calf a few hours before with its mother, a whale known as Infinity. Now it lay dead.

* * *

I talked to the biologist who performed what scientists call a "necropsy" on Infinity's calf. Like an autopsy on a human, it's an effort to determine the cause of death. Surprisingly, there's never been a TV crime show about that, the way there has been for pathologists and medical examiners.

In this case, the calf's death was quick, said Megan Stolen of the Hubbs-SeaWorld Research Institute in Melbourne Beach.

The gashes from the boat's propeller were the most dramatic injuries. But Stolen's exam determined that the deadlier damage was done by the blunt force of the boat ramming into the marine mammal.

I asked her if the injuries would have been nearly as severe if the boat had been going slower. She said a slower speed would have helped.

"The force of the boat against that animal is what killed it," she said. "The blunt force trauma depends on the speed of the vessel."

Our conversation turned to the calf's mom. Infinity was, she said, a "known" specimen, one that had been sighted over and over by biologists in recent years.

Three days after the calf turned up dead, an aerial survey team from the Clearwater Marine Aquarium spotted Infinity. The mom was 27 miles off Georgia's Cumberland Island, heading north at a good clip.

Turns out Infinity had been hit as well.

"We were able to notice that she did appear to be injured," Melanie White of the Clearwater aerial team told me. "The injuries were similar to that of a propeller strike."

The wound may have proven just as fatal as those that killed the calf.

"Infinity hasn't been seen again since that day," Stolen told me.

If you're scoring this at home, that's boaters 2, endangered whales 0.

* * *

"But wait," you say, "you're going too fast. How did the *About Time* get away with killing not one but TWO endangered animals while zooming through the water?"

Easy. They did nothing that's been classified as illegal.

This lack of a legal limit wasn't the result of some dopey oversight, such as the Florida Legislature not outlawing bestiality until 2011 because everyone was too embarrassed to talk about it.

No, this is the fault of the federal agency that's supposed to be protecting right whales and other marine mammals: the National Oceanic and Atmospheric Administration, or NOAA for short. The agency is, you might say, legally lackadaisical.

NOAA has known for years that—as with Florida's luckless manatees—boats kill and maim a lot of right whales. Research going as far back as the 1990s shows that, according to Southern Environmental Law Center science and policy analyst Melissa Edmonds (who, I can't resist noting, was named Melissa Whaling before she recently got married).

The two main causes of death for right whales are ship strikes and entanglement in fishing gear. Biologists say the population is so tiny, the loss of even a single whale—especially a breeding-age female—pushes the entire species closer to extinction.

But this NOAA seems to move more slowly than the line of animals waiting to board the ark built by that other Noah.

In 2008, the agency passed a regulation limiting the speed of big cargo vessels in areas along the Atlantic Coast where right whales are known to be swimming. But it hasn't done the same with vessels smaller than 65 feet—in other words, boats the size of the *About Time*.

"They're not regulated," Stolen told me.

In its cargo ship rule, NOAA said it would "continue to consider means . . . to address vessel classes below 65 feet should it become clear these vessels warranted regulation."

Yet so far, it's done exactly (wait, let me double-check my math—yep, carry the 2, that's right) nothing to make those smaller vessels slow down.

"The agency is extremely overdue in publishing a rule to address this threat," Edmonds told me. "They were supposed to publish a report assessing the effectiveness of the rule by 2019. They didn't finish it until 2020."

That 2020 report said that after the speed limit rule took effect on the big ships, most of them actually obeyed it, and deaths went down. Meanwhile, though, "between 1999 and 2012, small vessels were involved in at least 11 collisions with right whales resulting in injuries."

One of the 2020 recommendations: Impose speed limits on vessels smaller than 65 feet. The report called the need for better rules to protect right whales "urgent." Maybe the day they published the report was Backwards Day, because the agency has been acting like it's the opposite of urgent.

Last year, the feds promised to publish a proposed speed limit by this May, then take public comment on it and have a rule in place by December, Edmonds said.

Yet May is now over and we're halfway through June. Something tells me Santa's going to get here long before any help for the right whales arrives.

In the most recent three years that NOAA has been dragging its feet on this issue, Edmonds said, "eight whales have died or been seriously injured by vessel strikes. Three of these were calves."

There's a scientific theory called "cryptic mortality," she added, that says that for every right whale that is confirmed dead, there are probably two more that died in the ocean and were not found. That means the number of whales killed while NOAA dithers is likely to be much higher than the official number.

NOAA has not one but two mascots, an owl and a sea lion. I would propose replacing them with the banana slug, one of the slowest creatures on earth.

I contacted NOAA to ask why it's taking so long to put up new speed limit signs around the right whale habitat.

The regulatory change is under review by a division of the Office of Management and Budget, according to NOAA spokesperson Katie Wagner. Once it's done there, the agency "anticipates publishing a notice for the proposed rule in the coming weeks."

The famous last words, "remain calm, all is well," were implied, but not stated.

Because of the loooooong delay in official action, the team that watches the calving ground has been trying to persuade the smaller boaters to voluntarily slow down, according to a recent story in *FloridaPolitics.com.*

I don't think it's going well. As we saw with the manatees, some boaters really do not like being told to ease off the throttle.

I base that conclusion on a conversation I had with Shane Ryan, the captain whose boat ended both Infinity's and its calf's lives. The crash ended the boat too. The *About Time* was totaled—a $1.2 million loss. It's now being rebuilt, he told me.

Ryan had never seen a right whale before, and he didn't see the calf he killed until after he'd hit it. It was a speed bump that seemed invisible under the surface.

When I mentioned dropping the boat speed to save the whales, though, he rejected the idea "100 percent." I didn't quite follow his argument, but he contended that a slower boat is more vulnerable to bad weather, and that anyone urging slower speeds was "uneducated."

"I won't listen to any speed regulations," he told me. "I'll take the ticket. I won't risk the lives of my passengers to listen to some tree hugger."

So most likely any effort to regulate boats of less than 65 feet will not be, in the immortal words of Bruno Mars, "smoother than a fresh jar of Skippy." Maybe it will even touch off a new Infinity War.

But I think it's worth doing anyway, because the world would be a lot poorer with fewer whales in our ocean.

In the face of this kind of defiance, I think the key is to encourage reporting and enforcement. My suggestion would be to reward the captains for reporting a strike, the way Ryan did, but to penalize the boat owners for injuries or deaths among the whales.

If a captain hits a right whale and reports it, the captain will get a $1,000 reward. This would ensure that biologists would be able to include that collision in their counting.

Meanwhile, though, the owner of the boat would be penalized commensurate with the price of the boat, multiplied by the number of victims. That means the death of Infinity and its calf would have resulted in a fine for the boat's owner of $2.4 million.

How's that for an incentive to slow down?

No matter what NOAA decides, I just wish they'd hurry up. When they finally publish that speed limit, I'm sure everybody, even some boaters, will say, "About time!"

———————

Postscript: NOAA finally proposed the speed restrictions in 2023, and it touched off a firestorm of protests from boaters, boat manufacturers, and members of Congress, who proposed cutting NOAA's budget to hamstring enforcement. One of the more, um, interesting arguments against the slow speeds: There are so few right whales left, the majority of commercial fishermen never see them, so what's the point of slowing down for something you never see?

34

Feeling Hot Hot Hot

Florida Phoenix, November 17, 2022

When anyone asks me what's the coolest thing I've ever covered, I always tell them about the sea turtle: I once witnessed a loggerhead turtle crawl onto a Sarasota County beach in the dark of a new moon, dig a hole, and lay a bunch of eggs.

That night, I was riding with a couple of volunteers who patrolled the beaches marking turtle nests so they could be protected from beachgoers. Around 2 a.m. we spotted this one. We watched the mama turtle pull herself out of the water, find a good spot to make her nest, and then start laying.

When she was done, she covered the nest, dragged herself down to the surf, and began swimming back out to sea. As her flippers stroked through the black water, green lightning flashed from the tips—brilliant streaks of bioluminescence.

You can see how that transcendent experience left me feeling emotionally invested in the annual turtle nesting season reports. This year's season, which just ended, delivered both good news and bad news.

On the one hand, as the *Fort Myers News-Press* recently reported, "Hurricane Ian couldn't wash away the best turtle nest season ever in Southwest Florida. Nesting season runs from May 1 to October 31 and luckily most of the nests had hatched by the time the big storm destroyed the local beaches."

On the other, the turtle hatchlings from those nests are likely to turn out to be just one gender: all girls.

Having a lot of female turtles is not a bad thing in and of itself, of course. For instance, it's a safe bet that, while migrating, the male turtles never want to stop for directions, then waste a lot of time paddling the wrong way. Females won't have that problem.

But if you've studied basic biology—or ever visited The Villages—you know what happens when a population has a really large gender imbalance.

In The Villages, for instance, there are 10 women for every man, which has led to such consequences as a thriving black market for Viagra. Those women have to be very, very determined.

"But how do you know that the turtles are all going to be girls?" you ask. "Are you clairvoyant? And if so, why haven't you picked the winning Powerball numbers, collected your big check, and moved to Cassadaga, the Psychic Capital of the World?"

I am not clairvoyant. I don't even own a Magic 8-Ball.

I know the gender of the turtle hatchlings because this is not a new phenomenon. Just ask Bette Zirkelbach, who for the past 11 years has managed the Turtle Hospital in Marathon. The hospital cares for a lot of juvenile sea turtles during nesting season.

"We have not seen a single male juvenile turtle in the past four years, which is frightening," she told me.

What's behind this extreme lack of turtle-boys, whether teenage mutants or not?

I'll give you a clue, folks. It's also the name of a Robert DeNiro–Al Pacino crime movie: *Heat.*

* * *

Listen, I don't want to rile up Governor Ron DeSantis' semi-hysterical gender-identity army. I don't want his hand-picked Board of Medicine and Big Donors to announce a new rule that sea turtles MUST identify as males no matter what they are or what their parents want.

Sea turtle sexuality doesn't work the way ours does (not that the way gender works in humans seems to matter to the governor's minions).

Unlike humans, baby sea turtles don't start out with chromosomes that grant them a specific gender. Instead, the circumstances of their eggs' incubation—specifically, the warmth of the sand—decides whether they will be boys or girls. Warmer sand equals more girls.

Florida plays an outsize role in the reproduction of loggerheads such as the one I saw so many years ago. Scientists estimate 90 percent of all the Atlantic Ocean's loggerheads lay their eggs on Florida beaches. Then the ones that hatch here come back years later to lay their own eggs.

But something funky is happening on those beaches, and it doesn't involve James Brown.

Starting in 2002, a Florida Atlantic University professor named Jeanette Wyneken began monitoring sea turtle nests on Palm Beach County beaches

Florida Atlantic University professor Jeanette Wyneken with a recent-ly hatched sea turtle. Photo courtesy of Florida Atlantic University.

to check the temperature of the incubating nest. As soon as a new nest appeared, she or one of her team of researchers would insert a probe that would stay there as long as the nest lasted, measuring the temperature.

"Our goal was to find out what was the normal sex ratio," she told me. "I thought it would be one of those two- or three-year projects—that's all."

Twenty years later, Wyneken's team is still at it. They kept checking nest temperatures because what they found was so alarming.

The first year, she said, they found 65 percent of the hatchlings were female, which in retrospect was a pretty good number. The beaches had been cooler because 2002 brought a lot of rain, she told me.

But the next year it was drier and the females made up 95 percent of the mix. The year after that, the females made up 98 percent.

In the years since then, she said, they have found "100 percent female years, 99 percent female years, 98 percent female years. There are very few years where we've gotten even 10 percent males. It's worrisome."

This year, she said, a rainy April and May led to two nests of males hatching, "but outside of those two nests, we haven't seen a male since then."

The mysterious disappearance of the male turtles is really no mystery at all. Not if you're paying attention.

"The turtles are telling us a story," she told me, "and it's not just about turtles."

* * *

Climate change is making everything in Florida hotter.

And not in the fashion sense, either.

Florida was already pretty warm from being located so close to the equator. But gradually, thanks to the greenhouse effect, our days are getting warmer. So are the nights. The farmers' fields are growing hotter. So are the theme parks, the fishing piers, the skate ramps, and the drive-thru lines.

So, too, are our beaches. And that's important not just because when you cross the sand to the refreshment stand you have to run reeeeeeally fast (a move often referred to as "hot-footing it").

Remember how the temperature of the sand determines the gender of the turtle hatchlings? Hotter beaches mean fewer male turtles. Only on the rare occasions when the sand cools down—say, because of heavy rains—do the males reappear.

The dwindling number of males is further proof that climate change is not, as a certain not-yet-indicted Palm Beach club owner/presidential candidate once contended, a Chinese hoax. It's as real as your rising property insurance rates.

But if the sand gets too hot? The hatchlings don't hatch at all, Wyneken said. Or if they do hatch, they exhibit a sideshow variety of defects: no eyeballs, or a missing jaw.

If the weather is getting too hot to produce male sea turtles, she said, "then it's too hot for insects and too hot for plants and too hot for us, too."

However, as we learned from Jeff Goldblum in *Jurassic Park,* "Life, uhhh, finds a way."

According to Kate Mansfield, who runs the Marine Turtle Research Group at the University of Central Florida, the sea turtles may find a workaround for the havoc we humans have caused.

The turtles could start their nesting season earlier to avoid the heat of the summer or could show up later in the season, once the weather becomes more temperate.

There's a downside to that second option, Mansfield noted. The later the mama turtles lay their eggs, the more likely they will be destroyed by a hurricane. Climate change is making those stronger.

"It's a Catch-22," she said.

* * *

For 12 years, Florida's chief executive has been someone who can't even bear to speak the words "climate change."

First it was eight years under Rick "I'm-Not-a-Scientist-and-I-Don't-

Care-about-the-Seas-Swallowing-My-State" Scott. Even as storm surges around Florida crept higher and the temperatures rose and more people suffered from heat-related ailments, Scott kept dodging the issue whenever it came up.

Then it was four years under DeSantis. He's been fine with spending millions protecting waterfront property from being inundated but refuses to do anything else.

Worse, DeSantis and our fine legislature made sure last year that our local governments are locked into burning fossil fuels rather than switching to greener energy sources.

The most recent election guarantees that streak of denial will go to at least two years. That's when DeSantis will officially become a candidate for El Supremo—er, excuse me, president.

I asked Wyneken about how she deals with Florida's officially sanctioned support for making climate change worse. She told me that she's calculated her own carbon footprint and encourages everyone she meets to do the same.

As a result, she tries to lessen her personal contribution to the world's greenhouse gases in every way she can—limiting her driving trips, for instance.

But it's difficult, she admitted. For instance, she has to drive an SUV, not a more sensible vehicle, because sometimes she's transporting full-grown sea turtles. And when she does, she has to run the air conditioning for them.

My suggestion for those of us who are concerned about this would be to recruit some of those extremely determined women in The Villages. They've got the resources and the will to deal with the men in that community, so that means they'd be up for the challenge of dealing with this situation too.

We could get them interested in helping by showing them a series of super-cute pictures of the turtle hatchlings. Those things are so cute they could break the official Cute-O-Meter. Close-ups are particularly compelling, I've found.

Once they're convinced that we're facing a major sea turtle crisis, I'm sure they will hop in their fancy golf carts and hit the road to take care of the problem.

They'll caravan to Tallahassee. They'll track down those useless legislators who won't lift a finger to halt our spiral into a sweltering hell. And then those women will crank up the heat on THEM.

And if they need directions, they'll stop and ask—unlike us men.

35

Fly Like an Eagle

Florida Phoenix, March 16, 2023

It's been a while since I went on a tour of the Florida State Capitol, the esteemed winner of the Most Phallic Public Building in the World contest.

So, you'll have to forgive me if I am unable to tell you exactly where to find the Well of Nincompoopery. I can only assume its existence from the behavior of our fine legislators, who seem to drink deeply from this well whenever they're in session.

Based strictly on the ridiculous bills they've sponsored this year, some of them aren't just sipping the well water. They're soaking in it.

There's a bill to protect Confederate monuments from ever being torn down! And stop any attempt at rent control in the least affordable state! And ban the flying of rainbow flags in state buildings (but not Rebel flags)! And dictate the use of pronouns! (This is where Daffy Duck would look at the camera and say, "Pronoun trouble!").

The bills that struck me as the biggest evidence that there's a Well of Nincompoopery in Tallahassee are a pair that came out in favor of water pollution.

The bills—HB 1197 in the House and SB 1240 in the Senate—would forbid any local governments from "adopting laws, regulations, rules, or policies relating to water quality or quantity, pollution control, pollutant discharge prevention or removal, and wetlands."

Bear in mind that these bills are being put forward at a time when our beaches are plagued by a months-long red tide toxic algae bloom fueled by pollution in stormwater runoff.

Meanwhile, Lake Okeechobee is so choked by a blue-green toxic algae bloom fed by pollution that the U.S. Army Corps of Engineers had to stop releasing lake water to the east coast—twice.

Worst of all, a recent court decision found that the state Department of Environmental Foot-dragging—er, excuse me, "Protection,"—has failed for the past four years to clean up the pollution sources degrading our springs. You can bet the springs aren't the only Florida waterways being neglected.

Yet here come a couple of elected lawmakers saying they want to get rid of local regulations aiming for cleaner water and protection of wetlands.

Environmental groups have named these bills the worst of the session. Given all the other kooky stuff that's been proposed, that should tell you a lot.

"These bills are a direct threat to our state's environment and public health," said Cragin Mosteller of the Florida Association of Counties. "By stripping local governments of their ability to protect, preserve, and regulate water use, this bill puts profits over the beauty and safety of our communities."

Rachel O'Hara of the Florida League of Cities agreed and rattled off for me a long list of important municipal ordinances that would be invalidated. She also told me, "I can't make heads or tails out of what problem is supposed to be addressed by the bill."

Who would be such big nincompoops that they would push these pro-pollution bills? The sponsors are two guys from the same place, Pasco County: Representative Randy Maggard and Senator Danny Burgess.

And thereby hangs quite a tale, one involving an eagle nest, a swamp, and a house lot at a golf club. I've even got a soundtrack for it! Hang on, let me put on my DJ earphones.

* * *

Pasco County has long enjoyed a reputation as Ground Zero for Mind-Boggling Florida Weirdness, so our first record is Swamp Dogg's *Total Destruction to Your Mind*.

Do you doubt Pasco's bona fides? Exhibit A is the time Pasco deputies Tasered a runaway kangaroo. Exhibit B: The time the mayor of Port Richey was arrested after a gun battle with a SWAT team for practicing medicine without a license. Twenty days later, the acting mayor was arrested as well.

I can offer lots more examples, like that time the KKK adopted a highway. When people objected, Klan leaders promised to wear orange vests while picking up litter, not their usual white robes.

Pasco was once a hotbed of Mafia activity. Now it's known as the Nudist Capital of America, because there are more nudist resorts there than anywhere else. There's even a Bare Dare 5K, aka "the largest clothing-optional race in North America."

Pasco is also known for producing lots of clean water. In fact, other local governments tried to suck the whole place dry back in the '80s and '90s.

So why would a couple of Pasco politicos want to put the kibosh on water pollution regulations? Especially since one of them—Maggard—is vice chairman of the newly created Water Quality, Supply and Treatment Subcommittee as well as a former chairman of the Southwest Florida Water Management District?

In a recent *Miami Herald* story, a reporter tried to pin Representative Maggard down about his motives. He said he filed the bill because "he 'heard stories' about cities and counties requiring residents to obtain a water permit 'even if the water management district allows it' but, when pressed, could not provide an example."

Hey, I can think of an example—the specific one that REALLY prompted Maggard's bill.

It involves the Lake Jovita Golf and Country Club in Dade City, where his nephew was building a house and ran afoul of the rules.

This is the point where I cue up Sly and the Family Stone singing about how "It's a family affaaaaair . . ."

* * *

Zach Maggard was a standout Little League, high school, and college baseball player and, for a time, a minor-league catcher. (Our soundtrack now switches to John Fogerty rocking out: "Put me in coach, I'm ready to play . . .")

But he never got called up to the Show and retired from the national pastime in 2013.

Corporate records show he's now senior vice president and chief lending officer at the Dade City–based BankFlorida.

One of the bank's directors, by the way, is his dad, Dale Maggard, co-owner with the representative and their father of Sonny's Discount Appliances and a business partner of Agriculture Commissioner Wilton Simpson.

The registered agent for the bank happens to be another of Dale Maggard's sons, Matthew Maggard, who is the longtime law partner of Senator Burgess.

I assume the bank's hold music is Sister Sledge's "We Are Family," so we'll play that next.

Soon after Zach Maggard bought a lot in Lake Jovita, neighbors noticed something disturbing. A large eagle nest on that property, one that had been used year after year by the formerly endangered birds, suddenly disappeared.

"In 24 hours, a nest that had been there for 27 years was suddenly gone," neighbor Kevin Bohne told me. "It was pretty heartbreaking."

(This is where we'll play the Steve Miller Band's "Fly Like an Eagle.")

The nest didn't just fly away. Something or someone had removed it. The nest, and the trees that held it up, had been legally protected from disturbance by any construction.

"As long as the sticks were there, the trees were protected for five years," explained Kim Rexroat, the Audubon Florida eagle watch coordinator for Pasco, referring to the eagles' nesting material. "Once the sticks were gone, the trees weren't protected anymore, and it was okay to take them down."

Outraged eagle advocates called in officials from Pasco County, the Florida Fish and Wildlife Commission, and the U.S. Fish and Wildlife Service. They all showed up to investigate what had become of the nest.

That's when they realized that the lakefront wetlands shown on Maggard's building plans didn't match the wetlands they were seeing.

"They'd mapped out the wetlands wrong," Rexroat told me.

Now I'm cuing up Etta James' "Damn Your Eyes."

* * *

Bohne said everyone else in the Lake Jovita subdivision has done a good job of following the development rules so they can coexist with wildlife. They understood that protecting the wetlands helps keep their lake clean, so they wanted to do things right, he said.

But Maggard's approach was—oh, let's say "different."

"It was, 'Just get it done and do it, and don't care about the neighborhood,'" Bohne said. "These people are trying to manipulate the system. They don't care about the law."

I had an interesting on-the-record chat with a Pasco County building official who worked on the Maggard case. When we talked, he seemed as nervous as a man walking a tightrope in combat boots. He gave me an honest appraisal of what he found while avoiding saying anything critical of anyone involved.

"The wetland lines were not right," he said. "I required that a delineation be made by the state. It showed there was a wetland impact by the construction."

He then fielded alarmed reports that Maggard's construction crew was cutting down trees that weren't supposed to be cut, he said. He went back out with the county forester and they worked that out.

"I allowed him to remove some exotics—some camphor trees," the building official said. "He had to keep the native trees."

The big fight, though, involved a planned 12-foot "walkway" down to the lake that would cut through the wetlands. The building official could tell it wasn't a walkway but rather a concrete driveway for a boat ramp.

Nevertheless, he said, "I tried to work with him."

The building official suggested making the path out of a permeable material so water could continue to flow through it. That way, he said, it would comply with the wetland protection section of the Pasco County development code.

"He said, 'Nope,' and it got kind of nasty," the official told me. "He went over my head."

When I asked what happened next, he paused, choosing his words very carefully.

"It got approved," he said finally. "I didn't approve it."

Maybe now is when I should mention that the county commissioner for the area covering Lake Jovita is Ron Oakley. He has a sister married to Dale Maggard, which means she's the mother of Zach Maggard.

This seems like a good time to play Queen's "Under Pressure."

* * *

This, then, is the real reason Representative Maggard wants to take away from cities and counties their power to protect wetlands and combat water pollution: Because his nephew did some improper things, got caught, and yet pretty much got away with it.

Meanwhile Senator Burgess is apparently going along with Maggard's misguided mission as a favor to the family of his law partner. It's not because he has some deep-seated desire to rob the public of clean water. Heck, he's the former mayor of Zephyrhills, aka "the city of pure water."

Let's listen to Marty Robbins croon about "Cool, clear water . . ."

I talked to Representative Maggard this week about how this Lake Jovita situation involving his nephew turned into a legislative attack on all 67 counties and 400 or so cities across the state.

He acknowledged that his nephew's case had inspired the bill and demanded to know how I'd heard about it (it's common knowledge in Tallahassee). Once environmental groups began trumpeting how awful his bill was, he told me, he received "20 or 30 phone calls" from people who claimed to have had similar experiences. He also drew support from some powerful pro-development organizations, he said.

Our discussion was a little confusing because he kept using the word "duplicitous" to mean something other than "deceptive." When I finally asked him if he meant people were lying, he said no.

"To me, duplicitous means you're duplicating something," he said. (I was tempted to quote Inigo Montoya from *The Princess Bride* and tell him, "I do not think it means what you think it means," but I didn't think he'd get the joke.)

Maggard told me he's in favor of protecting our sources of clean water from pollution, but "why do the customers, the consumers, the citizens have to go through all these hurdles?" He didn't see the connection.

To Maggard, we should have only one agency protecting our water, even if that agency is doing a terrible job. I expect he's also opposed to requiring a second handrail on all staircases. Probably supports closing county sheriffs' and city police departments because the Florida Highway Patrol already exists. Why have a National Guard when we've got the Army?

Get rid of all that "duplicitous" stuff!

I don't know whether other legislators have drunk so deeply from the Well of Nincompoopery to vote for these idiotic bills. We can only hope that the process of wading through several "duplicitous" committee stops will slow them down too much to pass.

In the meantime, Bohne and Rexroat told me there's good news in Lake Jovita.

The eagles came back and rebuilt their nest. The mama bird promptly used the new nest to lay a couple of eggs, which recently hatched. Here's hoping those eaglets take flight soon—and then go peck the head of whichever duplicitous nincompoop tore the old nest down. If you're the one, I'd like to close by dedicating this NSFW Cee-Lo Green hit to you.

Postscript: The conversation I had with Representative Maggard remains one of the funniest in my 40-year history as a reporter. As for which Cee-Lo song I linked to, it's the one that the Muppets spoofed by showing a coop of chickens singing, "Cluck You."

36

A Little Fish Story

Florida Phoenix, August 10, 2023

This is a fish story. Not as big a fish story as, say, Jonah and the whale, or Chief Brody versus the shark in *Jaws.* It's actually about a pretty tiny fish. But, as with Jonah and *Jaws,* it's a fish story with an excellent outcome.

Fifty years ago, a Florida man named Nathaniel Reed worked as assistant secretary of the U.S. Department of the Interior. Reed was the son of a New York theater producer but he grew up far from Broadway. He spent his childhood fishing in Hobe Sound, collecting butterflies, and jotting notes on all the birds he saw around Jupiter.

The grown-up Reed was alarmed by reports of wildlife disappearing around America, so he gathered a group of like-minded federal officials at a Chinese restaurant off Constitution Avenue in Washington. In between egg rolls and moo goo gai pan, they jotted down the wording for what would become the Endangered Species Act, which passed Congress by a nearly unanimous vote in 1973 and was signed into law by Reed's Republican boss, Richard Nixon.

"We had the fervor of youth and a sense of high ethical standards for how man should treat his fellow creatures on spaceship Earth," Reed told me years later.

The earliest list of endangered species included such well-known critters as the Florida panther, the manatee, and the alligator, but the feds soon added others. One they put on the list in 1973 was a 2-inch yellow and green fish called the Okaloosa darter.

As the name implies, the Okaloosa darter lives in small streams in the Florida Panhandle counties of Okaloosa and Walton. It swims in short bursts of motion. In other words, it darts.

At the time of its listing as endangered, biologists said there were fewer than 1,500 darters left. It was circling the drain.

Now here we are five decades later and there are an estimated 600,000

An Okaloosa darter, recently removed from the endangered list. Photo courtesy of the U.S. Fish and Wildlife Service.

of them darting around in those Panhandle streams. I'm no math whiz, but even I can tell that's a vast improvement over 1,500.

The species is doing so well that, just last week, the U.S. Fish and Wildlife Service declared that the Okaloosa darter would no longer be on the endangered list.

The little fishy made a big comeback, baby!

How did this happen? Well, as the old anglers like to say, it's quite a tail. Er, tale.

* * *

Lately the environmental news around Florida seems remarkably grim.

Our coral reefs are baking like a Thanksgiving turkey in an oven set on too-hot-to-survive. Our seagrass beds are dying nearly statewide, leaving our manatees to starve to death by the hundreds. Our unchecked water pollution is fueling a rich soup of toxic algae that, in addition to being bad for us humans, may also be killing our state animal, the panther.

And I haven't even mentioned the leprosy outbreak.

That's why you'll have to forgive me for making such a big deal about this teeny-tiny fish. The survival of the Okaloosa darter seems like a beacon of bright light amid so much darkness.

Its rebound seems especially remarkable given its history.

For filling me in on this part of the story, I have to thank my friend Bill Kaczor, a former Associated Press reporter who covered some of the earliest controversies involving the darter. He dug up a bunch of fascinating 1970s stories, none of which involved Donna Summer or disco balls.

One story, carrying Bill's own byline, was headlined "Okaloosa Darter 'Costly' Minnow." That 1975 story begins, "The tiny Okaloosa darter may become known as Florida's million-dollar minnow."

That's how much state and federal money could be spent on keeping it from going extinct, he wrote.

Another story, this one from 1974 from my hometown paper, the *Pensacola News Journal,* warned that the darter was nearing extinction—but illustrated the story with a line drawing labeled "costly darter," as if that were its name.

That story quotes Okaloosa County commissioners referring to the darters as "those darn bullheaded minnows."

The commissioners were upset because a pair of modest bridges that they had planned were not allowed by wildlife officials. The simple box culverts they expected to install beneath the bridges would block the darters from traveling through the creeks. Instead, the Florida Department of Transportation had to build the bridges bigger, adding $940,000 to the cost.

A story about this particular controversy was headlined "Okaloosa Darters Muddy Progress on Highway 85 Cutoff Bridge," making the fish sound like a particularly aggressive sports team. I can just imagine the cheerleaders chanting: "Go, Darters! Block that bridge!"

"It looks like fish are more important than people," one bridge advocate harrumphed.

Some stories noted that the darters had "no economic value" of their own, making their protection seem pointless to a lot of hardheaded Panhandle residents. But other stories said that they were food for bass and bream, two popular freshwater sport fish.

Speaking as a hardheaded son of the Panhandle who has eaten his share of fresh-caught bream and bass, I'd say that makes them important indeed. Cook up a mess of filets, hand me a plate, and I'll say, "Fill it to the rim with bream," or "I'm all about that bass."

* * *

The little darters were lucky in one respect: 90 percent of the six clear streams where they live is held by a single owner, the federal government.

In fact, their landlord was none other than Eglin Air Force Base near Fort Walton Beach. It's a place for testing bombs with names like the "Massive Ordnance Air Blast." I bet they've got one they call something like "the

Super-Dee-Duper Hyper-Exploding Ultra-Big Bang," but that's probably classified.

Eglin has two major claims to fame: At 640 square miles, it is the largest air base in the world. And it's where the Father of Gonzo Journalism, Hunter S. Thompson, began his literary career.

If you're not familiar with ex-Airman Thompson's body of work, such as *Fear and Loathing in Las Vegas,* just remember that Thompson's personal motto was, "When the going gets weird, the weird turn pro." I think that could also be Florida's official motto.

Here's something weird: The place for blowing up those bombs used to be a place for growing trees.

The land was once Choctawhatchee National Forest, created in 1908 by President Teddy Roosevelt. In 1940, when Teddy's cousin Franklin was president and wars in Europe and Asia loomed, FDR turned the national forest into a big military base.

By then, the darter was already in trouble.

In the 1930s, federal workers began building red clay roads crisscrossing the property. For the road base, they dug clay from borrow pits—more than 100 of them. The old borrow pits and the crumbling clay roads dumped sediment into the streams, smothering the places where the darters lived, fed, and spawned.

The alteration of their habitat is what led to the darter decline. Thus, when the darters were put under federal protection in 1973, the military determined that the borrow pits and roads were the first places on the base that had to change.

Not right away, mind you. Nothing in the military moves that fast. Air Force officials took about 20 years to pivot from destruction to reconstruction.

But once they got going, they made a lot of progress, with help from the Florida Fish and Wildlife Conservation Commission and the U.S. Fish and Wildlife Service. You could say they were all swimming together toward a common goal, not unlike a school of fish.

* * *

I talked to two biologists who did a lot of the work on saving the darter: Michael Hill, now retired from the state wildlife agency, and Chris Metcalf, acting chief of the Panama City office of the federal wildlife agency.

Hill said that as they worked, they still ran into scorn from some people who didn't understand the point of saving such an insignificant animal.

"You couldn't eat it, so who gives a crap about it?" Hill told me was the attitude they ran into. But Hill said he called it "the poster fish for endangered fish" because the biologists had to come up with fresh strategies for pulling it back from the brink of extinction.

In 1994, Eglin officials committed more than $3.6 million to end the borrow pit problem. Meanwhile, Hill and Metcalf labored to fix other aspects of the darters' disappearing habitat—for instance, the railroad trestle no one remembered.

"There used to be a system of train tracks for moving things around the base, and one of the trestles was built over one of the darters' creeks," Metcalf explained.

At some point, the trestle fell into such disrepair that it collapsed. Meanwhile, erosion made the culvert that had been beneath it too high for the stream to reach. In effect, it had become a dam, blocking the fish, which meant it had to be removed and relocated.

"We didn't even know there was a trestle under there until we started digging everything out," Metcalf said. "Then we removed the culverts and reconnected the stream that had flowed underneath. Within days, the darters were moving up through the stream."

Another problem: the base's golf course water hazard.

"There were 10,000 golf balls in it when we drained it," Hill said. They cleaned out the muck on the bottom, too.

They also focused on a stream at the course where the darters had been seen years before, although none lived there anymore. The biologists figured they could restore the stream flow and attract the fish. But how?

The stream ran beneath a wide path to the fairway where the golfers often drove their carts. That meant the biologists couldn't just eliminate the pathway. Instead, they put in a very special culvert, one nearly 200 feet long.

A culvert that long would be dark like a cave, Metcalf said. Unlike some politicians I could name, darters don't like the dark.

In order to show the darters that it was safe to swim through the long culvert, they built a series of manholes with Plexiglas covers. That would allow sunlight to penetrate the culvert's gloom so the fish could see it was safe.

In effect, Hill said, they built skylights for the fish.

"Within two days, the darters were already moving from downstream to upstream through the culvert," Metcalf said. "It just opened up this whole area."

Metcalf and Hill were both fairly happy with the solution, which Metcalf called "pretty nifty." By the way, if you are thinking that "Skylights for Fish" would make an excellent name for an indie rock band, I would say you're absolutely correct.

I asked both Hill and Metcalf what they learned from the restoration project, something that we could apply to other endangered species.

"One thing we learned," Metcalf said, "was to think WAAAAY outside the box."

* * *

Justin Johnson, who's the chief of fish and wildlife at Eglin, called the skylight solution "smart people addressing a challenge," which I think sums up the whole effort.

Johnson told me they had to deal with other obstacles—beavers, for instance, that built actual dams that had to be removed. Overall, though, mostly what they were erasing were thoughtless human intrusions on the natural landscape.

By repairing the darter habitat, they enabled the fish to fill it with a piscine population boom. Johnson is hopeful that Eglin can apply that tactic to some of the 10 other endangered species that live on the base, too.

"The point is that recovery is attainable," Johnson said. "It does happen, although it doesn't happen often."

When I mentioned that it took 50 years from listing to recovery for the darters, Metcalf pointed out that they were correcting mistakes made even further back—nearly 100 years, in fact.

The darter story takes on added importance because there's been some chatter lately about how Nat Reed's law, the Endangered Species Act, may itself be endangered.

"Conservative administrations and lawmakers have stepped up efforts to weaken it, backed by landowner and industry groups that contend the act stifles property rights and economic growth," an Associated Press story reported recently. "Members of Congress try increasingly to overrule government experts on protecting individual species."

The chairman of the House Committee on Natural Resources, an Arkansas Republican and former Razorback football player named Bruce Westerman, called the act "well-intentioned but entirely outdated . . . twisted and morphed by radical litigants into a political firefight rather than an important piece of conservation law." He promised changes would be forthcoming.

I wish every one of these naysaying nincompoops could see the success of the Okaloosa darter the same way the Air Force does—as a major victory.

At a ceremony at Eglin last week that for some reason did NOT involve dancing, the current assistant secretary of the Interior, a Florida native named Shannon Estenoz, told the *Northwest Florida Daily News* that the way to look at this is the way a child would:

"If you want to understand the real magic and connection of the Okaloosa darter, take a four-year-old down to the streambed and just listen and watch them when they spot an Okaloosa darter—the wonder and delight of seeing something living scurry."

Recalling Bill Kaczor's story about the "million-dollar minnow," I asked Johnson how much saving the darter had cost the taxpayers. He estimated the price was about $200,000 a year for the past 30 years or so. Hey, it's the Six Million Dollar Fish!

But bear in mind that's a total of $6 million out of a federal defense budget that's currently totaling $1.77 trillion-with-a-T per year.

I think you could fairly call that a drop in the bucket—or maybe a little fish in a very, very big pond.

Part Five

LOOKING BACK,
LOOKING FORWARD

37

The Unlikely Tree Hugger

Florida Phoenix, January 5, 2023

We buried my dad last week. Oscar Pittman had a good, long life. He'd just turned 87, and he and my mom had celebrated 67 years of marriage.

Dad loved to tell stories and make people laugh. When I was a kid growing up in Pensacola, I used to hate going with him on trips to Sears or anywhere else because we were bound to run into somebody he knew. They would get to talking and what should have been a 10-minute shopping trip always turned into an hour.

I thought I knew all of my dad's stories, from set-up to punchline. For instance, there's the one about the two Baptist deacons discussing a fishing trip. One deacon brags that the fish he caught was so big, "if I hadn't seen it, Brother, I wouldn't have believed it." The other coolly replies, "Brother, I didn't see it."

After the funeral, though, my mom told me a story about my dad that I had never heard before. It showed me a different side of him than the one I knew. It concerns Florida's all-important wetlands.

Let me explain.

There was a good turnout for Dad's funeral service. Many of the chairs were filled by the scads of surveyors he had mentored. My dad spent 55 years as a registered Florida land surveyor. He even taught courses on the subject at Pensacola State College and the University of West Florida, despite lacking a college degree himself.

Surveying is a noble and historic profession, one that's perfect for folks like my dad who are (A) good with math and (B) need a job that allows them to take long walks in the woods.

George Washington was a land surveyor before he became a general and a president. So were Lewis and Clark, dispatched to explore the Louisiana Purchase (not to be confused with Owens and Clark of the TV show *Hee Haw.*) So was Henry David Thoreau before he began hanging out by a certain pond.

The author and his father in 1981. Photo courtesy of Craig Pittman.

Some of Florida's earliest white explorers were government surveyors hacking their way through thick swamps and forests to lay out railroad lines and county boundaries. These days, though, surveying tends to be tied more to the state's real estate industry.

My dad made a good living off all the development in the Panhandle. But he didn't necessarily hold the developers themselves in high regard.

One of them, a man I'll call O'Malley, had hired him to lay out a new subdivision, but he had a problem: He couldn't think of a good name for the subdivision. I guess "The Wilderness" was already taken.

Knowing that Mr. O'Malley was pretty sold on himself, Dad said, "How about calling it O'Malley Acres?"

Mr. O'Malley thought that was a BRILLIANT idea.

Anyway, the story mom told me isn't about Mr. O'Malley but another developer who sounds a lot like him. This guy—let's call him Bombastic Bob—was pretty sure he was king of the world and everything in it should bow to his implacable will.

There was something BB wanted my dad's help in bending to his will. And my dad didn't want to do it.

It involved a place known as Floridatown.

* * *

Even if you're a Florida native like me, you've probably never heard of Floridatown. No, it is not where all the Florida Men (and Women) live. They hail from all over Florida, especially Pasco County.

Floridatown is an unincorporated area in Santa Rosa County, lying right on the shore of Escambia Bay. According to Pensacola historian Brian Rucker, an entrepreneur from Georgia named William Barnett founded it in 1822, laying out lots and calling it the Town of Florida. I guess he was the original Bombastic Bob.

This Georgian's Floridatown "was the first real estate development outside of Pensacola in the early American period," Rucker told me. Barnett built a sawmill there and set up a ferry for crossing the bay. The ferry ran until cars and trucks replaced it in the 1920s, he said.

In the early 1900s, there was a rather grand establishment known as the Floridatown Hotel, sometimes called the Andrew Jackson Hotel. Both it and Barnett's sawmill are long gone.

My grandmother once told me about a wooden dance pavilion built near the bayfront in Floridatown by her father, my great-grandfather. She said he inserted small electric lights among the polished parquet floorboards. That way, at night, when the twinkling lights were switched on and the overhead lights switched off, the dancers felt like they were floating among the stars.

Now there's a county park with a playground, basketball court, picnic tables, and a fishing pier. People go there to marvel at the sunset. Some even have weddings. Because Floridatown sits on the edge of the bay, there are saltwater marshes there.

That's where, in the 1990s, this particular developer wanted to build his subdivision—smack in the middle of those marshes. According to my mom, he wanted to hire my dad to lay out a high-priced subdivision atop all the wetlands.

She says Dad's response was to shake his head and say, "You don't want to do that."

* * *

To say I was surprised to hear this is an understatement. It was as surprising as it would be to hear an announcement from Tallahassee that Governor Ron "Woke-Won't-Work-on-Me-because-I-Hit-the-Snooze-Button" DeSantis will lead a televised ceremony commemorating the 100th anniversary of the Rosewood Massacre.

My dad was not a member of the Sierra Club or the Audubon Society. He'd done work for destructive developers before. In fact, I'd seen that first-hand.

Back in the early 1980s, I spent a summer as a lowly grunt on one of my dad's survey crews. It was hard work. I collected enough blisters on my hands in just the first day of swinging a machete to qualify for a Guinness record.

Our big job that long, hot summer was laying out a new subdivision on land that was half swamp, half hog pen. The name of the subdivision to be built in this hellish location: Paradise Bay.

Live in Florida and you'll never suffer from an irony deficiency.

Because I was just a dumb college student, I told one of my co-workers that summer that I didn't see how anyone could build anything on that site besides a duck blind.

He snorted and told me that with enough fill dirt, you could turn any wetland into something temporarily dry and call it a subdivision. Print up some glossy brochures with pretty pictures and the buyers will believe it's prime real estate—at least until the yard turns into a lake. We laughed and kept on working.

At some point after Paradise Bay but before this Floridatown job came along in the '90s, my dad apparently learned that wetlands are important. They recharge our underground aquifer. They serve as habitat for a lot of important species. They filter out pollutants from stormwater. And they provide a sponge-like barrier against floodwaters.

I can't claim any credit for this change in his attitude. I didn't start writing about the loss of Florida's wetlands until after he'd retired from surveying in 2000. This is something he apparently figured out on his own.

The wannabe developer, my mom told me, didn't want to hear my dad's objections. He wanted to hear how much it would cost him to get that survey that he needed to proceed with his plans.

Dad didn't say no. Instead, he quoted him a price that was so outrageously high that the guy would go away.

That didn't stop Bombastic Bob, of course. He found a less scrupulous surveyor who was eager to collect a paycheck and the development proceeded.

The fancy subdivision got built atop the wetlands, and people bought those houses. Put in enough fill dirt, print up enough glossy brochures, you know the rest.

And then, a few years later, the storm came.

* * *

I well remember 2004, the year Florida got clobbered by four hurricanes in six weeks. The storms stomped across our landscape like a flamenco dancer wired on Red Bull, leaving quite a trail of destruction.

The last of the four, Hurricane Ivan, smacked the Panhandle around pretty hard. The winds only qualified as a Category 3, but Ivan had a massive storm surge. The surge was so big it took out the Interstate 10 Escambia Bay Bridge, which had been built 13 feet above the water.

One American Meteorological Society study noted that "Escambia Bay acted as a funnel and channeled the storm surge." A Federal Emergency Management Agency report said that the highest surge "was 16 feet in Floridatown at the north end of Escambia Bay."

The Floridatown wetlands that had once lined the bay could have soaked up that surge. The houses that had replaced them didn't do nearly as well. Too much of what the surveyors call "impervious surfaces."

Ivan wasn't the only storm to swamp that once-swampy area either. Hurricane Sally did it again in 2020.

"It's not a good place to live because of the storm surge," Shelley Alexander, the environmental programs coordinator for Santa Rosa County, told me this week. "Floridatown winds up underwater after every storm event."

The county is now planning to build a "living shoreline" along that area to try to fix this perpetual problem. The plans call for an offshore breakwater to disrupt the waves and a "marsh sill" that will be filled with native plants.

Funding is coming from federal dollars that are in DeSantis' budget for "resilience" projects. These projects are supposed to help waterfront communities cope with rising sea levels—and, in this case, really bad development decisions.

* * *

Of course, by the time a massive wall of gray water was rushing toward the residents of Floridatown in 2004, Bombastic Bob had raked in his profits and moved on to other developments. That means it's up to us taxpayers to foot the bill for fixing what he did wrong.

This isn't just a story about my dad, of course. This is a story about what's been happening to our wetlands for years, something that has recently accelerated.

Two years ago, in the waning days of the Trump administration, the U.S. Environmental Protection Agency gave its blessing to Florida taking over the issuance of federal wetland destruction permits.

A year later, the EPA under the Biden administration was waving a big old red flag about a lot of the wetland permits that Florida had issued. The

EPA said that the state was letting way too many marshes, swamps, and bogs get paved over.

As if to underline its point, EPA officials last week announced they now have a broader definition of wetlands to be protected than the, er, um, "business-friendly" one the Trump administration put forward.

Of course, the builders and developers hollered like somebody had left a burning bag of poop on their porch. Saving wetlands would inconvenience them and possibly slow down their plans for making a profit the way Bombastic Bob did. Can't let that happen!

Listen, my dad was no sandal-clad tree hugger swooning with joy at the sight of a butterfly. He was a hardheaded businessman in boots and khakis. As a child of the Great Depression, he was determined to provide for his family the only way he knew how.

But even he could see that constructing a subdivision atop wetlands was a bad investment for the future. Burying them under fill dirt to build frequently flooded homes is pure foolishness.

Yet the folks in charge of Florida's wetlands seem to be in a rush to let all the Bombastic Bobs keep doing exactly that, over and over again. They say they're protecting the environment, but to paraphrase that Baptist deacon in my dad's old joke: Brother, I'm not seeing it.

38

A Burning Issue

Florida Phoenix, April 27, 2023

Longtime Floridians are accustomed to the threats posed by water and wind. So often are we hammered by hurricanes and floods that I know people who refuse to take a storm seriously if it's not at least a Category 3. They regard anything below that as an excuse to throw a hurricane party, nothing more.

But 25 years ago, we were hit by a calamity of a different kind:

Fire.

In 1998, we endured six weeks of wildfires that were so bad, an entire county had to evacuate its 40,000 residents. All lanes of Interstate 95 and Interstate 4 closed down. Foot-long ash fell from the sky. Billboards melted in their frames. Some 10,000 firefighters from across the nation joined forces to combat blazes that ravaged a total of 860,000 acres. Despite their efforts, more than 300 homes were destroyed.

How bad was it? In a speech beamed by satellite to television stations across the state, then-governor Lawton Chiles asked Floridians to appeal to a higher power for help.

"'I hope you will join me in praying for rain," he said. "We have to hold on until the rain comes." (Can you imagine anything like that happening today? Governor Ron "God-Made-Me-More-Special-than-Other-Men" DeSantis would be too busy with his international "book tour" to come back home and help his constituents.)

Because newspaper editors love anniversary stories the way I love barbecue ribs, several Florida newspapers—*Florida Today, TCPalm.com,* and the *Daytona Beach News Journal*—ran "25th anniversary of the wildfires" stories last week.

I didn't need these journalistic reminders. I was one of several dozen reporters who covered the conflagration when it happened, and my memories of this event remain vivid. It's one of the worst disasters I've ever seen— even worse than the current legislative session, believe it or not.

Every interview was done in a rush because we didn't know which way the flames might jump next. Sometimes it was hard to hear responses to questions because helicopters thundered overhead, headed out to dump an entire pond on the burning forests. By the time I got home, the smell of smoke permeated all my clothes like an especially acrid cologne: Brut-ally Burnt-Up.

One Flagler County resident told me he'd built his sturdy block home to withstand another Hurricane Andrew—but he wasn't ready for this.

"We built for wind and storm, but nobody could build for fire," he said. "Fire will walk right through anything."

The *Florida Today* story on the anniversary emphasizes how much fire-fighters learned about fighting wildfires thanks to this heartbreaking event. You know who didn't learn anything?

Florida's developers.

* * *

Fire is as essential to the natural Florida landscape as it is to the name of the funk group Earth, Wind & Fill in the Blank.

"The vast majority of ecosystems in Florida are fire-dependent," said Hilary Swain, director of the Archbold Biological Station in Venus. Our landscape evolved to embrace fire because "lightning strikes are part of our long-term history going back millennia."

People who don't know this about Florida often look at all fire as if it were a destructive force, Swain said. They don't understand that regular fires that sweep through the pinelands, prairies, sand hills, and grasslands "are like winding up an old watch," she said.

The fires renew the energy of the place, restarting the growing season, spreading some species—saw palmetto, for instance—and thinning out what's become overgrown. The new growth even does a better job of sucking climate-warming carbon dioxide from the atmosphere, she said.

One mark of a longtime Floridian, Swain said, is that you drive by a stand of trees with blackened trunks and a vigorous burst of underbrush sprouting around them, a place that burned just a couple of months before, and you say, "That was a good fire."

Burning up old growth and forest debris also lessens the risk of wildfire, she pointed out. It's only when safe fires have been suppressed that we risk the wild, uncontrolled kind.

Some primitive part of the human brain recoils from any fire that humans don't control. It's OK when you've got a nice blaze warming you up

The first-ever prescribed burn in Florida, conducted at Falling Waters State Park. Photo courtesy of the Florida Park Service.

in a fireplace or cooking some 'smores by a campfire. When those orange tongues are bouncing willy-nilly from pine to palmetto, we freak out like the Monster in the movie *Young Frankenstein* seeing a flame flickering from his thumb.

That's why, for decades, you never heard a forester or a park ranger say anything nice about a fire. In the 1920s, the American Forestry Association dispatched its "Dixie Crusaders" across the South to warn everyone about the evils of fire. That became the gospel for decades.

"Fire was taboo back then," recalled Jim Stevenson, a longtime Florida park naturalist. "We thought the worst thing you could do was have a fire in a state park. We'd risk life and limb to put one out."

* * *

When the South's population of bobwhite quail declined, the owners of bird-hunting plantations near Tallahassee and Thomasville, Georgia, hired a federal biologist named Herbert L. Stoddard to figure out why.

Stoddard's studies found that the plantations needed regular fires to create the kind of habitat that quail favored. Suppressing the fires had messed that up.

Stoddard and a scientist named Ed Komarek established Tall Timbers Research Station near Tallahassee to study the ecology of the Panhandle's

Jim Stevenson, who worked on that first burn.
Photo courtesy of Jim Stevenson.

piney woods. Komarek persuaded Stevenson that conducting a regular "prescribed burn" would have ecological benefits for the state parks.

In 1971, Stevenson convinced his park service bosses to let him try one at Falling Waters State Park near Chipley. They chose that park because it was near Tallahassee and had the right mix of fire-sensitive species, Stevenson told me.

Leading the burn 52 years ago was Komarek's wife Betty, a Florida State graduate with a degree in botany who had co-founded the Birdsong Nature Center in Georgia. It was rare in those days for a woman to supervise a bunch of male park rangers, but her experience at Birdsong made her well-qualified.

"She was the fire boss," Stevenson recalled. "The burn went well, and we were off to the races." (Somehow we never see a salute to Betty Komarek during Women's History Month, but clearly we should.)

These days, park officials know that approximately 300,000 acres of the park system needs regular burning. Prescribed burns are a routine management practice throughout the state's parks and forests—except when it upsets nearby residents.

* * *

The firefighters who dealt with the 1998 disaster learned a lot, said Jim Karels, a onetime forester and firefighter who served as head of the Florida Forest Service from 2008 to 2020. One thing they learned was that there was a great need for regular prescribed fires.

"We do better with prescribed fire: the equipment is better and the management of it is better," Karels told me. "We were more isolated then, but now we have agreements and compacts in place to help each other."

However, he noted that one major problem is that "we still build in the wildland-urban interface."

In other words, developers are still scattering crop after crop of suburban homes that shouldn't burn amid the multiple stands of need-to-burn forests.

That's a problem because "people coming down here from up North—say, New York—don't know about wildfires or prescribed fires," said Karels, who's now fire director for the National Association of State Foresters.

Please join me in humming "Smoke Gets in Your Eyes" by the Platters for this next part of the column.

I asked Jane West of the smart-growth group 1000 Friends of Florida if she's seen this problem with builders plopping down houses too close to where the landscape needs to burn. Her "yes" shot out as fast as a 10-year-old racing to flag down a passing ice cream truck on a hot day.

Local and state government agencies often approve of building subdivisions too close to parks, forests, and wildlife management areas, she said. Then the residents become hot under the collar the second they smell that first whiff of smoke from a prescribed burn.

"The residents get outraged . . . and the next thing you know, they end up shutting down the prescribed burns," West said. By not allowing the regular burning to proceed, she told me, "that's setting it up to become a wildfire."

When I asked West for an example of what she was talking about, she brought up a project from the Jacksonville area from a few years back.

On land that had been used for growing timber, the Edwards Creek Preserve (yes, that's right, "preserve"!) sought a rezoning from rural to planned unit development. That way, its owners could build 790 single family residences.

The property was adjacent to the Timucuan Ecological and Historic Preserve as well as the Pumpkin Hill Preserve State Park, both of which needed to hold regular burns.

Instead of blocking the development or forcing it to be built as far from the two natural areas as possible, she said, the city council imposed an odd requirement: The developer had to disclose to the first buyer of each home site that there would be prescribed burns going on at certain times of the year. That was it.

Only the first buyer of the property got the notice, West told me, and "there was no requirement to disclose anything to subsequent buyers."

Plus, she said, the notice was "just a single piece of paper" provided to the buyer amid the cascade of documents presented at closing. The warning was likely to get lost amid the sea of other paperwork involved, she said.

Then West referred me to a fire expert named David Gordon from Quest Ecology in Wimauma.

"In my experience, developers do very little [to deal with wildfires] so it's put upon the agency landowners to install expensive fire breaks," Gordon told me. "When development goes in, you can no longer burn when the wind is coming from a particular direction because then it will put smoke on those residents."

As homes, stores, hospitals, and other human features are built next to forests, that can close the "burn window" for when and where a prescribed burn can take place, Gordon told me.

"It makes it more and more difficult," he said, "and things don't burn as often as they need to."

* * *

"Well," you may be thinking, "this is an interesting discussion, but what does this thing that happened 25 years ago have to do with things that are happening now? I mean, didn't you just write a column about heavy rains and flooding in Broward and Palm Beach Counties?"

This is the point at which I refer you back to the *Florida Today* anniversary story.

"This year, similar heat, drought, and other factors that set Florida ablaze 25 years ago are aligning," the story notes. "They are driven by the same climate cycle, although to lesser degrees. Meanwhile, other risks have grown. Today, 7.6 million more people live in Florida than in 1998, many at the fringes of where overgrown forests and newer subdivisions meet."

In other words: Say hello to 1998, Part Two!

As of two weeks ago, two-thirds of the state was suffering from moderate to extreme drought conditions, making those areas ripe for a wildfire to erupt.

All the trees knocked down by Hurricanes Michael, Ian, and Nicole can make for good wildfire fuel, too, especially in the places where prescribed burning has been limited by houses built too close to the woods.

Fortunately, we've had a little precipitation recently that lessened the fire threat somewhat. But it seems silly to me that we rely on the storms that bring us all those lightning strikes to also drench the debris-strewn landscape so it won't burn.

Why not push the builders to be more mindful of the fire risk they're leaving for the residents, just as they should be mindful of building in areas that flooded during hurricanes? We never do either one, though. Our elected officials, many of whom were elected with the builders' support, repeatedly grant the developers everything they want in order to maximize their profits and then walk away.

So, until we get into the full-fledged thunderstorm season next month, I'd recommend you heed the advice of the late Governor Chiles: Say a prayer that the good Lord sends us some wildfire-quenching rain.

39

96 Hours

Florida Phoenix, October 13, 2022

Jesus had some good advice for Florida developers: Don't build a house on the sand. It won't stand up when a storm hits.

"The rain came down, the streams rose, and the winds blew and beat against that house, and it fell with a great crash," the Son of God said in Matthew 7:27.

But Florida developers don't like anyone telling them what to do, not even a deity with the power to walk on water. So they have been building houses, condos, and a lot of other stuff on our sandy barrier islands for more than a century.

If you saw the pictures of all the beach communities devastated by Hurricane Ian, you saw a lot of buildings that "fell with a great crash." Yet a lot of the people who survived the storm are vowing to build back better, build back stronger, and build back in the exact same place they got wiped out before.

I'm not here to mock the survivors and their determination not to be beaten by adversity. What I am going to do is suggest that some places that held buildings were not the appropriate places to put human dwellings—not in a hurricane-prone state where mandatory evacuation is a drill we should all know by heart.

You know how that happened, though, don't you?

Builders trying to exploit a hot housing market for big profits ran roughshod over common-sense regulations intended to protect the public. Meanwhile, our elected officials went along with whatever the developers wanted.

A good example of what I am talking about is found in the recent case of Joanne and Bill Semmer v. Lee County and Southern Comfort Storage.

The case, Joanne Semmer told me this week, started about six years ago and involved a 7.58-acre property that contained a boat storage warehouse called Southern Comfort. The area had long been a working waterfront dominated by the seafood and shrimping industry.

But developers wanted to replace the warehouse with a marina, townhouses, and a high-rise resort called Bay Harbour, promising it would boost everyone's property values. To do that, however, the developers needed a change in the county's comprehensive plan for future growth.

Turns out, though, that the developers had a problem. The hurricane evacuation time for that area was already bad, and the occupants of Bay Harbour's 100-foot-tall tower would make it worse.

"I said, 'That's not an appropriate place to put a high rise,'" said Semmer, whose home sits 140 feet from the Southern Comfort warehouse, and whose brother Bill owns property nearby.

The county commissioners gave the comp plan change their blessing anyway. Then, after a hearing in Tallahassee, so did Governor Ron DeSantis and the three elected officials who make up the Florida Cabinet: Attorney General Ashley Moody, CFO Jimmy Patronis, and Agriculture Commissioner Nikki Fried.

Where, you ask, is Southern Comfort? On San Carlos Island in unincorporated Fort Myers Beach. It's one of the places that Hurricane Ian all but obliterated with a roaring storm surge of more than six feet.

The Bay Harbour site is at a busy intersection where vehicles line up to cross over the Matanzas Pass Bridge to the mainland. It's the same route residents of Estero Island use to evacuate—in other words, a crucial spot.

Semmer's home across the street was one of the many places on Fort Myers Beach that Ian nearly washed away. When I called her, she was exhausted from trying to deal with all of her losses. She said things would have been far, far worse if Bay Harbour had been built before Ian hit.

If I were the elected officials who gave Bay Harbour the green light, I wouldn't feel too Southern Comfortable about that decision now.

* * *

Lee County officials waited to issue a mandatory evacuation order for coastal areas until 7 a.m. Tuesday, September 27—a little more than 24 hours before Ian ripped up everything in sight after making landfall on Wednesday, September 28. A lot of people said that wasn't nearly enough time for everyone to flee a storm just a shade less powerful than a Category 5.

If you watched the proliferation of post-hurricane news, you probably saw at least one of the reports about our thin-skinned Outrager-in-Chief, Governor DeSantis, batting away complaints about the evacuation time.

"They were following the weather track and they had to make decisions based on that," he said in an interview with CNN that, as usual, turned into him heaping abuse on the reporter who dared to question him. "But you know, [at] 72 hours, they weren't even in the cone."

Actually, part of Lee County was always in the cone of uncertainty—an especially apt term in Ian's case. But that's not my point.

Evacuations are not supposed to be like passengers fighting over space in the lifeboats as the *Titanic* sinks beneath the waves. They're supposed to go in a very orderly series of steps.

"Governments have to plan how to get all these people out of here," explained Ralf Brookes, who represented Semmer in her and her brother's case against Bay Harbour.

Florida used to have a statewide planning agency, the Department of Community Affairs. That agency required counties to ensure evacuation times from flood-prone zones known as Coastal High Hazard Areas would be less than a day, Brookes pointed out. The law said the development density in those areas should not make the evacuees need more than 16 hours to get away from a Category 5 storm.

But when Rick "Look-at-My-Navy-Hat-Not-My-Hands" Scott was governor, he and the legislature killed that planning agency as dead as if Michael Corleone had called for the hit. They claimed that by trying to steer development away from places it shouldn't occur, the agency was ruining Florida's economy.

In the 12 years since that unjustifiable homicide, local governments have been allowing more and more development in those Coastal High Hazard Areas. Thus, evacuation times have been getting worse.

How bad are they now? According to Lee County Attorney Amanda Swindle, the current evacuation time for Lee County in case of a Category 5 hurricane isn't the legally required 16 hours but 96 hours.

Yes, I said 96. As in the number of tears Question Mark and Mysterians sang about.

"It is a long way off" from what the law requires, Swindle admitted.

That's four days—or about three more than the residents got as Ian veered their way.

And Lee is far from the only county that has allowed too much development to pile up in a place where people can't easily outrun a storm.

* * *

A four-day evacuation time. Think about that in the context of Ian. That's pretty much the same as saying: "We're never going to get everyone clear. Some people will die."

After dropping that particular truth bomb at the August cabinet meeting, Swindle noted that Lee had a lot of company in its rapidly sinking boat.

"Out of 45 counties in Florida's coastal areas, only nine of those counties" can meet the 16-hour standard, she told the state's top officials, who, for some reason, did not scream in dismay and swoon.

I did the math (don't laugh, I occasionally remember how a calculator works): 80 percent of the state's coastal residents live in places where there's too much development for them to safely flee a storm.

That's pretty dire. It sounds like a lot of local governments have been gambling with people's lives to benefit the builders who fuel their campaigns. It's almost as if they care more about money than their own voters.

In fact, it sounds like maaaaaybe the coastal counties should stop letting developers pack more residents into those death tra—er, excuse me, condos, townhomes, et cetera.

Instead of saying something like that, though, Swindle told the cabinet how wonderful it was that there's a loophole in the state's 16-hour law.

"Otherwise, development in these counties would essentially be held hostage, unable to develop or redevelop their property until the county can somehow magically meet those evacuation times," she said with a smile.

Thanks to this loophole, she said, Lee had allowed a lot of other projects to be built in the coastal high hazard area that made the evacuation time so bad. Nobody had bothered to challenge any before Bay Harbour came along, she said.

She then went on to claim—with a straight face—that Bay Harbour constitutes "smart coastal growth."

To me, it sounded about as smart as Herschel Walker debating his bathroom mirror.

* * *

How did the Lee County Commission get around the law in approving Bar Harbour's change to their comprehensive growth plan?

The same way state and federal wetlands permitters get around the laws that are supposed to protect wetlands: By promising to make up for any problems.

It's called "mitigation," and it's the Get Out of Jail Free card of property development in Florida.

"Listen," builders say, "I'm destroying 100 acres of wetlands, but through mitigation I'll make up for the damage. I'll preserve some land elsewhere or pull weeds from another swamp or write a check to someone in the mitigation business."

Then they get their permit, even though the "mitigation" rarely makes up for the wetlands that are lost.

In the case of hurricane evacuation, the loophole in state law says developers can get around that evacuation-time standard by offering to mitigate whatever they have added to the time.

They can do that by building new storm shelters, donating land for storm shelters, or donating money for storm shelters. In other words, it's all about shelters, not about making it any easier to get off the island. It just gives people more places they can go.

It's as if your child said, "I'm hungry" and you give him a plate with nothing on it. You've equated an empty gesture with one that actually deals with the problem.

* * *

Here's the reason the governor and cabinet got involved in this dispute: An administrative law judge named Suzanne Van Wyck listened to Semmer's objections to the comprehensive plan change, as argued by Brookes. Then she dismissed most of them.

But she ruled that Semmer was right about one thing. The judge agreed that the development would add to an already overburdened hurricane evacuations system, in violation of state law. She said that the comp plan change could stand only if the developer helped Lee County get its evacuation time down to 16 hours. That would be the only possible mitigation.

For some reason, the Lee County commissioners didn't welcome someone being ordered to help them get their evacuation problem fixed. Instead, they appealed the case to the governor and cabinet, sitting as the Administration Commission.

I called up my friend Charlie Whitehead, a former Fort Myers newspaper reporter who became a community activist. He's always had a reputation for telling it like it T-I-iS. He's also one of Semmer's neighbors. He, too, was totting up all that he'd lost in Ian's powerful surge.

"The reason the evacuation times are so bad is that the Lee County Commission never met a developer they didn't like," Whitehead growled. "Our commissioners believe what's good for the developers is good for Lee County."

We also talked about the timing of the cabinet hearing one month before Ian.

"It's just so Florida," Whitehead said with a chuckle, "that they did this right before a John D. MacDonald–style *Condominium* hurricane hit."

* * *

At the cabinet meeting, Swindle admitted that the county doesn't even know how much or what kind of mitigation the commissioners might require for Bay Harbour.

She said the impact might even be so minimal that they wouldn't require anything at all, a comment that drew a sharp rebuke from Attorney General Moody, who said it wasn't believable. (I found it completely believable.)

Russell Schropp, representing the developer, told the cabinet that his client was only willing to make up for what his project added to the evacuation time—not the whole thing. He mentioned building "an on-site shelter"—as if that should solve everything.

Semmer was there to warn everyone that a vote to overturn the judge's ruling was a vote to put people's lives at risk. She also said developers all over the state were watching to see how this case turned out.

Later, when I talked to her, Semmer had her own grim suggestion for how the developer could make up for all the new residents: "How many more body bags do they want to buy?"

Ultimately, DeSantis said he was going to side with the county, calling its position "reasonable." So did the other cabinet members—including Fried, a Democrat who seldom agrees with DeSantis.

Fried explained that she was voting to toss out the judge's ruling because "this would be a very bad precedent for any future development in the coastal counties." You can't let anything get in the way of building more houses on the sand, despite what Jesus said.

I tried to contact the governor and cabinet members to ask them if, seeing Ian's destruction, they now regret voting 4–0 to approve even more construction out there.

None of them got back to me. Gee, I hope I gave them enough time!

Schropp also didn't return my calls seeking a comment on whether this client—who before the storm sold the land for $18 million—plans to proceed with the development now.

Brookes said he wouldn't be surprised if Ian just hurries up even more overdevelopment by sweeping away the old working waterfront.

"Are the builders who have always been part of the Florida scene going to buy up all these lots from the insurance companies at bargain basement prices and then build taller building projects with many more times the density?" he asked.

You know the elected officials will be bowing to whatever those developers want. So, here's my suggestion. They should approve building in those areas that Ian destroyed, but with one requirement. Every single would-be buyer should get a photo showing exactly what that spot looked like after Ian hit.

Then, if they still want to buy there, give them the phone number for Dial-A-Prayer. They're going to need it, because if another Ian hits, the only one who can help them is Jesus.

40

The Green Wave

Florida Phoenix, November 24, 2022

Back when I was a kid in Pensacola, the church that my parents and I attended held services three times a week. We were there every time the doors were open: Sunday morning, Sunday night, and Wednesday night.

I liked the Wednesday sessions best because every couple of months we'd have a "song service." That meant we didn't have to pretend to pay attention to some dour preacher warning us against the evils of rock'n'roll and long hair on men.

Instead, the congregation would holler out page numbers from the *Baptist Hymnal.* Then the grinning choir director would lead us in vigorous renditions of songs like "Wonderful Grace of Jesus" and "The Old Rugged Cross." One request that came up every time: "Count Your Blessings."

I have been humming that hymn quite a bit lately, and not just because of the Thanksgiving holiday. It's been stuck in my head ever since the election results came in.

No, I don't mean the reelection of a governor who broke his promise to fix our toxic algae bloom problem, supports destructive toll roads, and constantly kowtows to developers. (To be honest, though, maybe I should be grateful about it, because it guarantees I'll have a lot to write about over the next two years.)

Instead, I'm talking about what the voters did in six Florida counties.

They voted to tax themselves to buy environmentally sensitive land.

In Alachua, Brevard, Indian River, Nassau, Pasco, and Polk counties, voters said yes to either a sales tax hike or a property tax hike to pay for saving swamps, forests, beaches, and waterways from being torn up by bulldozers.

Let's take a minute to appreciate how counterintuitive that is.

In Florida, our politicians are constantly promising more tax cuts. I keep expecting one to promise he or she will personally turn off the air conditioning in all government offices and leave the employees sweltering as if they're in a state prison.

Yet these voters opted to tax themselves MORE.

And they did it because they wanted to save some greenery in an ever-increasing sea of gray asphalt.

Marveling, I called Clay Henderson, a longtime Florida environmental activist whose new book, *Forces of Nature,* is a history of land preservation efforts in the Sunshine State. He had a theory about these votes:

"People are frustrated by the amount of growth and the pace of growth," he told me. "This is something that they can do about it."

* * *

Henderson and I are far from the only ones who noticed this "green wave" (which turned out to be more genuine than the "red wave" we were all promised). Traci Deen of Conservation Florida, a statewide land conservation group, spotted it too.

"Floridians don't always agree, but we do find common ground in the land and water we share," Deen, a sixth-generation Floridian, wrote in a recent *Tampa Bay Times* op-ed piece. "It's a great love of place. It's part of our ethos, our Floridian ethic, our heritage, and our legacy."

This green wave has been rolling through Florida longer than you may think.

Nearly 40 years ago, Henderson helped spearhead the nation's first voter-approved land-buying project. Volusia County's 1986 Endangered Lands program used a $20 million bond issue to buy 34 properties—water recharge areas, parks, and so on.

Volusia voters approved a new version of the land-buying program called Volusia Forever in 2000. They approved it a third time in 2020.

That kind of longevity speaks volumes about the way people feel toward those natural lands that are part of what make Florida special, Henderson said. They have "this sense of ownership."

By his count, there are now 19 of these local-voter-approved land-buying programs going on around Florida.

Some, like the one in Volusia, have been renewed more than once. The Brevard County program is another three-time winner, according to *Florida Today.*

"Brevard County voters . . . approved extending the Environmentally Endangered Lands Program, known as EEL, in a decision that could potentially double the roughly 28,000 acres of managed conservation land under the program," the paper reported this month.

That's one popular EEL. It passed with the approval of more than 70 percent of the voters. That's better than the first vote in 1990 (61 percent) and the second in 2004 (69 percent).

How much of a tax are they voting for? According to *Today,* "the owner of a single-family home in Brevard with a taxable property value of $200,000 would pay $29.30 a year."

Think of all the things you could buy for $30 (besides a $30 gift card). You could get a nice turkey for Thanksgiving. Or some of those "flame-less candles" that are really just flashlights. Or two of the "Pull-My-Finger Santa" toys.

Yet seven out of 10 Brevard voters decided to spend it on saving rivers, forests, swamps, lakes, and beaches. Sounds like a good bargain to me.

* * *

I found the ballot results in Polk County particularly fascinating. It's one place where the push to save the environment ran into pushback.

Yet, according to the *Lakeland Ledger,* the proposal passed with 58 percent of the vote.

There's always a lot going on in "Imperial" Polk. Just this week, for instance, a fugitive arsonist whose car had been stopped by deputies tried to sprint across Interstate 4 toward the T-Rex at the entrance of Dinosaur World, only to be shot in a particularly sensitive spot.

"We changed the looks of his groin forever, if you know what I mean," Sheriff Grady Judd announced rather proudly.

Polk is the pockmarked heart of our destructive phosphate mining industry. But it's also home to some key environmental features. They include the Green Swamp—the source for four major rivers—and the Lake Wales Ridge, an ancient sand dune running up the spine of the state.

To preserve some of those gems, Polk voters approved a land-buying program in 1994. It proved extremely successful, allowing the county "to acquire more than 25,000 acres, including what is now Circle B Bar Reserve, a 1,267-acre tract near Lakeland that has become one of the state's most popular birdwatching sites," the *Ledger* reported in July.

But that program expired in 2015. The county commissioners didn't want to continue it, according to Suzanne Lindsey, a Winter Haven native who chairs a group called Polk Forever that pushed for a new land-buying program.

The commissioners thought it wasn't necessary anymore (I'll tell you why in a minute), but it turned out they were wrong, she said. That's why the Polk Forever group went to the commissioners this year and asked them to put a new land-buying measure on the ballot.

The vote was close—3 to 2. The ones who voted no (one of whom is a developer) both said they supported the concept but felt that (A) the timing was wrong and (B) the tax levy (20 cents per $1,000 of taxable property) was too high.

But the other three commissioners said it was up to the voters to decide those questions and gave it a green light.

That wouldn't be the last time the measure would hit objections.

* * *

The vice chair of Polk Forever is Marian Layton Ryan, who's been a staunch Central Florida environmental advocate since the 1980s. I asked her to tell me her group's secret of success.

"Our secret was that we pushed every button we could to get the word out," she said.

That included everything from running radio ads on the country music station to putting on a traveling art show that displayed images of the landscapes being saved. They also handed out brochures and palm cards touting the proposal.

Ryan said people in their group went to every club meeting, special event, and festival in the county that they could, making their case face-to-face whenever possible.

That's how they found out they had a potential opponent in the local Republican Party, Ryan said.

"We knew we had problems early on because their clubs weren't returning our calls," she said.

The Polk County Republican Executive Committee never officially announced its opposition, she said, but had advised local Republicans to vote against the measure.

The chairman of the Polk GOP, J. C. Martin, told WFTS-TV he was voting against the Polk Forever proposal because he wanted to see "a more comprehensive plan for the county's lands before another tax is passed."

I tried contacting Martin to ask him about this, but apparently he was too busy to call me back. Perhaps he was out searching Haines City, Frostproof, and Eagle Lake for more drag shows that the governor can prosecute.

Ironically, the people running Polk Forever included Republicans as well as Democrats.

"Our board is very diverse," Ryan said. "It includes Republican hunters and fishermen, along with longtime bunny-huggers like me. This is definitely a bipartisan issue."

One hunting guide working with Polk Forever, Travis Thompson, summed up his thinking for WFTS: "If we don't do this today, these lands will be written as other things. . . . These lands will become houses."

* * *

The reason the 2015 Polk commissioners didn't think they needed to continue the land-buying program is that the year before, voters statewide had just approved one.

In 2014, 75 percent of Florida voters approved an amendment to the state constitution that said the legislature had to spend a certain amount of money buying environmentally sensitive land. Amendment One was expected to raise $22 billion over the next two decades.

Surely there'd be plenty of land preservation going on using that money, right?

Wrong. Our fine legislators, who always pay close attention to whatever developers want, paid absolutely none to what the voters wanted. Instead of buying environmentally important parcels, they blew millions on salaries, insurance, and new vehicles. Amendment One turned out to be Legislature One, Amendment Zero.

You'd think, as politicians, they'd be compelled to support something so popular. You'd think they'd even run on that: "I helped to save that swamp where you like to go look at migrating birds and that lake with the good fishing! Vote for me!"

But I know of only one recently elected legislator who made land preservation part of her pitch: Lindsay Cross, a Democrat, who just this week was sworn in as a new member of the House.

During the campaign, Cross made sure to play up her work with the Tampa Bay Estuary Program and her time as executive director of the Florida Wildlife Corridor organization.

Both political parties, she told me, usually treat the environment as nothing more than one of several bullet points on the back of a campaign brochure. But when she was campaigning, the voters she talked to understood that it's more important than that.

"It's something they were really excited about," she said. She noted that the destructive 2017–2018 red tide outbreak was "recent enough that people know what clean water means."

At some point, surely some smart Florida candidates will copy Cross and turn "saving forests from bulldozers" into a major talking point.

On my more optimistic days, I even picture a majority of our legislature embracing the green of the environment instead of the green of campaign cash, because it's what the voters want.

In the unlikely event that happens in my lifetime, I'll bust out the old *Baptist Hymnal* and start bellowing "Count Your Blessings." For now, though, all we can do is offer fervent prayers that our so-called leaders will someday see the light.

41

Our State Bert

Florida Phoenix, November 4, 2021

There is nothing our Florida legislators enjoy better than picking state symbols. They have given us a bunch, from the official state sand (Myakka fine) to the official state play (*Cross and Sword,* last performed in St. Augustine in 1997).

Sometimes their choices have resulted in rhubarbs. They fought over which pie to pick (Key lime beat pecan). They resisted naming the panther our state animal even though it had been chosen by schoolchildren (some lawmakers favored the gator). And every few years—this year included—somebody brings up the idea of changing our state bird.

Contrary to what you may have heard, Florida's state bird is not the construction crane. It is the common mockingbird (*Mimus polyglottos*), known for its ability to mimic everything from other birds to cell phone chimes. It's also known for being everywhere in the South, from the swamps to the suburbs. I can hear a couple of them chirping in my front yard right now.

The Florida Legislature selected the mockingbird in 1927, and then Arkansas, Mississippi, Tennessee, and Texas copied us because, like I said, mockingbirds are everywhere. Seeing our mockingbird choice mimicked, ironic though it may be, bothers a lot of folks.

In 1999, 10,000 schoolchildren proposed changing our state bird to the Florida scrub jay, an endangered species that exists only in Florida. That choice didn't fly then or when it came back up in 2000.

Then, in 2009, 20,000 kids voted for the osprey, which is not endangered but looks cool when it dives straight into the water to grab a fish. All three attempts at change were shot down (gun pun intended) by Marion Hammer, the tough-talking National Rifle Association lobbyist who also happens to love mockingbirds.

Now here comes Republican senator Jeff Brandes, representing part of Pinellas County, once again raising the idea of ditching the mockingbird. "He wants a bird that 'immediately says Florida,' like orange juice does as the state drink," the *Tallahassee Democrat* reported, failing to mention that oranges are not native to Florida.

Several people have asked me what I think about the latest bird brouhaha. You know what I think? I think it's not worth thinking about.

If I ran the legislature, I wouldn't waste the taxpayers' money fighting over state symbols (well, maybe Key lime pie, but only if I get to eat some). Instead, I would be calling for the immediate repeal of what's been the most damaging piece of legislation passed in the last 30 years.

I am referring to the little-known Bert J. Harris Jr. Private Property Rights Protection Act of 1995.

I have a theory that the longer the name slapped on a bill, the worse the bill will turn out to be. This is my Exhibit A. The real name, I think, should be "The Developers Can Do What They Want Law." Isn't that clearer?

The act is strictly for the birds, in the sense that it's for killing them and every other bit of the environment.

I have lost count of how many times over the years I have heard local government officials say some variation of this sentence: "Gee, we would really love to reject this terrible development that none of our constituents want, but we're worried we will get socked with a lawsuit under the Bert Harris Act and have to pay millions of dollars and raise taxes."

When the legislature first passed the Bert Harris Act 26 years ago, the law "had a big chilling effect" on local governments trying to control growth, recalled Jim Beever, a retired regional planner and biologist from Fort Myers.

The Bert Harris Act was supposed to protect the poor, beleaguered landowner from burdensome government regulations by granting them the right to sue for damages if, say, a zoning change hurt their plans for their property.

Instead, it became a cudgel for developers who wanted local officials to say yes to the most destructive of projects.

"There weren't a lot of Bert Harris Act cases," Beever told me, "but whenever developers wanted to fill a lot of wetlands or build on the water side of the mean high-water line or up the density on a piece of land, that's the law the city or county attorneys would cite, and say, 'If you don't give them what they want, you will have a Bert Harris Act suit on your hands.'"

And then the local government would cave.

* * *

You will not be surprised to hear this law was sponsored by a state representative from Lake Placid named (well, DUH) Bert Harris Jr. He was a grower
of cadmiums and citrus who devoted his life to promoting agriculture.

This was, as the old folks like to say, way back in the long-time-ago—
back in the days when Democrats controlled the Florida Legislature and
the governor's mansion. In the mid-1990s Harris, a Democrat, chaired the
House Agriculture Committee, meaning he was pretty influential.

In a 2012 interview, Harris said his namesake bill was born one day when
he bumped into another representative named Ken Pruitt on an elevator.
Pruitt was a water well contractor from Port St. Lucie, which means he benefited from new development.

The two of them started talking property rights versus regulations—you
know, like you do—and pretty soon they had worked up a bill that Pruitt
insisted on naming for his co-sponsor. Together they pushed it through
both houses and persuaded then-governor Lawton Chiles to sign it, which
I think may be Walkin' Lawton's biggest boo-boo.

One legal analysis published in 1995 said that the new statute "has stirred
fears that it will empty the public purse and roll back decades of work in
environmental protection and growth management," but assured readers,
"If properly implemented and applied, the measure will have none of the
above effects." (That was the point where I started laughing. Hindsight is
hilarious!)

I should mention that that legal analysis was written by a couple of lawyers who represented developers and the real estate industry and an attorney working for Chiles who then began working for the state's biggest
developer.

They got one thing right, though. This law was a reaction against all the
new laws Florida passed in the 1970s and '80s to protect the environment
and control runaway growth. I mean, how dare local governments try to
save even an acre of forest or swamp!

This was, by the way, a completely unnecessary law. Under the Fifth
Amendment to the U.S. Constitution, any time the government takes your
property, say, for use as a road right-of-way, then you have to be paid. It's
called a "taking," and it's an established piece of the law just like the Second
Amendment (which Marion Hammer loves more than mockingbirds).

But, under the Bert Harris Act, the definition of a taking expanded to
cover a whole lot more than just the government seizing your land. Instead,
if the government imposed some regulation that was so burdensome it pre-

vented you from using your land in a way that you wanted to use it, then that counted as a taking too, and the government had to pay you.

And by "the government," I of course mean "the taxpayers." Because all that money comes out of our pockets.

There is irony here. The Bert Harris Act was supposedly created to protect family farms and ranches. In reality, it has rewarded the speculators who wipe out farms and ranches, explained Wayne Daltry, who before retirement was Lee County's smart growth coordinator.

Meanwhile, the landowners, who didn't want to change a thing but just wanted to enjoy their woods or prairies, were out of luck, Daltry told me. The law gives them no tools to block a developer with designs on the property next door, someone ready to use the Bert Harris Act to clobber any local government standing in the way.

The law itself is a mess. A 2015 analysis published by the *Florida Bar Journal* said that "there appears to be a great deal of ambiguity as to what is protected under the act, how it should be applied, and what exactly constitutes a vested right, an existing use, or an inordinate burden." The only way it could be more confusing is if it were written in Esperanto.

As a result, when Bert Harris–related lawsuits do hit the courts, they tend to be lengthy and expensive. One such suit, Pacetta v. Town of Ponce Inlet, "spanned over a decade with multiple appeals . . . costing millions in attorneys' fees," according to one analysis I read. It reminded me of the lawsuit in Charles Dickens' novel *Bleak House* that went on for so long that people were born into it and died out of it.

The Ponce Inlet case didn't even involve something local government did, but rather something it did not do—namely, that it did not pass new rules to allow a boat storage complex to be built. Oh, the horror!

Because the law is so poorly written, the legislature keeps tinkering with it, trying to get it right. When I was chatting with Eddy Labrador of the Florida Association of Counties about this, he suggested a creative solution: apply a version of Bert Harris law to the people who make our laws:

"Imagine if the Legislature did that to itself," he said, "where every time they passed a bill that affects a business, someone could file a lawsuit and demand damages."

The most recent changes that the legislators made took effect in October. The new version tips the scales even further toward developers, because why put the onus on the folks with the bulldozers to pay for things when you can stick it to the taxpayers?

* * *

Like the law it amended, the 2021 reform bill had a faintly ridiculous name: "The Relief From Burdens on Real Property Rights" bill.

But it was more vicious than it sounded.

The Bert Harris Act required a property owner to give 150 days' notice to the local government of a potential lawsuit, along with handing over a valid appraisal showing the amount of supposed damage done to the property value. This new law cuts that notice time down to a mere 90 days. And there's no longer any need for a valid appraisal, just a signed statement about the value.

There are other provisions that hurt local government and taxpayers, such as the one that says any property owner who wins gets to collect attorney's fees starting from when the claim was filed rather than when the suit started.

The really sneaky part of the latest Bert Harris changes had Tallahassee trying to overturn a court decision involving Lee County.

A developer sued Lee under the Bert Harris Act, but then sold the property in mid-suit. An appeals court ruled that the sale ended the lawsuit and thus Lee County won.

This new legislation, though, says that a property owner who sells his or her land during a Bert Harris Act lawsuit can still win the suit.

Yes, that's right, the legislature says someone who doesn't even own the disputed property any more can still collect damages from the taxpayers over an obstacle to its development.

When I asked Daltry about lawmakers trying to overturn an appeals court decision to benefit a developer who lost, he quipped, "It's always cheaper to buy a legislator with campaign contributions than to do the right thing."

And Governor Ron DeSantis, a graduate of Harvard Law School who claims to be a friend of the environment, was OK with that. He signed the Bert Harris changes into law, with nary a concern about the local taxpayers who will bear the burden or for the legal ruling that was overturned.

The thing we should do is stop trying to rewrite the Bert Harris Act and just repeal it. That should be a bipartisan shoo-in.

To the Republicans now controlling the legislature, I say: The Bert Harris Act is a law written by Democrats with a Democrat's name on it and it hurts taxpayers, so why would you want to keep it? To the Democrats I say:

Here's another mistake of the past that needs to be junked like a Confederate general's statue.

Not only is the Bert Harris Act confusing and expensive, but it ties the hands of local governments as they try to combat climate change. How can they tell people not to build homes in areas that more frequently flood if the Bert Harris Act says they can't impose such "burdensome" regulations?

But I doubt the legislators will take my suggestion. This makes the Bert Harris Act the perfect symbol—of how screwed up Florida's state government can be.

42

The Lake That Sued

Florida Phoenix, April 28, 2022

Some people have accused me of being down on Florida because of all the bad stuff I write about—the shady politicians, greedy developers, and rapacious road builders. You know, the usual suspects.

Nothing could be further from the truth! I revel in opportunities to highlight the many ways Florida leads the nation. If I had a big foam finger with "Florida No. 1" written on it, I'd be shaking it like a Polaroid picture every chance I got.

We've got the only state park system that's won national awards four times. Our beaches frequently top the list of the best in the United States.

And everyone knows we've got the world's funniest police blotter items, such as "Florida woman pulls gator from yoga pants during stop." That story inspired Dave Barry and Carl Hiaasen to join forces and record a song titled "She Had Turtles in Her Trunk and a Reptile in Her Pants."

So, when I heard the news about our lakes, I was ready to do a fist pump. They're No. 1 in the nation! Woo-hoo!

For pollution, that is.

Cancel that fist pump.

"In a new study examining water quality across the U.S., Florida ranked first for the highest total acres of lakes too polluted for swimming or healthy aquatic life," WLRN-FM reported last month. "That means water can have high levels of fecal matter and other bacteria that can sicken people or low levels of oxygen or other pollution that can harm fish and other aquatic life."

The study, by the Environmental Integrity Project, was based on Florida's own reporting of its water quality progress (or lack thereof). Apparently, our report card is chock full of F-minuses.

That should tell you what a reeeeally terrific job the state Department of Environmental Protection has been doing protecting our environment over the past 20 years. I would suggest we throw the DEP a ticker tape parade for making us No. 1 but, judging by its record, the agency probably wouldn't make anyone clean up the confetti afterward.

(I asked the DEP for a comment on the study. The response sounded like one hand clapping.)

With the state regulators apparently asleep when it comes to pollution, is it any wonder some amateurs are ready to try fixing things?

That's why I wasn't surprised last week to read in the *Fort Myers News Press* that there's now a drive to pass a new constitutional amendment to say that in Florida, clean water is a right of all citizens.

"This is a legal tool whose time has come," Joseph Bonasia, a Cape Coral retiree who's spearheading the amendment's petition drive, told me this week.

To understand how this movement started, you have to go back to 2018, Orange County, and a passionate guy named Chuck O'Neal.

* * *

O'Neal runs a residential investment company and heads an environmental group called Speak Up Wekiva. I first encountered him in 2015, when he sued to stop the state's first bear hunt in 21 years.

The suit failed, allowing the state wildlife commission to proceed with what was supposed to be a week-long hunt. The hunters killed 304 bears in two days, including 36 lactating mother bears. The public backlash meant that was the end of bear hunts in Florida, although the bears probably would have preferred fighting it out in court.

As with the bear suit, O'Neal has seen his organization's efforts to protect the Wekiva River from pollution run into repeated roadblocks. He got frustrated with the system, which—SURPRISE!—seems weighted toward the folks with all the money.

"We're basically handcuffed here at the local level when it comes to protecting our water supply," he told me in 2020.

Then O'Neal went to a two-day conference where one of the speakers was Thomas Linzey, senior legal counsel for the Center for Democratic and Environmental Rights. Linzey talked about a growing worldwide movement to grant human rights to natural features, such as springs and rivers.

O'Neal invited Linzey to his house. With some other environmental activists, they drafted a proposed change to Orange County's charter that wound up on the ballot.

Meanwhile, though, Florida legislators, looking to protect their favorite contribu—er, I mean "constituents"—moved to stop the "rights of nature" gang from upsetting the balance of power in Florida. In this case, "balance" means the developers hold the steering wheel and sometimes turn it this way and sometimes turn it that way.

Representative Blaise Ingoglia, a homebuilder (of course) from Spring Hill, filed a bill that would ban local governments from granting "any legal rights to a plant, an animal, a body of water, or any other part of the natural environment."

Ingoglia delivered this oh-so-persuasive argument for passing his bill: "We are stopping local cities and counties from doing something that will hurt business, the taxpayers, the tax base."

Yes, God forbid we hurt business, y'all—unless of course it's a business like, say, a theme park that opposes something the governor supports. Then it's "release the Kraken!"

The bill failed, but Ingoglia snuck the language into another bill, the "Clean" Waterways Act. Although supposedly based on the recommendations of Governor Ron DeSantis' Blue-Green Algae Task Force, the bill was so unlike those recommendations that environmental activists begged DeSantis to veto it and start over.

Spoiler alert! He did not. That noted champion of (pretending to be a fan of) the environment instead signed it into law.

Nevertheless, Orange County's voters passed the charter measure by 89 percent. That's a pretty clear indication that they prefer clean water to developers destroying a public asset to make a private profit.

* * *

Now O'Neal is using the charter change to sue a development that would destroy about 100 acres of wetlands. The lawsuit, which he filed on behalf of two lakes, a marsh, and a couple of streams that rely on those wetlands, marks the first suit of its kind in the country, according to *The New Yorker*.

The idea of nature having rights was first proposed in a 1972 law review article headlined "Should Trees Have Standing?" by a University of Southern California professor with the ironic name of Christopher Stone.

Stone's argument was endorsed in an opinion by Supreme Court Justice William O. Douglas, which prompted an attorney named John Naff to poetically spoof the idea in the *American Bar Association Journal*:

Great mountain peaks of names prestigious
Will suddenly become litigious.
Our brooks will babble in the courts,

Seeking damages for torts.
How can I rest beneath a tree
If it may soon be suing me?

In other words, not everyone's a fan of the rights-of-nature movement.

For instance, a Seattle-based professional "Statler and Waldorf" imitator named Wesley J. Smith wrote a column for the *National Review* in reply to *The New Yorker* story on O'Neal's lawsuit. His main argument was—hang on, let me make sure I've got this quote exactly right—"Bah."

Smith then expounds on that: "What about the lost jobs if these development projects get scrapped, the consequences of preventing natural resources from being harnessed for human benefit, and the greater deleterious impact on humankind if environmentalist radicals are empowered with the legal standing to impose their ideology on the rest of us by court order?"

Somehow "lost jobs" wound up at the top of his list, yet "clean drinking water" gets not even a mention. You'd think a clean water supply would count toward Smith's stated goal of "harnessing" natural resources for human benefit.

* * *

According to O'Neal's suit, filed in February, the development would "adversely impact the lakes and marsh who are parties to this action," causing injuries that are "concrete, distinct, and palpable."

In other words, they'd screw up the ecology. As Marvin Gaye would say, "Mercy me!"

How many times have you seen developments pave over Florida's precious wetlands and obliterate an ecosystem? Now, the ecosystem is trying to fight back. But it's an uphill battle, to say the least.

During the first hearing on the case Tuesday, an attorney for the DEP argued that that charter vote doesn't matter because of Ingoglia's skullduggery.

"It is not up to local governments to decide whether the state government has made adequate provision for the environment," he told the judge, according to *Politico.*

If all those polluted lakes in Florida did have a voice, this is the point at which they all would have screamed, "Objection!" The judge has not yet ruled on the defendants' motion to dismiss O'Neal's case.

* * *

While the DEP's attorney is busy babbling like a brook on behalf of a developer, Bonasia and his organization are pursuing something that's both bigger and simpler.

Their group: Florida Right to Clean Water. As of April 11, they'd filed the paperwork with the state Division of Elections to try to amend the Florida Constitution in the 2024 election. This is their second try after a scattershot effort last year failed.

This time, rather than calling for lakes and rivers to have rights, their amendment would simply spell out that all of us—22 million thirsty humans squeezed into the Sunshine State—enjoy the right to clean drinking water. If something threatens to pollute it, we humans can sue.

"It's not giving rights to nature, but it's spelling out that humans have a right to nature," Bonasia told me.

Bonasia is a retired English teacher from New York, so he knows the importance of words. He emphasizes that the amendment wouldn't just say that humans have a right to clean water, just like they have a right to post pictures of their meals on Instagram. (I post pictures of my shirts, because they tend to be more colorful than my food.)

Instead, the amendment will guarantee that clean water is a fundamental right, like life, liberty, and the pursuit of happiness.

Bonasia says his group knows it's not going to be an easy battle.

They figure they will need $15 million to collect the necessary 891,589 signed and verified petition signatures to qualify for the ballot. They also have to convince those stone-faced justices on the Florida Supreme Court that the ballot language meets legal requirements.

Karl Deigert, a former charter boat captain who's working with Bonasia, figures the group needs volunteers in all 67 counties collecting 30 signatures a day each to get enough for the ballot.

If you want to sign the petition, donate or volunteer, their website is https://www.floridarighttocleanwater.org/. But bear in mind that this is going to be a long, hard slog to 2024.

"We certainly anticipate opposition," Bonasia said, rattling off expected objections: "Oh, that's just those goofy Rights-of-Nature people," or "It's going to harm the economy!" or "It's going to create a lot of lawsuits."

I worry that their biggest opponent will be apathy. Some people think that as long as you can turn on a faucet and get something liquid to squirt out, the water supply is fine. They don't notice the connection between pollution, toxic algae blooms, and lost tourism and fishing business.

Plus, there's a long history of legislative conniving to undercut constitutional changes.

Florida's voters have frequently gotten so ticked off at their legislators for not doing their jobs that they have approved constitutional amendments to force them to do what's right. There was one to limit class sizes, another to require the state to spend a lot of money on buying environmentally sensitive land, and one to give ex-felons their voting rights back.

Each time, our lawless lawmakers have subverted it somehow. Just this month, they ignored a 2010 citizen-driven constitutional amendment to require fair redistricting in order to pass a gerrymandered map demanded by our cheat-to-win governor.

In this case, Bonasia said, there's nothing the legislature can do. The amendment automatically takes effect if it passes. Meanwhile, enforcement is up to the citizens who figure they can't do any worse at cleaning up our waterways than the DEP did.

If this passes, says Linzey, Florida will become the first state in the United States to approve such a measure. That means I'll be shaking my foam finger again. Woo-hoo!

I do hope that Bonasia and his allies pull off this near-miracle. If they do, I bet we'll see a whole bunch of our destructive developers dancing around to dodge all the lawsuits, hopping around like they've suddenly got turtles in their trunk and a reptile in their pants.

––––––––––

Postscript: In July 2022, a judge ruled that—as the Orlando Sentinel *put it— "the arguments for the lakes and connected streams didn't hold water legally." Meanwhile the petition drive for a statewide right to clean water fell short for the 2024 ballot, but the backers said they'd try again for 2026.*

43

Teach Your Children

Florida Phoenix, June 9, 2022

We expect so much from our teachers these days. I blame Harry Potter for this.

Harry's teachers at Hogwarts use wizardly magic to make things happen and never have to worry about running out of supplies. Clearly, we expect the same from the humans working in Florida schools, despite the distinct lack of sorting hats and snowy owls.

Some people act as if our teachers are so powerful they must be stopped from passing along their secret knowledge. No talking about racial inequities! No "inappropriate" books in the school library! No mentioning anyone's sexuality!

Why, those insidious wizards might even snap their fingers and turn our kids into some creature wrapped in rainbows! (News flash: That is NOT how being LGBTQ works.)

But if there's a gunman around, one so scary even the cops won't go after him, let's give these same teachers guns to shoot at him. Even though we don't trust them to teach straight, we trust them to shoot straight. No to talking about race, yes to racing to fire back!

As we're all debating the caliber of our teachers, and the caliber of weaponry they should be packing, I just want to make one small point about our educational system.

I think that one of the things we should be teaching our kids in Florida is . . . Florida. Specifically, the part of Florida that lies outside the classroom.

* * *

Why do we send our kids to school? I mean besides the fact that keeping them out is illegal.

We send them so they can learn what they need to know to secure their own futures, as well as that of our state. That's why we pay teachers to help them learn all about math, science, literature, languages, history, and civics.

These are all very important subjects. (Well, maybe not algebra. Don't get me started on that.)

Florida does require fourth-graders to learn about Florida history, geography, and government. Back when I was in the fourth grade—roughly the Jurassic Period—that meant we were required to learn all 67 counties and locate them on a map, as well as memorize a few other bits of trivia, such as how to spell "Juan Ponce de Leon."

Our only discussion related to the Florida outside our classroom was whether the weather was suitable for running laps in P.E. class. Coach Grant made us run a LOT of laps. (I'm glad he wasn't armed—he might have fired a few shots to make us run faster.)

But the environment is pretty important here, too.

Our beaches, springs, swamps, forests, estuaries, and aquifer, not to mention our amazing native species—these are all things we should be teaching our kids about as well.

Remember that Florida's environment is the foundation of our economy. As we learned during the 2010 BP oil spill, and then during the lengthy red tide algae bloom of 2017–19, any damage to the environment leads to major damage to our economy.

Plus, nature is cool! I vividly remember back in 19mumble-mumble, when I was around 6 or 7, my parents and I spent a couple of weeks driving around and camping at various Florida state parks.

That trip lives on in my memory in part because it was so much fun, and in part because it's when I "accidentally" slipped and fell into the Suwannee River. I call it my Florida baptism.

Yet despite the environment's importance and its awesomeness, according to Jennifer Jones, president of the League of Environmental Educators in Florida and a professor at Florida Gulf Coast University, "The state of Florida really lacks a focus on environmental education."

Florida's Department of Education and Department of Environmental Protection used to work together to encourage teachers to give lessons on Florida's environment, she said. Not anymore.

A few of what she called "teacher-champions" do their best to get the kids to see what a wonderful place we live in. But they're the exception, not the rule.

You'd think their parents would make sure their children had some idea of how delightful Florida can be. Yet, as the Chamber of Commerce likes to point out, roughly 900 new people are moving here every day. Most of them have no idea what they've gotten themselves into—er, I mean, where they've landed. They think Disney is the alpha and omega of the state's attractions.

"A lot of the kids we work with have never been on a boat before," said Peter Clark, founder of Tampa Bay Watch in Tierra Verde. "Or never even been to the beach."

Katie Mastenbrook, who runs Tampa Bay Watch's Marine Education Center, told me that she and her staff see kids going from "trepidation, to fear and being nervous, to excitement, to being inquisitive, and then joyful. . . . I have been with many children when they are having their first experience holding a fish, going on a boat, seeing a dolphin in the wild, and you can really just see their mind turning."

I posted something on Facebook about my Suwannee River dunking and got a huge response. Turns out a lot of my fellow Florida natives went through some similar formative experience.

"I was fortunate to have a mother who took me and my sisters to the beach and to parks including the Everglades," wrote one.

Another said, "As a kid I swam in a huge Lakeland lake (saw snakes but not gators), frolicked through mucky orange groves barefoot, swam way out at Ormond and Daytona (pre-*Jaws* and sunscreen)."

"We grew up with a sturdy tree fort in the pine rocklands and a mango grove," a third one recalled. "Our trails and paths through these woods were well worn. We were almost always barefoot."

Not all memories were golden. One of my friends warned me, "If it's Florida and a good 20 percent of the article doesn't touch on mosquitos or some other sort of biting bug, you're writing a lie."

I told him that the skeeters tore me up as a kid too, but now ignore me. Probably after so many bites, my blood tastes like the mosquito equivalent of a wine-tasting spit bucket.

Most of my environmental education came from my mom, an avid backyard birder; my dad, who took me hunting and fishing (carrying a gun or a cane pole is the Southern man's excuse for enjoying a walk in the woods); and my Boy Scout troop, with whom I went hiking and canoeing, although not often enough to suit me.

The problem with all these sun-dappled recollections of frolicking outdoors is that they date to the long-time-ago. Back then, kids routinely spent hours playing in their backyard or exploring the woods or creek near where they lived. Sometimes they'd catch critters that would wind up in a box in their bedrooms.

Karen Johnson of Nature's Classroom in Hillsborough County. Photo courtesy of Hillsborough County.

This was pre-cable, pre-streaming, pre-video game, and that world is gone. There are a few environment-themed video games, but they're not quiiiiite as popular as, say, *Minecraft* or that *Mario Kart* game that teaches you how to survive a drive on I-95 or I-75.

Those memories also date to a pre-asphalt-everywhere Florida. Good luck finding some woods or a creek near your suburban sprawl split-level these days. You're more likely to find a retention pond and the landscaping for a model home.

Children today "have no connection anymore to their own backyards," said Karen Johnson, who's in charge of Nature's Classroom, a Hillsborough County program in Thonotosassa. "Kids don't have the knowledge we gleaned by playing in our backyards."

* * *

I was happy to talk to Johnson, now in her 23rd year of running Nature's Classroom. Her program should be considered a model for the rest of the state.

Nature's Classroom sits on 365 acres of land along the Hillsborough River. The land is owned by the Southwest Florida Water Management District and leased by the school district. Every sixth-grader in the Hillsborough school system makes a visit.

"They hear about the challenges facing the environment and learn how the health of the river affects us all by influencing things such as our drinking water supply. Most importantly, students learn how their actions now and in the future can impact the environment in the community," WTVT-TV reported last year.

Since the program began in 1969, more than 300,000 grade school students have passed through its gates. One of them was Johnson, herself.

"I was a sixth-grader out here in 1976," she told me. "It had a huge impact on me and my classmates."

One of the first things kids hear when they visit is: No staring at their phones. There's too much real life to look at. Then the teachers keep them so busy they don't miss their electronic distractions, she said.

What they learn about the river, habitat, species, and so forth includes lessons from science, math, and language, "all of it interwoven together," she said. Meanwhile, Nature's Classroom staffers work with visiting teachers on ways to extend the outdoors experience into their indoor schoolwork, she said.

The students can visit with a one-eyed hawk, a rescued bobcat, an alligator, a flock of deer, and a black bear of somewhat mysterious origin. These are not the kind of neighbors that most Florida kids have these days.

As far as I'm concerned, this menagerie beats the heck out of the standard classroom hamster.

* * *

Few states have made the environment a full-fledged part of their curriculum. Three that do are Maryland, New Jersey, and California, according to Stacie Pierpoint of the North American Association for Environmental Education.

In 2016, Oregon's voters approved spending money from the state lottery to provide all fifth- or sixth-grade students in Oregon access to a weeklong Outdoor School program. The program is voluntary, but it's open to all, even home-schooled kids.

Making environmental education a guaranteed part of the Florida school system might require an Oregon-style voter initiative, too. You know how much our legislature hates those, but it may be our only avenue for making a change.

Our legislators and governor don't seem to be too concerned about the lack of lessons on green topics. While they've banned certain subjects (ones not actually taught below college level), their additions have mostly been

Kids in the Nature's Classroom program paddling boats on the Hillsborough River. Photo courtesy of Hillsborough County.

focused on teaching kids that Communism is bad and money (and knowing how to spend it) is good. Well, duh.

So maybe it's up to us parents to step in and play teacher on this subject.

If I were designing a Florida environmental curriculum, the students would get to splash in a spring, tube down a river, search for pretty shells or shark teeth on a beach. There would be a wintertime field trip to a manatee viewing center, such as the one by the Tampa Electric Company power plant in Apollo Beach.

They'd learn key Floridian survival skills, such as how to read a hurricane map, how to remove sandspurs (lick your fingers first), and why you always walk in the shade instead of the sun (it's 10 degrees cooler).

The kids would read such Florida classics as Robb White's *The Lion's Paw*, Marjorie Kinnan Rawlings' *The Yearling*, or Patrick Smith's *A Land Remembered*. Come to think of it, that last one would make a good name for the whole course.

A few modern works might sneak in too, such as Carl Hiaasen's *Hoot*—which, I hasten to add for the Moms for Liberty crowd, is about burrowing owls, not the scantily clad waitstaff at Hooters.

The most important thing the students would learn is that natural Florida is special and, if we have to fight to keep it, that's worth the effort.

"When you learn to love the environment, you want to protect the environment," Clark said. "That becomes extremely important when they're voting adults later on."

If you're a parent, tell your kids that Florida has plenty of strip shopping centers, storage buildings, and big-box stores, but a dwindling number of creeks and rivers and swamps. It's going to take some serious civic-minded magic to make sure the latter don't all disappear under the former—say, at the snap of some developer's fingers.

Maybe some kids who remember the wonder of their first river baptism will turn out to be the wizards who can save us all.

ACKNOWLEDGMENTS

Every story in this volume exists because some editor trusted me to tell it, and in many cases found ways to improve my writing. I'd like to thank *Florida Phoenix* editors Diane Rado and Michael Moline, *FORUM* editor Pam Daniels, *Flamingo* editor Jamie Stephenson Rich, *CrimeReads* editor Dwyer Murphy, and *Legal Examiner* editor Roy LeBlanc, all of whom repeatedly put up with my shenanigans, bad puns, and pop culture obsessions. I'd also like to thank all the folks who submitted themselves to my annoying questions. You're the real stars here. Well, except for that ONE guy. You know who you are, buster.

Craig Pittman is a native Floridian, an author, a journalist, and a podcaster. For 21 years, he covered environmental issues for the *Tampa Bay Times,* winning state and national awards. He's now a columnist for the *Florida Phoenix* and co-hosts the *Welcome to Florida* podcast. He is the author of seven books, including the *New York Times* bestseller *Oh, Florida! How America's Weirdest State Influences the Rest of the Country.*